• THE •
NEPHILIM
IMPERATIVES

SECOND COMING CHRONICLES—VOLUME II

Second Coming Chronicles—Volume I
The Rapture Ready Dialogues: Dark Dimension

· T H E ·
NEPHILIM
I M P E R A T I V E S
DARK SENTENCES

TERRY JAMES

Anomalos Publishing House
Crane

Anomalos Publishing House, Crane 65633
© 2007 by Terry James
All rights reserved. Published 2007
Printed in the United States of America
07   1
ISBN-10: 0-9788453-6-6 (paper)

EAN-13: 978-0-9788453-6-0 (paper)

Cover illustration and design by Steve Warner

All biblical references are from the King James Version.

A CIP catalog record for this book is available from the Library of
Congress.

ABOUT THE AUTHOR

Also by Terry James: The Rapture Dialogues—*Volume I of the Second Coming Chronicles* (VMI/Musterion Press, 2006); Are You Rapture Ready? (Penguin, 2004); *Foreshadows of Wrath and Redemption, Forewarning,* and Foreshocks of Antichrist (Harvest House); *Earth's Final Days, Raging Into Apocalypse, The Triumphant Return of Christ,* and *Storming Toward Armageddon* (New Leaf).

James is a frequent lecturer on the study of end-time phenomena and interviews often with media on topics involving world issues and events as they might relate to Bible prophecy. He is also an active member of the Pre-Trib Study Group, a prophecy research think tank founded by Dr. Tim LaHaye. Much of his work can be accessed on the highly popular Web site www.raptureready.com.

ACKNOWLEDGMENTS

My love and thanks to those closest to my heart for their support during the writing of this book: my wife, Margaret; Terry James, Jr.; Nathan James; Jeanie Hedges; and Dana Neel, who does a terrific job as publicist.

Special love and appreciation to Angie Peters—who is in the middle of that family I love so much—for her indispensible work as editor on this and all of my books.

Profound appreciation to David Wilson for invaluable research and description involving aviation, aircraft, and other matters of flight. Thanks, also, to Christopher Mangan in New York City for his research input.

And my gratitude to Todd Strandberg, my partner in our Web site, raptureready.com, who is also a part of my supportive, close-knit family.

Last, but not least, many thanks to Tom Horn and his wife, Nita, whose kindred spirits to mine in bringing this book to publication mean so much.

CHARACTERS

Christopher Banyon	Pastor of St. Paul Presbyterian Church
Susie Banyon	Wife to Christopher
Alan Cranston	Morgan Lansing's boss; Vice president of advertising for Guroix, Tuppler, and Macy
Kristi Flannigan	Morgan Lansing's friend
Musahad Kahlied Afgani	Prisoner at Guantanamo; Unwilling operative of George Jenkins
George Jenkins	Blake Robbins's boss; Covert operations director, Department of Defense; Chief liaison between joint American-EU project and Transportec
Clark Lansing	Mark and Lori Lansing's son; Morgan's brother; Writer for the *New York Examiner*
Lori Lansing	Daughter of Laura and James Morgan; Morgan's mother
Mark Lansing	Former marine captain and Delta pilot; Son of Clark and Jennifer Lansing; Lori Lansing's husband
Morgan Lansing	Copywriter for Guroix, Tuppler, and Macy; Daughter of Mark and Lori Lansing; Clark Lansing's sister
Casandra Lincoln	Morgan Lansing's friend
Laura Morgan	Grandmother of Clark and Morgan Lansing
David Prouse	Grandson of Dr. Prouse; Criminal defense attorney
Dr. Randall Prouse	Doctorate in theology; Biblical archaeologist

Blake Robbins	Covert operative for black projects with the Department of Defense; Civilian corporate job with Transportec; Marine reserve major
Nigel Saxton	British Intelligence Services (MI7) agent
Yusfi Shabatt	Arab guard assigned by Islamics to provide security for Mt. Moriah Muslim holy sites
Hans Sheivold	Scientist within the Colorado mountain covert operations complex
Wayne Snidely	Assistant to the secretary of defense
April Warmath	Assistant to George Jenkins
Bruce Wilson	Clark Lansing's boss; Editor of the *New York Examiner*

Jerusalem—Midnight, January 1, 2000

Yusfi Shabatt hated this duty. But it was better than going on the Hamas raiding parties that usually meant death to most of those who tried to kill the Jews. Guarding the golden-domed place of the stone was easy. Although he was supposed to watch for Jews who might try to destroy the Al-Aqsa Mosque, and the Dome of the Rock, he knew better. Other than an occasional gathering of the Jew-dogs to try and place a temple cornerstone, as they called it, the Jews posed no threat. Many times he had been called upon to commit acts that the leaders could then blame on the Jews.

His thoughts, and standing, wearied him. Yusfi leaned the Russian-made automatic assault rifle against the wall of the guardhouse and sat upon the hard surface of Mount Moriah with his knees up while he nodded. He would get some sleep this night of darkness, lit only by the occasional stars that peeked between the sky-spaces in the growing cloud cover.

His eyelids dropped the moment he rested the back of his burnoosed head against the stucco and stone wall. However, rumbles of thunder caused him to come to full consciousness, his dark brown eyes glistening with the lightning illumination of the gathering storm. This meant rain. He would have to go to the hut a few dozen steps nearer the divine mosque.

Before he could rise, he saw in the distance, almost at the center of the flat surface of Moriah, a strange thing. He retrieved the weapon and started walking toward the spewing light that seemed to be erupting from the ground.

Lightning flashed brightly, making visible with daylight clarity the area toward which he moved. He saw it then: a huge, human-shaped figure but four times taller than a human. It was black and looked to be boiling. It sparked brilliant, dagger-like shards of light, and the spectacle caused the Arab's mouth to drop in amazement.

Another figure appeared suddenly—as large as the other, but so bright that it hurt Yusfi's eyes, causing him to shield them with his forearm. He let the rifle slip from his grip. He didn't notice it falling to the ground, his eyes now wide with astonishment.

The two monstrous creatures clashed, accompanied by an earth-vibrating clap of thunder.

Yusfi Shabatt stood paralyzed, mesmerized by the spectacular battle that raged at the center of the Mount's surface. The figures, their bodies firing bursts of light and further illuminated by the horrendous lightning that occasionally made the surrounding places like midday, grew to enormous size, rising from the top of Moriah to the lightning's very source.

The rain began cascading while the wind blew in gale force, causing Yusfi to go to his knees and lean into the palms and heels of his hands in order to maintain his position on the ground. Still, he watched the monsters wrestling at the Mount's center. They seemed to explode with each crash in their own lightning-producing clashes.

A blinding bolt leaped from the heavens, joined by a thousand other flickers. The result was a massive strike that knifed through the combatants and an explosion of thunderous sound that caused Yusfi to hold his ears in pain. He looked to the place where the figures had struggled. There lingered a beam of light that spread near the top to form what looked to be a crossbeam upon the radiant column of light. It looked like a gigantic cross, he thought while witnessing the scene that changed in less than a second.

The Arab was dumbfounded by the evolving visions at the base of the cross of light. Two infant-like figures seemed to float in viscous liquid, their beautiful little faces cherubic, their eyes glowing with colors that held Yusfi's own eyes transfixed upon them. The children began growing from infancy through toddlerhood and the teen years, then into young adulthood. They stood while the fierce winds blew about them and lightning viciously fractured the tumultuous clouds above Moriah.

Within moments, all changed back into the night as it had been before the storm had come.

Tora Bora, Afghanistan—January 18, 2000

Yosri Fouda fumbled with the tripod, becoming frustrated that the knob wouldn't tighten to affix the camera at its apex. He was a filmmaker, not a mechanic, he grumbled, growling his displeasure through clinched teeth.

Ziad Jarrah nudged him aside, frowning in concentration while he shook the camera so that its bottom screw hole accepted the bolt jutting from the top of the tripod. He twisted the camera, and the action accomplished the attachment Yosri Fouda wanted.

"One shouldn't attempt such difficult tasks without proper degrees," the Saudi said in Arabic, looking into Fouda's eyes.

Everyone in the dark cave chamber laughed, causing Fouda to shake his fist in the air and then draw his hands together in a prayerful pose, holding them aloft. The laughter grew louder and then subsided when a tall human form walked into the chamber from an adjoining tunnel.

"It is good to laugh," Osama bin Laden said, seeing the faces grow somber upon his entrance. "We shall laugh much more. The Zionist devils will not be as amused," he said, walking toward Mohammed Atta and handing him some pages of text in Arabic.

"Allah is great!" one of the men shouted in Arabic. The others picked up the chant.

"Allah be praised! Allah is great!"

"Death to the Zionists! Death to the Jew! Death to America!"

Yosri Fouda carefully framed the shouting men, who gesticulated wildly, thrusting fists into the air and holding hands that were pressed together over their heads in a gesture of praise to Allah.

Osama, who at 6' 5" stood a head taller than the tallest of the celebrants, had moved out of camera range. His eyes dilated, becoming solid black while he watched the gleeful laughter and prancing of his fellow conspirators. A guttural snicker came from deep within his throat when Mohammed Atta began to read from the pages before the camera.

"Allah be praised, for he is great," the Saudi began. "Our deaths are but entrance into life eternal. Allah be praised. We are chosen to bring everlasting glory to Allah and his mighty prophet Mohammed. So let it be! The eternal realm of Allah and his prophet is come at last. I pledge my life, my will, my all, to the great god Allah!"

Osama bin Laden ducked his cloth-wrapped head, bowing his thin frame into the tunnel and exiting the chamber, leaving the filming process behind.

The al-Qaida leader emerged into the frigid White Mountain air momentarily, his gaze liquid pools of black. As he looked to the peaks to the north, a sinister smile crossed his illness-emaciated face.

A brilliant white disk hovered silently to the right of the tallest spire. It darkened slightly, then grew to the brightness of the sun. The disk shot upward at incredible speed, then vanished.

ONE

New York City—Tuesday, September 11, 2001

Blake Robbins glanced at the clock on the wall next to Megan Kafka's desk.

"Eight forty-one," he said beneath his breath, before taking his first sip of black coffee from his second cup of the morning. Time to finally settle in at the computer and get started.

He made his way through two small offices to his own corner office on the north side of Two World Trade Center Tower. He stopped to look out the huge window, noticing black specks in the distance. The freighters moved imperceptibly upon unusually blue Atlantic waters, from his eighty-eighth floor perspective. This was going to be a beautiful, clear day, he thought, contemplating the plane ride to D.C. a little later in the morning. He had already booted up the computer, and the most recent instructions from the European Union interlocutors in London were electronically etched upon the monitor screen. He pulled the chair so that it rolled far enough from the desk for him to slip between its burgundy leather-covered arms.

He placed the mug to the right of the mouse pad and began manipulating the mouse. The text scrolled, and he read the day's negotiating points for dealing with the United States Department of Defense and Boeing's defense contractors.

"The black projects relevant to the transactions must be integrated within the general appropriations, if we are to move forward. Priority is that the devices involved in the R technology be included. Allies must trust each other."

Blake intertwined his long fingers with the dark hair that thickly padded the back of his head. He stretched and reached to retrieve the mug while keeping his eyes trained on the screen.

Meagan Kafka interrupted his concentration. "It's 8:45," she said from his office doorway. "The car will be waiting."

"Just got to make a couple of notes. Tell the driver I need fifteen minutes, will you, Meggie?"

"Flight's at 9:45," the secretary said with a tinge of urgency in her voice.

"I know, I know. I'll try to make it ten minutes."

He again put his fingers together at the back of his head and stretched his body before bringing his hands down and rubbing his eyes with his index fingers. While he read the text, he heard a rumbling noise, and the screen went dead. The office around him darkened; the light no longer streamed into the room from the large windows.

Blake looked to his surroundings, trying to make sense of the strange, growing darkness.

When he looked back at the monitor, his eyes met blood red text against the screen's blackness.

Megan stopped stuffing the several portfolio pouches with papers her boss would need for the meeting with the Pentagon and Transportec people. She looked puzzled, cocking her head in curiosity, as she heard a rumbling and felt the building vibrate. She reached to take her cup of tea from the credenza behind her desk, sipped the liquid, and returned to filling Robbins's attaché case.

Megan again sensed something was wrong and walked through the other offices to that of Blake Robbins.

"Blake." She saw the top of Robbins's head just above the high-backed chair. The secretary moved to his side, getting no response.

"Blake?"

His face was a mask of nonexpression, his eyes staring at the screen.

"Kingdom come," Megan whispered the words she read.

"Blake!"

She shook her boss's shoulders. His pupils were fully dilated, with none of the blue iris showing around the black._

"Blake! Something's happened in the building! We need to find out!"

She shook him again and tried to make him look at her instead of at the screen. "*Blake, what's wrong?!*"

Looking out the windows of the executive's office, her eyes were drawn to the North World Trade Center Tower 120 feet from her own building. She screamed, "Oh! My Lord!"

Smoke and flaming debris showered from the windows high on the building's south side. She again tried to get Robbins's attention but gave up and ran out of his office. Opening the door leading into the hallway, she saw people fleeing their offices, their faces projecting the puzzlement and fear that clutched them.

"Somebody said a plane hit Tower One just above us!" a man holding a cell phone to his ear shouted to the others. "We've got to get out!"

Megan ran back through the offices into that of Robbins, where he sat, still staring at the screen.

"Tower One has been hit by a plane or something, Blake! They're saying we need to get out…*Now!*"

She tried to tug him from the chair, but his body was rigid and could not be budged. So she ran to find help in getting him out. In the hallway milled confused, excited people. Someone was yelling that the South Tower wasn't affected, that it hadn't been hit by whatever had struck the North Tower.

"Would a couple of you guys help me get my boss out of the office? He can't move for some reason," Megan said to a large black man, who shook his head "no."

"Sorry, but we've got to get to the top and see if there are some helicopters or something we can use to help those up there in Tower One." He hurried in the direction of the steel fire door leading to a stairwell.

The people seemed eerily quiet, despite the hallway traffic. There was no panic, just a rush to get to the elevators and stairwells at the skyscraper's center.

Megan trotted through the offices again, finding Blake walking toward her, staring straight ahead. He had put on his suit coat and walked in his normal stride, passing her without a word. His eyes still looked like black marbles.

"Blake!" she shouted while he continued past her desk and opened the door to the hallway.

"*Blake!* Wait!"

She grabbed her purse from the credenza and ran to catch up.

"Where are we going, Blake? What are we going to do?"

The young woman expelled the questions between inhalations of trying to catch her breath while they entered the elevator and ascended toward the top of the tower.

"We're going up, not down?" she asked in a perplexed tone.

His face seemed that of a mannequin. Megan's eyes filled with tears, fear welling within her thoughts.

"Where are we going?" she asked him again.

Robbins didn't acknowledge that he heard her or that he was even aware she shared the elevator with him.

"You're scaring me," she said, softly whimpering the words. Robbins remained transfixed on some unseen point of reference directly ahead.

Megan never had been on one of the tower's elevators with less than a dozen people. Now there were only Blake Robbins and she moving quickly up the shaft in the large conveyance. The fact that they did not stop even once poked at her troubled thoughts while she watched the illuminating numbers move across the top of the elevator: 90, 91, 92, 93, 94...

At 109, the elevator stopped, the doors opening to a group of men in business suits and others in work uniforms.

"The doors to the roof are locked, if that's what you've got in mind," one of the maintenance men said. "It takes a special code to get up there, and we don't have it."

"It will take about ten minutes to get the electronic locks opened," one of the maintenance men was saying to several of the businessmen. "And, that's if they will let anybody up there. Not likely to do that...All that radar stuff and the lure to the crazies, you know?"

Blake Robbins didn't seem to hear the man's words, walking past the four men and opening the door to the building's top floor. While they ascended the steps, several men and women met them on their way down.

"They've locked the doors," one woman said while they continued to climb.

Megan looked into the woman's troubled eyes and smiled her acknowledgment and concern.

"Blake, they say the doors are locked," she said while Robbins made the turn on the stairwell to climb the last series of steps.

He said nothing, taking the last few steps, then turning to push a door that opened into a wide walkway that led to a row of double doors along one wall. The words, "To the Roof," were emblazoned in large, red, illuminated letters above the doors.

Robbins stopped in front of the centermost pair of doors and stood staring straight ahead for several seconds, his arms straight down at his sides. Megan looked at his strange expression, then, seeing he was not going to do so, tried the doors herself.

"See? They're locked, just like they said." Frustration began to overwhelm her anxiety. "See—these, too," she added, trying to open several of the other doors.

Robbins continued to stare straight ahead, oblivious to the woman's presence.

"We better get down right now," Megan pleaded, putting her right hand on his forearm.

The skin felt unlike flesh; rather, it was solid to the touch beneath the flannel suit coat's sleeve—like wood or stone.

"Blake! What is wrong with you?!"

Megan pulled her hand away and stared at Blake's eyes. They appeared cold, black, and nonhuman—like the eyes of a shark.

"The doors won't open. They're locked," Megan said with irritation.

Robbins walked forward and reached to the handle on one of the massive doors. When the door swung outward toward the roof, she blinked, was frozen in place for a moment, and then hurried through the opening to just behind Robbins before the door swung back to the closed position.

Blake Robbins strode without hesitation toward the south side of Tower Two, the secretary breaking into a jog every few steps to keep up.

She looked back to the north, seeing the inferno blazing skyward, Tower One's roof obscured by thick, black smoke.

"My Gosh! Those poor people," she said, the tears coming again with realization of the magnitude of the catastrophe. "What are we doing? Where are we going? Do you expect a helicopter or something?"

Robbins continued walking, stopping finally when he reached the roof's barrier that was its southern, outer perimeter. His black, pupil-filled eyes stared toward the Atlantic's horizon.

Megan saw it then. It seemed to swoop from high above, its engines screaming while it banked, almost as if it would roll. It straightened slightly at the last second, closing in on the skyscraper at 590 mph.

Her already-shocked brain couldn't react in time to prepare for the impact. The huge, fuel-laden 757 cut a swath through the tower, and the building lurched northward, making the secretary sense that it would topple toward its blazing sister tower. Tower Two sprang back toward the south, throwing her to the roof, then straightened to its proper upright position.

She struggled to her feet, the skin of her knees torn and her leg bruised from her fall. Her eyes went to Blake Robbins, who had not been moved from his stiff-legged stance. He continued to stare toward the Atlantic.

A monstrous fireball boiled upward, turning the southern sky into a massive sphere of reds, oranges, and yellows while causing a hot wind to sweep across the roof. Megan fell to her knees, the heated air singing her hair, burning her face, and causing her to gasp for breath. She looked upward at her boss, who raised his arms, lifting his hands skyward.

He spoke in a growl that crawled from somewhere within, in a language the secretary couldn't understand. Suddenly, Blake Robbins wasn't there anymore.

5:30 p.m., Tuesday, September 11, 2001

Her eyes failed to penetrate the coagulant air outside the thirty-seventh floor window.

All of the Lower East Side of the city seemed locked in fog. But it wasn't fog. The stench of smoke and dust that billowed from the World Trade towers' collapse had hung and swirled thickly while she traversed on foot the twenty-two blocks from midtown Manhattan to her apartment building three hours earlier. She didn't see improvement while she held the cell phone to her right ear and spoke.

"Clark, have you told Mom and Dad? Were you able to get them?"

Morgan Lansing pulled her gaze from trying to see the street below, which teemed with fire trucks and emergency vehicles moving toward the carnage that once was the 110-floor twin World Trade tower buildings.

She sat on the edge of the bed, beginning to pat and rub a huge rottweiler's dark head. The dog nuzzled her roughly, trying to get her full attention away from her conversation.

"No, Peanut! No, no!" she scolded the year-old canine but continued to scratch and rub his head and ears.

"No problem," she said into the phone's mouthpiece. "It's just Jeddy, wanting me to pay attention…"

A young woman walked through the doorway, and Morgan cut her eyes toward her while her apartment mate sat on the end of the bed and began rubbing the dog, who moved to her side, welcoming the unfettered attention.

"It's terrible outside. But our building is safe. There's no problem," she reassured her older brother, Clark Lansing, who issued words of caution.

"Yes, my dear big brother, we'll be very careful." She hesitated when her only sibling interrupted. Then she spoke again.

"I know they're worried. Tell them I've been trying to call. I'll keep trying until I get through, okay?"

Morgan listened a moment longer, then said, "Yes…yes, I'll be careful. Love you. Bye." She stood after pushing the "off" button on the cell phone.

"Mom's been trying to get me. Clark said if I would stay off the phone long enough, maybe they could get through." She rolled her eyes.

"You know the cell towers must be melting down. They'll get through," Casandra Lincoln said, pulling gently at one of the rottweiler's ears.

"Guess so," Morgan said, again looking out the window before turning to face the girl. A feeling of gloom suddenly saturated her senses.

"I've been on this great job exactly one day and now this. Cassie, what do you think this means...I mean, to our jobs?"

"Our jobs might be the least of our worries, according to all of the news guys," Casandra said. "They're saying we can expect there to be more attacks."

Morgan considered the words. "Well, according to Mr. Cranston, the agency will be open for business tomorrow," she said, again sitting on the bed beside the dog, who, standing between them with his chin resting on the bed, enjoyed the petting by both girls.

"Guess advertising must go on," Morgan's roommate said, then stood and walked to the bedroom door. She added, before leaving the room, "I don't know, M, just got a funny feeling things won't be the same after today."

2:15 a.m., Wednesday, September 12

Casandra Lincoln was fitful in attempted sleep. Light from some unidentifiable source kept waking her while she tossed first onto her left side, then onto her right. They were only dreams...troubling dreams that kept pulling her to the surface of consciousness every few minutes, she thought, trying to see the amber numbers on the digital alarm clock.

"Two twenty-one," she read, then plopped her head back into the hollowed-out place in the soft pillow. She raised her head and fluffed the old feather pillow that had been her faithful friend since childhood, then tried to settle again.

Noises from outside her window, emanating from the city that never slept, sounded strangely different while she drifted toward unconsciousness. The change brought her head up from the pillow, and she turned to try to hear the altered sound.

Growling. Very deep, and low in volume. Was it Jeddy?

The apartment door was locked, barred, and dead-bolted. The window, at this level, was protected from any intruder, unless he had Spiderman capabilities. The thoughts ran quickly through Casandra's awakening brain. She sat upright, again craning her head to listen to the growl that came from Morgan's room. She flipped the cover aside and swung her legs over the edge of the bed.

Finding her soft slippers on the floor, she stepped into them and stood, pausing to hear the growling noise that, this time, was louder than before.

Casandra moved cautiously to Morgan's bedroom doorway in the semidarkness. The small apartment was lit only by the smoke-muted city lights that streamed in through the narrow spaces that surrounded the blinds and curtains of the window in her friend's room.

Chill bumps covered her arms and the back of her neck while her eyes tried to penetrate the darkness. She wanted to speak, but the words wouldn't come. *Morgan.* But the name was only thought, not spoken.

She stepped inside the room and froze with terror when a threatening growl leaped from the rottweiler's throat and trailed off to become a guttural sound that continued at a low, angry level with each breath the dog drew.

The animal stood on Morgan's bed, facing Casandra. Its eyes glowed yellow within their sockets, surrounded by black, bristling fur that blended with the heavy shadows. Its snarling mouth curled tightly, the thick canine teeth gnashing slightly within its massive jowls while the growling continued. The dog's muscles bulged while it bowed and stiffened in preparation for attack.

The faint light revealed Morgan's form, but Casandra, her mind in panic mode, couldn't take her eyes from the dog's eyes and teeth, seeing the girl only through peripheral vision. A sudden movement to the right of the dog broke the transfixion. A black mass seemed to emerge from the lump in the bed that was Morgan Lansing's body. The horrendous sight formed into the shape of a human-like being. The creature appeared to stand in the bed beside Morgan from the thighs up, but its bottommost part penetrated the mattress while its head turned toward Casandra. It moved through the mattress and box springs, emerging fully beside the bed near the wall with the window. The monstrous creature stood almost to the ceiling, its hideous round eyes glowing red while it stared at Morgan's apartment mate. Then the humanoid mass leaped through the wall and was gone.

Casandra Lincoln's senses darkened to unconsciousness in the moment of her collapse to the bedroom carpet.

Near Ketchum, Idaho—5:24 p.m., September 13, 2001

He finally got through the phone maze created by the crisis in New York, after an hour of trying.

His sister was crying, and Clark Lansing strained to hear her words through the static of the cell phone against his left ear. He struggled with equal determination to see the road ahead.

"What happened to her?"

He stared hard through the brief openings created by the slapping windshield wipers while he questioned Morgan.

"I don't know, Clark. She was just lying there when I woke up."

His sister's words came between sobs.

"What does her doctor say?"

"They can't figure out what caused her to collapse. Maybe a stroke or something..."

"A stroke? At twenty-four?"

"They really don't know, yet," Morgan said, managing to control her emotions. "One of the best neurologists in New York is running some tests."

The cell reception broke apart and then reconnected.

"You there, Morgan?" he asked.

"Yes. I'm here."

"Listen, Sis. We'll likely lose the cell. If we do, I'll call you as soon as I can, okay?"

"Okay."

"Love you, Sis," he said, listening for her response but hearing none.

The rain slackened, and the road in the distance became visible again. His thoughts leaped ahead to his meeting with Jabard Sowell, the rancher he had contacted a week before. He questioned his own reasoning ability...driving through the barren reaches of Idaho in a raging storm, looking for Bigfoot. His little cabal—a close-knit group comprised of several classmates at the Princeton School of Journalism—would laugh him off the planet. Even if he got an interesting story from the back woods farmer-rancher, what could he do with it? What respectable publication would take a story on Bigfoot? Maybe *The National Enquirer* or one of that sort. But not a respectable rag…

Something other than the quest for a paycheck drove him to investigate. He knew what that something was. The nightmares. They were so real that he could reach out and touch the creatures.

When he had watched Sowell interviewed on the CBS documentary, upon hearing the rancher's descriptions, he knew he must go to Idaho. Now, he would give Sowell a heads-up that he was within a few miles.

Daylight was in its final throes of extinguishing while the Ford Explorer topped the hill and rounded the curve on the narrow road. Clark reached to the console to retrieve the cell phone. He glanced at the piece of paper he held between his thumb and index finger against the padded steering wheel and started to push the buttons of the phone with his right thumb. His eyes darted between the note with Sowell's phone number, the phone's number pad, and the now sharply curving road.

Light burst with vision-debilitating brilliance. Instantly blinded, his right foot stomped the brake. He fought to control the steering wheel when the braking caused the front wheels to turn, the antilock system reacting to take control from the driver in order to assert command of the Explorer's direction of travel. The right front tire hit the gravel just off the asphalt, and the vehicle fishtailed before straightening. Clark gained control and slid the Ford to a stop in a shallow ditch well off the roadway.

The thunderstorm had passed, and the headlight beams cut through the mist caused by the drizzle aftermath. Had it been a lightning strike? There had been no thunderclap such a burst should have caused.

Clark put the Explorer in reverse and tried to back up. The rear wheels spun, but the vehicle remained in place. He put the shift in drive, and the Ford's rear wheels again spun without moving the vehicle.

He put it in park and opened the door, stepping onto the thick grass that covered the ditch. He examined the rear tires. They were stuck, almost to the top of the rims.

The front tires looked to be on solid ground, but the ditch's surface, just beneath the grass, was obviously too soft to provide traction.

What had caused the burst of light? It couldn't have been lightning. The storm had moved on, and he could no longer hear even the faintest hint of thunder.

He scanned the surroundings after retrieving a flashlight, shining the light around the area to look for some rocks, or logs—anything that could provide something to put beneath the tires.

When he stepped carefully through the soft terrain to the right side of the Explorer, he found what he needed. Stones, almost flat, and in a cluster. They should do the job.

He squatted and began gathering the stones between his left forearm and chest. A rustling noise caused him to look to the forested area further off the road.

He picked up the flashlight from the foot-high grass and aimed the beam into the trees. Small saplings fronted the larger, thicker-trunked varieties beyond. Clark moved the light's beam slowly back and forth, his eyes straining to pierce the blackness.

Satisfied that the sound was only a normal noise of nature, he laid the light aside and again began picking up rocks. Holding as many as possible against his body with his left arm, he fetched the flashlight from the grass, stuffed it in his right pocket, and reached to get a few more stones that he could hold in one hand against his stomach.

The Explorer's lights beamed ahead through the fog-like mist; then he saw it. A dark, human form in the headlights!

"*Who is it?!*" Clark's shouted question echoed but elicited no response. He dropped the stones and thrust the flashlight in the direction of the form, which had moved toward the forest, away from the vehicle's beams.

"Who are you?!" he yelled again, searching with the flashlight to find whatever, whoever was watching him from the darkness of the wooded copse.

A high-pitched shriek from behind caused him to instinctively whirl around. The flashlight beam framed the creature in the distance. The nearly black, human-shaped creature appeared huge, even from this distance of one hundred feet. It stood erect, its massive head and shoulders rising and falling while it again shrieked.

Its face looked to be more than a foot wide and hosted a gaping mouth with fang-like canine teeth gnashing angrily. Fiery, orange-red eyes blinked and glared at him. Paralyzed with the shock of the beast's threatening, Clark could do nothing but stare back. When he finally began shuffling with trepidation toward the creature in order to see what it was, it turned and, in the next instant, could no longer be seen. It was as if it had simply vanished!

Over the Atlantic—Sunday, September, 2001

The government 737 moved at 590 mph through the late-morning sky at thirty-seven thousand feet above the calm, cool Atlantic. Blake Robbins closed the cabin door and lifted the receiver to his ear.

"Yes, sir?"

"Blake," the familiar voice of the assistant to the secretary of defense, several times removed, said. "How's the flight, so far?"

"Great, sir. Just fine."

"Good! Good!"

There was silence for a moment, except for a muffled conversation, which Robbins took as George Jenkins talking to an assistant.

"Blake, I'm sorry I wasn't available to personally brief you before your trip," the covert operations director said, pausing again to issue orders of approval to an underling. He returned his attention to Robbins.

"But, we are secure with this phone, so thought I would give you a few thoughts."

"Yes, sir," Robbins acknowledged.

"The project, as you know, is set for a major test near the end of the month. The president is acutely interested in the results. I spoke with Mr. Rumsfeld, and he informs me that the man is counting on the R technology to perform to good effect against the enemy."

An uncomfortable silence prodded Robbins to say something.

"Yes, sir. The techno—"

"And, we are all depending on you to convince those involved at Brussels of the importance of this effort," Jenkins interrupted.

The younger man decided it best to say nothing, listening for Jenkins's next words.

"The technology has worked at every level tried so far. But, we just don't know how it is going to do at pinpointing and extracting the targets from these caves. So, I want to say again that the project peripherals have to be made to understand that we expect some unforeseen ramifications of this in-theater experimentation."

"Yes, sir. We will fully prepare them for that probability," Robbins assured the chief liaison between the joint American-EU project and Robbins's company for about the fifth or sixth time he thought while letting his eyes roam the cabin walls in a look of frustration.

America's European Union allies, at the second tier of governing authority, would make no promises that "Operation Scotty" was foolproof. It was his responsibility to give warning of the unknowns involved. Jenkins had not ceased to remind him of his duty in the matter since the moment the DOD clandestine operations chief enlisted him from the ranks of the technology's civilian producers.

His duty, from an overall perspective, was a mystery to him. Jenkins had used dormant military obligation to wrest him from his civilian corporate job with Transportec. Technically, Blake Robbins was a marine reserve major. In fact, he was a covert operative, answering strictly to the assistant secretary for black projects as part of the Department of Defense. Patience wasn't his strong suit, and he fought the urge to ask his American government superior for details of the mission to Brussels.

His being a part of the project was itself an enigma beyond which his mind could explore. His last memory of that horrendous day of the attacks on the World Trade towers…knowing nothing until a week later…the sudden consciousness, arising abruptly from the dark nothingness produced the moment he heard the rumble in his eighty-eighth-floor South Tower office.

Blake Robbins did know one important factor in the mix of the unknowns. He was alive while almost three thousand of his fellow World Trade towers workers—including his personal assistant, Megan Kafka—were not. He was—he was told—a product of the technology's success. He should make its best salesman.

George Jenkins walked in a short, brisk stride after putting the phone receiver back on its cradle. April Warmath followed him, scribbling notes on the stenographer pad as best she could while he dictated.

"Get Lambert and Gravner on a conference call. Set it up for three thirty my time. Tell them the demonstration is set for Friday of week after next. No one else is to be privy to the call. There is no clearance high enough to include anyone else."

His gruff expression made it clear to the young woman that she had just been included in, most likely, an illegal operation of some sort. While the fact was somewhat ego building, the downside was troubling. She knew a lot...maybe too much.

Near Los Angeles, California—The Following Tuesday

"You look tired, dear. You aren't getting sick, are you?"

Lori Lansing looked up at her son and felt his left cheek with the back of her left hand.

"No, Mom. I'm okay. Just a little jet lag, most likely."

Clark Lansing gripped his mother's hand and kissed it. "I'll be fine," he said, then bent to pick up the suitcase and laptop. "A few hours of sleep and everything will be cool."

Lori hugged him and reached to pat his cheek. "Well, your room is ready, and the office is yours when you need to work," she said, admiring her 6'2" son while they walked toward the interior of the house.

"The bedroom will be fine for working. I don't need a lot of room," he said.

Clark was the spitting image of his father at that age, she thought. "Your father and I are happy you chose to stay here for a while."

"Yes. Well, I needed to get off the flying circus for awhile," he said.

"Daddy will be glad to see you," she said from in front of him while they ascended the stairway.

"Heard anything from Morgan?" he asked, trudging behind her with the cases.

"She hasn't called in a week. She's not very happy with her mom."

"Oh? What have you done to her?" Clark asked in a feigned accusatory tone.

"Preached at her, I guess," she said, without hesitation.

"About the not going to church thing again, huh?"

"Well, young man, it wouldn't hurt either of you to go to church," she said sternly but with an amused lilt to her voice.

"I've got to call her tonight. Do you know if she's at the apartment?"

"She's there, so far as I know," Lori said. "What do you need to talk to her about?"

"Oh, just stuff," he said, turning sideways to get through the door to the bedroom of his teenage years.

Fifteen minutes later while he carefully hung clothes from the suitcase onto the clothes hanger bar in the closet, the troubled thoughts returned. Probably just eating too late at night, or irregularly, or something, he thought, smoothing the cloth on a sports coat sleeve. But why his sister? Why was Morgan always the center of the nightmares? And, why always the same dark entities? Did the nightmares have something to do with the creature—or whatever it was—he saw those several years ago in Idaho? That's when the nightmares had seemed to start up again.

And, what about the creature? The eight-foot beast that walked upright, like a human, not like an ape, or a bear?

Memories of his meeting with the rancher-farmer that September night in 2001 played through his brain for the thousandth time. The inexplicable way in which the giant vanished right in front of his amazed eyes. Or did it? Was the sudden disappearance actually a trick of the darkness and the misty rain that obscured what really happened to the creature? Or—had he, in fact, seen it at all? Was it all a figment of his imagination?

Jabard Sowell didn't think it was Clark's imagination. The old man hadn't flinched when he told the rancher about the incredible thing that had happened to him on the way to the meeting that night.

"About eight feet tall, you say? That's about what I got figured, too," the rancher had said, squinting one twinkling-blue eye and looking directly into Clark's thoughts.

"Disappeared, you say?" Sowell asked the question while walking and shining the flashlight beam on his big barn thirty feet or so away.

"Com' 'ere…I got somethin' to show you."

Clark followed him to behind the weathered, gray structure, where Sowell knelt to lift a five-foot-square piece of quarter-inch plywood from the yellow-green grass.

"Tell you one thing, young fella, wasn't no ghost varmint that made this."

The old rancher shined the powerful flashlight beam into the huge depression. It was a human-like footprint, at least twenty inches long, ten inches wide at the front, just behind the toes, and more than three inches deep. The footprint of a giant!

Clark's life—at least his sleep-life—hadn't been the same since that night. There had been the dreams from the time he was ten years old, through age eighteen or so. But, they were few and far between. The giant things, dark and boiling, and the small, pale-gray creatures that sometimes stared at him with huge, black, glistening eyes. But, they were just nightmares of an over-active boy's imaginings. And, his dad had always gone to great lengths to reassure him, walking him through every dark place in the house, shining light into the crevices.

Still, he remembered the troubled look from his mother each time her son described the dreams. But, she, too, always did her best to assuage his fears. But lately, the dreams were intense, waking him up, bathing him with cold sweat of terror. His little sister, Morgan, was always at the center of the nightmares.

"Atten…Hutt!"

The voice! Clark whirled, came to the military position of attention, and saluted stiffly.

"Hey, big guy!" Mark Lansing said and rushed forward after returning his son's salute. There, right hands came together only briefly, hearty hugs taking the place of the handshake that just wouldn't do the job.

21 Club, New York City

Morgan sat, awaiting Bob Rashing's return to the table. She was uncomfortable being at dinner alone with a man twice her age, an important client of Guroix, Tuppler, & Macy. But, Alan Cranston had assured her the man was okay. The vice president for the advertising agency's creative department told her the firm needed to put its best foot forward in trying to land the account, that of one of the largest dog food manufacturers in the world.

She was, Cranston told Morgan, the natural choice to go to dinner with Rashing because she owned a rottweiler. Maybe—if all went well—Rashing would even like to put Jeddy in commercials. Cranston would consider having such a campaign pitched in that direction.

Still, the sudden request that she accompany the K-9 Excel vice president for marketing to dinner, and to some of New York's sightseeing spots, made her apprehensive. She wasn't at the level of account executive; rather, she was a copywriter still learning the agency business. But, she trusted her boss' judgment, and he vouched for Bob Rashing's character.

He was a nice-looking man, she thought, watching him make his way past the tables of 21 Club. His graying temples framed a darkly tanned face just below slightly thinning, dark brown hair. He was a little less than six feet tall, she surmised. Almost handsome. But, more than twice her age...Fifty, Alan Cranston had informed her.

"Sorry, honey," Rashing said, taking his seat across the small table. "Some business that had to be taken care of in Atlanta."

He had, somewhere between leaving the table to take the call, and returning ten minutes later, decided that she was now to be addressed as "honey," not "Miss Lansing." The decision made on his own to become more familiar was abrasive. Could it be that she was growing up in the New York fast-track life? Becoming more assertive? Normally, she would prefer "Morgan." But, she—not him—would decide when to become more familiar.

"I'll make it up to you. We'll have breakfast sent up to the suite in the morning," Rashing said with a broad, toothy smile.

"Breakfast?" was all that would come out. She felt her face redden. He sat smiling at her, as if he had said nothing out of line. A chiming sound in her purse interrupted her silent processing of his words.

"Excuse me," she said, retrieving the cell phone from the purse.

"Sis?"

"Clark!" Hearing her brother's voice after she answered made her nearly laugh out loud.

"What's that noise?" Clark asked.

"Oh, just a bunch of people at 21 Club," she said, with a happy tone in her voice.

"21 Club?! Boy, we are living high, aren't we?"

"Yeah...That's me. Living high!" she said with animation in her voice. "The agency asked me to go to dinner with a client..."

She listened to her brother for a few seconds, then cut her eyes toward Rashing, who looked with an impatient glare back at her.

"Yes. A client. He's about dad's age," she lied, knowing her father was sixty-four. She glanced again at Rashing, whose own complexion took on a darker, more reddened tone.

"Oh. Yes, I'm enjoying dinner very much. Mr. Rashing...Bob...just invited me to spend the night in his hotel suite."

She giggled, her nose crinkling when she heard her brother's words.

"Here, you want to talk to him?"

She thrust the cell phone toward Rashing, who picked up the white cloth napkin, wiped his mouth and hands, threw the napkin on the table, and got up and strode away.

"Guess not," she said with another giggle.

"Looks like I'll have to find my way home, my dear brother. Seems Bob is no longer interested."

They picked up the conversation an hour later when Morgan had entered the small apartment, been greeted by Jeddy, and settled into an overstuffed sofa in the living room.

"I'm thinking about getting out of New York, anyway," she said to Clark while stroking the rottweiler, who lay on the sofa beside her, his massive head in her lap. "Maybe I'll try an LA agency. I'll probably get the boot, after tonight. The guy was furious."

Clark listened to his sister's words, wondering how to broach the subject that was, even in his own proximity to the matter, ludicrous to contemplate. He searched the darkness of his old room, now so foreign to him. Too much time, far too many miles between him and home. They had to talk about it.

"Morgan, I have something to ask you. You're going to think I've lost it."

She heard in Clark's voice a familiar tone and sat more erect on the sofa, causing the dog to sit up from his lying position. Something was worrying her big brother. Somehow, inexplicably, she knew what was coming.

"Remember the first time you told Mom that a cloud-man...a dark, cloud-like man was standing in your room? You must have been about... what? Five years old?"

Morgan felt a flush of uneasiness, a bit of chill traversing her spine and the back of her neck.

"Yes. I remember."

You told me a couple of years ago that you have the recurring dream but not quite as often. Have they—do you still have those kinds of dreams?"

Morgan said nothing, and Clark sensed her troubled consideration of the question.

"You've got to talk about it, Sis. I'm having the dreams again, more than ever. Are you having them?

"You okay, Morgie?"

"Umhummm," she affirmed. Her brother wasn't convinced.

"I know what they're like. So, you don't have to feel...funny...about telling me. I, of all people, understand."

Again she was reticent to talk about the things of the nightmares.

She asked, after several seconds of silence, "How long will you be in LA?"

"I'm taking a week off. I'll fly to New York on Tuesday."

"I'm coming home, Clark. Can we talk about this then?"

9:00 p.m., Tuesday

"Morgan, I'm telling you the truth. I didn't tell him you would…entertain him…Not like that. We don't do business that way."

Her silence caused Alan Cranston to say more. "Look, the guy isn't even at the level to make decisions on whether GT & M gets the account. Don't worry about it."

"I'm not worried about that. I *am* worried about the thought of your using me as a perk!"

Cranston's eyes shifted from side to side while he sat in his fifty-sixth-floor office, his brain in overdrive, trying to defuse, with the phone call, the situation he had created. The agency's principals wouldn't like losing the young woman they had put three years into, training her to assume account executive duties. Besides, it was really true—Morgan Lansing's familiarity with canines, and her love of them, was one reason she had been chosen to be placed in the firm's training program.

"Look, Morgan. Just take tomorrow off, okay? Let's let things simmer down a bit. What do you say?"

"Well, I say that copywriters are a dime a dozen in New York. Why are you even bothering with me? I'll go home and find something a little less…demanding."

"Come on, Morgan. Don't be like that. You know we are like a family at GT&M. We don't want to lose one of our own," the creative director said in his best cajoling voice.

"Really? Do we send one of our own out to service clients—like a hooker?"

"Look, I apologize. I just had no idea Rashing would think he could…"

Morgan interrupted, "Tell you what; I'll take you up on your offer and take that day off. I'll go running with Jed and let you know if things have…simmered down."

"Fine! Great! We will talk Thursday," Cranston said with a tight-lipped smile.

Washington, D.C.—9:30 p.m., Tuesday

Her life of late was less than the good times promised by Wendel Clay. The spacious hotel suite, since coming to live with him, had turned into anything but the love nest she had envisioned when talked into leaving her own efficiency apartment closer to her job at the Pentagon.

April Warmath finished her calisthenics with yoga position stretches to soft, dreamy music. Her eyes closed while she swayed, and she reached to extend each muscle to its fullest.

She walked toward the large bathroom three minutes later, mopping the damp glow of exertion from her pretty face. She was always glad when the exercises were finished. They had never been fun, but she had been faithful to them since her late teens. At twenty-six, they were ingrained, and she felt incomplete when she couldn't do the nightly exercise ritual.

At first she had felt a little sheepish, well…cheap, actually, she remembered while she looked into the brightly lit bathroom mirror, seeing the ivory-hued, oval face, framed in part by the raven black hair pulled back and piled neatly atop her head. Her eyes, green and beautiful, nestled within long ebony lashes. But she no longer felt diminished by the live-in situation with her lover. The effects of her Midwestern upbringing were fading, and she must move on in the new life she chose for herself.

Wendel was seldom home any more. His time away from Washington, from her, was becoming more intrusive. He had assured her they would spend more, not less, time together now that his corporation had assigned him to be full-time lobbyist. Maybe he didn't foresee that his services as one of Transportec's attorneys would be needed. But he had not made any effort to explain things. She was expected just to accept it and be prepared to fulfill his desires whenever he showed up. Most angering of all, she suspected his time out of town really was spent with the wife he had promised never to see again.

She would make the move on the upcoming weekend…

What would her father say, her living as a "kept" woman? But, she assured herself, continuing to dab the tiny perspiration beads from her face, she wasn't a kept woman. She had a job. A very important job within one of the nation's top covert operations. The office, with George Jenkins as its director, had received, as a result of the war on terror, tremendous Pentagon black budget funding for carrying out…for carrying out exactly what? She didn't yet know but was about to find out. Jenkins had told her just six hours earlier that soon she would receive clearances necessary to know the ultra-clandestine project's darkest secrets. The thought gave her leverage, thus self-confidence that she didn't have before today.

Wendel was wrong if he thought she couldn't walk away from such plush surroundings. She had power with Jenkins, and the potential was positively exquisite: the ultimate aphrodisiac.

The door to the bathroom was open while she looked at her image in the huge mirror, the indirect lighting barely illuminating the large master bedroom behind her. She gently patted her face, holding the towel with both hands. Raising her chin, she continued to dry her slender neck, her eyes closed in the moment of relaxation.

When she again opened her eyes to see her image, she startled at what she saw behind her. A dark, shadowy figure stood glaring at her, its red eyes glowing ember-like, its long, thick arms reaching toward her.

April twisted, at the same time shrieking as she faced the monstrosity. But, nothing was there!

Her heart pumping wildly, she hurried into the bedroom, her panicked mind racing.

Who? What? What had she seen? She did see it! She did!

She searched every corner of the room, and, determining that all was well, slowly made her way back to the bathroom, looking with fearful apprehension into the mirror.

Her eyes widened when she saw the image, and she started to scream, putting the towel to her open mouth. But, in the next instant, she slowly lowered the towel, her face taking on a placid expression. A subtle smile took the place of the look of horror while she continued to stare, unblinking, into the mirror.

THREE

11:48 p.m., Tuesday

His latest segment was due in two days. "Phenomena or Phonies?" was the title he wanted for the series. The *New York Examiner* wanted it titled "Monsters on the Loose!" They were paying the freight; it would be "Monsters on the Loose."

But, for now it was sleep. He was dog-tired after his flight from JFK, then the reunion with his parents. Despite promising himself a week free from work, he had a full day's writing tomorrow, so he had to get sleep. Sleep that more and more often evaded him these days.

Information gathered over the past six months swirled slowly within Clark Lansing's drifting mind while he lay with the back of his head on the pillow, staring at the ceiling. A slow-motion collage of all he had investigated formed—as it always did—while he sought sleep that tugged at his fatigued brain.

Bruce Wilson's words echoed for the thousandth time within his memory while he kneaded the bridge of his nose and yawned, the yawn becoming a full-body stretch.

"This series will catch attention for the very reason that the elite snobs at the *Times* and all the others view all of this as foolishness. Limbaugh is right! They are losing touch—have already lost touch—with the country."

Wilson had moved about his tiny, thirty-first-floor office in Manhattan that day in September of 2001, gesticulating by flailing his short, thick arms to make his point.

"There's too many of these reports to be just imagination. Readers want to know the truth about them. Somebody needs to look into these…whatever they are. Might as well be us," he had said, appealing to Clark, whom he had used as a freelancer for three years.

Clark's fascination had grown with the proliferating reports of the creatures called "Bigfoot," "Yeti," "Sasquatch," "the Abominable Snowman," and other names. There had been the two personal…were they encounters? The first with the creature on the road that night in September of 2001when the rancher had shown him the footprint near Ketchum. The second, less than a week ago, when camping with two friends in Oregon, near where the creatures had supposedly been spotted. He thought he had photographed the beast that night while it turned and fled toward a thicket of trees. Like on the road in 2001, it had seemed to vanish in the camera's flash. And, when he examined the digital camera's recorded shot, all he found was an image of the thicket.

As intriguing as the personal…*encounters*…were, however, it was the visceral understanding that the monsters in Idaho and in Oregon were, in some strange way, a part of his lifelong nightmares that drove him to find the truth about the creatures.

Reporting on the war on terror and the U.S. invasion of Iraq, as well as writing about other news events, interrupted his plans to explore the matters involved with the nightmares and his encounters. Now, he was back on track, and, after a week's rest, he would again pursue the story full time. Bruce Wilson and the *Examiner* were willing to pay, and there just might be a book in the future from researching and writing for the series of articles.

But, for now it was sleep that he needed. Sleep was all that mattered…

Clark felt the veil falling, but still—against his will—his conscious mind wrestled to maintain control. His spiraling thoughts moved from his childhood room to somewhere…somewhere he didn't recognize.

His sister, her hair the same colors as the sunlight that reflected off of it, ran toward him. She was no more than six years old. She ran and ran toward her big brother, who turned to look back at her while she sped after him.

The sky turned a deep gray, almost purple, and a chilling wind replaced the warmth of the field of weeds and flowers through which he trudged, his baby sister trying to catch him.

Again he turned to look at her while an icy blast from the impending storm blew against his face flesh. Things became slow-motion, then, Morgan's arms reaching out to him while she ran, slower, ever slower…

The figure seemed to spring from the weeds behind her—or just to explode into existence—without warning. A boiling, dark, man-shaped monster. A giant: its black, menacing arms stretched toward the little girl; its huge, powerful hands and fingers grasping her and lifting her from the field.

He ran after the thing that held his sister while it moved away at a speed he couldn't match. His legs were heavy, so very heavy while the roiling cloud-monster grew smaller and smaller in the distance.

Clark sat upright, blinking his eyes to clear his vision. Another of the nightmares! Just another bedeviling nightmare.

He laid his head against the pillow, trying to regain his sensibility. He was thankful they were just nightmares. Just as much as he wished beautiful dreams were real, he was grateful, now, that the nightmares involving the cloud-like giants attacking his sister were only dreams. The good dreams were rare these days, he thought, now sitting on the side of his school-days bed. The nightmares were the norm, and always Morgan was at the center of them.

He stood and rolled his head around to relieve the stiffness of his neck. After a few motions of his arms to limber his body, he walked barefooted into the hall, stopping to flip on the light switch of the room that had been his sister's.

His mother hadn't changed things much, and Clark looked around, mentally reminiscing. They had been close for siblings of different gender and six years apart in age. She was a seventh grader when he left for his first year at Princeton. She had cried the day he packed off to New Jersey.

He made his way in the dark down the hallway and stairs leading to the first floor, after switching off the light in Morgan's room.

He hadn't been hungry at dinner, despite his favorite food of fried shrimp his mother had prepared for him. Now, at the hour of almost 3:00 a.m., he was hungry. It might not be good for his sleep the rest of the morning, but the shrimp called to him from the refrigerator.

Again upstairs, after microwaving the leftovers and grabbing a can of soda from the refrigerator, he sat in front of the laptop that rested on the desk he had used to accumulate a nearly straight-A record during his years at Berklon High School.

The desk lamp's light made seeing the laptop screen difficult, so he pushed the off button on the lamp's base. Better…

He scanned his e-mail, deleting 95 percent of the new messages. Mostly junk, he thought, seeing the new e-mail prompt that announced Bruce Wilson's message. "Someone called for you," it read.

Clark opened the new message and devoured its typically brief contents.

"Sexy-sounding girl wants to talk to you about your dream," the first line read. "Don't think it's a porn come-on, though…Gave her your e-mail address."

The sign-off line was the familiar "BW –Exam."

Clark replied, "Thanks. –Lansing"

He looked over the new messages again. One from Morgan, a few from friends, three or four from familiar sources asking him about his research on Bigfoot sightings. Nothing that smacked of a sexy-sounding girl.

He smiled. Morgan might take exception to that assessment. But, Bruce Wilson knew her voice; the phone call wasn't from his little sister.

Sleep tugged at him, and his body ached with feverish sensations reminiscent of times when he knew he was coming down with something. He downed a couple swallows of the soda and switched off the laptop. Maybe the e-mail of the girl Wilson told him about would be there when he woke up.

It came quickly. The sleep that sent its wave of nothingness within moments of shutting his eyes. Just as quickly, he was awake again, and he sat on the bed's edge in the total darkness of the room. But, the room wasn't dark. A red glow coming from the direction of the desk caused him to strain to determine the strange light's source.

He stood over the desk and read the words on the otherwise dark monitor screen of the laptop.

"The kingdom cometh" the text read in crimson letters.

Clark tried to clear his head of sleep, mouthing the three words several times. The screen…how could there be text on a monitor that was inactive? That was turned off?

He looked at the computer again, and the message was gone, the screen again dark. His brain was fully lucid again, having thrown off the drowsiness after awakening. Had he been dreaming? Dreaming that he saw the cryptic message in blood red text?

Central Park, New York City—3:20 p.m., Wednesday

The rottweiler strained at the leash, his powerful stride forcing Morgan Lansing to run faster than she intended.

"Jeddy! Peanut!" She shouted while trying to rein in the canine a bit by pulling on the leather strap around her wrist.

Cleopatra's Needle jutted seventy-one feet into the air just ahead, the imposing ancient obelisk standing on Greywacke Knoll, between the jogging path and the Metropolitan Museum of Art. The heavy overcast sky gave the thirty-five thousand-year-old, 244-ton Egyptian monument an eerie presence. The vacant asphalt path that curved out of site around the bower would be forbidding if not for the rottweiler's aura of confidence and the protection he provided.

Morgan's own running slowed when the dog finally got the message.

"Good boy!" she said between puffs of trying to catch her breath. "Let's walk for a minute," she added, pulling more firmly on the collar until Jeddy broke the slow trot and began walking. He turned his huge, black-and-tan head to see if his human mother was now okay with the pace.

They rounded the point where the vegetation impinged upon the walker/jogger line of view for continuing down the pathway. "Okay, Peanut! Let's try again," Morgan exhorted, both she and the rottweiler breaking into a slow trot.

No sooner had they cleared the area that obstructed their line of sight, than a jogger, headed in their direction, burst into view.

When he saw the dog, he seemed startled and jumped from the path to his right. His right foot clipped a large stone, and he tumbled headlong into the grass, managing to break the violence of the fall with a controlled, athletic roll onto one shoulder, then into a sitting, upright position.

Morgan stopped, and Jeddy lunged to one side, as surprised as his mistress with the development.

"Oh no!"

Morgan's gasp of concern made the rottweiler come to her and stand stiffly while glaring with suspicion at the fallen man. The dog emitted a low, deep growl that was renewed with each breath he took.

"No, Jeddy, No. Mommy is okay," Morgan assured. Jeddy sat against her leg but continued glaring at the stranger, who tried to get to one knee, then stand.

She wanted to go and help him but thought better of it. "You okay?" she asked from the pathway.

The man said nothing but rather, after failing at his attempt to stand, sat with his feet flat, knees bent upward, exploring his right ankle with his fingertips.

"I—I'm so sorry," Morgan said, trying to see the problem with the ankle. "Can I do something?"

"I'll be okay," the injured runner said, continuing to manipulate the hurt.

She walked to the edge of the jogging path, nearer to the fallen runner. "I'm so sorry," she said again.

"Why? It wasn't your fault," he replied, glancing at her, than starting to rise. "Just a Robbins moment, that's all."

"A Robbins moment?" she echoed, reaching to touch and stroke Jeddy's head to assure him everything was okay.

"Just a clumsy move on my part," he said, wincing when he tried to put weight on his right foot. He took a few unsure steps, frowning slightly with each.

Jeddy began the guttural growling again, and Morgan held the leather strap tighter, bending to place her hand on his right shoulder and pull him toward her. "No, Peanut, it's okay."

"Quite a dog you've got there," the tall man said, looking with a wary eye at the canine, whose dark brown eyes never moved from their fixation upon the runner.

"Rottweiler...beautiful animal," he said, making him instantly more friendly in the view of Jeddy's owner.

A very handsome, as well as friendly guy, she concluded. "Thanks. Sorry if we frightened you."

"No—like I said, just a Robbins moment."

"Don't think I've heard that," she said, her blue eyes sparkling with her inquisitive thoughts.

"That's just a joke among the Robbins family," he said, grinning, and mopping his face and arms with a hand towel. "I'm Blake, Blake Robbins." He walked back and forth, trying to exercise the hurt he apparently felt in his right ankle. "That's what we always say when we do something stupid: 'A Robbins moment.'"

"Oh," she said, liking the funny, self-abasement of the family joke.

"Well?" he asked, drying the sweat on the back of his neck with the towel and glancing into the eyes that looked at him with interest.

"Well, what?"

"What's yours?"

"My what?" Morgan asked, then realized what he meant by the question. "Oh, I'm Morgan, Morgan Lansing."

"And this big guy?" Robbins gestured toward the dog.

"Jeddy."

"I thought you called him Peanut or something."

"Oh, that's just a nickname. His AKC name is Jed."

"Like Uncle Jed of *The Beverly Hillbillies*?"

"Well, a little more sophisticated in its significance, I hope."

"Heck, I like Uncle Jed," he said, without breaking a smile.

"Okay..." Morgan said, not knowing what else to say.

"We New Yorkers are sometimes a little too sophisticated, don't you think?"

The question took her off guard, and she felt uneasy with the straightforwardness of this stranger's manner. At the same time, his cobalt blue eyes seemed to betray someone with whom it would be easy to be friends.

"Maybe I better not make that judgment. I'm not from New York," she said, watching him sweep back his thick, black hair with fingers of both hands.

"Do you think you'll be okay? I mean, is your foot or ankle going to be all right?" Morgan's question was both out of concern for him and for the need to get the run in before the afternoon sun got too low.

"Oh, gee, I don't know," Blake Robbins said, trying to walk and limping badly. "I don't know if I can make it to my car or not."

"Where are you parked? Maybe we can help get you there," she said, but really wanting to finish her run, then get to the apartment before dark.

"I'm right over there, Eighty-first and Eastside," he said, pointing toward the obelisk and the big building behind it.

"You actually drive in this city?"

"Not really. But I do ride in private rather than public transportation," Robbins said, beginning to limp beside Morgan, who urged Jeddy to begin walking ahead of them.

"Here, put your arm around my shoulder," she said, positioning herself beneath his arm and walking slowly behind the dog.

"I really appreciate your help, Morgan. I know you're not from New York now. Not many people here would give me a shoulder to lean on."

"I haven't found that to be true," she said, watching the grassy terrain that required some careful negotiating to traverse. "New Yorkers are pretty nice people, I think."

Soon they emerged from the trees and vegetation, and he pointed to a dark car a half-block away. "There we are," he said.

Morgan saw only a limousine, long and black, parked along the curb.

"Martin!" Robbins shouted and raised his left arm, motioning for the limo driver to drive their way.

"A limo?!" Her words were blurted, without thinking about them.

"Yes. Is there a problem?"

The car rolled to beside them, and a man in a chauffeur's dark uniform emerged from the driver's side.

"No. I've just never known—personally—anyone who rides around in a limo." She restrained the dog, who stood and stiffened, the growling coming again while the driver walked around the front of the car.

"Well, you're about to become a person who rides around in one," Robbins said, taking his arm from around Morgan and reaching for the rearmost door handle. The chauffeur beat him to it and opened the door.

"That is, if you'll allow me to give you a lift home."

Morgan said nothing for a few seconds, looking at the handsome face and considering his offer.

"No, but thanks. I've got to finish the run." She nudged Jeddy to begin their walk back toward the park's pathway.

"Thanks for the help," Robbins said, standing beside the open limo door while the chauffeur held its handle. "Maybe we can see each other again?"

The question wasn't rhetorical. He was fumbling for words to ask her for a future meeting. She realized that but acknowledged his invitation only by turning her head to look back briefly while she and Jeddy walked toward Cleopatra's Needle.

Near Los Angeles—3:25 p.m., Wednesday

Clark Lansing didn't know where to go next with the story. He had reached the juncture where facts involved with the Bigfoot investigative reporting must merge with speculation about where it was all going. The dilemma confronting him was one that would separate the respected journalist from the purveyor of pulp, and even the money a story that would interest a massive body of readers might produce wouldn't be worth alienating his brothers and sisters of the mainstream press. Writing from the wrong slant could mean being blackballed from all but the most fringe tabloids.

He had gone over the personal encounters a hundred times in his mind. The creature he saw on the road that stormy night in Idaho had been real. The twenty-plus inch, three-inch deep footprint was real. Jabard

Sowell, the rancher that showed the footprint to him, was not one to lie or perpetrate a hoax. The creature was real—or appeared to be real. Why did he always go back to the obviously imprinted thought, "appeared" to be real?

The giant whatever it was had just seemed to disappear. Did that mean he hadn't really seen it? Or had he imagined the creature that might have been as tall as nine feet?

Then, there was the camping trip just weeks ago in Oregon. The three of them had seen it. His friends had described exactly the same creature. A giant, more than eight feet in height, weighing—who knew? Something like that would have to weigh four, five hundred pounds? Probably a lot more.

The wrestler, Andre "the Giant," he remembered from a story he once wrote on professional wrestling had weighed more than five hundred pounds at one point. Such a creature as they had seen was at least a foot taller than Andre, who had been seven feet, five inches.

There had been no footprints; they had searched. Why had the rancher discovered a footprint, but they had discovered none? Probably the difference in ground material. The camping area was thick with underlying vegetation, and the area had been without rain for some time.

While he had investigated hundreds of reports of sightings and encounters with similar creatures, he could rely only upon his own senses as far as how to discern the genuine from the hoaxes.

Knocking on the bedroom door facing disrupted his thoughts.

"How's it going, Son?" Lori Lansing asked from the doorway.

"Oh! Okay, Mom. Pretty good," he said, putting out his hand to take his mother's. She stood over him from the back of the chair and bent to hug him and kiss his cheek.

"Sure is good to have you home," she said, glancing at the computer screen. "How's the story coming along?"

"Kind of at an impasse, but things will work out," Clark said, turning the chair, then standing to embrace his mother. "I'll have it finished by deadline, one way or another."

"Daddy wants to tell you something about what happened—about

the dreams you're having. There are some things you need to know." His
mother's tone was troubled, and he turned from stacking some papers on
the bed to give full attention to her words.

"Oh? Like what?"

"I'd rather he tell you, sweetheart. Can we talk this evening? Will you
have time to take a break after dinner?"

"Sure, we can talk then, if Dad wants."

His cell phone chimed, and he searched beneath the papers scattered
on the bed to find it.

"Hello?" He looked at his mother, who smiled, kissed him on the
cheek, and left the bedroom.

"Yes. I'm Clark Lansing. Who's speaking, please?"

"That's not important, now," the young female voice said. "What is
important is that you please listen very carefully, Mr. Lansing."

"Okay. Yes. What is it?"

"I've got some information about something that I believe will be of
interest to you. About your investigation involving the creatures."

Clark said nothing, his thoughts moving swiftly in their search
through the things he had researched over the past few months and years.
"Yes?" was all he could manage in response.

"I have access to certain clandestine information. I'm worried about
the matters I'm talking about. I need someone to share them with because
I'm afraid that I might be harmed, if, if I don't…"

She let the thought die.

"Are you in government?" he asked, his mind continuing to race.

"Yes."

"What branch; what department?"

She said nothing.

"Look. It's okay. Just a reporter's abrasive curiosity. You tell me when
and if you want to, okay." He hoped he could preempt her cutting the
conversation short. He had heard in her voice the apprehension that
might make her hang up. "You just tell me what you want me to know at
your own pace, okay?"

"There are some, within the darkest reaches of…certain government black operations…who are carrying out inhuman experiments. There is such an experiment scheduled this Friday. They are using prisoners from Guantanamo to…to carry out antiterrorism experiments. They have already used…some kind of creatures in these experiments. But, now, they are going to use human beings."

"Experiments? Can you tell me more about these…experiments?"

"No. I can't stay on this phone any longer. I'll call you tonight."

There was a click, and the line went dead.

Andrews Air Force Base,
Outside Washington, D.C.—7:22 p.m., Wednesday

George Jenkins thumbed through a portfolio of papers, taking time occasionally to initial a page. He sat near the rearmost portion of the Gulfstream 5, the desk tray built into the back of the seat pulled down so he could do the last minute approvals.

"Takeoff time is 1940, Mr. Director."

The lieutenant colonel stood in the aisle several rows forward toward the cockpit, talking to be heard above the whine of the auxiliary power and air-conditioning units attached to the jet.

"Thanks, Tom," Jenkins said, without looking up from his task of signing the appropriate pages.

The pilot moved aside to allow a young woman to pass. She came to where Jenkins sat, turned toward the right, and began stuffing her small cloth bags in the overhead luggage bins.

April Warmath sat in the seat directly across from the DOD assistant director and smoothed the skirt of her impeccably tailored business suit.

"We take off at 7:40," Jenkins said without looking at the girl. April said nothing but began fumbling through her black and tan leather purse until she found the object of her search.

"I got these for you," she said, handing a roll of antacids to Jenkins, who took them, tore open the package, and chewed two of the tablets.

He glanced at her and started to speak. His words wouldn't come. She watched his face take on the familiar, pale, glazed-eyed look. She had seen it before: the countenance of a person who was hypnotized. She knew to do nothing but simply wait out the attack.

Jenkins eyes went from blue-gray to black, the pupils expanding to full dilation.

The DOD director's lips moved, but she heard nothing. His fists clutched the papers, wrinkling them. She reached to gingerly remove them from his hands, looking nervously into the glistening eyes. She straightened the sheets and replaced them on the small desk-tray.

"Make the call, Miss Warmath," he said between clinched teeth, the words issued in a deep growl that frightened her.

"Yes, sir," she said, moving back to the seat across from his.

Jenkins's eyes appeared to return to normal but then rolled upward, until mostly the whites of the corneas were visible. His head fell backward, then forward, before straightening. He seemed to be aware of his surroundings again, and he looked at the girl, who sat with an expression of amazement, staring at him.

"Did I…did I say anything?" he asked, anxiety in his question.

"Yes, sir. You said for me to make the call," she replied, still startled from witnessing one of her boss's "episodes," as he called them.

"Then do it," Jenkins said gruffly.

New York City—7:30 p.m., Wednesday

"You can see her, now," the caregiver said, smiling at Morgan, who rose from the chair in the waiting lounge and followed the woman down the long hallway. Rooms on either side served as living quarters for people in various stages of physical and mental disability. Most in these rooms were hopeless, Morgan had been told. But, this was Cassie, and Morgan would never give up on her friend.

She smiled brightly when she saw Cassie Lincoln's face, although she wanted to cry. The young woman, only a couple of years older than herself, gave no facial indication that she knew her best friend had walked into the room.

"Hi, Cassie!" Morgan bent to kiss Cassie's cheek and hug her, feeling the frail frame of the young woman who had once been so athletic. "Have they had you busy today, sweetheart?"

She took a chair directly in front of Cassie, sitting as far forward on the seat as she could. She leaned farther to take the unmoving girl's hands in hers.

The doctors said it was best to just talk to her as much as possible when visiting. Normal, conversational topics, in normal, conversational tones. Morgan could at least do that for her.

She, for some reason, felt guilty that Cassie had fallen ill on her bedroom floor that night in 2001. The physician in charge of the case said it was an unavoidable cerebral accident. An aneurism had burst, and the girl, though unresponsive, and for all practical purposes vegetative, nonetheless still retained what they believed to be viable brain function. However, she wouldn't respond to anything they did to try to stimulate her to self-motivated physical or cognitive activity.

So she would come to this little world of Casandra's and tell her everything she knew, for as long as she could.

Cassie stared straight ahead, her face expressionless. At least the caregivers had applied a bit of makeup to the thin face that was still beautiful. Morgan reached to touch the face and pat it gently with her fingertips.

"Well, let me tell you about my life," she began in a light tone that was more for her own spirits than for Cassie's.

"There was this guy, named Bob. He took me to dinner last night. 21 Club, no less! He's about fifty. Can you believe it? Fifty!"

Morgan pulled a tissue from a box of tissues on a table near them and wiped away a bit of moisture that had formed on one corner of Cassie's mouth.

"You know what the guy wanted? Well, we can only guess. But, he the same as said he expected yours truly to spend the night in his hotel suite. Said he would have breakfast sent up by room service next morning."

She giggled, looking into Cassie's unblinking eyes.

"Well, Clark—you know, my brother—called me on my cell while this guy was hitting on me…"

She reached again to dab at the moisture on the girl's lips.

"I mentioned to Clark the fact that the guy wanted to bed down his baby sister, and, well, needless to say, the date was over." She again giggled and squeezed her friend's hands.

"Bob is—was—a client. Don't know if he still *is* a client…"

Morgan stopped what she thought was to be just rattling on, considering that she was, in effect, talking to herself. Made no difference, she decided; the doctor had said talk to Cassie. So she would talk.

"But, that's not the interesting meeting with a guy. This afternoon— while Peanut and I were running in the park—I met this guy." Morgan became reflective, looking for the right words to express the meeting and the man.

"His name is Blake Robbins, Cassie. And he was gorgeous!"

Morgan sat more erect in the chair, squeezing her friend's hands in a gentle way.

"This guy was about six feet, three inches tall, or so. Dark, almost black hair. Had the bluest eyes you've ever seen, girl. Like looking into the ocean from twenty thousand feet. And a body like a cross between a fashion model and a world-class swimmer."

Morgan reached to push behind her friend's ear a strand of hair that had fallen across Cassie's face.

"Jeddy and I were plodding along, rounded a corner, and this guy— Blake—saw Peanut and jumped to one side. He tripped and hurt his ankle. Anyway, we talked, and I helped him back to his car, a limo! Can you believe it? With a chauffeur and the whole thing!"

She looked into Cassie's unblinking eyes, thinking how her friend would have said, had she been able, "So, when are you going to get to the interesting parts?"

"He offered Peanut and me a ride home…" Her words trailed off. She had regretted not taking him up on the offer ever since turning to walk away from him. The disheartening realization finally had taken root. She would never see Blake Robbins again.

Near Los Angeles—7:00 p.m., Wednesday

Mark Lansing grabbed Lori after she had placed a goblet of iced tea on the table next to the big leather recliner. Her squeal of surprise turned to laughter, and she put her arms around her husband's neck while she sat in his lap. They kissed several times in a playful way, then in a lingering way reminiscent of younger days, Lori thought with inward delight.

"You guys at it again?"

Their son's question was accompanied by a disbelieving chuckle.

"Want me to come back, later?"

"Just sit down over there and learn something or two, wise guy," his father said, then kissed his wife again.

Lori pushed away and straightened her clothing. Both husband and son grinned at her effort to regain decorum.

"Mom's still got it, huh?" Clark said, still poking at his mother.

"Indeed!" Mark agreed.

"And both of you are going to get it with a broom handle," Lori said, laughing, leaving the big den to return to the kitchen.

"So, Dad. What's the mystery meeting about?" Mark asked, taking the glass of tea handed him by his mother when she returned a moment later.

"These…things…you've been researching, Clark. What's the latest on them? I mean, what's the latest verdict? Do they exist, or not?"

Clark shifted in his chair, his father's question causing a degree of uneasiness.

"Why, Dad? I didn't know you knew…didn't know you knew what I was researching."

"I didn't know, not exactly. But, I had some idea. You've been fascinated with…" Mark let the verbalization of the thought die.

"We have something to tell you, Son," Lori broke in, sitting in the twin leather recliner beside the one in which her husband sat.

Mark and Lori glanced at each other, each wanting the other to begin. Mark did so.

"Son, we've told you about the times your mother and I had to deal with some…strange goings-on in government."

"Yes, I remember that you said you couldn't talk much—"

"Right," Clark's father interrupted. "We had no choice. If we had talked too freely, some in government wouldn't view it too well. Your grandfathers could have lost their pensions and suffered in other ways"

"But, there are things, Clark…" Clark saw the agony in his mother's expression while she tried to find the words. "These dreams you've been telling us about. They…"

"They are a lot like the kinds of dreams, or whatever, I had back in those days," said Mark.

"Whatever? You said 'dreams or whatever'…"

His father sat forward in the big recliner, his elbows on his knees. His eyes searched the den's wooden-tiled floor for the right words.

"They weren't dreams. They were…something other. They weren't of this world," Mark said, slowly raising his head to look directly into his son's eyes.

"Yet they have been here all along."

FOUR

The warm front forced the Canadian September weather to retreat, and New York City sweltered under heat reminiscent of mid-August. The walk from her Sixty-eighth Street apartment building seemed longer today, but a sudden, cooling breeze refreshed Morgan, and her step quickened.

Her office building loomed in the sunlight that filtered between the other skyscrapers. She had made up her mind and, as always, looked forward to starting her workday by meeting Kristi Flannigan at the corner of Seventy-second and Madison Avenue so they would walk the final blocks together.

"Well, she returns!" her friend, a pretty native New Yorker smiled, walking to meet her, then grabbed Morgan's arm and gave her a quick hug.

"Must be nice to take off in the middle of the week like that," Kristi said above the busy city noises, stepping off the curb with her friend to cross with the "WALK" light.

"It was nice. I could get used to that," Morgan said while she hurried in quick strides beside Kristi.

The expansive sidewalks, crowded with people of every description, never ceased to amaze her. The city teemed with pedestrian traffic this beautiful September morning while they neared the building that housed Guroix, Tuppler, & Macy on its forty-seventh floor.

"How did the dinner date go?"

The question took Morgan somewhat aback, and she couldn't answer, causing Kristi to explain.

"I heard Lucinda Watson telling somebody. He's a big shot at the dog food company, right?"

Morgan would have been incensed but for the fact that Kristi was, next to Cassie Lincoln, her best friend in the city. "I would have told you, but it was after work, and you had already left. Alan said it was important that we be hospitable, and I was the one who knows about the dogs."

"Well?"

"Well…the guy expected a little too much hospitality," Morgan said. "So, I found my way back to the apartment by myself."

"I would kill Cranston."

"Yes, let's do," Morgan agreed, laughing at her friend's well-known volatility.

They rounded the corner in front of their building and saw a number of people going out of their way to avoid someone holding a large placard. Some looked irritated as they skirted the man dressed in a white robe from the neck down. Others smiled or laughed, shaking their heads while moving further along the sidewalk on their way to their jobs. Most paid no attention at all.

The sight wasn't all that strange in Midtown. The loonies and the more serious protestors always hoped for the ever-alert New York press.

Morgan and Kristi prepared to give the small man a wide berth while they tried to get to the steps leading to the building's main door fronting Madison Avenue. When they side-stepped to go around him, the man jumped to block their way, his eyes wide, his expression of urgency exaggerated by the heavy wrinkles above a mostly white beard that reached his chest.

Morgan thought for a moment that he would strike her with the placard he held aloft by a 1 X 3-inch board. It stated in blood red letters: "The kingdom cometh!" The man moved forward, causing both Morgan and Kristi to back up. Others surrounding them gawked at the scene that was weird, even by New York City standards. The old man's expression became even more wide-eyed. He pointed by extending his free arm and the crooked index finger of his right hand at Morgan's face.

"Daughter of man! Child of darkness!"

The old man's words hissed at Morgan, who could only stare back at him with a puzzled gaze, her face emotion-reddened beneath the straw yellow hair. The words seethed at her again, in a steam-like whisper. "*Daughter of man…Child of darkness…*"

The robed man seemed to choke, his eyes bulging. He dropped the placard to the concrete and grabbed his throat with both hands, gagging—his tongue thrusting from the open mouth. His face went from red to almost purple, and he dropped hard to the sidewalk.

Morgan stood staring down at the fallen man while the onlookers gathered around them.

"Come on, Morgan." Kristi tugged her friend from the crowd. "Let's get out of here."

Near LA—7:05 a.m., Thursday

He had been unable to link to the Net since 5:00 a.m. Clark Lansing tried unsuccessfully for it seemed like the one hundredth time to get someone on the line to explain and fix the problem. Finally, he was informed that it was a regional problem that had nothing to do with his computer.

He cursed almost inaudibly, pushing himself away from the laptop. There was so much research and writing to do…so much.

He paced the bedroom carpet, trying to draw upon facts he had filed in his mind. Where to go next with the story?

When he heard the e-mail chime, he clenched his fists and punched the air. "Yes!"

He sat again and moved to beneath the tabletop. The first e-mail prompt to meet his eyes was from an address he hadn't seen. A rush of excitement bathed his tired brain.

"The creatures—your book—need to talk."

Clark opened the e-mail and devoured the message in a quick scan.

"There is a story the American public must know—involving the giant creatures—your nightmares. I'll call again at 9:00 a.m., Thursday, Pacific time."

The girl! She would call in…Clark checked his wrist for the watch that wasn't there, then looked to the clock on the laptop. "Seven ten," he considered, hating the thought of having to wait an hour and fifty minutes to hear again from the young woman who had cut the conversation short the night before, the person who said she worked for a dark project within a clandestine agency of the U.S. government.

His brain reeled from what his mother and father had told him and now thoughts of what this woman—apparently a DOD leaker—wanted him to know. He had come home for a few days to reflect and finish the story that was already all but written. This sudden surge could constitute information overload. The vacation was over before it began...

His anxious pondering was short-circuited by his cell phone ringing.

His sister's name and cell number popped on the tiny screen.

"Morgan?"

"Yep. It's me!" Morgan sat between a drawing board and her small desk, a plastic cup of Coca-Cola between the fingers and thumb of her left hand.

"You okay?" her brother's inflection made her know the early morning call was troubling to him.

"I'm okay. Just had to talk to my big brother for a minute."

"Good. I'm glad," Clark said, pleased more than she could realize that she had called him.

"Just wanted you to know that I've slept on it and decided I'll stay with the agency. At least for a while."

"Good. That's really good," he said without considering the enthusiasm in his voice.

"Well, I thought you wanted to see me!" Her tone was playfully chiding.

"Oh, no, Sis. It's just that my life has suddenly become a bit chaotic, and I'm going to have to leave. I'm waiting on a call now. I'm sure I'll have to do some traveling, so wouldn't be here for you..."

"Where you going?"

"Honestly, I don't know, yet. Got this mysterious call from this person about my research for the story and, hopefully, for a book."

"The hairy giants?"

"Yeah. A woman in some government office—a DOD person, I take it—wants to tell me things that she says the public needs to know."

"The DOD?"

"Department of Defense," Clark said. "I really don't know more than that. But, I'll let you know once I can. We'll get together in New York as soon as I can get back. Got a lot to tell you—things Dad and Mom have told me about these nightmares, all of that."

"I've got some pretty weird things to tell you, too," Morgan said then sipped hard on the Coke. "This old man, dressed like some Old Testament guy—a prophet or something—out of all the people on the sidewalk in front of the building this morning, he picked me out. He stood in front of me, pointed a finger in my face, and called me something like, "daughter of man, child of Satan…or the Devil." I can't remember what. Then…" Her voice choked with emotion. "Then he fell to the sidewalk. I don't know if he fainted, or died, or what."

Clark said nothing, awaiting his sister's next words. She broke the silence, remembering more details.

"He held a sign, you know, tacked to a board—like one of those political placards. It had painted on it, 'The kingdom cometh.'"

Clark felt a strange flush of anxiety ripple through his emotions. He saw again in his mind's eye the blood red sentence on the black, lifeless screen: "The kingdom cometh."

Twenty-three minutes later, Clark sat composing the finishing touches on the block of writing he had assigned himself. The rest of the three hours he had set out for work on the project would be spent searching the Net for specific accounts of encounters with the creatures called Bigfoot, Yeti, Sasquatch, and other names, depending on the area of the world where people allegedly had the encounters. Of course, anything that one might find on the Internet was suspect. He would have to carefully follow up with phone calls and e-mails. He would save the trail for the most likely to produce proof of what was reported.

Bruce Wilson wouldn't mind the expense of travel, if the result was, at a minimum, spectacular. The editor of the *New York Examiner* preferred that expenditure for travel produce stupendous results, but he would settle for the mere spectacular. Travel, at the moment, didn't appeal to Clark. Especially not to Nepal, where one intriguing report had it that a mid-mountain climbing camp had been destroyed by at least two ten-foot tall creatures. The Sherpas, the Tibetan burden carriers for the climbers of the Himalayas, could only scream "Yeti!" according to the British mountaineers, who all witnessed the creatures disappear into the heavy snowfall after wrecking the camp. The Himalayas had held no attraction in his wanderlust during his usual love of travel and certainly did not now. Even the Fouke Monster reports were more alluring than traveling halfway around the planet to trek the freezing mountains of Nepal. Yes, the swamps of southern Arkansas would be preferable.

The cell phone rang, snapping his thoughts to the call he had been waiting for. Yes! The area code displayed was that of D.C.

"Clark Lansing," he answered, trying not to sound anxious.

"This is the person who called you before—"

"Yes, I recognize your voice," Clark said, reaching for a ballpoint and notepad. He wished he had prepared to record the woman's words. But, he couldn't risk her having devices that would detect such recordings—thus likely to cause her to refuse to talk.

"Please listen carefully, Mr. Lansing. I have only a few seconds to tell you where to come in order to…observe this travesty. Are you prepared to take this down?"

"Yes. Proceed."

The young woman's inflection betrayed that she was reading the information. She gave the directions for two minutes, then warned, "This won't be easy to do, Mr. Lansing. But being as discreet as possible is absolutely critical. They mustn't know you are watching. Do you understand?"

"Yes, I understand. But, will there be anyone who can give me specifics? Show me the area, so I don't give away my position? I know nothing of Colorado wilderness areas. I've never been there…"

"Just get to Alamosa as quickly as you can. You will receive help from there."

"Alamosa" he said, scribbling the instruction. He started to speak again but heard a click. She had hung up.

New York City—6:28 p.m.

Jeddy lay near Morgan's chair while she stroked the keys on the computer keyboard. The crunching sounds while the powerful jaws gnawed the nylon bone made her turn to the dog.

"Peanut, we are going to have to get you some quieter bones to chew on."

The rottweiler stopped chewing and raised his ears in a quizzical look, then, determining "Mommy" was just making idle chitchat, went back to gnawing the bone he held between his huge front paws.

Alan Cranston had asked her to do something she didn't think she could handle. Why did she agree to do it?

He probably just wanted to make her forget her anger over being propositioned by an executive of one of the agency's best-paying client companies. Probably had nothing to do with wanting her to give ideas on the dog food account because she was somewhat knowledgeable about dogs.

Still, the idea that they might use the Peanut in a commercial was appealing. Her father always teased her by saying that the honors her beloved rottweilers won at the dog shows were really her victories, not the dogs'. She was a bit competitive, she surmised, smiling inwardly at remembering her dad's fun poking.

Alan wanted some ideas for how to pitch the company. He needed her input on a creative concept for the company's next new campaign. She had about a week. Why had she agreed to take on the project? She might be selected as account executive for the company's campaign, but did she want that kind of pressure?

She mentally chastised herself for having such a slothful attitude. Her father and mother would never approve of such laziness.

A Mozart masterpiece chimed on her cell phone, and she moved to the sofa to retrieve the phone from her purse.

She didn't recognize the number but decided to answer.

"Hello?"

"Is this Morgan? Morgan Lansing?"

The voice—it couldn't be! How could he know?

"Yes."

"This is Blake Robbins. Remember? From the park?"

"Oh, yes. The guy with the sprained ankle."

"The same. I was worried I wouldn't be able to find you."

"And how did you?"

"It's a long story, and I've only got a minute. Mind if I tell you the details later?"

Morgan didn't respond, hurried thoughts crisscrossing within her mind.

"I hope there will be a later, that you'll let me see you again. Do you think that's possible, Morgan? I really want to see you again."

Blake Robbins was a man of straightforwardness. It would normally be off-putting, but his inflection told her—or she thought it told her—that there was nothing egocentric in his questions.

"Maybe…I don't know. Yes, I suppose it's possible," she stammered, thinking how very much like an ambivalent female she must sound.

"I'm interpreting that as a 'yes.'"

Silence again.

"We can meet wherever you say. Or, I'll pick you up. Whichever is best for you," Robbins said.

"Okay, I'll meet you at…Westside Restaurant. It's on the northeast side of Broadway—

2020 Broadway, at Sixty-ninth Street. You know where that is?"

"I'll find it."

The line was again silent, before he broke in.

"Could you make it in an hour and a half?" Robbins asked.

"An hour and a half? I…I think so," she said, her mind again reverberating with the rush of thoughts.

"Great! See you there at eight. Thanks for agreeing to meet me. Bye."

"Goodbye," Morgan said hesitatingly, looking through a dazed expression at her cell phone while she closed its case.

THE NEPHILIM IMPERATIVES 57

Lori stood at the open closet door inspecting her son's clothes by holding a hanger by its hook and rubbing her thumbnail over a spot she thought she had found.

"Is there no way you can put off this trip for a day or so? These things need to go to the cleaners."

"They'll be okay, Mom. I'm used to hopping to when the boss man says 'jump.' There's hardly ever time to tend to clothes."

Clark folded a T-shirt and put it in one corner of the worn, leather suitcase. He picked up a pair of briefs and folded them carefully before placing them on the T-shirt.

"Well, they should at least give you a little time," Lori said, trying to remove wrinkles from her son's blazer with sweeps of the palm of her right hand.

"Does this trip have something to do with the Bigfoot investigation?" She walked beside Clark and placed the blazer on top of the cheap clothes bag lying flat on one side of the bed.

"Somewhat, I guess. The person said the stuff she wanted to tell me about involved my nightmares—the creatures, that sort of thing."

"How could she know that? I mean, how could she know about the nightmares?"

"Don't know…I guess I must have mentioned them in a story somewhere. I don't remember. Probably did…"

"Daddy and I are worried about you going to look at something to do with government secrets. We've got some experience in those things, remember. The creatures, they're real. But, they aren't some form of life that is…the kind of life everyone thinks they might be."

Lori laid her face against her son's back and embraced him in a lingering hug while he continued to look at arm's length at a shirt that he was folding.

"They are spirit, not flesh and blood, son. Interdimensional, not terrestrial, or extraterrestrial."

"Well, whatever they are, I'm going to get the story, if a story is to be gotten. You worked in molecular biology, Mom. You always gave it all you had, right?"

He put the shirt in the suitcase, then turned to hug his mother with both arms. "You uncovered some things they don't want us to know. Then they put you and Dad in a box of silence. I'm going to open that box. Find out the truth about what's going on, about the nightmares."

Lori reached to her son's neck and pulled his head down, then kissed his cheek.

"These are not earthly monsters, Clark. They're monsters beyond any you can imagine. You must not approach them without the Lord going before you."

Mark returned his mother's kiss by pecking her on the cheek. "Mom, I'll follow in your and Dad's footsteps in pursuing this as far as I can. But, don't ask me to accept that religious stuff. We've been through all that."

"We took you to Sunday School and church. What happened?" Lori looked into Clark's eyes, tears forming in hers. "Why do you and your sister not believe?"

"It's not your fault, Mother. You and Dad did the Christian thing. You raised us in church. But, when the professors at Princeton addressed the fallacy of religion, of all religions, not just Christianity, all of that stuff in Sunday School looked...I'm sorry, Mom, don't get upset. It just all started to look pretty fried. I'm sure Morgan feels the same way."

Lori wiped the tears from her face with her sleeve. "That's what I thought, too, but your grandmother didn't give up. She prayed for me. She's praying for you, Son. And so am I."

"Sorry to get you out tonight, but I didn't think you would refuse because I know you're dying to see this guy."

"You know it!" Kristi Flannigan said, her eyes wide with delight. "You mean he called you, and you never gave him your cell number?"

"A little scary, huh?"

"Not if he's made of the studly stuff you describe, girlie. Nothing scary that I heard in your critique."

"Well, maybe my assessment was off. Hope you aren't disappointed," Morgan said while they stepped off the curb onto the Sixty-ninth Street crosswalk." All I knew is that I wasn't going to meet him alone," Morgan said.

"I'm not Peanut, but maybe I'm frightening looking enough to keep him from assaulting you."

"Yeah, well, he's probably a serial killer, with my luck in men," Morgan said while they moved onto the sidewalk.

Morgan and Kristi walked through the restaurant's main entrance while Blake Robbins sat watching them from the back of the dark limousine just out of their sight. The chauffeur glanced into the rearview mirror.

"Sir?" he said in a British accent. There was no response to the implied question while the driver looked at Robbins's face. His eyes appeared to be black, his pupils fully dilated.

"The time is not yet. Drive on," he said in a growling voice that sounded as if it reverberated within an echo chamber.

Colorado—10:35 a.m., Friday

The C-130 Hercules dipped its right wing and began a sharp turn in preparation for lining up on the short landing strip that began not fifty yards from the trees that forested the high-mountains wilderness to the west. George Jenkins stood outside the Humvee, his elbows on its top, the large field glasses trained on the rapidly descending, camouflaged aircraft.

A man in a black jumpsuit got out of the driver's side and put his binoculars to his eyes, watching the tires of the bird contact the concrete, sending puffs of blue-white smoke behind.

"Right on time," the man said, continuing to follow the C-130 while it made its brief roll out, then turned from the runway onto a narrow taxi ramp.

"Yeah. Let's go," Jenkins said, opening the passenger side door and ducking inside the Humvee.

A large truck painted in camouflage moved toward the plane, which had ceased its forward movement, its four propellers having whirled to a stop. A number of black jump-suited men leaped from the truck's canvas-covered cargo area, their M-16 weapons pointed skyward.

The driver pulled the Humvee to within one hundred feet of the air-craft and the troop transport vehicle. Jenkins glared hard at the Hercules while its rear portion swung downward. He watched while eight of the weapon-wielding men ran up the loading ramp. They disappeared from view for several minutes, then again appeared at the top of the ramp. They closely herded a number of shackled people dressed in bright red clothing. The entourage was on the ground within seconds, and moments later the prisoners and the troops were out of sight inside the back of the canvas covering of the truck.

George Jenkins spoke into the small phone device he had just unfolded.

"Our Guantanamo guests have arrived," he said matter-of-factly into the phone, then snapped it shut.

Crestone Needle stood bathed in blood red relief against the Colorado skyline, jutting in 14,197-foot, vertical, spike-like peaks. It was considered, Clark Lansing learned on the ride to Alamosa, the most difficult climb of the fourteen thousand-foot-high mountains in the state. The creeping afternoon shadows of the many other peaks within the Sangre de Cristo range painted stark contrasts of reds and purples along the entire range of slopes that spanned seventy miles into vanishing perspective.

Clark wondered what could possibly induce anyone to want to scale such a devilish, dagger-like slope. For that matter, why would anyone want to climb any mountain, anywhere?

"These mountains are good preparation for attempting the Alps, the Himalayas around Everest, and the rest," the young man sitting next to Clark Lansing said with a tone of authority, in an upper-crust British accent.

"Are you a climber?" Clark asked.

"Yes, I've some experience," the man of about thirty said, clearing his throat. He continued, "Actually, I've come to prepare for a climb in the Swiss Alps late next spring."

Clark grunted amazement with a raised eyebrow but said nothing, looking again out the SUV's large window at the towering spires of Crestone Needle.

"What, if I may ask, is your purpose in coming to the area?" the man inquired.

"Oh, just a reporter looking for a little color to serve as background for a story."

"Fascinating. You writing about climbing?"

"No. About something of a more fictional nature." Clark said no more, and he could sense the Englishman's restlessness for more information. He felt compelled to add to the explanation. "It's more of a science fiction type project."

"I see." The man again cleared his throat, before asking his next question. "May I ask about the nature of your project? I mean, may I know a bit more about what you are doing?"

"When I tell people, they usually move away from me. There's no place for you to get away. You sure you want to know?"

Clark's deadpan tone made the man's own eyebrows rise in curiosity. He said through a clenched-teeth smile, "Well, I shall try to remain calm."

"I'm looking for Bigfoot. At least for evidence or lack thereof."

"I see. Yeti, that's what the Sherpas call them, you know?"

"You believe they exist?" Clark asked.

"I don't know, really. I supposed one should keep an open mind in these matters," the man said, a curious lilt in his tone.

"Yeah, well, most don't keep an open mind, I'm afraid. Glad to meet somebody who does for a change."

"Name's Nigel Saxton," the young Brit said, offering a large, callused hand to Clark.

"Clark Lansing. Nice to meet you."

The SUV slowed, and Clark's attention went to a group of buildings of Tyrolean architecture, toward which the vehicle moved. He recognized one of the structures as the one he had looked at on the Internet. It was to be his home for the next several days.

"Welcome to Alamosa, gentlemen," the driver said after pulling the Suburban to a stop at the curb of the wide walkway in front of Clark's hotel. He sucked in the thin but pristine air of the high Colorado terrain after stepping from the vehicle. Winter was already asserting its leading edge in this high-mountain place, he surmised, feeling a brisk breeze chill in his upper body beneath the light jacket.

Before he could retrieve his battered suitcase and garment bag, he saw them disappearing through the entrance to the hotel lobby, carried by a short, thin young man. He lifted his laptop from the floorboard where he had sat for the trip into Alamosa and followed the bellboy.

"Thanks," Clark said once inside, pulling his wallet from his back pocket and taking from it a $5 bill. He offered it to the teenager, who had placed the bags just inside the lobby.

"No, thanks, Mr. Lansing," the boy said, shaking his head and waving Clark off with both hands, indicating that he wouldn't take the gratuity. "It's already been taken care of."

"You know my name?" Clark asked.

"Yes, sir. I've been expecting you. I was told to have you wait here in the lobby. She should be here any minute."

"She?"

"Yes, sir," the boy said, looking around the lobby. "She was just here. Oh! There she comes!"

Clark's eyes followed the direction the teenager's index finger pointed.

"Mr. Lansing?" The tall beauty smiled through the question. "Are you Clark Lansing?"

"Yes," he said, taking in the vision of the long-legged female with stunning green eyes set within the loveliest face he had seen in some time. Her coal black hair swept back to a piled swirl gave further sleekness to her statuesque perfection. She was even more pleasant to the senses than her soft voice had been on the phone.

"I'm April Warmath," she said, offering her hand.

Clark took it, noting the long, lovely fingers, tipped with equally beautiful manicured nails laminated in red polish.

If she was a leaker, she surely wasn't one who feared for her job. If she was the girl who had the secrets to divulge, all eyes of whatever department she worked for must be drawn to her, no matter where she appeared. How could she possibly feel confident in greeting him so openly?

The thoughts ran through his mind, then dissipated when he again looked into the stunning green eyes.

"There's a lot I want to tell you, Clark. May I call you Clark?"

"What? Oh, yes. Please do," he stammered, still dazzled by April's arresting features.

"Brett, will you please see to it that Mr. Lansing's bags are put in the Humvee?"

The teenager dutifully trundled off with the bags, minus the laptop, which Clark refused to give him.

"I hope you don't mind, Clark, but, I believe you will be pleased with accommodations a bit closer to the...the matters involved."

"Sure. Fine with me," he said, following her while she moved toward a side door. They stepped through it, putting them near the vehicle in which his bags were being loaded.

"Where are we going?"

"Over there," she said, pointing toward the tallest and sharpest of the jagged peaks. "You will find this trip interesting," she said before ducking into the driver's side of the Humvee.

"What's this all about?" Clark asked after several minutes on the rough-surfaced road leading away from Alamosa. "You said you had stuff to tell me, to show me, about Guantanamo prisoners?"

April Warmath looked at her passenger, then again at the steadily ascending roadway.

"We've checked you out, Mr. Lansing...Clark." She looked again at him, her tone matter-of-fact when she spoke.

"You are the one we want to use to get the news of the atrocities to the public."

"We? Who's we?"

"Amnesty Universal," she said, glancing at the road, then again at him.

"What are they doing to the prisoners?"

"Textbook reporter, huh?" April said without changing her solemn expression. "Who, what, why, when, where, et cetera."

"Well, you chose a reporter. What did you expect?" His tone and expression matched hers.

"Touché."

"So, is this what it's to be, a verbal fencing match? Miss Warmath— April—I didn't fly out here to engage in semantic jousting. Your time is valuable; so's mine. Can't we just get down to it?"

"Mmmm. A man who likes to get right to it. I really like that." She turned to look at him, a beautiful eyebrow raised sexily, her voice playful.

"How much progress have you made on these Bigfoot inquiries?"

"Not enough. It's slow going," he said, his curiosity piqued about where she was going with the line of questioning.

"Why do you ask?"

April glanced briefly at him, then back to the twisting road upon which she steered the oversized vehicle. "I think maybe you will begin to make progress, once you see with your own eyes what you've come to observe," she said.

New York City—4:40 p.m., Friday

The air conditioner wasn't doing its job, Morgan considered while standing over the copy machine fanning her face with a file folder, waiting on the machine to reproduce the document. She was unsure about her ideas on the K-9 dog food account. The ten-page document would either convince the agency's powers that be of her ability to handle the account—or show them how amateurish and unprepared, thus unfit she was to be a part of the $55 million account. Winning the account would mean more than seven million dollars in media commission for Guroix, Tuppler, & Macy. What did she think she was doing, thinking she belonged in any position other than that of a budding copywriter?

But, she reminded herself, it was Alan Cranston who wanted her to do the creative thinking on acquiring the account. He insisted he thought she had what it took to serve as account executive…

"Morgan!" The whispered but excited greeting startled her out of her thoughts about Cranston.

"You won't believe who just walked in?" Kristi Flannigan's eyes were wide while she gripped Morgan's arm and squeezed.

"Who?"

"That guy—Blake Robbins!"

"What?! How do you know? You've never seen him," Morgan responded.

"Paul Guroix introduced him to Cranston. I heard the name. He's just like you said: tall, dark, and handsome. You weren't lying about him being studly, kiddo!"

Morgan's senses heightened, the cold flush of emotion racing through her. Coincidence that the guy would show up at her place of work? Or...

"Oh! There you are."

The agency's president walked into the copying room with Robbins flanking him.

Guroix said with a broad smile, "They said you were likely in here. Good! Good!"

Kristi glanced at her stunned friend, then left the room.

Morgan made quick eye contact with Blake Robbins, then glanced to Paul Guroix.

"I believe you two have met," the agency's CEO said, continuing to smile. Morgan said nothing, trying to make sense of the situation.

"Hi, again, Morgan," Blake Robbins said, his tone one of contrition. "I'm so sorry about last night. A critical matter had to be attended to, and there was no way of getting in touch. I tried your cell several times but kept getting your voice mail."

She said nothing, but thought, "Liar. I checked. No messages from you."

"Please forgive me?" He held out his right hand. "Friends?"

She took it but with reluctance, feeling the large hand's cool flesh, the long, strong fingers nonetheless gentle while they held hers.

"Mr. Robbins has just signed with GTM on behalf of his corporation. Transportec is quite a wonderful client to have join us."

Morgan didn't at first hear Guroix, her gaze transfixed upon the man who continued to hold her hand. When she realized the executive was speaking to her, she removed her hand from Robbins's and looked at Guroix.

"Sir? I'm sorry. What did you say?"

"I said Mr. Robbins has just signed with us on behalf of Transportec. GTM will be representing his corporation in matters of public relations, advertising and marketing, the whole thing. Isn't that exciting?"

"Oh. Yes, sir, that is exciting," she said smiling subduedly, first at Guroix, then at Blake Robbins.

"I'll tell her the rest," Robbins said, his intense gaze seeming to penetrate into her core senses. "I signed with the understanding that you would be the primary liaison between this agency and Transportec."

She said nothing for several seconds, then said, "Why me?"

"I feel like we know each other already, you work with the agency, and you are the one I want to do the work."

His matter-of-factness rendered her unable to respond.

"Please agree to help me—to help Transportec."

His soft manner and the sincerity of his plea disarmed her growing apprehension.

She looked to Guroix, who continued to smile and beam with pride over having acquired the account. He nodded approval to his new account executive for Transportec, Inc.

"I've got a few things to do, so I'll leave you two to discuss business," the executive said before exiting the copying room.

Morgan felt her emotions begin the climb toward panic. Left alone with him…She glanced her alarm at the agency president's back when he left.

Robbins's look of sincerity made her glance side to side in her nervousness. "Morgan, I know my apology is weak, but last-second exigencies demanded I break our date."

"Exigencies?" Her raised brow and inflection made him laugh.

"Please excuse me. I've been bogged down in all these meetings with diplomats and corporate heads. My language hasn't adjusted back to the real world."

Morgan didn't smile much, but she did smile. The momentary expression encouraged him.

"The…matters…that caused me to have to break the date involved some of the things I want you to explore with us—that is, with Transportec."

When she said nothing, her expression remaining noncommittal, Robbins spoke again.

"If you agree to take us on for your agency, you will learn, I think, that I had a good excuse for standing you up last evening. And, I did try to let you know as far in advance as I could."

"Okay."

Morgan knew she sounded disinterested in his excuses. She responded exactly the way she had intended.

He laughed, seeing she wasn't to be easily swayed. "Okay. I agree my standing you up is inexcusable. Will you please forgive me and let me make it up to you?"

"I—I'm not sure," her stammered words surprised her.

"Look, let me buy dinner tonight. I'll take you home when you finish work this afternoon and pick you up at, say, seven?"

The discomfort of the intervening silence forced her decision. "Uh, okay."

"Great! Cipriani, the Rainbow Room? Will that be okay?"

"What did you tell him about the guests from Guantanamo?"

George Jenkins's words came between chews of the tuna sandwich he held between his fingertips. He glanced at the young woman, then to the tabletop for a napkin.

"Just what you told me to tell him," April Warmath said with surprised irritation, "that Amnesty Universal is concerned about the treatment of the Guantanamo prisoners."

"What was his reaction?" Jenkins wiped his mouth while putting the question.

"Quite skeptical, I think. He probably thinks we—that is, thinks Amnesty Universal—is trying to use him for its own purposes. He's a purist. Doesn't intend to be made a reporter lackey for anyone's cause. That's how I read him so far."

A knock on the heavy, metal door interrupted Jenkins's thoughts as he was about to pose his next question to the girl.

"Yes! Come in!"

His shouted words caused a uniformed man to open the door.

"Yes?" Jenkins said gruffly.

"Sir, one of the newest of the prisoners has gotten free," the soldier said.

"Free? Is he out of the compound?" Jenkins scowled the question at the military man.

"No, sir. There's no way he can get out of the compound."

"Is he chipped?"

"Yes, sir. They've all been profiled and chipped."

"We have plenty of 'em to waste. Let's get him with the RAPTURE."

Jenkins issued the order in an excited tone, then manipulated several switches and buttons inset in a panel within the tabletop. A row of monitors on the wall several feet in front of the DOD deputy director lit up. He spoke into a small microphone he pulled from the console.

"Don't waste time bringing this guy back. Let's zap him."

April winced inwardly at what her boss' words likely meant to the prisoner. She wasn't sure. But, she had heard stories, terrible stories.

Kristi Flannigan examined her friend carefully, reaching to flick a strand of Morgan's light blonde hair to its proper position. Jeddy watched the ritual with his huge black and brown head cocked to one side, his ears forward and brow wrinkled, unsure of what the fuss was all about.

"Well, I'll tell you one thing. If he stands you up this time, it's his loss. You are ravishing!" Kristi emphasized her compliment by standing back, hands on her hips, and giving Morgan one more visual inspection.

"I don't know what I would have done if we weren't the same size. I couldn't afford this, that's for sure," Morgan said, turning to look in the full-length mirror against the wall to her right.

She walked in front of the mirror. Jeddy followed and sat down at her right foot, looking admiringly up at his mistress.

"What you think, Peanut? Is Mommy ready for the Rainbow Room?"

The rottweiler shifted and growled a happy sound, hearing his pet name.

"Oh, my dear, Mommy is definitely ready," Kristi said, standing behind Morgan and admiring her friend while Morgan looked at her own reflection.

"Cipriani's—the Rainbow Room…Rockefeller Center! My, we've come a long way from McDonald's!"

Morgan looked at Kristi's reflection and giggled. "Yep. That is, if he doesn't stand me up again."

"Yeah, well, like I said, he's a fool if he does." Kristi moved behind her friend to smooth the midnight blue evening gown that sparkled in the apartment light.

"So, are you going to take the account executive job for his company? You know, that will be a high-pressure position."

"Oh, I'm not sure of that. I'll have to find out more about all that's involved," Morgan said, making a last adjustment by pinching the snug-fitting dress on either side at its strapless top and moving it back and forth.

She turned to face Kristi, who continued to look her up and down.

"You think this is all just to have a date?" she asked, with concern.

"Well, he's a guy. And he's human. He likes what he sees," Kristi said, then became more comforting. "Listen, girly. You are talented and can handle anything that the account involves. Just relax and enjoy the attention."

Jeddy growled and let out a subdued bark, shifting his weight while he leaned against the floor-length evening dress.

"See, Peanut agrees, don't you, big guy?" Kristi bent to pat the dog's head.

"Thanks for the loan of the dress. And for staying with the Peanut tonight," Morgan said, hugging Kristi.

"I'm a little envious. But, I'll get over it," she said, returning the affectionate hug.

Jeddy stiffened, the black fur on his thick neck standing up. He moved in a threatening posture to the door just as someone knocked.

Clark Lansing studied the laptop computer screen, his eyes moving over Bruce Wilson's e-mail message.

"April Warmath is a graduate of Colgate, 1999. Major: international relations. Hmmm…Didn't know there was such a degree. Maybe political science…She apparently went to work with Defense right out of college. Very unusual, seems to me."

Clark thought so, too. Right at the time of the change from Clinton to Bush. Must have had extraordinary pull to survive the transition. Someone at Defense—an entrenched bureaucrat, or something.

Clark's eyes returned to the screen.

"Her resume says little else. No mention of Amnesty International or Universal, or whatever they call it…That's all I got. –BW"

A knock at the door caused him to instinctively click out of his e-mail.

"Yes?" He shouted at the small room's rough-hewn door several feet away.

"It's just me, Clark!"

April. He closed the laptop and moved to the door.

"How's the room?" She put the question in an upbeat tone, awaiting his invitation.

"Great! Just great. Come in," he said after realizing she was waiting.

"These are a little bit rustic, but they will do," April said, looking around.

"It has high-speed internet; that's all I need," he said, closing the door.

"You aren't hard to please, Mr. Lansing. Hope I can please you as easily with the story I believe is in these mountains."

Clark said, with a solemn expression that portended serious questions, "Hope you still think so after I've asked a few more of those Journalism 101 questions."

"Of course. Shoot!" she said, her smile fading to a more businesslike demeanor.

"Why call me, a freelance journalist, to rat on a department you're working for?"

"Because we believe you are, in fact, an independent, fair-minded, freelance writer who will help us change the way of doing things by this government."

She smiled and, before he could pose his next question, said, "We've done some checking, Clark. We didn't just pick you at random. We know, for example, that you did some good writing in support of investigations into the treatment of prisoners by the military at Gitmo when the military was taken to task for allowing the abuse of those prisoners, posing them for pictures, and all of that."

Clark absorbed and digested April's words before responding. "Yes... Well, you know then that I found little of substance to support the charges that it was a military-wide, a government-wide abuse. Just a few rogues. Just a dereliction of the higher-ups' obligations to keep a better handle on things at lower echelons."

"And, that's the point. You didn't join with your fellow journalists, who seemed to proceed writing about the abuses from a common template. You were fair-minded and just reported your findings."

"And, what if I find things other than you insinuate in this case?"

April smiled, seeming to soften. "We're willing to accept your findings, Clark. As I said, our research shows that you are fair-minded in your reporting."

"What about these hairy, giant creatures? You said I would learn interesting facts involving my nightmares, the facts about these..." He paused, searching for the word he couldn't avoid that sounded kooky, even to him. "...these Bigfoot anomalies. What do they have to do with the matters involving the Guantanamo prisoners?"

April sat in a chair near the bed, upon which he had taken a seat at one corner.

"Once you know what's going on, you'll see how it all fits. That's why we know you will report on this from the right point of view," she said, after crossing one long denim-wrapped leg over the other at the knee and smoothing the material.

A loud thump at the door startled him as he was about to pose his next question.

"That is Brassi, an associate," April said. "We have some TV for you to watch."

"It is wonderful to have you with us this evening, Mr. Robbins," the small, graying man said with a mild accent. He bowed slightly toward Morgan. "And you, Miss Lansing."

She smiled at the maitre d'. "Thank you," she said with a hint of uncertainty.

Morgan glanced nervously up at Blake Robbins, who held her slender arm in the crook of his own muscular one. She wondered what she was doing in the Rainbow Room at Rockefeller Center, whose elegance she had nothing in the way of experience to compare to, in the company of this VIP, who had to be the most gorgeous man in New York City.

"We have your favorite location prepared," the man said with a twinkle in his expression.

"Thanks, Giavanni," Blake Robbins said, beginning to follow the maitre d'.

"This way." He motioned for the two to accompany him to one side of the entrance. He snapped his fingers, and a man in a formal, white jacket and black tie hurried to lead the way to their table.

"Have a wonderful dinner," the maitre d' said, admiring the beautiful, young woman in the glittering dress while she and Robbins moved with the waiter toward a raised dining area and huge floor-to-ceiling windows that overlooked South Manhattan.

"This is probably my favorite vista in the city," Robbins said, walking past their table and standing beside Morgan. "From here you can see both the Empire State Building and the Statue of Liberty."

He pointed with a wave to another section of the gigantic windows. "From over in that area, we would be able to see the east and west, the Hudson River, the Bridges, Queens, Brooklyn, and New Jersey. But, this is my favorite. These skyscrapers are jewels in the night, aren't they?"

"Breathtaking," Morgan said, seeing the golden-hued dome of the Empire State Building shimmering above the other structures. "Just breathtaking," she repeated in a whisper, transfixed on the light show from their sixty-fifth-floor perspective.

"Yeah. I've always thought it was pretty cool," Blake said while they turned back to the elegantly laid table. He held her chair until she took her seat.

"Yeah, cool and breathtaking," she said with a subdued laugh.

After ordering drinks—Robbins's favorite wine—he sipped from the long-stemmed glass and dabbed at his lips with the cloth napkin. Morgan saw in the bluest eyes she had ever seen a question he was about to pose.

"Morgan, I don't like to spend a lot of time getting to the point when something is on my mind. So, may I get to my thoughts up front, so we can both relax and enjoy each other's company this evening?"

She fingered the tall stem of her own wine glass and glanced at the dark burgundy liquid before looking again into his eyes.

"Sure."

"I've discussed this with Paul Guroix. Just to clear it in case you wanted to make the decision tonight."

"What decision?" She blurted her question and immediately was sorry she had posed it at that moment.

"I don't mean to intrude into your privacy, believe me, Morgan. But, the situation demands that I move rather quickly. I'm on a tight schedule with these matters. If there is a way I can get you to answer with a yes over dinner tonight, I was hoping to move forward with my plans within two days."

She looked at him with an unchanging expression. "Yes?" she said, with touches of both puzzlement and impatience in her question

A waiter arrived and both looked to him. He laid the elegantly bound menus in front of each, then made his recommendations for the evening's cuisine.

"Thanks, Montgomery, we'll take it from here," Blake said, nodding.

"Very good, Mr. Robbins. Thank you," the man said, bowing slightly, then leaving.

Robbins again looked at Morgan, and said, after taking a sip of the wine, "We—that is, Transportec—are involved in some highly classified

matters that we are developing for this country and certain nations in
Europe. Whoever works with us in public relations in this effort will have
to be thoroughly informed and will have to have some degree of government clearance. And, he or she will need to be involved in a quite up close
way, in order to understand the purpose, mission, and so forth of the
technology and our part in it."

He paused in order to—she thought—gauge her reaction. She pur-
posely remained silent and tried not to change expression.

He again sipped the wine, wiped his lips with the napkin, and smiled
slightly. "Well, I expected some reaction, I guess, from such a revelation.
I see you're not impressed."

"Well, not yet, anyway. I'm listening," she said, her eyes sparking
with the reflected light of the candle flame that flickered at the center of
the table.

"You will need to be available to travel with me—with us—to get
that up close perspective I mentioned. I assure you that I—we—chose
you carefully from among a number of people who were considered for
this…assignment."

"Why me? I don't have any experience in…government secrets and
things like that."

"You are a blank Word document, a new, unblemished canvas. That's
exactly what we need. To start from scratch, so to speak, in bringing
someone into these matters. We need someone without preconceived no-
tions."

"And, you just picked me because I'm a blank page?" Morgan's tone
was mildly incredulous.

Blake smiled. "Guess the analogy lacked finesse. The bottom line is,
I—*we*—want you to handle public relations for us. Will you accept?"

Light beamed upon the jagged crags of the cave that narrowed the farther
the troops moved into its interior. It swept side to side to expose any
possible hiding niche within the cave walls. The thick, hard-composition

heels of the soldiers clattered on the inner-mountain floor and echoed off the solid rock walls while they proceeded.

"Should be just around the corner," one of the men said, his words caroming throughout the cave tunnel and the now more expansive chamber.

The light next struck the man in a red jumpsuit, his back to the high wall that comprised the rearmost of the chamber. His black eyes glistened with hatred and fear while he tried to see through the agonizing brightness of the beam concentrated upon him.

He shouted curses in Arabic and reached to pick a stone from the cave floor. He flung it at the troopers, who easily avoided the projectile.

"We've got him on camera!" one of the soldiers shouted. Another framed, in the camera's viewfinder, the escapee, who continued to search around his feet for more rocks. The light blinded him, and he covered his face with his right forearm while shaking his fist with his left hand at the men who tormented him with the light.

While he again began searching his surroundings, a burst of brightness exploded from the corner of his right eyebrow. His entire body glowed with a thousand points of dazzling, colored lights. He opened his mouth to scream, but there was no sound. The sun-like radiance grew even brighter, then instantly dissipated.

The troops, who had donned protective eyewear moments before the light burst within the cave, rushed forward, removing the black-lensed goggles. They surrounded the place where the prisoner had stood against the wall.

The screen in front of Clark Lansing, April Warmath, and the man she called "Brassi" projected the place where the man in the red jumpsuit had stood. He was gone. It was as if he had never been there.

"What is this?!" Clark's tone expressed his astonishment.

"Well, it's not an episode of *Star Trek*," April said. "As you can see, the man vanished."

"It's not a camera trick, Mr. Lansing," the muscular man with the shaved head said. "It's technology they've developed for use against…anyone they choose to use it against."

"Who?" Clark asked, looking at Brassi. "Who has developed this?"

"Watch. You still haven't seen the true horror of the thing," April said, directing his attention back to the large screen inset in the wall.

The scene displayed was that of a room that looked to be a science lab. At its center appeared to be a large round platform on the tiled floor, with a rounded overhang suspended from the ceiling, positioned directly above the platform.

"Watch," she said, her own eyes affixed in a fascinated stare at the screen.

Light exploded from a single ignition point at the very center of the air midway between the rounded platform on the floor, and the suspended covering above. The entire area between the two round devices filled with excruciatingly bright points of colored lights.

The room became unrecognizable when the light reached the brilliance of the sun. Then the light was gone, and something appeared atop the platform at its center. Barely visible wisps of smoke arose from the glob.

"What's that?" Clark asked, thinking the disgusting-looking mass of pink and red that bubbled at the center of the circle was what April Warmath was about to confirm.

"The man in the red jumpsuit. From the cave," she said.

Near Crestone Needle, the Rocky Mountains, Colorado

Lighted spots of varying colors flashed or remained glowing in pinpoints upon the high, vast wall. A huge map of the White Mountain region of eastern Afghanistan, where the Afghan border meets Pakistan, dominated the screen that reached fifteen feet high and stretched forty feet across. George Jenkins pushed a small lever forward with his finger and thumb tips, and the scene on the screen marked "Tora Bora" in blazing red letters drew closer and closer to Jenkins's eyes while he squinted to try and lessen the discomfort caused by the brightness.

The graphic next combined computer-generated topographical features with satellite real-time video to give the DOD deputy director as clear a view of the region as had ever been possible. The technology was just put into operation within the past twelve hours, and Jenkins gloated cerebrally that he was the sole person—at least for the moment—besides the president and the chief executive's closest advisors to be allowed to play with the latest and greatest spy-toy. The president and Jenkins's advisor-competitors were in D.C., and he was here in the Colorado mountains, the only place on earth the technology existed, for now, at least. He smiled with smug satisfaction while jockeying the lever back and forth, then manipulating several toggles and buttons to maneuver the satellite cameras. His thoughts ran the gamut, beginning with the creatures. Then there were the ongoing experiments, extracting the terrorists, who were now Guantanamo prisoners, from this godforsaken region. Next would come the payoff.

His thoughts melded somewhere in the center of his brain with the darkness he couldn't control. Black, wave-like shivers rippled his body, and his eyes became black, glistening orbs while the minion had its way with his mind.

Remembrance emerged from the evil matrix, and Jenkins was again in the subterranean cavern the moment the subjects were brought before him—the moment the groundwork began to be laid for the masterful plan that would bring to the Oval Office the head of America's number-one enemy on a silver platter.

The director of the dark ops project saw not fear but rather contempt glaring at him from the prisoner. The man, dressed in a crimson jumpsuit, stood, his hands shackled behind his back at the wrist by steel bands connected to chains that loosely hung to their attachments at each of his ankles, which were confined by the same type of metal bands.

The Afghani looked with disdain around the room, seeing for the first time marvels of which he had not dreamed. Western technological magic pulsed and blinked silently, and his visage for the first time metamorphosed slowly to display uncertainty.

"I understand you speak English. Your name is…" Jenkins looked at a document he had been handed moments before by a black-uniformed guard.

"Your name is Musahad?" Jenkins looked at the prisoner after posing the question.

"Yes," the bearded man answered.

"You've been given a cell by yourself, Musahad. You've been allowed to keep your hair and your beard while the other prisoners have been shaved. Have you wondered about that?"

Jenkins's question was, itself, issued with a tone of curiosity.

The Afghani said nothing. He lowered his eyes to avoid those of his inquisitor.

"Says here," Jenkins said, flipping a page of the document, "that you are mujahedeen, that you are Taliban. Is this true?"

Still, the prisoner stood mute, his eyes affixed somewhere on the tiled floor upon which he stood.

"You have a brother; his name is Yusef Kahlied. Is that true?"

Musahad Kahlied raised his head slowly, letting his gaze meet that of Jenkins. "Yes," he said in a quiet tone.

"I have some bad news for you, Musahad. Your brother faces a death sentence, I'm afraid."

The black ops director squinted in concentration, watching the prisoner's unchanging countenance.

He spoke again after several seconds of studying the Afghani's expression.

"He's about to be shot by firing squad, Musahad. He was caught after setting an IED that killed some women and children in Pakistan."

Jenkins reached to the console in front of him and flipped a toggle switch.

"See, here's your brother," he said pointing to a large screen. The prisoner turned his head to the right to see the scene that displayed his brother tied, with hands behind his back, to a large pole. Soldiers were preparing for their firing squad duties by checking their AR-15 weapons and chambering rounds by pulling back the bolts of the receivers.

"You can stop the execution, Musahad. All you have to do is agree to undertake a mission for us."

The prisoner said nothing, lowering his eyes to stare at the vacant floor between himself and George Jenkins behind the console board.

"Have nothing to say, huh?" Jenkins said in a soft, almost amused tone. "Old Yusef will just go to get his seventy-two virgins and be with Allah, right?"

Musahad Kahlied remained silent, eyes turned downward.

"I'm afraid Yusef won't get those 72 virgins, Musahad. He—and all your other brothers…" Jenkins again paused to thumb through the several sheets of the document he held. "Five of them, I think, all will go straight to Satan, I'm afraid, Musahad. You see, the people in Pakistan have been ordered to round them up. As a matter of fact, they've already rounded them up."

Jenkins flipped a toggle, and another screen came to life beside the one showing Musahad Kahlied's brother affixed to the pole.

"Yes. These are your brothers, aren't they? And your father. Yes, your father, too."

The prisoner looked at his father and brothers, who were all bound with their hands behind their backs, standing side by side against a high stone wall somewhere in Pakistan. His eyes widened, his mouth gaping open. Tears began to stream down his face.

"Got some more bad news, Musahad," Jenkins said, flipping yet another toggle, lighting up another video broadcast from Pakistan.

"Recognize what's going on here, Musahad? As you see, it's not a pretty scene."

The screen displayed a number of huge hogs being herded into a pen.

"These will be killed and rendered. There skins will be removed, in preparation for your father and brothers, Musahad. These skins will be the burial apparel—the robes—your father and brothers will be wrapped in once the firing squad has executed them, in their turn."

Musahad's face contorted, and he screamed, as if in pain. He cried out, "No! No!" in Urdu.

"Before their execution, each will have his body shaved. The blood and oil from the pigs will then be poured over them, in preparation for their deaths. Guess you could call it an anointing, as part of our little burial ritual."

The Afghani dropped to his knees, weeping, bowing before George Jenkins, who smiled tightly. The DOD assistant director then spoke in a consoling tone.

"Now, now, Musahad. We don't want to send your father and brothers to the great Satan for eternity. You, alone, can save them from this...unfortunate end."

The DOD black ops leader motioned to the guards standing behind the Afghani without saying anything. They moved forward and lifted the prisoner to his feet.

Musahad Kahlied lifted his face, tears streaming down his cheeks. "Please," he said in a quiet, pleading voice. "Do not do this."

"It is all up to you, Musahad," Jenkins said in a tone as soft as that used by the Afghani. "You must make the decision."

The horn sound blasted, the *ooga-ooga* sound that tore him from the thoughts of pleasures of dealing with the heathens. Jenkins reached to the console and pushed a button. A small monitor among a row of monitors of equal size popped alive with a man's face.

"Yes?" Jenkins question was tinged with irritation.

"Sir, Mr. Snidely is on monitor three," the man in the black uniform said from the screen of the monitor in the middle.

Jenkins switched the monitor off and switched on the one to its right, where the screen filled with the image of Wayne Snidely. Jenkins recognized the backdrop behind the assistant to the secretary of defense as part of the situation room at the center of the Pentagon's basement.

"Yes, Wayne?"

"Are you alone?" Snidely's words cut the air in an inquisitor's fashion.

"Take him to the cell," Jenkins said to the guards. He watched while they hustled the prisoner from the nerve center of the complex.

"I'm alone now, Wayne. What's up?"

"We have decided to move more quickly than expected. We want one more test with the hybrids. We will just have to take the chance, regardless of how that turns out."

"But, we know it works with the hybrids. We need more testing with the human subjects," Jenkins said with frustration.

"If we can get him, even in a state of…disassembly…we can still use the DNA to prove the job has been done."

Jenkins paused, glaring at the screen.

"Well?" Snidely said with impatience.

"Very well," Jenkins said, finally. "We will get the test set up."

Clark Lansing's eyes popped open. Faint, diffused light filtered through the curtains on the wall to the left of the bed. He blinked, trying to grasp his reality, finally remembering it was the cabin-room. He was in Colorado, the area of Crestone Needle. He was here for a story or research that might lead to a story.

He struggled to an elbows-supported position on the mattress, continuing to try to understand his surroundings. His mind wouldn't completely clear, and he wondered why his circumstance eluded his clouded sensibility.

The floor was rough when he stood from the right side of the bed. Not cold, but rough and tolerable, like the weathered wooden planks he had felt on the floor of the cabin at the deer camp in Arkansas while hunting with his father as a teenager.

Why was the floor of wood? There had been carpet.

The quandary gave way to a more profound one. The entire wall of the cabin seemed to come apart, to disintegrate before his amazed eyes. A green glow grew into a bright mist that caused his vision to blur, his surroundings to become indistinguishable.

He stood now on surface of another sort. At first it felt like thick carpet-grass of a plush lawn, but it melted, or smoothed to a flat, hard surface.

Still, he couldn't distinguish his surroundings, and now he seemed to be swept by an indefinable something. Not a harsh wind but rather the hard surface upon which he stood, itself moving him in conveyor-like motion through the greenish fog toward a rift, a split in the distance.

He was at the same time separate, and an ambient part of the bright fog, until he was conveyed through the split and found himself standing, or hovering. He couldn't tell which. Yes. Hovering well above the strange scene within the vast, oval chamber.

A lab. Yes! A laboratory, with instruments—technology—he had never seen. Circular walls and himself suspended somewhere above a table. No. Two tables, side by side. Operating-type tables.

The gigantic room pulsed with an amber glow that seemed to have a life of its own. Now men and women in white lab coats moved about, checking console boards and lighted screens 360 degrees around the high, rounded walls.

His eyes seemed drawn then to the tables like a camera zooming in for a close-up, drawing the white-sheeted tabletops closer, ever closer. Human forms, covered from the waist down, lay atop the tables that looked to be constructed of stainless steel, as they glinted in the constantly blinking, colored lights around the walls and the bright, operating room-type lights suspended above the subjects of attention.

Closer, ever closer to the subjects. His view seemed to lock, then, in close-up of the individuals who lay side by side, each upon his or her own operating table. His attention was drawn to the several people who moved in, dressed in surgical garb, their faces covered with surgical masks. Two of those people held instruments of a configuration he couldn't determine. The long, thin, cylindrical tube-like devices shone with a red, pulsing glow and were tipped, it appeared, by electronically produced light.

His attention went again to the subjects on the table. They were face up, their noses and mouths covered with masks that apparently were part of the anesthesia machinery to which the masks were attached by several thin, tube-like lines. He saw that the subject on the right was a much longer form beneath the sheet that covered the body from the navel to the feet. A man. The other subject, a woman.

One of the figures dressed in surgical garb approached the unconscious woman. The person removed the anesthesia mask. Clark's gaze went instantly to the face. The face that he loved so very much. His sister! It was Morgan's face!

Clark's vantage changed in the next instant. He now viewed the scene from a new perspective. Dark, boiling masses invaded from everywhere within the chamber. They moved through the floor, the walls, the rounded ceiling. The masses were humanoid in form, and they towered over the white lab-coated humans in the chamber. The despicable creatures surrounded Morgan and the other subject. They seemed to invade the bodies, reaching long black finger-like projections through the chests and abdomen of the unconscious man and of Clark's sister.

Clark struggled to free himself from the position high above the scene. But his struggle was in vain. He was locked in an inalterable state of powerlessness. A distant chime disrupted his concentration on the horrific scene below. The chiming became distinctive and louder. It caused him to tumble toward the hard surface of the laboratory chamber, his mind thrust again into consciousness with another shrill chime of the cell phone.

Clark fumbled for the cell phone on the nightstand, his fingers running over several other objects before finding the leather-covered instrument. He hesitated before answering, wanting to clear the cerebral cobwebs.

"Hello," he said in a groggy tone.

"Clark. Is that you?"

Morgan! The voice of his sister helped pull him the rest of the way from the nightmare.

"Sis? Yes. It's me."

"Didn't sound like you. Are you okay, big Brother?" Her question harbored a hint of a giggle, knowing her brother's notorious sleepy-headedness upon first awakening.

"Where are you? Are you okay?" His question retained the concern from the dream he had just exited.

"I'm good. I'm in New York. Where did you think I would be?"

"Oh. Just had a crazy dream. The black, smoke-like things, again."

"Oh, those…"

"You were in the nightmare. You were on an operating table in some laboratory or something. I was watching it all from above. Some guy was on another table beside you. These…weird things…were reaching inside you both. Right through the skin, into your bodies."

"Creepy! Well, I'm fine. As a matter of fact, I have great news."

"Let's hear it. I can use some good news after that episode, believe me."

Clark stood from the side of the bed and reached to the night table to check the time. The travel clock read 5:58.

"Sorry to wake you up, but I'm leaving soon, and I don't know when I'll have a chance to call."

"Oh? Leaving? Where you going?" He reached to boot the laptop on the little desk.

"I really don't know, yet. Oh, Clark! I've been promoted. I'm an account executive now. I've been assigned to handle public relations for… Well, I can't say just yet. But, it's a major corporation that is tied to U.S. Department of Defense contracts, that sort of thing."

Clark sat on the chair at the desk and began manipulating the mouse to retrieve his e-mail.

"And you don't know what this travel will involve yet?"

"All I can say, all I know, really, is that I will be gone for no more than a week or two at a time. I can still have my apartment in New York."

"How did this come about? That's quite a rise from copywriter to account exec in charge of a corporate PR situation."

"Don't you think your little sister can handle it?" Her tone feigned disappointment.

"We are Lansings. We can handle anything," Clark responded, remembering their father's encouraging, only half-joking words so often spoken while the two of them were growing up.

"As well as anyone and better than most," Morgan added, the same words her dad always added to the statement of confidence building.

"What about the Peanut?" Clark asked.

"He'll go with me wherever I go. Wouldn't have taken the job otherwise."

"Who's going to see after you? I mean, beside Jeddy?"

"I'm a grown woman, now. Guess you haven't noticed."

"Who's looking after you?" Clark asked again, more insistent.

"There's this really terrific guy I've met. Clark, he's the most wonderful guy."

"A guy? Who? What has he got to do with this new job?" His growling, interrogating tone irritated her, but, at the same time, she understood her brother's ever-present guardianship over her.

"His name is Blake Robbins. He has a top position with the company that has the defense contracts."

"And, he is the one who'll watch out for you?"

"Well, he'll be close by while we travel."

"WE? He'll travel with you?"

"Yes, my sweet, wonderful, but overly concerned brother. He will be traveling with me, and that's all."

Clark was silent for several seconds, then his tone became serious and softer.

"Morgie, that is YOUR view of things. I'm not so sure about his…"

"Where are you?" She interrupted. Her question was as much to change the subject as to satisfy her curiosity.

"I'm doing something I can't tell you about right now. I'd have to kill you…"

"Okay, so long as you keep the phone turned on," she said with a sigh.

When they hung up, Clark's thoughts went back to the scene of the nightmare. His mind recalled vividly the face of his sister. And, to his surprise, the face of the one on the stretcher next to her was etched firmly in his memory. The eyes of the male face were open, unlike his sister's on the other table. The eyes were black. Not just the pupils and the irises, but the entire eyes were black…

The rottweiler's dark forehead wrinkled when his mistress called his name. He stood from his lying position and cocked his head, trying to understand Morgan's words.

"Ready to go for a walk, Peanut?"

The dog stretched and shook, then trotted to Morgan's side, seeing the leash they always used for their constitutionals around the building.

"Now, Peanie, I want you to be on your best behavior this morning. We will have a new friend walking with us. Well, you've met him but only a couple of times. Remember the guy who fell when we were jogging in the park?"

She attached the leash to the canine's collar while explaining. "I want you to become friends with him. His name is Blake. We will see him quite a lot because Mommy will be working with him."

The rottweiler cocked his head again, trying to grasp the meaning of her musical inflection while she talked.

"You wait and see. You will come to really like him." Morgan smiled at her silliness, talking to Jeddy as if he understood every word. But, then, he often surprised her with his grasp of things. If "Mommy" liked Blake Robbins, Jeddy could learn to like him…

Five minutes later, the dog led Morgan from the elevator onto the lobby floor. People stepped aside, unsure the young woman had as firm a grip on the leash as necessary, in case the rottweiler was hungry or just didn't like their looks. Morgan smiled appreciation when one person said, "What a beautiful animal," and silently nodded "no" with a smile when another asked, "Will he bite?" Of course, she knew he would, under the right circumstances.

Typical of busy New Yorkers, most just sidestepped and moved ahead to whatever their next pressing matter involved.

The morning sun was up but low in the sky, and its most brilliant rays slanted painfully into Morgan's eyes. She tugged on the leash for Jeddy to stop, and before he could respond, his great strength jerked her forward from her position when she tried to plant her feet on the sidewalk just outside the building's main front door.

"Peanut!" She said, struggling to find her sunglasses in her purse. "Hold up a sec."

The dog obediently stopped, although anxious to get to his familiar places of business.

The rottweiler ignored the people walking by them, for the most part, each pedestrian giving him wide berth, eyeing him warily or admiringly—sometimes doing both.

"We need to wait here for a little," she said, after finding and placing the dark glasses on the bridge of her nose. She walked to him, taking in the leash by winding it around her right hand.

"Now, I want you to be on your best behavior, Peanut," she said, kneeling, without letting the right knee of her denims touch the stone-imbedded concrete of the sidewalk. "He's a really nice guy. We mustn't act badly."

Jeddy sat, listening intently but still antsy to get on with his routine. He licked at her right cheek when she got too close trying to straighten the rounded collar at the back of his thick neck.

Morgan's face lit up in a wide smile when she saw him standing on a corner fifty feet down and across the street. She stood and raised her left hand, bouncing up and down on her toes and waving to get Blake's attention.

"Blake!" she shouted in controlled volume, wanting his attention but not wanting to make a spectacle in front of the increasing number of pedestrians. "Over here!"

She watched him cross with the foot traffic, his tall figure easy to follow, since he stood at least a head above most. He raised his hand and smiled while he crossed, acknowledging he had seen her.

Jeddy suddenly stood from beside Morgan's right leg and strained forward. He bristled and emitted a low growling sound.

"Jeddy!" Morgan scolded. "Sit!" She knelt by the dog and held his leash close to the collar. "No, Jeddy. It's okay, it's okay." She stroked his head and ears while she assured the rottweiler.

Blake Robbins stopped a few yards in front of them, waiting for Jeddy's mistress to lay the groundwork for the dog to accept his company.

Jeddy relaxed but kept his eyes upon Robbins, who returned the favor, eyeing the rottweiler warily.

"Is he okay with me now?" Blake Robbin's words were halting, unsure.

"He'll be okay. Just approach him gently. Hold your hand palm-up if you want to let him get to know you," Morgan said, surprised that Jeddy had spotted Blake so soon in the crowd, then immediately had gone into the bowed-up, pre-attack position.

"Good boy," Robbins said, squatting and reaching his long fingers toward the dog's muzzle.

"That's a good fella," he said while Jeddy strained to smell the offered fingers. The dog relaxed a bit and sat, turning his head to look at Morgan, as if asking, "Did I do okay?"

She patted and hugged him, kneeling, like Robbins, and smiling, first at the dog, then at Blake.

"He will get to know you and like you," she said.

"So will his mom, I sure hope."

"I like you," she said with an overemphasized and teasing inflection.

They stood, and he moved slowly around the rottweiler to take Morgan's hand. He surprised her then with a quick, gentle hug.

A rush of not unpleasant, though startled, emotion ran through her body.

"Thanks for inviting me on your morning walk," Blake said.

"Thank Jeddy. It was all his idea," Morgan jokingly lied, her nose wrinkling in a coquettish expression.

"Well, Jed, you and I are going to get on just fine," Blake said, again kneeling and reaching carefully to let the dog smell his fingers, then patting the rottweiler gently on the nose and head.

"You really think he will get to like me?" Robbins looked up at Morgan and realized her attention was elsewhere, her mouth slack, her eyes unblinking in an expression of disbelief.

"What's wrong?"

He got to his feet and looked in the direction she was staring.

"Oh, no!" Morgan's words were issued in almost a whisper.

"What's wrong, Morgan?"

"That man…" She pointed at a crowd of people walking, passing each other. Just behind them was a little bald man with a long white beard. He was dressed in a white robe…white clothing that she could see hung from his shoulders to the sidewalk.

He held a placard. The same words as before, in blood red letters painted upon its surface: "The kingdom cometh."

The prophet-like figure raised his hand and pointed at her and Blake. Though the noise was great from the early morning rush, she heard the angry-looking man shout, "Beware, daughter of man! Beware. The kingdom cometh…Beware!"

"What's wrong, Morgan? What do you see?" Robbins reached to hold her arm while she continued to stare, as if in shock.

He gently shook her arm to get an answer. She blinked, her thoughts cleared, and she looked into his eyes.

"What? Oh, I don't know. That little man with the sign." She looked at the pedestrian crowd again. The robed figure and his sign were gone.

Crestone Needle, the highest of the spires, jutted into the bright Colorado sky just ahead. The big chopper thumped its way northwestward, its powerful engines at near full throttle while it leaned into the wind that had kicked up sometime in the mid-morning hours.

His conversation with Bruce Wilson, before catching the helicopter to an unknown destination, replayed in Clark's memory.

"What's this all about? What does this have to do with the Bigfoot reports?" Bruce Wilson's gruff question was laced with swear words. He was clearly not happy with the expenses his reporter was accruing on this trip.

"All you've told me so far is that you've had a look at some government videotape about some *Star Trek*-type thingamajig. You can't even verify its authenticity. You say it could be faked," Wilson growled, then paused to hear his reporter's retort.

"Yeah, well, it sure appears to be the real thing. It's just that the stuff I find on the Net about teleportation is antithetical to the current knowledge of the physics involved."

There was silence on the line for several seconds.

"What the hell, exactly, does that mean, Lansing?" the editor in chief of the *New York Examiner* said, finally.

"What I saw, or thought I saw, defies a law of physics."

Again the silence.

"It's impossible that the technology is authentic, huh?" Wilson said after a few more uncomfortable seconds.

"It's the Heisenberg indeterminacy principle that presents the problem," Clark said.

"The what? What the blazes is that?!"

"The Heisenberg indeterminacy principle...Has something to do with individual molecules and momentum," Clark said. "Has to do with quantum physics and the theory of molecular or atomic particle movements through space and time. In other words, I don't know exactly what it means. But, according to what I've been able to gather from what I read about attempts at teleportation and that sort of thing, it is not possible, based upon present technologies."

Again, silence reigned over the cell linkage.

"Then why the ruse? Why are they stringing us—stringing you—along?" Wilson's tone had mellowed to one of curiosity rather than angry impatience.

"That's what a reporter's job is, isn't it? To investigate these things and find out the answers to the cover-ups and all that?"

"Yeah, wise guy. And you ain't doing such a hot job of it so far, despite all the big bucks we've been throwing into all of this travel."

"We'll just call it off, and I'll stay at my own expense. I will sell it; I guarantee you," Clark retorted with feigned irritation, knowing Wilson was blustering.

"No, no—we'll see this thing through to the end."

"Okay. But, we're taking chances talking by cell like this. Don't think we should talk again until I can get to a land line—one not located here."

A sudden jolt shook Clark from his memory of earlier in the morning.

"Sorry about that," the military 'copter pilot said over the ship's intercom. "There are some strong bursts going on between these mountains. Everything is fine."

Clark looked around at the men and women who accompanied him on the flight from just outside Alamosa. Each seemed busily engaged in reading materials or looking at laptop screens. None seemed perturbed over the turbulence. Obviously, he surmised, the trip was almost routine to them.

He watched the sharp-edged rock formations whisk by, deep crevasses between their angry projections providing beautiful, though deadly reminders of how close he was to death, spared only by the pilot's skills and the chopper's mechanical integrity.

But he couldn't think of the lethal consequences of pilot error or mechanical failure. He had learned long ago to tune out such things when helplessly encased within the planes or choppers that flew him to assignments around the world. He recalled his father's words: "Better above the madness than down there in the madness."

His Dad had often taken his sister and him along on flights when Delta allowed such privileges. Usually, it was to deposit them for summer visits at their grandmother's house in Santa Fe or at their other grandmother's in San Antonio. Flight was second nature. Still, he had seldom flown through such rugged terrain with such powerful winds whipping violently about the big helicopter.

Thoughts of April Warmath brought his mind back into his remembered conversations, the conversations they had while awaiting this trip deeper into the rocky crags of Colorado.

She was a beauty, and he did all he could to make himself forget she was almost mesmerizing in her loveliness. He was a reporter with a story to write. He had to get past his attraction to her unintentional allurement to his lustful side.

"You are taking a risk, Clark. I can't lie to you," she had said on that brisk, early morning while the two of them walked in the copse of trees just behind the vacation cabins.

"What kind of risk?"

"More than just a risk of your job, I'm afraid."

"You mean like a James Bond type risk?" Clark had said with a chuckle.

"You aren't that far off. There are people who are part of the project who would...do whatever necessary to protect their efforts. And, I do mean they would do anything."

"Well, I've got some experience with danger," he said, speaking with a best-he-could-muster James Bond-like voice that displayed teasing bravado. "I was in the mountains of Afghanistan while the fighting with the Taliban was going on in 2003."

"Looking for Bigfoot?"

He was pleased she could return the banter and felt closer to her in that light moment.

Clark said, after several seconds of studying the pretty face, "Yeah. Osama bin Laden."

April's demeanor seemed to melt just a bit, and a rapprochement seemed to have been accomplished. They turned from their face-to-face discussion, then began walking slowly down the little path leading deeper into the forest.

"So, if I'm asked, I am to say that I'm there to gather information, so I can report that America is being well served by the goings-on in the area. Is that the story?"

"Yes. We've got clearance for you to check out what they will allow. And they will allow you to check out the technological control nerve center that was completed about a month ago. They will allow you a look, to some extent, at least," April said, her face turned downward toward the path while they walked.

"But the thing I'm actually here to do is investigate the treatment of the prisoners from Guantanamo…From Gitmo?" Clark said, like his companion, watching the path just in front of them while they walked.

"We've got to make the world aware of these abuses. If we don't stop this torture, then we're terrorists every bit as much as those who flew those planes into the Trade towers."

"What about the creatures? When will I get to investigate them?"

"The creatures are part of this horror. You will see."

The helicopter leaped in a sharp upward lurch, leaving Clark's stomach somewhere below. The violence served to snatch his mind from the pathway conversation. He watched the walls of the mountains from his porthole seat as they climbed, hoping with all that was within him that the pilot hadn't suddenly realized he must gain altitude to avoid crashing.

He watched, then, while the chopper topped the rim of a peak, and a deep depression opened into an expansive valley. From nine thousand feet, he could see the several silver-blue lakes, surrounded by a lush forest that looked to spread for miles to the north and west. Gargantuan peaks of lavender and dark purple-shaded gray surrounded the evergreen floor toward which the copter now descended. Within two minutes, the bird swung its tail toward the northeast, then settled onto a landing pad he had not seen on the way down.

The huge blades rotated to a swishing stop, and when Clark's turn came to disembark through the sliding door on the side of the big helicopter, his eyes met those that were familiar. They were the beautiful green eyes of April Warmath.

SEVEN

Christopher Banyon sucked in the desert air, letting his breath expel slowly through clenched teeth. The Hungarian Vizsla walked beside his master while Banyon surveyed the terrain composed of plateaus and hills that ascended in the distance to become high ridges. He once thought it would be good to have no trees to interfere with seeing as far as he cared to look. He had gotten his wish, and the winters spent here in Central Arizona provided the warmth he had longed for, even as a seventeen year old chopping wood in the forests of his native Maine.

It was always good to come back to the winter home, knowing the snow would soon start flying around the Mitford house. He would return to Maine for the two weeks surrounding Christmas—would do it for the children and grandchildren. Arizona just didn't seem right for Christmas time. But, then it would be back to near Phoenix to settle in the desert home, far from the forests where he long ago had to chop wood for the fireplaces that were the only sources of warmth during those bone-chilling New England winters.

He touched the stick he held in his right hand to the dog's nose, and teased the canine, who jumped and snapped playfully at the piece of wood.

"Get it, Klaus!"

Banyon threw the stick as far as he could manage. The sleek gold-and–rust-colored animal surged forward in a powerful charge, tearing up the sandy soil when he applied paws and claws to brake. He returned to his master, waving the stick and teased Banyon, staying just out of the man's range so that he couldn't grasp the toy. But, the dog didn't have the patience to continue the game of keep-away. He wanted the stick thrown again, so let his master take it from him.

Christopher tried to throw the stick farther than before. He felt the twinge in his seventy-four-year-old shoulder and massaged it with his left hand, rotating the shoulder, then stretching and flexing the throwing arm to lessen the discomfort. He thought of all of the former major league pitchers his age. What must their shoulders feel like? He smiled and clapped his hands toward the dog, who raced toward him with the stick between his teeth in a distinctive expression of canine joy.

"Good boy, Klaus! Very good!"

Banyon went to one knee and embraced the Vizsla, who licked his master's cheek before Christopher was able to avoid the dog's affectionate action. He wiped the just-kissed skin with the shirtsleeve of the hurting shoulder and ruffled and hugged Klaus' neck.

Something caught his attention in the distance, and he stared past the dog nestled against his chest. The sky above the sand-colored ridge was in the lavender-gray state of late afternoon, so the oval object hanging above the promontory's center stood out in a bright point of light.

He squinted to focus better. It wasn't a star; it was too early for a star to appear so starkly. A planet? Venus? No. Too large for a star or planet…

"What do we have here, Klaus?" Christopher stood, still watching the gleaming object in the sky toward the southwest. The ridge was no more than a mile; he knew from previous hikes in the area.

"Come on, boy. Let's have a look-see," he said, beginning the trek toward the raised terrain and the glowing object that appeared to hang in the sky above the ridge.

The anomaly seemed to expand horizontally, its light diffusing somewhat while they drew nearer the upraised terrain. When they were within a football field's distance from the sloping outcrop, the glimmering shape contracted into what looked to be a perfect sphere, grew blindingly bright, and shot upward and out of sight at phenomenal speed.

Christopher stood, looking up, stunned by what he had witnessed. Klaus whimpered and shifted from his sitting position beside his master, glancing nervously upward at the man.

Again able to see his surroundings after following the sun-bright light, Christopher looked at the ridge. A chill of realization ran up his spine. It looked very much like another site from long ago. No. It looked *exactly* like that place in Qumran in 1967—the cave of the Dead Sea Scrolls!

Was he delusional? Had he and the dog been in the desert so long that he was now seeing things? Was this a mirage? He turned to look behind them. This was not the desert of America's great Southwest. This wasn't Arizona. But how? It was Qumran, the Middle East. Banyon looked at the slope leading to near the top of the small mountain. There! Near the top! A black hole. The cave…

George Jenkins and two underlings walked in hurried strides down one of the five small tunnels leading to the huge cavern that housed the three-story metal structure. The building under construction was to be identical to the one in Cheyenne Mountain, which housed NORAD, the joint security defense facility for the U.S. and Canada. Like the Cheyenne facility, this one, when completed, was expected to be capable of taking an almost direct hit by a five-megaton nuclear strike and surviving. But, it was deeper and farther into this mountain. The structure was believed to be set within much more dependable granite and was sitting upon a series of massive springs that could absorb either nuclear shock or an earthquake of considerable magnitude.

"Do you have things ready for the test, Gerald?" The tone of Jenkins's commanding question left little room for a negative response.

"Yes, sir," the small, thin man in the white lab coat and Day-Glo orange construction helmet said. "We are good to go at 1530 hours."

Jenkins said nothing but stepped up the pace toward the gigantic cavern.

"Sir, we are a bit confused on the subject of the test," said the other man—a short, corpulent scientist who struggled to keep up with the two men.

Jenkins cursed, looking toward the first man who had spoken. "I thought you said things were on go."

"Well, sir, we never received orders on exactly what…who…the subject is to be for this particular test."

"Incompetents. I'm surrounded with inept fools," Jenkins complained in a seething whisper to himself while he stepped up the pace once again.

Momentarily, the three men passed through an opening that would be, when finished, a three-foot thick, hatch-type blast door of carbon steel and titanium. They hurried through the towering skeletal framework of the structure that would serve as headquarters for the new, more secure North American Defense Command. They came finally to a doorway, through which they stepped into another small tunnel. They entered a door to the left and walked through several large rooms.

Lights behind opaque paneled ceiling sections flickered on automatically when they entered the office of Jenkins's choice.

"The subject is one of the hybrids," Jenkins growled, searching through the center drawer of the desk. "Number sixty-one," he said, looking at the piece of paper he had retrieved from the drawer.

He looked at the men with a perplexed expression. He tried to speak but couldn't.

They watched while their superior struggled, as if choking. His face reddened and his eyes bulged, the large blue veins of his neck and forehead seeming to try to burst through the skin. Jenkins's pupils dilated black while his face contorted with rage.

He stood behind the desk, gripping the head rest of the high-back desk chair. He seemed to calm, his complexion becoming a bit less hypertensive in appearance, the shaking transforming into calm, deliberate purpose of movement.

"Go, and do as I have bid you."

The words rumbled from the throat in deep, ominous resonance, the face taking on a shadowy pallor that chilled his associates.

The men had seen him this way before. They said nothing but glanced apprehensively at each other, nodded in his direction, then left the room as quickly as possible.

Jenkins sat in the chair, his back straight, his arms rigid upon the desk, glaring toward the door the men had moments before exited. The fluorescent lights dimmed on their own, a dark, boiling mass materializing between Jenkins and the door. It transformed into a human shape that towered almost to the room's ceiling.

The door opened again, and a tall, feminine form, dressed in a white jumpsuit, walked into the semidarkness. April Warmath's eyes, like those of George Jenkins, glistened, their black, inhuman appearance dominating the lovely oval, ivory-hued face.

The hulking, cloud-like being stepped toward the woman and in the next instant was sucked into her body, as if a smoke-vapor vacuumed from the room.

"The man, Clark Lansing, is secured," the woman said in a quiet, emotionless tone.

"We shall not underestimate his cleverness," Jenkins said from behind the desk. "He believes that he is to report on human rights violations by the government?"

"Yes and that he will be given proof of the creatures and their part in the technology," the woman said.

"We must step up the timeline for the ignorant human political agents. We must keep them forging ahead with the teleportation imperative. They must be kept busy so that they have no time to consider that there are other imperatives."

"They have accepted, without question, that they are the beneficiaries of reverse engineering," the voice emanating from April's mouth said. "There is no one among them capable of making the connection to either creation of Nephals or the taking away."

"It is a brief human time span before the merging begins. Will the female be within the compound soon?"

"Soon," the woman said, a momentary smile of ominous intent crossing April Warmath's pretty face.

LaGuardia, New York City

Morgan smiled when she saw Blake Robbins step from the limousine.

"There he is, Peanie," she whispered with anticipation.

The rottweiler's ears perked, his brow wrinkling while he tried to know his mistress's meaning. When she sounded like this, there was always fun to follow for him. He sat up from his former Sphinx-like lying position beside her while she stroked between his ears with her right hand.

She watched while two men in business suits stepped from another car and walked the several yards to where Robbins stood speaking with a man who had ridden with him to the airport.

Her nerves were on edge, and her heart palpitated uncomfortably within her chest. But, it was the good kind of nervousness, not of dread. Like the times she traveled with her father on trips around the country as a reward for getting top grades in junior high and high school over the years.

"You comfortable, Miss Lansing?"

The copilot of the Gulfstream 5 asked the question from several feet away, smiling, but with his eyes on the rottweiler, who eyed him back.

"Yes. Just fine," she said.

"Great. We should be taking off in about twenty minutes," the man said while turning and heading toward the cockpit.

The sky was overcast, the September wind unusually brisk. It could start raining any moment, Morgan thought, seeing Blake and the men walking the aircraft parking ramp from the cars' temporary parking area.

He was indeed a good-looking guy. He stood a half a head above the other men and moved with athletic grace. She wondered if his tripping in Central Park could have been other than it appeared. Could such a grace-ful body have tripped over its own feet? Of course, the first sight of Peanut had made more than a few people commit foolish-looking actions.

She reached to scratch behind the dog's ears. "You are a fearsome beast," she said, causing the canine to look at her and shift on his sitting haunches. "Aren't you, Peanie?" she concluded, laughing and hugging him.

She watched the men until they stopped just before reaching the folding ramp that led into the G-5's fuselage. The conversation appeared somber. They were discussing matters of top secret importance, no doubt, she surmised. What in the world was she doing in the middle of such company?

Morgan watched Blake move up the steps and through the airplane hatch opening. He paused to speak to the copilot, then looked in her direction, waving before turning back to the shorter man to speak.

"How's everything? You and Jeddy comfortable?" Robbins's question, after he walked over to them, was of a greeting sort, but it was somehow genuinely meant to check on her level of comfort, she thought, holding the dog's collar. Jeddy's throaty grumbling while Robbins approached caused his mistress to jerk lightly on the collar.

"Shussh!" Morgan admonished the rottweiler, looking up at the man she would accompany to Denver.

He moved carefully along the wall of the cave, bent slightly to avoid contacting the roof with his head. Christopher Banyon looked behind him for the Vizsla, but the dog hadn't followed him into this confining passageway.

"Klaus, come here, boy," he said softly, snapping his fingers in the direction from which he had come.

The dog must have been afraid of the shadowy corridor leading deeper into the cave, he concluded, bending farther forward as the cave passage got smaller with each foot traversed.

But, it wasn't dark. Not totally, he considered. Why was there light this far into the cave? And the cave—was it the same…No. Impossible! That cave was half a world away, in the Middle East.

Yet the interior was familiar, very familiar, and now the illumination increased, his surroundings becoming clearly visible. To the right, the deep crevasse. It appeared to be the same he remembered from those decades ago when he and Susie had entered the cave, had experienced…whatever it was they had experienced…

The tunnel soon shrank in dimension to a crawlspace. Something within drove him forward; although, he would soon reach the point that his body could no longer move on hands and knees. Soon he would have to snake his way toward the glow in the distance—mist-shrouded light fluorescing along the narrowing walls far ahead.

After a few more yards, however, he had slithered through the narrowest point, and the tunnel enlarged to become a passageway through which he could walk without bending.

Now the pathway became brighter, and the foggy iridescence dissipated the farther along the corridor he moved. Within several more steps he stood inside an enormous chamber with light that forced him to put his hands over his eyes to shield them from the pain-producing radiance.

The scene before him was surreal. The huge cavern gleamed with chrome-like stainless steel, from its oval walls and rounded ceiling to the floor upon which he stood. A futuristic vista of lights emanated from inset positions within the mirrored walls. Many white-lab-coated men and women moved about the gigantic room. They paid no attention to him while he stood dumbfounded just outside the cave tunnel's mouth from which he had emerged seconds before. The room seemed to flare in flashbulb fashion at various points within the vast chamber. He tried to make sense of the bursts of white lights, but they vanished the moment after exploding, leaving him momentarily blinded before his sight returned to take in his strange surroundings.

He noticed, then, a screen of great expanse upon one wall above the colored lights that were indicators of the controls. The screen was alive with an overhead camera shot of two tables, upon whose surfaces two human forms lay, face up.

People in surgical garb approached and left the human forms atop the operating tables, and either conferred, attached wires to the bodies, or moved quickly out of camera range to perform other duties.

The camera zoomed toward the two bodies that were the subject of attention, their heads partially covered with gleaming metallic devices. Several wires ran from their bodies, connecting with each other and with something near the stainless steel-looking floor in an area hidden from the view of the camera lens.

Closer, ever closer, the lens zoomed in on the two subjects, who lay head to head, the glimmering chrome-like helmets less than eight inches apart.

Christopher Banyon's eyes widened with the scene before him—the realization that he was looking at Mark and Lori Lansing's now-grown children.

Musahad Kahlied sat without so much as a twitch, his dark eyes glaring at the guard who stood at parade rest with the M-16 at the ready. His hate-filled stare gave way to a brow furled look of concern when the man in the white lab coat held the Afghan's head steady with his left hand and injected the special chip within the skin beneath his right eyebrow, near the middle of his forehead.

"I'm watching them prepare him now," George Jenkins said into the phone's mouthpiece.

Jenkins squinted to better see the up close view one of the cameras framed within the monitor's screen.

"They are just about finished. We will ship him within the hour."

The voice of Wayne Snidely made him grit his teeth with contempt. "The Secretary is wanting to know what…exactly…the procedures are from this point, Jenkins. I mean, how do we know this thing is going to work?"

"I told the Secretary and the others who have knowledge of the operation that there are no guarantees. We think it will work. We just aren't sure. The hybrids have been successfully transmuted. But, the humans have worked in very few cases, as the Secretary and the others well know."

"It's got to work, Jenkins. The president wants bin Laden's head on that platter. Or his DNA, or something to verify…"

"You will get something. I'm not promising exactly what," Jenkins interrupted. "I'm told the DNA will be there, no matter in what condition the package arrives."

Their conversation ended moments later. Jenkins sat in the semidarkness, his angry thoughts forming into a verbal outburst when he reached to push a button on the console in front of him.

"Musahad." The Afghani looked around, then at the direction on the ceiling from which he thought the voice projected.

"Musahad. Remember what's going to happen if you fail at any point to carry out our instructions. Your entire family...all the males...will be executed and wrapped in those swine skins. Do you understand?"

The prisoner shook his head in the affirmative, then lowered his eyes.

"Good. Siegfried."

The black-uniformed man in charge of the guards came to attention when Jenkins snapped his name.

"Get our friend on his way to his beloved homeland."

EIGHT

The darkness was total, and Christopher Banyon had to make his way back through the cave by feeling along the tunnel wall. The sharp ridges of stones caused pain to his fingers, whose skin felt as if it were being lacerated while the fingers tried to do what his eyes couldn't. His hand jerked back automatically when it touched something cold and slimy.

He stopped forward movement, then reached to try to determine the disgusting thing he had touched. He sensed, in the next instance, the presence of…what, he couldn't determine. Something that closed in on him, surrounded him. A large, hateful presence, both behind and in front of him.

He reached to touch the unseen entities, but his hand felt nothing. Yet they bumped him, breathed on him—a fetid smell of the cadaverous sort. Their breath was hot, and the stench seemed to permeate his very soul while he tried to inch forward against the rock wall. He had to get out of this hell-like place of darkness.

Deep-throated growling accompanied the stench of the beings that bedeviled him. He forced his way past the creatures, or through them, and felt their groping, scratching raking at the flesh of his arms, of his face.

He reached again for the rock wall to gain perspective, to assess his place in this black world that now seemed all-encompassing. The wall was no longer there, and he would have to take the chance. He stepped forward into an abyss. His body turned and tumbled while he kicked and screamed, trying to grab something—anything—that would help break his fall to his doom.

Dripping blood red words flashed before his mind's eye while he plunged into the blackness. Many frantic voices screamed in cacophonous, echoing shrieks: "The kingdom cometh!"

"Reverend Banyon."

Light pierced Christopher's brain, causing pain to reverberate throughout his skull. Had he hit bottom?

"Christopher—Reverend Banyon!"

A strong hand gripped his bicep, lifting him to a sitting position. He felt something warm and wet move across his face. A hard, furry object pressed against his jaw, the tongue again licking him.

"He's okay, boy," the deep male voice said while the bright light continued to assault Christopher's eyes. "He's okay, boy."

"You gave us all a bit of a scare there, Reverend," the deputy said, kneeling beside Banyon, whose head began to clear.

"That's some pooch you have their, sir. He brought us right to you."

Christopher looked at his surroundings, illuminated by the big flashlight the officer held. He was sitting in the sand...on the desert floor, he surmised.

"How long have I been here?" His words were forced, as were his movements while he made a labored attempt to stand.

"You take it easy, sir. Let's just let you get to feeling a little better before you try to get up," the deputy said.

The Vizsla would not be held back. Christopher embraced him, finally realizing that his constant companion had indeed proven that a dog was man's best friend—or, at least, that Klaus was his best friend.

"This area isn't covered by NORAD security because we are already within the innermost perimeter of the new complex."

April's whispered words broke the near silence while they traversed the 150 yards from the rough-hewn cabins toward the sheer rock façade of the mountain.

"We have twenty minutes before the tests begin. That's plenty of time to get to the chamber." April reached to take Clark Lansing's hand. "It gets really dark just ahead. I know the way quite well, so don't let go of my hand."

Clark had no intention of letting go of the hand. She could lead him anywhere, he thought. This was a fascinating girl, and he found it increasingly difficult to keep his professional thoughts separate from the personal, the longer he knew her.

The area indeed grew darker by the second. He felt her crowd closer, her hard, yet feminine, form nudging him one way and then the other while they moved with care toward their objective.

April put her arm out to stop him. "This is where it might get tricky," she whispered. "Hope they haven't changed the codes."

Clark could see nothing but felt her movements while she obviously manipulated something upon the rocky surface. He heard a mechanized sound, something droning to a stop.

"Come on," April said, hooking her arm through the crook of his and tugging at him to step forward.

They walked a few feet forward, and she again manipulated the wall in front of them. The wall slid apart, and subdued light presented a long hallway that seemed to disappear in perspective.

"There are no cameras or sound or movement sensors in this part of the complex. We should be okay." She tugged at him, her long legs beginning a quick walk down the hallway.

"What happens if we get caught?" Clark's question was lighthearted, but he was only half joking.

"Boiled in oil," she said in a deadpan tone. "If we're lucky."

He thought that surely she was joking. At least he hoped she was joking...

"You're not afraid, are you?" She glanced into his eyes while they walked, her arm locked within his.

"Yes, I am, as a matter of fact."

"Well, don't be. I'm quite a talker when caught red-handed. Always have been."

"I'm counting on that," he said, her wit assuaging his concern to a degree.

Still, questions kept nagging at his thoughts. Why could they get this far into a top secret complex without encountering even one security guard? And, no cameras, no sensors? Why not? She had said it was the innermost perimeter. Then, why was he himself not more carefully scrutinized upon entering the complex? He had not undergone any security clearances that he knew about. He wanted to ask but wouldn't.

He would put his reporter's insatiable appetite for answers on hold for now. He wanted to get to the bottom of the Bigfoot question. He was promised that he would be allowed to do so in exchange for reporting about the horrendous treatment of Guantanamo Bay prisoners. He would be given proof of both the truth about the prisoners and truth about Bigfoot.

April pointed a credit card-size device at a panel of lights affixed to the wall on the right of the elevator doors. They hurried through the split that developed when the doors parted.

Clark could hold the question in no longer. "How are we doing this without encountering security? Looks like they would be swarming us by now."

"Help from the inside. Don't question it. Just be glad that there are those who are with us," she said, leading the way out of the elevator when it whirred to a stop.

"My biggest worry was encountering someone before we entered the complex. Security has been diverted to other areas while you and I do this."

"What about my look at the NORAD technologies for detecting potential weapons that can disrupt the nation's electronics?" "Like I told you, that will be a quite shallow introduction to the system. That's scheduled for day after tomorrow. Just enough to give you something to—they hope—praise the DOD," April said. "It provides a legitimate reason for our having invited you to come here. But, what we will look at now is why my group—not the Department of Defense—chose you. We want to expose what they are doing to the Guantanamo prisoners to get to the American and world publics."

She stopped in front of an electronic sliding door after they had walked through several short corridors. She again pointed the device at a panel of small lights. Ceiling lights activated automatically when they entered the room filled with monitors of various sizes. Four control boards in a squared configuration sat at the room's center. April punched several buttons that activated the monitors. She slid a rheostat to a position that dimmed the ceiling lights to the level she wanted.

"You've been here before, I take it," Clark said, watching her manipulate the room's gadgetry.

"Work here most days, actually." She pushed another button, and a large screen appeared above the smaller monitor screen when the walls slid apart. The big screen lit momentarily, giving view of a chamber somewhere deeper within the mountain complex.

"Here we are," April said. "This experiment was conducted earlier—this afternoon, to be exact." She manipulated the control board in front of them. A voice emerged from the speakers surrounding the large screen.

"This is hybrid number sixty-one," the narrator said. The camera panned from the ceiling and floor devices, which Clark recognized as the teleportation apparatus, to show a huge, hulking figure that emerged from the shadows of the otherwise darkened chamber.

Clark's mind spasmed when the creature became fully revealed at the center of the teleportation device. The monster was the same as he had seen those years ago on the winding Idaho road! Bigfoot!

He sat in rapt silence while the narrator continued.

"We will disassemble hybrid sixty-one and reassemble in this exercise and follow the experiment up with Prisoner G-103."

The creature stood at least eight feet tall, Clark surmised, his eyes affixed upon a being he had never been sure he had actually seen. It stood, its arms much longer than what should be normal length, he thought. At the end of each arm was a massive, hair-covered hand hanging limply to just above what must be the knee, he analyzed.

The beast's body was gigantic, with large muscles beneath thick, reddish-brown hair. The torso was great in length, like the bulging arms, and connected to short but thick, powerful-looking thighs and calf muscles. The musculature moved in ripples with the being's slightest movement while it stood with its huge feet upon the slightly raised platform of the teleportation device.

The unidentifiable entity stared straight ahead, with wide, red eyes that seemed to glow, as if a light projected from somewhere within its cranium. Its broad face, which looked to be covered by leathery skin not unlike the face of a mountain gorilla, was human-like, yet far from human. The nose had nostrils that flared across its broad face. But this was no gorilla. It was something unlike anything Clark had seen, except on that curving, mountain road in Idaho and in his nightmares.

"Proceeding in five, four, three, two, one…"

When the narrator said "zero," the entire space between the top of the teleportation device and the platform upon which the beast stood became alive with a million points of dazzling lights of every color. The agglomerate mix of beast and light points became so bright that it caused the image presented on the monitor screen to intensify, extinguishing the picture.

"What happened?" Clark asked.

"Watch," April Warmath answered, still looking at the screen, which now dimmed, revealing the transporter apparatus minus the creature.

Clark watched intently while the screen continued to display the device upon which the hybrid had stood. His vigilance was rewarded when the space between the device's top and circular platform again lightened to a vision-blurring effulgence before the points of colored lights again dominated the screen in the shape of the giant.

The beast stood again upon the platform. It was agitated, and it opened its cavernous mouth, displaying teeth of enormous size, with fang-like canines. Its eyes glowed fiery red, the nostrils flaring while it screamed, its massive head turned toward the top of the transporter.

"The creature was sedated and controlled electronically before being subjected to the RAPTURE," April said. "Its molecular structure—every atomic particle of its body—was taken apart, then reassembled. So, when it was reconstituted, the instrumentalities they used to keep it under control were no longer in the mix."

They watched as the hybrid lumbered from the platform, gargantuan body tense and deadly while it looked for the way out of the laboratory.

Two flashes of laser-like light shot from the side of the monitor's picture, contacting the beast's head. It became instantly tranquil, the muscle-rippling arms dangling harmlessly at its sides.

"They've got it under control. Seems the test was successful. But they always are with the hybrids. The true test will be the human subject, that will come next," April said.

"Rapture? What's that? Is that the name of the device?"

"Rapid Atomic Particle Transmolecular Unification Reassembly Energizer," April said. "The DOD's most secret project."

"Then what am I doing here?" Clark's tone was genuinely incredulous.

"That's just the point. You aren't supposed to be here. But, it's the only way we can get the word out of the horrors perpetrated by the government on these Guantanamo prisoners."

"That's just great. If I get caught, I'll have to disappear like that… thing…just disappeared."

"Like I said, there are others who are even now out there keeping us from being discovered, keeping the wrong people from finding out that I've got you here watching the replays of these experiments."

Her words weren't very comforting, and Clark tried to put from his mind the consequences of being discovered. His reporter's curiosity took over.

"This Rapid Atomic thing—what's its purpose, as far as the Defense Department is concerned?"

"Many uses, I suspect. But, for now, they hope to extract a certain terrorist from the mountains of Afghanistan using the RAPTURE," April said.

Clark asked, after analyzing her words, "Osama bin Laden?"

"Oh! Here we are again," she said, not answering him. She watched two black-uniformed guards bring in a small, dark-skinned man in a red jumpsuit.

"This the prisoner they're going to use next?"

"Yes. It's against every agreement and convention in existence. The poor man is about to be torn apart, literally. God only knows if they can bring these poor souls back together, each time they perform these experiments. It works about 25 percent of the time—success in reassembling the human body, I mean."

"Not good odds, huh?" Clark quipped, watching the guards rough up the little man, whose eyes expressed fear while they glanced at the top and bottom of the device within which he stood.

"They've threatened to boil him in swine fat, and then bury his body wrapped in the skin of a pig. That's the ultimate fear for a devoted Muslim. So, he will do as they say."

Momentarily, the RAPTURE chamber ignited, and the prisoner's body was seen as only the shimmering display of colored light, the screen again whiting out before dimming again to show the empty apparatus.

"We'll see what they've done to him," April said, swearing in the process.

The technology again did its work, and when the video cleared, the prisoner stood on the platform. He dropped to his knees, and the guards rushed forward to lift him by putting their hands under his armpits and dragging him from the device.

"Well, this one seemed to work. It will only encourage them to more boldness in using the prisoners," April said with disgust.

Clark, though dumbfounded that he had just learned that the Bigfoot creature did exist, could only think of one question overriding the importance of his new knowledge. "You didn't answer my question. Is this all about Osama bin Laden?"

At just after midnight, the red and green lights caused an eerie glow to partially illuminate the four men who stood fifteen feet from the right wingtip of the C-130. George Jenkins looked at Musahad Kahlied's dark, worried face.

"Hope you don't disappoint us, Musahad," the deputy director for covert operations said. "We wouldn't want to have to see your brothers and father go to Allah wrapped in swine skins."

The smaller man said nothing, his eyes now showing fear rather than the anger they had projected for most of his month and a half at Guantanamo Bay, and then as prisoner at the mountainous complex in Colorado.

"Tora Bora is nice this time of year, I'm told, Musahad. You will be among friends. I should have thought you would be jubilant about rejoining your terrorist friends."

Jenkins's humiliating words were facetiously pleasant in tone. The Afghani lowered his eyes upon the mocking abuse.

"Think about it, before you consider just getting lost in those mountains, Musahad," Jenkins said. "This thing implanted in your head will tell us where you are. All it will take is the push of a button, and your head will explode. Then your father and brothers go straight into the boiling pig oil."

The deputy director's words cracked sharply. "Got it, Musahad?"

The prisoner nodded slightly in the affirmative without looking up.

The director of covert operations glanced at the big guard beside the Afghani. He nodded, a gesture meant to send them on their way.

Jenkins and an associate began walking back toward the Hummer fifty feet away from the right wing of the C-130. The bird's four engines began grumbling, the propellers twisting powerfully into a steady drone while several black-uniformed guards hurried Musahad Kahlied into the aircraft.

"Put the fear of God in 'em, Mashburn," Jenkins said once the two were seated in the vehicle. "That's the answer to dealing with them."

"You think he can get close enough to affect the target?" The lieutenant colonel watched the bird's landing lights illuminate their surroundings, and the C-130 begin its taxi to the end of the runway.

"He's well known by the mujahid. He was captured among a lot of confusion a month and a half ago. The bunch there in Tora Bora won't suspect he's a plant. At least that's our belief, our hope. They'll put him in some well-worn mujahid clothing—like the ones in which he was captured. It will look like he's just found his way back to them."

"How will we know when he's with the target?"

"He's wearing the transponder. It will give an electronic pulse when he has made' physical contact," Jenkins said. "The device has a button to push, giving us acknowledgement by satellite he's with the target."

"You think he will follow through?"

"He thinks his whole family—the males, at any rate—will be killed by boiling in pig broth, then will be buried in the swine skins," Jenkins said with a sneering chuckle. "There's nothing worse than that to one of these fanatic Islamic jihadists. I'm confident that this has every chance of succeeding."

The engines roared to takeoff speed while the two watched the C-130 lift, its position lights becoming pinpoints in the distance against the black Colorado night.

Morgan examined the cabin, touching the wood of the small desk in one corner. Blake Robbins's words, spoken just before he left the guest house, replayed in her mind.

"Your being with me in this project means so very much to me, Morgan," he had said, his sincerity exuding from the eyes that pierced her thoughts now, eyes framed by the handsome, perpetually tanned face beneath the almost black mane of hair that swept back in seeming perfection. His scent lingered in her nostrils, in her senses now while she touched the desk, without really knowing that she touched it.

Then he had kissed her. A light brush of her lips with his. Her heart had fluttered. She felt it. Had he felt it while he held her close in that lingering moment that she didn't want to let go of while she wandered the cabin's rustic interior examining but not really examining the small suite that would be her home for the next...how long? She didn't know. Didn't care...so long as Blake was with her.

Was Blake Robbins to be her...her...love interest? Her mate in life? She smiled at her audacity. He moved in circles somewhere among the stratospherics of life, as high as these majestic Colorado mountaintops.

She was...just another girl? Another of many?

Still, he had picked her to be with him in the project. Had chosen her from among many, no doubt. That had to count for something.

"Come here, Peanie," she said, holding out the leash in the direction of the rottweiler. "Better have our walk."

Jeddy stood from his lying position at the end of the bed. He stretched before hurrying to Morgan so she could hook the leash to the collar around his thick neck.

She was glad to be walking with her canine "son," as she liked to call him. This was an eerie night in an unfamiliar place. Eerie, because the fog had set in, and its mist glowed in halo-fashion around the basketball-sized globes that attached to the top of high poles. The greenish glow made one think of things better reserved for nightmares from which one could awaken.

Jeddy pulled her along at a slightly faster pace than she wanted to move, and she tired of straining to pull back on the leash. "Peanut! Let's slow down," she said, knowing he wouldn't slow down until he had marked every light pole and tree trunk within the fogged-in compound.

Finally, the dog became curious about the vegetation that was sparse because of the late season but which nonetheless offered unexplored hidden places that had to be investigated.

Jed smelled several of the shadowy niches, snorting and shaking his head when his nostrils sucked in things that made him sneeze. Still he tried to mark each spot he found interesting.

"We're just about out of ammunition, aren't we?" Morgan asked, watching Jeddy go through the ritual for the third time in less than thirty seconds without successfully making his mark. The rottweiler was through with preliminaries and now wanted to find his stride, as was their normal walking habit every evening and morning. Morgan surveyed the path ahead and saw that it branched into multiple pathways, several leading into open areas with buildings and few trees and one leading into a heavily wooded area. She preferred the others, but Jeddy chose the more intriguing pathway to the right, and she let him have his head. He pulled her in the direction of the leaf-denuded trees of thick trunks and high limbs, whose smaller branches extended into the night, exaggerated in their finger-like appearance by the foggy glow of the lights on the poles.

The trees clustered closer together the farther they moved along the narrow path. The last light pole receded behind them, and the path way faded to black in the distance.

"This is far enough, Peanie," she said sternly, beginning to apply the brakes with the rubber soles of her jogging sneakers. The dog stopped, but his head was high in the air, looking down the path, his broad neck stiff and bulging. He emitted an ominous growl—one that made even his mistress's flesh crawl with chill bumps.

"You're scaring me, Peanut," she said, scanning the darkness ahead. The dog bristled, the fur on his neck standing on end while he bared his teeth, the cavernous growling breaking the night air in expulsions of the canine's rage.

The darkness grew suddenly to obscure the trees and the trail in front of them. Morgan saw, then, the reason: a dark, gigantic form standing less than twenty feet from them. It was a creature that towered to almost twice her height, its eyes red like glowing embers while it straddled the pathway.

Fear paralyzed her. She tried to scream but nothing would come. Jeddy burst from Morgan's grip at the moment the monstrous being crouched slightly, its huge arms and fisted hands preparing for the assault.

The rottweiler lunged with all his force into the beast's midsection, and the creature screamed its outrage, trying to grasp the dog, but failing. Jeddy caromed to one side of the pathway but instantly recovered and sank his teeth into the creature's left leg with a powerful bite.

The monstrosity shrieked, hitting the dog with a sweep of its left arm, sending Jed rolling and tumbling ten feet away into a thicket of underbrush.

The rottweiler was again on the beast before it could reach Morgan. He leapt high on the creature's back, tearing into the skin and muscles covered with dense, coarse hair.

Morgan, now recovered from her fear paralysis, saw the massive being twist to get the dog, who hung from its back, the canine's head and jaws shaking and twisting his head with all the strength he possessed.

"Jed—No! Come!" Morgan's command did nothing to deter the dog's attack.

But, he could hold the grip no longer, and the raging giant flung the rottweiler from its back with one powerful twist of its massive body.

"Come, Jeddy! Here, boy," his mistress commanded, and the dog broke off the attack to hurry to a defensive position between the girl and the monster.

Morgan backed away while the creature stood to full height and screamed. Now, though, it was clearly visible, all of its height and girth exposed to a light coming from somewhere behind her.

Beneath the pulsing nostrils that were hideous gouges in the vile face, the mouth gnashed with fang-like canines on either side of a row of huge teeth that drooled saliva with each enraged shriek. The eyes reflected fiery orange-red flashes in the light that framed it against the blackness of the forested area behind.

"Don't move, Miss! Just don't move!" The shout came from the direction of the light, and she half-turned her head to catch in her peripheral vision several human forms rushing toward her and the dog.

Morgan turned her eyes back toward the monster. It was no longer there.

NINE

Phoenix, Arizona—the Next Morning

"There's nothing wrong with me. Can't you just tell them to get me out of here?"

Christopher Banyon displayed uncharacteristic impatience. The overnight stay in Phoenix's Banner Good Samaritan Medical Center had not been restful. The Lord had things for him to do, and the thought of any more time wasted here taking medical tests of every description was not the course of action the Almighty wanted for him at the moment. He had stayed awake all night while they "observed" him, and poked him, and bled him. Things had to change, and Susie was absorbing the thrusts of his angst.

"You will just have to wait until Dr. Wilcox gets to you. Now you behave like a grown-up, Christopher Banyon!"

His wife was up to the task of taming his irritability, her tone at a decibel and with authoritative inflection he had seldom heard from his sweet Susie.

"You will leave when the doctor determines you are okay to leave. Now lie there quietly and let them find out what's going on," she said, unintimidated by his frown of frustration.

A large male figure filled the hospital doorway with a rap on the door facing, and they both broke into smiles.

"Randy!" Christopher tried to sit up in the bed but settled back to the pillow when Susie put a hand on his shoulder.

"Some guys will do anything for attention," Randall Prouse said sternly from the doorway, then moved to the side of the bed, gripping Christopher's hand after hugging Susie Banyon.

"Boy! What a life of leisure!"

Christopher laughed, thinking how his big friend's eighty-two years had dampened neither his robustness nor his sense of humor.

The archeologist asked the inevitable question, after talk of family and general topics concluded, "What happened out there in the desert, Chris?"

"There was this bright point of light, much bigger and brighter than a star. It moved to above a ridge. It just hung there," Banyon said, his tone and expression both confused and inquisitive while he looked at Prouse. "The thing just hung there, and I approached it. Then it grew tremendously bright and shot off into the sky. I looked at the ridge, and Randy—it was the cave. The cave at Qumran."

"Qumran? What do you mean?"

"I'm telling you, Randy. It was the same. The cave of the Dead Sea Scrolls. Once inside, it led to, to a cavern, a chamber of some sort. I'm convinced I really went in there, that it wasn't a delirium of any sort."

"And then they found you outside the cave?"

"Yes. Just out on the desert floor. Klaus, my dog, brought them to me. They said they could find no cave."

"What you think it means?" Prouse asked, taking a seat in a chair beside the bed. "What was in the cave? What did you see?

"I could see as clearly as I can see you now, Randy. It was a scientific center of some sort. I saw them very clearly, people on the operating tables. They were Laura Morgan's grandchildren. They were Mark and Lori Lansing's kids."

Prouse sat forward in the chair, his eyebrows raised in surprise.

"There were lab-coated people everywhere. And, there were the entities entering and leaving the place. They were entering the bodies of the people who were examining Morgan and Clark Lansing."

"Sounds like what was going on in '67," Prouse said.

"Yes. Exactly like Laura Morgan, that Jewish scientist, Gesel Kirban, and Lori described. Remember? The scientists, whoever they were, were performing the experiments on Lori and Mark. According to Laura, she had seen her daughter and Mark Lansing together that night on the apartment balcony in San Antonio. That was the last thing she remembered until awakening in the underground complex near Taos."

"Laura said her daughter and Mark were standing there looking into the sky at a UFO, or something…" Prouse interjected, his eyes reflecting memory of the discussions those decades before.

"Yes. She said it was a strange light that grew brighter until it blinded her. Then she doesn't remember anything until she woke up in the complex," Banyon said. "That's when Gesel Kirban also awoke from a coma. Laura said it was a spectacular light show that seemed to hover over him and bring him out of the coma. Then they found the chamber where all these figures were interacting with the scientists while they experimented on Laura's daughter and Mark."

The men reflected in silence, trying to make sense of what it all might mean.

"The minions are intent on using those kids," Susie Banyon's words broke the momentary silence. "The Lord is telling you that Satan, the minions, needs the children of Lori and Mark. It's not just a delusion; it's a vision, Chris. Don't you see? Their parents' genetics were tampered with all of those years ago. Even their grandfathers' genetics. Laura's, too, maybe."

Susie spoke again when the men said nothing while considering her words. "Whatever they started back then, they intend to finish now. We've got to ask the Lord to show us what he wants of you, Christopher."

The physician completed her examination by bending slightly to look into Morgan's eyes. She smiled and squeezed Morgan's left hand.

"You are just fine, Morgan. Last night's fright might stick with you in your thoughts and dreams for a time, but, physically, you are a very healthy young woman. "

"Can I have someone look at my dog? Jeddy took some pummeling by that…" she let the thought die.

"We have a couple of very good veterinarians on staff. They've looked him over. I haven't talked with them, but I'm sure he's okay. He sure looks like a big strong boy," the doctor said, helping Morgan from the examining table.

"We're so sorry for that…experience…you had last evening. We've put the orangutan in a more secure cage. You will be safe on your walks within the compound, we promise."

Thoughts filed through Morgan's brain, and she blurted the main thought before she could stop herself. "What I saw was no orangutan."

"Oh? Well, that's the animal we had to capture and lock up. Harry, our big male orangutan…"

"Morgan started to argue but could see by the doctor's expression of tolerant condescension that the story wouldn't change. The patient had seen a large orangutan, and that WAS the story. But, it was no ape that had tossed Jed as if he were a toy poodle. And they didn't capture it; it had disappeared.

The doctor patted Morgan's right arm. "I feel you are just fine, but, I want to run a few very minor tests. The animals we use for lab purposes are sometimes subjected to things that might prove harmful to us. So, just to be safe, I want to take a little vial of blood and a couple of other things. I'm sure everything is fine. But, we don't want to leave anything to chance. Okay?"

"But, I never was touched by…the animal," Morgan said, wanting to put the whole experience behind her.

"But your rottweiler did have contact, and you had contact with him. Plus we want to make sure nothing airborne might have…affected you in any way."

The woman opened a door into a small room. Blake stood from a chair in one corner.

"How's our patient, Doctor?" His tone was lighthearted.

"She's fine. We just need to do a little blood work—for precaution," the woman said, looking again at her patient.

"Could you be here around, say, nine-ish tomorrow morning?"

Morgan looked up at Robbins. He nodded yes.

"Guess so," Morgan said with resignation.

"Great! We'll see you then. Now, please don't eat anything after ten o'clock tonight, okay? Tea, without sugar, or coffee and water. Those will be okay but no food or soft drinks."

They stepped from the clinic onto the concrete walkway. Blake Robbins walked her toward the golf cart with the enclosed cab especially designed for the Colorado Rockies weather. Before reaching the vehicle, he stopped and turned her to face him with a strong, but tender grip on her arms.

Sunlight danced from her hair, and his eyes sparked with its reflection while he looked into her eyes.

"You are beautiful, Morgan Lansing," he said in a soft voice, glancing at the glints of gold atop her head, then at the face that looked upward at him with a mixture of surprise and curiosity.

She said nothing, but her expression changed to one of shyness, her emotion washing her thoughts of all other matters away in a rush of realization. Blake found her…beautiful…

He bent to kiss her, their lips coming together in soul-meshing warmth that seemed to seal them against the cold wind that began to assault the high Rocky Mountain valley.

Muted, purple and mauve-colored clouds obscured the surrounding mountain peaks, making the fleeting afternoon prematurely dark. Clark Lansing felt the first few flakes before he saw the flurry blowing against the thickening sky.

The biting wind pelting him with a mixture of sleet and snow added to his near-depressed state of mind. The only thing good about the trip so far was April's exquisitely lovely face, which projected against the screen of his mind's eye while he watched the flakes grow larger and more profuse by the second.

He had his story. He had seen the Bigfoot, Yeti, whatever it was. Or had he? For some reason, the memories of the experiments seemed unreal, like they were contrived science fiction staged for his entertainment. Not reality. Not something to hang one's journalistic reputation upon, not even for a rag like the one for which he currently was freelancing.

April had said he was really allowed into this top secret place to be given a look at America's and Canada's technologies to protect against—

specifically—weapons designed to disrupt national infrastructures. Magnetic Pulse Weapons. To prevent them from knocking out all things electronic in some sort of superbursts in space above the two countries.

But, he had not yet seen any of those preventative technologies—only the experiments with the...whatever they were. The Bigfoot creatures?

And his benefactors who gave him entry to the compound...Amnesty Universal. They wanted him to expose the abuse of Islamic prisoners from Guantanamo Bay, to tell the world that the prisoners were being used in diabolical, inhumane experiments through a technology like in *Star Trek*...the teleportation of things, of flesh and blood. Teleportation of the Bigfoot creatures, whatever they were.

"These are not earthly monsters, Clark. They are monsters beyond any you can imagine. You must not approach them without the Lord going before you." His mother's words interjected themselves without warning. He mulled them over and over while the icy precipitation pelted the skin of his face. Her words replayed again and again.

"Daddy and I are worried about you going to look at something to do with government secrets. We've some experience in those things, remember. The creatures, they are real. But, they aren't some form of life that is...the kind of life everyone thinks they might be."

Clark looked across the compound, to the complex of modern structures now almost indistinguishable through the opaqueness of the deluging, blowing snow. He looked upward at the mountains behind the complex, the peaks that disappeared into the clouds. The conversation between himself and his mother flooded his mind.

"We took you to Sunday School and church. What happened?" His mother had looked into his eyes, tears filling hers. "Why do you and your sister not believe?"

"It's not your fault, Mother. You and Dad did the Christian thing. You raised us in church. But, when the professors at Princeton addressed the fallacy of religion, of all religions, not just Christianity, all of that stuff in Sunday School looked...I'm sorry Mom. Don't get upset. It all started to look pretty fried. I'm sure Morgan feels the same way," he had answered.

"That's what I once thought, too, but your grandmother didn't give up. She prayed for me. She's praying for you, Son. And so am I."

Clark felt a sudden shock against his side. His cell phone. He pulled it from the pocket of the denim jacket.

"Hello."

"Clark, it's your grandmother," Laura Morgan said, bringing a smile to her grandson's face.

"What's going on, Granny?" He turned his back to the wind that came now in bitter gusts from the peaks to the north. He considered the oddity—his grandmother calling just as he was remembering his mother's words about her own mother—his grandmother—praying for Lori those years ago.

"Where are you?"

"Colorado. In the mountains," he said, opening the door to the cabin and walking inside.

"I've been thinking about you, sweetheart. Are you okay?"

Laura's words were, as always, soothing and calming in his frenetic world.

"I was just thinking about you, too. Great minds run in the same tracks," he joked.

"I haven't been able to reach your sister on her cell phone. Have you talked with her?"

"A couple of days ago. You sound worried. Anything wrong?"

Clark sensed his grandmother was troubled while she paused to search for the right words.

"Just have been having some bad dreams about you and your sister, honey. That's all. It just made me want to talk to you both."

"Oh? What sort of dreams?"

"What you've heard your parents and me talk about over the years. It's nothing, really. Just a silly old grandmother's nonsense," Laura said with a small laugh.

"About the events that happened in 1967? Grandpa and the aircraft incident, the Taos underground complex?"

"Yes. All of that. I've had nightmares about those for years. And, now, you and Morgan…"

Laura let the sentence die. Each was lost in their own thoughts for several seconds before Clark broke the silence.

"I'm okay. Morgan is flying somewhere on a new job. A really good one with her advertising agency. Some public relations stuff for a client."

"Do you know where she is going?"

"No. But, I'll be talking with her soon."

"Have her call her granny, okay?"

"Yeah. I will. Don't worry about us, Granny."

"Clark…" Her tone was quiet, almost a whisper. "Have you been going to church? Have you thought about things of the Lord, like we talked about? "

Again, there was silence—an uncomfortable one for Clark.

"I…I'm sorry, Granny. I'm just not at that point, yet."

"I'm praying for you, Clark. For both you and your sister, that you will accept Christ," she said in a trembling voice that betrayed her tears.

George Jenkins long ago had accepted their terms. But, in his private moments—the moments he was rarely privileged to enjoy—the same thoughts pierced his innermost being. Who were they, really? And, just as much a point of agonizing over, who was George Jenkins? Who had he become?

The nautical-motif clock above the model of the USS Constitution, which sat on a credenza against the dark, oak-paneled wall to the left of the desk, read 11:50. Ten minutes until midnight.

Always they came at midnight. Sometimes two, sometimes more. Always they came to collect their payment for services rendered—remuneration for seeing to it that George Jenkins was positioned in high places.

Not that it was something he didn't relish—moving within governmental power spheres. Especially the most covert power spheres of America and the European Union. It was intoxicating, and the things the…beings…didn't interfere with his own ambitions but rather would assure that he achieved his most coveted goal.

He would become top security chief of the Western world, putting the Islamics and all other diabolist enemies of Western thought in their place—in hell, where they belong. He, alone, would make decisions about the security procedures for the civilized world of the future. Presidents and prime ministers, popes and potentates would be at his doorstep. The human-like, yet otherworldly beings provided the technologies that would give him his power to control all who refused to comply. He would start his ultimate climb to that apex by handing George W. Bush Osama bin Laden's head in a bucket of ice.

Nevertheless, the shivers of fear always set in before the visitations. The tremors came now while he looked at the clock: 11:56…

They had an imperative that was not the same as that of the U.S. or of the European Union. Theirs was not the same as his own priority, which was to situate George Jenkins at the center of whatever eventuated, to be at the top echelon of controlling a world of increasing perplexity. Very few understood the nuances of the differing imperatives. He himself was uncertain of their objectives. None but he and a few understood that they were otherworldly. Otherworldly in the most profound sense.

The clock chimed in subdued tones that evoked sensations of things maritime. *Twelve midnight…*

He preferred them to indwell him. To take over his mind. To do whatever they did with him. Facing them directly like this, while in the fully conscious state, was difficult. No, was terrifying, and he wished now that they would do it the preferred way. Just take over and do whatever they must do to achieve—or make progress toward—their imperative, then return his brain, his cognitive powers, to him.

The fluorescent lights beneath the expansive plastic panels on the ceiling dimmed while the clock rang out. Jenkins's surroundings became barely visible. He stiffened in the chair behind the big desk.

The figures appeared to materialize, to emerge from the very air while they stepped into the almost totally dark shadows ten feet in front of the desk. His eyes strained to frame them. Three of them. Tall, exceptionally lean man-like forms that stepped forward and stood side by side, looking to be human triplets, yet more than human. Beyond human. Beyond earthly…

They wore black suits. Black, with white shirts and black ties. Thick, white hair covered the heads above the albino–like skin. Dark-lensed glasses set in black frames covered the eyes he had never been allowed to see.

The one in the middle spoke, the mouth a gash-like line that parted the pasty white skin. The black split moved unnaturally between lips that were almost indiscernible, so thin and pale like the surrounding facial skin were they. The being made no other perceptible movement. Like the other times, Jenkins felt somehow invaded—his individuality usurped, siphoned by the creatures.

The words, he could tell, were of a different language, alien from the English into which they were somehow translated in the space and time it took them to leave the hideous mouth and invade his ears.

"The Afghani is on his way with the promised technology. It is time to now accomplish the imperative agreed to by our covenant."

The words hissed while they entered George Jenkins's ears. They became incendiary at the center of his brain.

"Yes. We begin the process of bringing the subjects together tomorrow," he said.

Jeddy nuzzled Morgan's underarm with his nose, then sat up to an alert position on the carpet beside her bed, satisfied he had awakened his mistress.

Morgan stirred, then strained her arms and legs to a position of maximum stiffness, feeling the pleasure of the first stretch of the new day. She rolled onto her left side, and the rottweiler moved to nudge her with his nose again, then sank his teeth into the covers she had pulled up around her neck. He pulled on them, and they yanked from her grip.

"Peanie...please," she muttered. "Gimme a break."

The dog stood with his front paws on the edge of the bed and barked his demand that she wake up.

"Okay, okay. I'm awake; I'm awake!"

Morgan moved to a position on her right elbow and tried to fend off Jeddy's affectionate licking.

"You have doggie breath," she said, then hugged him. The response caused him to back off the edge of the bed, where he waited for his mistress to come to full consciousness.

Morgan smiled, her first cogent thought going to the face of Blake Robbins. They would use the day to become familiar with the complex and its surroundings; he had promised. No work, just getting to know the place.

She sat on the edge of the bed, then stood and stretched her body again, ending the exercise with a yawn.

Her second thought was of the creature on the pathway night before last. But, the day would not be dampened by that frightening memory. They had dealt with it. She must now think only of the day just ahead.

Blake's face obliterated all other thoughts, and she smiled inwardly. She bent, then, to give Jeddy another hug.

"Mommy's going to be gone for a while today. Not too long, though. I won't put you in your crate. So, you'll have the run of the place. I'll be back before you know it. Okay?"

The rottweiler growled, his way of acknowledging that he recognized she was talking directly to him.

"He really is wonderful. Isn't he, Peanie?"

She whirled around with movement befitting her years of gymnastic and ballet training, then broke into light calisthenics by touching her toes and stretching.

"Wonder what he has planned?"

Her voice was light, causing the canine to cock his head to try to comprehend whether the matter about which she spoke involved him.

Her cell phone's ring interrupted a pirouette she had begun.

"Mom!"

Morgan smiled and sat on the edge of the bed.

"We haven't heard from you, girl. Daddy and I were beginning to worry," Lori Lansing said from Pasadena.

"Oh, I'm great, just terrific!"

Lori heard the exultation in her daughter's voice, and said with a hint of amusement, "Where are you, sweetheart? You sound like you just won the lottery."

"Now, Mom. You know gambling is a sin," Morgan teased, standing again, and bending from side to side from the waist up.

"Don't sass me, Morgan Lansing."

"Oh, Mom. Things just couldn't be better," Morgan said, twirling in place, then falling onto her elbows upon the bed.

"Tell me about it. Where are you? Or is it still a secret?"

"Colorado. Somewhere in the mountains. I'm really not exactly sure where."

"Colorado?! What on earth are you doing there?"

"Just hangin' with the best looking guy on the planet," Morgan said, lying on her back and raising her legs straight out, then slicing them one over the other, continuing the impromptu workout.

"What guy?"

"His name is Blake Robbins. And he is some fine dude…"

"Well, I'm not so sure your dad will like that," Lori said, trying to keep from snickering. "Now who is this…dude?"

"Actually, he's an executive of a company that is a client of ours. I've been assigned to handle PR for them."

"PR?"

"Public Relations. I've been given the PR part of the account. It's a very hush-hush cooperative thing between Blake's company and some kind of a government combine. That's all I can tell you. Mainly, because that's all I know right now," Lori's daughter said, sitting again on the edge of the bed.

She held out her hand to Jeddy, and the rottweiler moved happily to her, accepting her petting affection.

"How long will you be there?"

"I don't know, but, I'll let you know more when I find out. That is, I'll tell you all I'm allowed to tell you."

"Well, is it really that secretive?"

"It seems to be," Morgan said, hugging the dog, then standing from the bed.

"Have you talked to your brother?" Lori's tone became one of concern.

"Why? You sound worried."

"Have you heard from him?"

"No. I've tried several times but get the old 'Your call has been forwarded.' I've left him a couple of voice mails, but he hasn't gotten back," Morgan said. She stopped the calisthenics and sat in a chair near the little desk in one corner of the room.

"Well, I guess he will get in touch when he gets a minute from his work," Morgan's mother said.

"Yeah. I'll keep trying to get him, too."

"Now, about this fine-looking dude—you be careful there, Sissie, okay?"

"You know I will, Mom."

There was silence between them for the moment; then Lori spoke.

"Sweetheart, have you…had anymore of the…dreams?"

Morgan said nothing, and the silence disturbed her mother.

"Morgan, have you?"

"Not really, Mom. Just very brief dreams here and there. Not like they used to be…"

Lori knew the hesitation in her daughter's voice meant she was holding back.

"Come on, Morgie. Tell me about it. You're not telling me something."

"It's not the dreams, Mom. I saw something here night before last. Something on a walking trail within this complex while Peanut and I were on our walk."

"What? What did you see?"

"They told me it was an orangutan. A huge…creature all covered with reddish-brown hair. They said it was their male orangutan they use in their experiments that had gotten loose. But, Mom, it was no ape. It was hideous—a man-like creature, a giant. It looked like some of the beasts in the dreams."

"They've got the section shut down for today," April said. "You were scheduled to be given a tour of the new antiballistic MPW measures facility. But that's on hold until tomorrow."

"Why the shut down?" Clark asked.

April spoke from deep within the recess of the huge, surrounding hood of the parka, its thick, luxuriant fur blowing with the gusts that assaulted the complex from the peaks to the north.

"Well, do I have to stand out here and explain it?" she inquired with an air of incredulity in her tone.

"Sorry. Come in."

April came into the cabin and knocked the hood from her head with her mittened hands. "Bottom line is, they have to recalibrate some things, and it's going to take most of the day. Maybe you can get a look tonight. I really don't know at this point," she said.

"Okay. I have some work I can catch up on, I guess…"

"No!" Her blurted interruption surprised even her, and she, for the first time, he thought, seemed almost shy, unsure of herself.

"I—I mean, I was hoping…" She was grasping for her explanation, and her demeanor changed to one of little girl-like innocence. She was, he considered, never prettier than in this uncharacteristic look of uncertainty.

He said nothing but rather waited for her fumbling to end.

"I was hoping, I mean, that you would be willing to…to go snow-mobiling with me. Look over some of this beautiful area with all this new snow."

April's wide-eyed look of pleading in the silence that ensued melted him, and all thoughts of work drained away. Without thinking about it, he pulled her to himself, their lips coming together in the passion-stirred moment that engulfed them.

When they parted, she let the words escape with a whisper, her face reddened, her eyes gleaming emeralds of approval.

"I take that as a 'Yes'…"

Mark Lansing had no sooner hung up from talking with his former Delta copilot and began the long walk down the hallway when the phone rang, causing him to reverse course and again enter his study.

"Mom! What's going on in San Antonio?"

His brows narrowed, his forehead wrinkling when he heard his mother-in-law skip the amenities to get straight to the point. Her voice betrayed her anxiety.

"I'm worried, Mark. I've dreamed about Morgan again. The night-mare last night was the worst yet. Have you heard from her?"

"As a matter of fact, Lori spoke to her this morning. She's fine. Just fine, Mom."

"I…I guess I'm going crazy. The dreams are getting worse, Mark…"

"What are they, still the ones about the things chasing the kids?"

He sat behind the computer desk and tried to remember where his wife had told him she was going to be shopping for the morning.

"Yes, like when the children were small. The cloud beings, black and hideous. I've just got to talk to Morgan, Mark. Where is she?"

"Colorado, in the mountains. I didn't talk to her, but that's where she is working on this new job with her agency. Some sort of public relations job that's just come up."

"Colorado? Did she say where, exactly?"

"No. Said she didn't know for sure. And, it involves some sort of government project, so didn't know if she would even be able to tell us more about it later."

"Clark is in Colorado," Laura said, as if thinking out loud.

"He is? How do you know?"

"I talked with him yesterday afternoon. He's in the mountains of Colorado; he told me. He wasn't forthcoming, either," she said.

"That's funny. Both of them in the mountains…in Colorado. And, neither of them can tell us much more than that?"

"When did Lori talk to Morgie?"

Mark thought about the question, remembering that the conversation took place just before Lori left on the shopping trip early in the morning.

"It was quite early. About five or so here, I think."

It was Laura's turn to figure the time in the silence of her worry. "I talked with Clark yesterday afternoon. Six thirty, I think. About five thirty Colorado time," she said finally, again falling silent, trying to make sense of the problem she instinctively knew was there.

"Clark told me he didn't know where his sister was," she said, finally framing the concern.

"Morgan told her mother that she hadn't talked to Clark," Mark said, now, himself, thinking out loud.

"Something is wrong, Mark. I don't want to worry you, but something is terribly wrong. They're both in Colorado, apparently working on things they can't tell us about…And, neither knows the other is there?"

The only thing Mark could think about was the creature, the ape-like beast that wasn't a beast. The human-looking animal Morgan told her mother the dog had attacked on the pathway. He calmed his rising anxiety with the knowledge Morgan had seemed okay as the conversation concluded—according to Lori. He didn't want to further disturb Laura and said nothing of the reported encounter.

"Yeah. I see what you mean. What do you think? What should we do?"

"Call those kids. That's what! I'll call Morgan when we hang up. You call Clark."

April Warmath tried the door when her patience ran short.

"Clark? You here?" she asked, poking her hooded head through the door opening and looking around the cabin room.

"Yoo-hoo! You here?"

Clark came from a door opening against one wall.

"Yeah. I was just looking for my cell phone. I don't know where it could be. Just vanished…"

April joined him in the search, getting on both knees to look under the bed.

"Don't see it. When did you have it last?" She stood and searched behind the nightstand near the headboard. Not finding it, she pulled the rumpled covers back and forth in a jostling motion, trying to dislodge the instrument if it happened to be hidden in the folds.

"Just great! That phone is my lifeline to my work. Where is the stupid thing?!" His frustration spilled over into his temper, and he cursed the situation while he, like April, continued to search the room.

"It will turn up. Housekeeping will find it and put it on the night-stand."

Her words did little to console him. He swore again, then pulled the heavy parka from the closet to the left of the bathroom door. April searched the bathroom and the closet while he put on the bulky garment.

"I'll call them, and tell…" April said, picking up her own cell and punching in some numbers.

"Housekeeping—is this Janice? Oh, hi, Jan. Listen, my friend, Clark Lansing, has lost his cell phone somewhere in his cabin—number 330. Can you make sure they make a special effort to look for it when they clean?"

She smiled, looked at Clark, and said, "Good, thanks a lot!"

Less than ten minutes later, Clark thought the yellow-and-red striped snowmobile was remarkably quiet while they traversed the fifty yards from the front of his cabin upon pristine snow that stretched in the distance as far as he could see. But, visibility wasn't all that good, because the blowing snow was so profuse that it challenged the windshield wipers to keep up. Within another five minutes, they had left the complex, which was now shrouded by the snowfall that continually painted an opaque curtain of white behind them.

The vehicle's cockpit was warm enough for the pair to pull the parkas' hoods from their heads. April was never prettier, he thought, seeing the ivory skin of her face reddened by the cold at the cheeks. She cut her eyes toward him.

"This is one of my favorite things to do. I'm a winter, you know?"

"A winter? You, personally, are a winter?"

She laughed, alternating her glances from his direction, then to the snow fields that rushed at them in the distance.

"That's my color. Fair skin. I'm a winter. My skin tone goes with certain shades of colors, and those colors mark me as a 'winter'."

"Oh…"

"Yes, well, I didn't expect you to be up on cosmetics and so forth. I'm also a winter because I love the wintertime."

"Yeah, well, I'm from California. That makes me more of a summer, I guess," he said, reaching to hold on to a handle protruding from the dashboard when the big sled ran across a few unforeseen snow-buffered bumps. Clark examined the inside of the snowmobile, turning to see the cabin behind them that was as large or larger than the cockpit.

"This is some snowmobile. When you said 'snowmobile,' I thought you meant an open-type motorized thing like I've seen them use on expeditions to the Antarctic or someplace."

"Oh, no. The government provides only the best. I have a friend in transportation who was happy to let me sign one of these babies out. Luke is a good friend…"

"Luke?"

"Luke Bledsoe. He can't resist my charm," she said, looking over at Clark and batting her eyelids in her best, feigned-sexy look.

"Bet he can't. I know I couldn't," he said, returning her banter in a more serious tone than hers.

"Whatever," she said giggling, then becoming wide-eyed and letting out a yelp when she hit a larger than usual snow mound. The machine ramped several feet in the air before landing with relative ease upon the downside of a long, gently declining hill.

"Woman driver," Clark said solemnly when the ride again smoothed. She hit him playfully on his arm with her fisted right hand, her mouth open in mock astonishment.

"That was masterfully done," April said, then broke into laughter.

"Hope there aren't any ravines you don't know about," he said, only half joking.

"No. I've been all over these areas. We're okay."

Snow blew in greater profusion the further they proceeded northeastward toward mountains that could no longer be seen. April braked the big snowmobile in another ten minutes to assess their exact whereabouts.

The snow became less blinding to the areas ahead when they stopped.

"It's over there," April said, pointing a gloved finger past her passenger to the right. "I want you to see this."

She revved the engine, then steered the machine at slow speed toward the region she had indicated. They stopped at the promontory above a vast valley landscape that stretched until it vanished in the agglomeration of opaqueness created by the snow veil in the distance.

"I just wanted you to see this, Clark. Is this not the most gorgeous view you've ever seen?"

He said nothing, and she turned from her own enthrallment with the view, feeling his eyes upon her.

"No. This is the most gorgeous view I've ever seen."

He gazed into her loveliness, his words bringing them together even before their embrace meshed their heavily clothed bodies. They kissed deeply, passionately, then she gently pushed him away.

"We're fogging the windshield," she joked weakly.

Clark reached to pull her to himself again, but she moved him back with a light touch of her outstretched right hand.

"Let's have some hot chocolate," she said. "Will you reach back and open that case?"

He did so with reluctance.

"Get the thermos and those big thermal mugs."

Clark pulled them from the case as instructed. April took the big thermos and opened the top. Steam filled the air between them, further covering the snowmobile's windscreen.

"Guess I had better get some defrost going," she said, manipulating several sliding levers set within the dashboard.

"It will just fog up again," he said. "But it won't be the hot chocolate."

"I do want you to see the valley a bit, first. Let's have the hot chocolate, then we'll…think about other things," she said, pouring the hot liquid into a mug, then handing it to him.

"I had the kitchen make this especially for us. Mazie—our chief cook—makes the best chocolate there is. See what you think," April said, pouring a mug for herself.

"Fantastic!" Clark's declaration was made facetiously, after a cursory sip. April's wide eyes narrowed in disapproval.

"No main course, no dessert," she said with a matter-of-factness that was reminiscent of his mother at the dinner table in early childhood.

"In that case, I'll be a clean-plater," he said.

"Clean-plater?"

"That's an award they gave us in preschool, as I remember. If you ate everything on your plate, you got a "Clean-Plater Award.""

She smiled, looking seductively into his eyes that stared back at her above the mug from which he sipped. She raised her own mug of hot chocolate in his direction.

"Cheers. Here's hoping you get that …Clean-Plater Award."

The defroster soon cleared the windshield of fog. The valley before them lay blanketed in white, the evergreens and rocky protrusions on the valley floor presenting a masterpiece of winter nature-art. Occasional nearby cascades of snow obscured part of the masterpiece, before slackening, thus returning the vista to its full magnificence.

Clark would rather look at April Warmath. And did so, drinking in her stunning profile while she admired the scene before them.

Then, her lovely features changed, distorted and blurred. Clark blinked to try to recapture clear vision. She turned to him, a look of perplexity on her face. He looked out the windshield and saw the panorama of valley snow-art waving in flag-like motion—a nauseating field of white, green, and grays. He looked back at the girl. She reached to take the mug of half-drunk hot chocolate from his wavering grip.

The sky brightened somewhat while he again looked to the dark lavender-gray roof of the valley—the thick snow clouds now lit by brilliant spheres. He squinted to see them, strained his undulating brain to make sense of the scene. He tried to speak, to form a question about the disks that pulsed with white and colored light while they hovered. The lights aligned in a triangular configuration, but then began whirling in his fading vision, becoming a blended, milky mixture that snapped to black.

Morgan suddenly felt uneasy while she tried for the fifth time to call Clark's cell phone. The answer was always the same after four or so rings. "Your call has been forwarded…"

The phone was always on or very near her brother. She had never failed to reach him on his cell, any time, night or day. The feeling was one of suddenly losing a part of herself—something without which she could not function.

"Peanie, Mommy will be back. I won't leave you in your crate. You be a good boy, okay?"

She knelt to hug the rottweiler, who shifted his front feet, unsure of what was expected of him. He became still when she issued the familiar instruction.

"Stay."

Jeddy's mistress stood, checked her features in the big mirror above the dresser, then turned again to the dog. "I'll be back in a couple of hours, and then we'll go for a walk, Peanut. Okay?"

The rottweiler whined, registering his request to go with her.

"Not this time. I'll leave the TV on," she said, turning on the set with a flick of the remote.

Ten minutes later, Morgan stood in front of the rustic log gift shop less than one hundred feet from her own cabin. She strained to see between the now sporadic snowflakes that came in occasional light showers. He was late.

She heard his approach, before she saw the horse turn the corner of a distant building. The high-pitched ringing of sleigh bells attached to the animal's harness told her Blake Robbins would soon keep his appointment with her.

Her heart beat faster when she finally could make out his face within the parka's hood. He smiled while he gave a quick wave of his free, mittened hand. She hurried to him, and he helped her into the sleigh's seat.

The clouds grew darker while they moved along the valley floor, toward the even darker forests of evergreen that nestled against the mountains miles in the distance.

Blake held the horse's reins in his left hand. He slipped his right arm around Morgan, nudging her to move closer. He looked into her eyes.

"Cold?" he asked, pulling the heavy blanket of tanned bear fur higher around her.

"You're nice and warm," she said, snuggling as close to him as she could.

They said nothing for a time, Morgan drinking in the breath-taking horizon of white, with the spruce, pine, and other varieties of evergreens helping to make it a magical landscape through which to slide behind the giant chestnut that tugged the sleigh without effort toward no particular destination.

Snow began falling in greater profusion, and Blake reached behind to pull the sleigh's top over them. Morgan looked to the horse, concerned that he had to endure the deluge. The animal, she realized then, was covered with a weather-proof blanket of some sort. He seemed none the worse for wear while he high-stepped through the snow, white puffs of his breath exhaled into the twenty-degree air, without evidence of exertion.

"This is kind of new to a California girl, isn't it?" Blake's question was visible, his breath, like the horse's, issued with white clouds into the frigid air.

"I've been skiing and sledding but never like this. A horse-drawn sleigh in all of this beauty…"

"I thought we had better take advantage of this opportunity. When I found out they keep a sleigh around for patrolling the areas nearby the main complex, I used my special influence to acquire its use."

"Special influence?" she said, laughing at the pomposity of his tone.

"Yeah, well, I begged, with great agony in my plea."

"I'm glad you used all of your 'special influence.' It's wonderful," Morgan said, laying her cheek against Blake's shoulder.

"They use the motorized things, the snowmobiles, for longer trips, I think," he said, holding her more tightly against his side.

Morgan felt his warmth even through the heavy winter clothing they both wore. Could this be the man she had thought about, dreamed about, discussed with her mother and her closest friends since she was old enough to be interested in boys? He knew all the right buttons to push, that was for sure. Maybe there was something to God's making love matches in Heaven after all…

She closed her eyes and held onto the arm he had removed from around her to reach beneath the seat.

"I've brought some hot cider for us. You like cider, I hope…"

"Yeah. Love it," she said, taking the thermos from Blake.

"There are a couple of Styrofoam cups under your side, in a sack…"

Morgan retrieved the sack, removed the cups, and opened the thermos. She poured the steaming cider into one of the cups and handed it to him before pouring some for herself.

Soon, Blake pulled the horse to a stop. They sat atop a sprawling ridge, high above a deep gorge of white. The expanse was broken near its center by a large stream that narrowed in perspective to a vanishing point among a thick forest of evergreens.

"It's beautiful, Blake. Do you come here with lots of girls?"

Her question was probing, not rhetorical.

"Only one who is important to me," he said, looking into her questioning gaze.

" Morgan," he said, moving toward her while pulling her to his lips. "You are the one who means so much to me."

They kissed, the rapidly dropping temperature about them unable to chill the heat of their embrace.

"Blake…I…" Morgan's words would not form. She struggled to keep her eyes open, and they met a surrealistic scene above the valley below them. A huge light appeared, at first brightening out their surroundings, then dimming to reveal a gigantic, glowing disk against the dark clouds. The object began its slow descent. It turned, like several wheels within other wheels. It was moving toward the valley floor.

The cold, white world surrounding her in her convoluting attempts at thought became a darkening, ambient heat that melted her confusion to nothingness.

The 737 shuddered on its way to the thirty-five thousand foot cruising altitude assigned it by the air traffic controllers at Phoenix International. The turbulence wasn't a surprise. The captain had warned shortly after takeoff ten minutes earlier to expect a bit of rough air before leaving the airspace over Arizona.

Some in the fully loaded tourist section gripped the handles of their seat armrests, their faces masks of fear. Some looked around the semidarkness, wide-eyed, analyzing whether to panic based upon reactions to the bumpy ride manifested by others.

Randall Prouse, seasoned by thousands of hours of plane rides both rough and smooth, paid no attention to either the bumpy ride or to his inexperienced fellow passengers. He was behind on a manuscript due at his publisher. He couldn't be distracted by the worries of others. Long ago, he had put his flying anxieties in the very capable hands of the Lord.

He glanced at the laptop screen, then to an open book lying between the keyboard, which was sitting atop the pull-down tray, and his lap. The sky was dark now, and he strained to read the words on the page. Tired of the stress to his eyes, he reached above to click on the small light that beamed directly downward.

The passenger to his right seemed to be dozing, so wouldn't be bothered by the light. Randy mused that the heavyset man, like himself, must be a regular flyer, with no indication that the bumping and swaying bothered him. Plus the man's breath that reeked with bourbon—the thing that drew Prouse's attention to the lightly snoring passenger—no doubt helped with the peaceful sleep.

The archaeologist sat back in the cramped seat and kneaded the bridge of his nose after removing his reading glasses. He stared out the porthole to his left, barely able to discern the glow from the position lights beneath the wing. Memories flooded his mind of things he and Christopher Banyon discussed before his departure for New York from Phoenix International.

Christopher had been uncharacteristically agitated, and Susie had looked at Randy with pleading in her eyes. He moved to allay both hers and Christopher's concerns.

"Chris, the best thing for you to do is to recover from…whatever made you pass out. If this is some sort of vision from the Lord—like those years ago at Qumran—don't you have faith that God will make that clear?"

"Listen to Randy, Chris. This worrying yourself and not eating or sleeping is going to hurt your health," Susie said with authority in her tone. "Just call Laura and talk to her about it. She won't mind."

"Yeah. Give her a call, Chris. Can't hurt anything. And, it will put your mind at ease that you at least followed up on the…episode," Randy Prouse put in.

"Laura probably won't want to hear about this. It will only worry her. No need to cause her sleepless nights, too. It's just that it wasn't like a dream, Randy," Christopher said, his eyes pleading for understanding. "It was real. It is as vivid now as when I was in it. One doesn't retain such vivid memories of mere dreams—does one?"

"Call Laura. She will want to know," Susie said.

Prouse's mind snapped back to his present with the flight attendant's question.

"Sir, can I get you something to drink?"

"Oh. Yes. Coffee, please. Black." he said, replacing the glasses on his nose and looking again at the work before him.

He wondered if Christopher Banyon had been able to get in touch with Laura Morgan. He would call as soon as they touched down at JFK to find out.

He forced his attention back to the screen and began typing: "The Temple Mount continues to be the greatest singular point for potentially igniting nuclear conflict in the world today. Moriah commands the attention of the international community's diplomats as no other..."

Something glinted in his peripheral vision from the porthole to his left, and he peered into the blackness that shrouded the big jet. Bright, oval objects shone brilliantly just in front and slightly above the plane's left wing. They remained in unwavering formation and grew brighter, larger in the black night sky.

Prouse removed the reading glasses and rubbed his eyes, blinking to clear his vision.

Still there! In unwavering positions just above and in front of the wing.

Did the flight crew see them? Did others see them? He quickly glanced at the seats in front of him. The backs of the seats were too high to see if the others were gawking at the spectacle. People on the other side of the aisle most likely couldn't get the same view as passengers on his side.

The lead object appeared to be slightly larger than the two flanking it. It changed color ever so slightly, turning a bluish white; then it changed again to a faint orange hue.

The three objects drew nearer the plane, and now he could see them with perfect clarity. These were disks. Vehicles unlike he had seen but had often read and heard about and had always believed existed. The disks were like Christopher had reported seeing above the plateau in the desert.

The craft moved away from the 737, then vanished. The sky was again deep black, except for the slightly illuminated left wing that glowed with the hue of the position light.

Prouse noticed the laptop's screen was as black as the sky outside the aircraft. Before he could reach to try and reboot the computer, his eyes widened in astonishment. On the inactive screen, the words glowed in blood red characters: "Beware the sons of God, daughters of men."

The generators were getting on his last nerve, despite the fact they were the very best money could buy. The noise, though half the level caused by less technologically superior machinery, was maddening in the partially darkened cavern.

The thin-framed man lay still while the two Egyptian-trained doctors worked above the Saudi on a hospital-type bed.

"Make haste. Remove these horrors from me," Osama bin Laden said in Arabic, raising his head so that his long-bearded chin met his chest in watching the proceedings. The doctor in charge said nothing but rather hurried to detach the intravenous tubes that attached bin Laden to the dialysis machine near one wall of the cave-room.

It was over for another half-day, he thought, as he, with the assistance of the doctor, swiveled to sit on the edge of the bed. "Another session in hell over with," the lanky terrorist grumbled to himself, allowing the two men who stood on either side of him to lift him by his elbows to his feet.

His blood was cleansed for the brief moment, and he had much to do this fall morning. Time to meet with his underlings for planning the attacks in Europe—plottings that had been thwarted earlier in the month by the heathens (CIA and MI5). But the next time it would work. The bombers would get through. Hundreds of the infidels would die in sacrifice to Allah.

"Exalted One." A small man, his voice raised with excitement, hurried through the cave's entrance to bin Laden, who continued to try to find his weakness-impaired balance.

"Yes?!" said the irritated leader, standing more than a head and a half taller than the man.

"He returns!"

"Who? Who returns, you little fool?" bin Laden said, gripping his temples with the thumb and fingertips of his right hand, closing his eyes tightly, and opening them several times to help clear his faltering vision.

"The Afghani Musahad Kahlied!"

Bin Laden removed his kneading fingers from his head and angrily pulled his arms from the doctors who had been steadying him.

"Kahlied?" The al-Qaeda leader let his knowledge of the Afghani file through his still reeling brain. "Kahlied was captured by the Americans more than two months ago."

"Yes, Exalted One. That is correct. But, he tells us he escaped. That he has much to tell you," the short Saudi said with excitement.

Bin Laden remained silent while the Arab looked up at his leader, who frowned in concentration.

"Where is he?"

"Just outside, sir. In the first chamber."

"Bring him to me. I will hear of this escape," bin Laden said, a slight, tight-lipped smile crossing his gaunt face.

Musahad Kahlied stood shaking, both from the near-zero-degree weather through which he had just come and from the anticipation of seeing Osama bin Laden face to face. He was the great leader of the jihad against all that was hated, the man who brought America to its infidel knees by crushing its towers of economic power. But, he was here to betray bin Laden to the great Satan, the Americans. When he grabbed the leader, they would both be...whatever would be done and would next appear in the American chamber. It was either Osama, or Musahad Kahlied's entire male family. His fathers and brothers...All would be boiled in swine broth and blood, then wrapped for burial in the swine skins. All would be lost, for Allah would not bear swine within the rituals of Islam. It was his great hero, Osama, or his own father and his brothers in hell with all the infidels, forever...

When the messenger left the tunnel to follow the order given by bin Laden to bring the Afghani, the terrorist paced slowly, his 6' 5" frame moving in unsteady steps, his right hand again massaging his aching temples.

He stopped and became rigid, his arms dropping stiffly to his sides, his fists clenched while his face rose toward the cave's ceiling. The two men walking nearby him lurched forward to catch him, should he weaken and begin to fall.

Bin Laden turned to face them, his face projecting his inner rage, his eyes black and glistening within their sockets.

"Leave me!" His command was deep and growling. The frightened men had seen the horrible eyes, the terrifying demeanor, many times before and bowed quickly, hurrying through the tunnel exit the messenger had left moments before.

When the chamber was empty except for the al-Qaeda leader, a dark, boiling, human-shaped figure stepped into the cave through a wall directly in front of the terrorist. Bin Laden said, while glaring through the shark-like eyes at the creature, "Yes, I understand."

The entity moved into the tall Saudi's body to assume his shape. Bin Laden walked to the cave's back exit and left the chamber.

"He is in the cave; isn't he?!"

George Jenkins was almost frantic while he grabbed and shook the technician by the collar of his lab coat.

"Now, you tell me that stupid rag head has let him get away?!"

"Sir, the sensors, the audio—all indicators were that the operative was about to be issued into the target's presence."

"What happened? We had him in our sights, and you let him just… vanish?!"

The short, overweight scientist spoke calmly, clinically. "Sir, we feel he got wind that something was wrong with the operative's showing up."

Jenkins cursed, turning to the desk. He slammed the side of his fist against its top.

"What shall we do with the operative, sir?"

The question, offered by another of the scientists, brought the black ops director to his senses.

Jenkins said, without a hint of emotion in his voice, "Kill him."

Mark was worried, and Lori, though troubled too, moved to ease his frustration.

"It doesn't help to wear yourself out by not getting some rest," Lori Lansing said, putting a hand on his shoulder while her husband looked at the monitor screen.

She kissed him lightly on the top of his head, then hugged him. "Nothing from either of them?" she asked, looking at the screen and seeing the e-mail prompts through which he scrolled.

"About a hundred spam but not a word from them. Where are those kids?"

"It's getting late, sweetheart. Let's get some sleep. We'll find out something tomorrow morning first thing."

"Yeah, okay. But, if we haven't heard from them by tomorrow, I'm going looking for them."

The phone rang, and Lori, startled, jumped. She unfurled her arms from around her husband's neck and retrieved the receiver several feet away.

"Mrs. Lansing? Is this Clark Lansing's parents' home?"

The gruff male voice hurled troubling thoughts through Lori's mind in an instant. Was it about the kids? Was one or both of them hurt? Was this one of those tragic calls every parent prays never comes?

"Yes, I'm Clark's mother. I'm Lori Lansing."

"Mrs. Lansing, I...I'm sorry for the late hour and this call. I'm Clark's editor at the *New York Examiner*. He's doing a story for us."

"Yes. Have you heard from Clark?" Her question was animated with hope. Mark turned from the computer and stood, then walked to her side.

"Actually, Mrs. Lansing, I was going to ask you the same thing. I haven't heard from Clark in several days. That's not like him when he's checking in while on assignment and so forth."

"You haven't heard from him?"

The angst in Lori's voice prompted Mark to reach toward the phone. "Let me talk to—

whoever that is," he said.

"Mr. Wilson, isn't it?"

"Yes. Bruce Wilson."

"Mr. Wilson, my husband, Mark, wants to talk with you."

Lori handed the phone to Mark. "Mr. Wilson, you haven't heard from our son? How long has it been?"

"About three days now. It's quite unusual of him to not call in, Mr. Lansing, and I just wondered if you knew how to contact him."

"We haven't heard from him and can't reach him by his cell phone. We haven't gotten any e-mails, either. It's been a couple of days, and we're becoming concerned. What kind of assignment is he working on?"

"I'm sure you know he's been researching the Bigfoot sightings and so forth."

"Yes. That's been something he's been into for several years now."

"Exactly. Well, he was contacted by this woman who is connected to the Department of Defense in some way. They flew to Colorado, to some secret-type operations they have out there in the Rockies. Not too far from Denver, I think."

"It has something to do with the Bigfoot question?"

"Yeah. But, it's involved—I don't really understand it all—something about a thingamajig that has to do with teleportation. You know, like that device in *Star Trek*, the Transporter, or whatever it was called. The thing takes things apart at the atomic or molecular level, or something, then reassembles them somewhere else."

Mark's mind raced with the disappearance of Colonel James Morgan—Lori's father—then his reappearance in the underground chamber near Taos. He also thought of his own father's disappearance in 1947 from the airplane...

"Defense Department, huh?" Mark asked after several seconds of analyzing the newspaper man's words.

"There's more...involving the treatment of the terrorists who are held in Guantanamo, in Cuba. This broad...this woman...he's with wants him to look into the matter of the way those Arab-Islamic types are being treated. Says it has something to do with their use in these teleportation experiments."

Both men were silent for a moment, each assessing things before Mark spoke.

"Look, Mr. Wilson, we haven't heard from him, either. When we do, I'll make sure he gets in contact."

"You think something's wrong?" Wilson said, his tone becoming softer in his concern.

"I don't know. I really don't know."

Randall Prouse punched in the numbers of his cell phone the moment the 737 shut down at the gate. The first two attempts failed to find a connection, but the third try netted success.

"This you, Chris?" Prouse said, putting his left hand over his left ear to hear his partner in the conversation in his right ear.

"Yes, Randy. It's me," Banyon said while sitting in his study, glancing at the French doors ten feet in front of his desk, seeing Klaus looking longingly at him through the glass.

He walked and opened one of the doors, allowing the dog into the room.

"Chris. There are some strange happenings again," Prouse said, glancing at the passengers who continued to stream past him in the aisle, heading for the exits.

"Oh? What happened?"

"Wish I knew. Remember the trip back in '67 over the Atlantic? That storm?"

"Very vividly, my friend," Banyon said, his interest piqued.

"We didn't have a storm. But, there were things going on outside the window."

"Things? What kind of things?" Banyon asked, before Prouse could get it out.

"UFOs. They were lights, and they were craft—or appeared to be craft. They moved close enough for me to get a clear look."

"UFOs? What happened?"

"The objects just came in close, and then moved away, before vanishing," Prouse said. "And, get this. I'm the only one who saw it, apparently. Nobody else seemed to notice!"

There was silence for a moment, both men analyzing Prouse's revelations.

"But this is even stranger. I looked at my laptop screen, and it was dead. The power was off. Yet, there were these words in red that glowed within the darkened screen. The words were 'Beware the sons of God, daughters of men.'"

Christopher said nothing, the words ricocheting in his mind.

"You there?" Prouse asked, thinking he might have lost the cell connection.

"Yes...Yes, Randy. I'm here."

"What do you think it means?"

"We've got to talk to those kids, Randy. This all revolves around them."

Nigel Saxton shrugged the backpack and let its canvas straps slide down his arms. He knelt beneath the overhanging ledge, then removed the mittens and unsnapped one of the many pockets of the backpack. He found the binoculars, popped the caps from each lens, then cleaned the glass with a soft cloth.

The coordinates were confirmed by the Global Positioning Satellite that maintained constant vigilance from its geosynchronous assignment more than six hundred kilometers above the western United States. His GPS receiver marked the spot as located in the valley between the mountains below.

He put the binoculars to his eyes and zeroed in on the mass of green, the evergreen forest that spread from near the center of the valley to the highest of the peaks to the west.

They had been tracking them for months, whatever they were. His government, although a United States ally, wanted to know what kind of technology was being hidden from them. Nigel Saxton was a mountain climber *par excellence*—the best among all of the agents at MI7, the newest and most secretive of British Intelligence Services. He, a young mountain climber training for an assault on one of the Himalayan peaks, would attract little attention in this region famous for helping prepare climbers.

Climbing to this spot to do the observation necessary to his mission was a piece of cake. He chuckled, amused at his use of American slang even in his thinking. Maybe he had been here too long already. Although only six weeks in America, it felt like an eternity, and he longed for the rainy skies and gales of bonny England.

The powerful glasses drew the scene closer while he pushed the automatic zoom button. Nothing. Just a thick forest of many varieties of evergreens. The GPS showed this to be the precise spot where the unidentified objects had landed on numerous occasions.

He would pitch his lean-to of miracle fiber that the MI7 eccentrics promised would raise the temperature, once he was ensconced within, by at least thirty degrees. One's body heat, deflecting off the inner-material's special composition, would, he was promised, keep him cozy, even in sub-zero weather.

Although the overhang and the surrounding rocky perimeter inhibited some wind from invading, it was already near zero and would when nightfall came, go well below. He would soon know if the brand-new technology—the material stretched around a collapsible fiberglass framework—was as good as the MI7 geniuses promised.

There were enough of their high-energy foods, packaged in dense, six-inch bars, to last a week, if necessary. The mini-water filter, another creation of the MI7 scientists, could give him an unlimited amount of drinking water, so long as the snow held out.

The high observation perch was well hidden. "Bring on the UFOs," Saxton said with a grin of satisfaction while scanning the terrain below with the binoculars.

"You got it ready?"

The man gripped the door knob to the cabin and glanced apprehensively at the shorter man, who held the long-barreled pistol at the ready.

"Yeah. Ready as I'll ever be," he said.

The snarling on the other side of the door made both men know they were in for a battle. The shot had to be on target. Tom Johnson would have to be quick with the netting.

"Okay, Willie. When I open, you better be quick," Johnson said, gripping the knob tighter and twisting it slowly.

Jeddy growled a guttural anger while he heard the men outside the door. He stood bowed between the bed and the dresser, ready to launch forward when the intruders entered.

When the door inched open, the rottweiler expelled a vicious, powerful growl that caused Johnson to hesitate.

"That's a bad dog in there, Willie. You sure you're ready?"

"Yeah. I'm ready, but I wish they'd a let us shoot the thing for real. You be ready with that net, Tommy."

"Don't know why they want the thing alive and unhurt. I'm with you; I'd rather plug it for real. Guess they don't want the place messed up with blood," Johnson said, opening the door again but only a crack, through which he then peered with one eye, trying to locate the dog.

"He's there beside the bed, Willie. Think you can hit him from here?"

"Need him turned sideways. Need a shot at his flank, if we can get it," the man with the dart pistol said, moving to look through the crack between the open door and the door facing.

"Don't think he'll turn from that position. He's just got room to face us head-on. Man! He's a big'un!" Johnson said, readying the heavy netting while again peering through the opening.

Jeddy backed slightly, his 115-pound, muscular body tensing for the attack, the black hair standing rigidly from just behind his massive head to near his docked tail.

"If you can get the net over him, that should stop him, Tommy," Willie Fletcher said. "Then, I'll plug him through the net."

"Sounds good. I don't think he can get outta between the bed and that dresser. I'll just fling it over the whole area. It will get him tangled up, I think," Johnson said. "Ready? Here we go!"

Johnson opened the door fully, Fletcher to his right as they entered. Jeddy leaped forward, snapping and growling while Johnson flung the netting at the canine.

The dog leaped upward toward the bed's top, his head and front paws ducking past the edge of the net, which fell to the space where the dog had been.

"Watch it!" Johnson screamed, cursing. "He's loose!"

The rottweiler leaped from the bed to near the door opening. The man with the dart gun swung to his left, trying to get a bead on the moving target. He fired at the dog, but the dart pierced the wall and stuck there. Jeddy escaped into the snow-cloud filled, winter morning.

His morning was off to an atrocious start. George Jenkins swore while reading on the computer screen the latest coded security message from the Pentagon: "The president and the secretary are most disappointed that you failed to get the target. We've put a tremendous amount of time and funding into making his capture a success. You are to meet with us in D.C. tomorrow at 0800 hours—the Pentagon. —W. Snidely, Ops chief liaison, DOD"

"Pimply-faced punk," he seethed. Jenkins grumbled another obscenity, then pushed back from the computer. The instructions meant he would have to leave by early evening at the latest. The Gulfstream-5, assigned to other government officials at the moment, wouldn't be available, which meant a charter. Arrangements, timing, rushing around like someone had ordered him to mop the floors. Treated like a janitor by Snidely and the others.

What did they want? To fire him? Not likely. He was the only person with the total picture of things. They knew it, too. He had seen to that little detail—deliberately keeping some things totally under lock and key, others locked securely in his brain. He had studied J. Edgar Hoover and had it figured—the way to make himself indispensable. Hoover was there until they took him out, toes-up…

His bitter ruminations were interrupted by the door swinging open after a light knock.

"Sir. He's signed, sealed, and delivered."

Jenkins watched April Warmath stride into the room. At least something had gone right, he thought.

"Where is he?"

"I don't know, sir. I thought you knew where he's being held," April said, perplexity in her voice.

"They've got him…" Jenkins left the rest of his thought unspoken.

"Who has him?"

"It's not for us to know, Miss Warmath," he said. "Get me a flight on a charter for D.C. I've got to leave by no later than 1700 hours."

New York City—2 a.m.

The nurse moved about the room, but Casandra Lincoln didn't appear to pay attention to her. Mary Bridges, a veteran of fifteen years at St. Bartholomew Rehabilitation Center, was most always in good humor. This early morning was no different. She hummed "Amazing Grace" while straightening around the bed, beside which Cassie sat in a wheelchair, staring, as she always did, toward the door.

Mary walked to the patient, bent to look into the girl's eyes, and smiled. "You feeling okay this morning, honey?" Her words were cheerful. She really wanted the girl to be asleep at this hour but had come to grips with the fact that Cassie always wanted to sit and stare at that door in the early morning hours. Maybe this was as good as any other therapy. Nothing else seemed to help, that was for sure.

The young woman's brain activity seemed normal on every technological gadget they had used to test her. The nurse had heard the neurologists talking. They were baffled about what was wrong. There wasn't a sign of stroke, of cerebral/vascular accident of any sort. No signs of any kind of poisoning. She had just suddenly, at twenty-five, ceased to do anything but stare when awake, with no signs that she understood anything, or knew anybody.

She didn't have much family but had lots of friends, and the company streamed in from around the country. Some contributed to her stay at

Saint B. But she knew—or seemed to know—none of them. Mary let her cogitations about the strange case die.

Her shift would be finished at 3:00 a.m., and she was ready to knock off, having worked a double shift. She looked at the chart she held and flipped through the pages.

"Looks like you are scheduled for a little bit of exercise tomorrow, baby," the nurse said. "I think we had better get a little sleep. Don't you? Need to be rested for that workout."

Cassie made no response, and Mary expected none. "Let's get you back in bed."

Neither did the young woman protest while the nurse turned the chair, then positioned it so that the transition from the wheelchair to the bed would be more easily accomplished.

Five minutes later, the job was done and Casandra Lincoln was tucked between the immaculate white sheets.

"I'll see you tomorrow, Cassie. You get some sleep, sweetie," Mary Bridges said, then dimmed the switch to the right of the door before she left the room, closing the heavy door behind her.

The room's semidarkened shadows surrounded the bed where the girl lay, still staring at the door the nurse had just exited. Her eyes blinked, her face reddened, and her body began a slight trembling that became more convulsive, her brown eyes turning toward the ceiling. Her eyes closed, her body violently twitching between the tightly tucked sheets that prevented her from tumbling from the bed.

The room brightened to the effulgence of the sun. The brilliance shrank to a ball of blindingly bright radiance. The sphere moved to directly above her spasming body. It hovered three feet above Casandra, projecting hundreds of thousands of light streams that touched every point of the girl's anatomy.

Mary Bridges sat at the small nurse's desk just outside the suite of rooms that surrounded her. She had completed the reports on the rehabilitating patients and would call a cab to take her to her Brooklyn apartment building—one of the perks of being a shift nurse when getting off after a late-night shift. The cab rides were on St. Bartholomew, and it was a welcome change from having to take buses.

She started to punch in the numbers while holding the receiver to her ear. Her face froze in amazement. Her mouth dropped open while she stared in disbelief at the door directly in front of the desk.

Casandra Lincoln walked through the doorway. No longer the pitiful, emaciating patient in the wheelchair, her pretty face glowed with perfect health. Her tall, slim body moved with the grace and suppleness of the young, beautiful woman she had again become.

Kristi Flannigan bolted from the elevator the second the doors slid open. She scanned the crowded entrance hall, her eyes searching wildly for the person who had moments before called to tell her she would soon be in the building's lobby. A group of people made excited noise in the right corner of the room. There were squeals of delight while the women she recognized as fellow workers at Guroix, Tuppler, & Macy hovered with enthusiasm around the object of their attention. It had to be…!

She hurried and jumped on her toes in the high heels, trying to see her.

"Cass! Cassie!" She waved her right hand in the air as she laughed at her ebullient attempt to get Cassie Lincoln's attention.

Cassie slipped through the circle of animated onlookers to embrace Kristi.

"Oh, Cassie!" Kristi said, tears flooding over her cheeks, her words choked back with emotion she couldn't control while they hugged each other in the moment of reunion.

Twenty minutes later they were nearly alone, the many greetings of their astonished GTM associates settling into an occasional passer-by coming to Cassie and giving a brief embrace and smile.

"I don't remember anything about that night, Kristi—just walking to Morgan's room. I don't even remember opening the door or whether it was open or closed, for that matter. She never closed it, so I guess it would have been opened."

"You remember walking toward the room, and that's all?"

"Well, I do remember the room was really dark, so I suppose I remember getting that far."

Kristi looked into the brown eyes of the girl who was one of her two best friends, thinking of what question to ask next.

"And then you remember nothing, until...you came out of it?" she asked, finally finding the question.

"I just woke up in that hospital bed all of a sudden. Felt great. More alert than I've ever been and nearly scared Mary to death—the sweetest woman on earth. One of the nurses who helped with my case."

They held hands. Kristi pulled Cassie's hands to her lips and kissed them. She wiped her eyes, then, with a tissue she had to find by rummaging through her purse.

"Where's Morgie?" Cassie asked when her friend had composed herself.

"I haven't been able to reach her on her cell in several days. I'm beginning to worry about her."

"She isn't working here any more?"

"Yes. She's still employed by GTM. But, she's got this really good position. Paul Guroix assigned her as public relations account exec for some top secret government project, some private company that has the patent on some top secret technologies. That's all I know. That's all Morgan knew, before she left."

Kristi blew her nose and tried to think more clearly.

"I guess we will hear from her when they let her contact us," she said, then smiled broadly, reaching forward for another embrace.

"I just can't believe you're okay, Cass. It's just so...wonderful..."

"The doctors can't believe it either. But...here I am!"

San Antonio, Texas

Laura Morgan answered at the first ring. She was initially disappointed that it was a male voice, having expected to talk to her daughter, who was supposed to call back. Her frown turned into a smile when she recognized the voice.

"Chris! Is that really you?!"

"The same old broken down preacher, I'm afraid," Banyon said, himself smiling with pleasure upon hearing the voice of the woman who was once his parishioner and who had long since been one of his best friends.

When the greetings settled, he asked, "Laura, how are the grandkids?" His tone, plus the fact that he first used her name, made her know the question was more than a conversational icebreaker.

"The grandkids? Why, Chris? You sound like there's something behind your asking."

"The last thing I want to do is worry you…"

"Go on…It's okay."

"I've had a very strange experience, Laura. It involves Morgan and Clark…"

Laura sat stiffly forward on the small desk chair.

"What sort of experience? What did the kids have to do with it?"

Banyon heard the angst in her voice and moved to explain in as soothing a tone as possible.

"Don't worry. Okay? It's just something that concerns Susie and me a bit," he said, then paused for her response. There was none.

"Remember back in 1967, all of that?"

"Yes," Laura whispered.

"Remember the experience I had in that cave in Qumran? The cave of the Dead Sea Scrolls?"

"Yes, I remember that it was a vision…of end-time things."

"Yes, well, this…experience…was like that. I was in the desert here near Phoenix, near the Estrella Mountains. I was playing fetch with my dog, Klaus, when I saw a glowing disk above a high ridge—a UFO of some sort."

He heard Laura's slight gasp, but she said nothing when he paused.

"Klaus and I went closer, to have a look. And, Laura, I was suddenly in that same place at Qumran, near the same cave. I saw it as clearly as I saw it back then."

"What does it mean, Chris?"

"That's not the half of it. Then I suddenly found myself inside the cave. It was the same as at Qumran but different. I moved through this long tunnel, with big chasms surrounding me. I went into this huge cavern. There were—" He searched for the descriptive words.

"What? What did you see?" Laura's heart raced. What this had to do with Morgan and Clark was all she could think of.

"Somehow I moved around the cavern—a huge, oval room."

"Like the one in Taos." Laura's words of interruption were matter-of-fact, not a question.

"Yes. Exactly like the one you described where you found Lori. It gleamed like polished steel. It was a gigantic lab of some sort. And…" he tried to find the right words and the least troubling way to express them. "I, I don't know how to say this in a way that won't upset you, Laura. But, remember, this was likely a forewarning, not necessarily something actually happening. That is, if it was a vision and not just a brain glitch or something…"

"Tell me, Chris. Just tell me!" Laura's words were panicked.

"I saw Clark and Morgan…on tables. Like operating tables, Laura. The dark things were, were…"

"What things? Not those monstrous cloud figures?" she said in words that became teary.

"It's okay, Laura. It's okay. Let's just think on it for a second. Okay?"

"Okay," she replied in a breathless, resigned whisper.

"I'm convinced this vision is from the Lord. You know, then, that He is with us. He will see us, those kids, through this, if there's anything to it."

"Yes…" Laura's whispered agreement strengthened her resolve, and she straightened in the chair. "The Lord will never leave us or forsake us."

TWELVE

The light ahead meant human comforts, and the rottweiler needed comfort, warmth, and food.

Jeddy had been through humans' trying to harm him. He wouldn't fall for it again. His canine instincts kicked into action the closer he got to the light streaming from the window. There was warmth and food within. But there were human things. Was his mistress there?

He sniffed the air, smelling good, food smells. Meat that could make the burning hunger go away. And there was warmth just inside the log cabin walls.

"Com'ere, feller," the human voice called to him. Jeddy sniffed the air and relaxed his bowed position in the foot-deep snow fifteen feet from the open cabin door.

"Come on, boy. It's warm in here," the old man urged while he stood in the doorway, framed by the fire-lighted cabin behind.

Instinct told the rottweiler he had nothing to fear from this human with the friendly voice. This would be good until he could find "Mommy."

"Good boy," the man said, kneeling slightly to pat the dog's huge head. Jeddy shook, sending the melted snow from his black fur.

The old man laughed and patted the dog again, letting Jeddy smell his hand. The dog gave it a gentle lick, telling the human that he returned the affection.

"My name's Ezekiel. But, if you could talk back to me, I'd let you call me Zeke. Can't tell me your name, can you? Is it okay if I just call you "Boy"?

Zeke walked to a cabinet near one wall. "Got some stuff here you'll like, Boy."

He pulled a sack from one of the shelves. "Been savin' this for some-body just like you," he said, pouring the dry dog food into a large pan he took from another shelf.

Jeddy ate his fill, feeling the satisfying warmth in his stomach while the food did its nourishing work. He lapped water from a big bowl the old man had placed beside the pan.

"Good to have company," Zeke said, patting and stroking the rott-weiler, who followed him to near the blazing fire in the stone fireplace. Zeke sat in a rough-hewn rocking chair, then sipped from a large mug of coffee he had retrieved from the hearth.

"Cold out here in the middle of the Rockies, huh, Boy? You must have come from a ways off. You just lie down on that bearskin there and get warm. You'll be good as new afore you can say 'peanut.'"

Jeddy raised his head, twisting it in curiosity, his black-furred brow wrinkling.

"Yep," Zeke said with a laugh, scratching Jeddy's head between his ears. "Afore you can say 'peanut.'"

Pasadena, California—the Same Hour

"Yeah, Chris. Mom—Laura—has told us everything."

Mark Lansing paced with the remote receiver, stopping to look down the stairway just off the upstairs hall.

"Lori's getting packed. We're going to Colorado to look for them."

Christopher Banyon was silent for several seconds, then said, "Mark, I really think you should hold off on that for just a day or so."

"Oh? Why?"

"I told you about Randy Prouse and those disks on his trip from Phoenix to JFK. Then the strange matter with the computer screen. Randy is part of this, whatever it is. He's in New York City to do a lecture at a museum on artifacts from Qumran. I know that Morgan worked there—in an ad agency, right?"

"Yes," Mark said. "Guroix, Tuppler & Macy."

"Randall wants to help any way he can. He and I have discussed it.

He will, with your and Lori's permission, do the legwork to look into what someone there might know."

"Randall is almost 83, Christopher. I know you've told me he's in excellent shape for an old guy. But, I don't want him risking his health by exhausting himself…"

"I agree. But, he has David—his oldest grandson—with him. David is an attorney in the Big Apple, you might remember."

"Yes. He always seemed to be a good kid. I remember all his questions about flying."

"He'll help Randy get around up there. Find out what's going on," Christopher said, waiting for a response.

"Well, Lori and I will accept any help we can get. It will save us a trip to Colorado, for now, at least. Chris, we are worried, my friend. Don't mind telling you…"

"Don't blame you. If it were my own kids, I…" He let the thought die. "But, let's think this thing through," Banyon said, trying to frame through his own concerned thoughts the facts involved and then the best course of action.

"Clark and Morgan haven't been heard from in—what? Three days?"

"Yeah. It's been about that long since Lori talked to Morgan or Laura talked with Clark."

"The kids have had dreams, or whatever they are, about the dark, cloud-like figures."

"The same kind of dreams or visions I've had since the time at Randolph Air Force Base. Even before that. Like those Lori's dad was having," Mark said.

"Yes and your own dad, the disappearance in 1947. What happened in that underground chamber at Taos. The cover-up, so that we couldn't get close to investigating. Even if we could, Laura and Colonel Morgan were threatened that if they ever pried into the matters…"

"Lori and me, too. They threatened us, in a backdoor sort of way, for many years," Mark said.

"Oh? You and Lori?"

"They hinted at getting my commercial pilot's license pulled permanently, if we didn't just let things drop. Lori had plenty of work in molecular physics projects, as long as she said nothing. The kids coming along kept her at home, so they lost that leverage. But, we've always worried about the kids. Been afraid there would be threats against them."

"I had that weird flashback of the vision I had in 1967. That was in 2001. The same day of the 9-11 attacks. Then, this…experience in the desert. That huge, stainless steel-looking, half-oval chamber. The kids…"

Struck with a conversation he recalled, Chris said, "Clark told us he saw the same scene in a dream. Only, it was his sister and someone else in a chamber of some sort. What's going on, Chris? I've got to find them. It's driving me nuts…"

"You and Lori aren't alone. We've got to work together to find them, Mark. We've all been brought together again in this thing, for some reason only the God of Heaven knows."

New York City—Same Day

David Prouse greeted his grandfather with a hug that made the elder Prouse wince with discomfort. Randall's oldest grandson stood the full 6' 4" that he himself had once stood. At 82, he thought, the temple begins to collapse. No, is already pretty much in a state of collapse, he corrected the thought…

"What's this all about, Grandpa?"

The younger Prouse, a twenty-nine-year-old criminal defense lawyer by training, and one who was viscerally determined to get to the heart of matters by nature, walked with his arm around his grandfather while they talked.

"Wish I knew," Randall Prouse said when they stopped at one of the gigantic entrance ways to the Empire State Building. "There are things going on I can't wrap my old gray sponge around."

David laughed, remembering fondly the funny terms his granddad always used. He was amused, too, because he considered his grandfather one of the brightest bulbs on the planet.

They entered through the Fifth Avenue side, the elder Prouse scanning the vast lobby. His eyes first met the sign for Finesse Jewelers against the south side, then people moving in every direction, or standing in crowded lines, boarding and disembarking from the famous old building's escalators that led to the elevators. The lobby floors and walls were of luxuriant black and gray marble, their beauty appearing like flowing molten lava. The marble was broken in zigzag patterns, with maroon lines that gave the structure, finished in 1931, the elegance he had heard about—the architectural gravitas rightfully belonging to one of the most recognizable landmarks in the city. David ushered his grandfather to the part of the building that had always fascinated him most. "This display is terrific, huh, Grandpa?"

Randall looked at the black-and-white photographic display of Fay Wray in her scenes of the most famous of all movies involving the building, *King Kong*. He mused over another photo that showed the great beast, in a later version of the movie, holding Ann Darrow as the gorilla curiously tinkered with her clothing. A commemorative plaque to Fay Wray completed the tribute.

"Went to see it as a kid," the elder Prouse said. "Got a little woozy in those scenes where Fay huddled on the ledge." He spent time reading, mouthing the words, "'Was beauty that killed the beast.'"

They walked toward the elevators. "Well, it's a long ways from the Regions Bank branch lobby in San Marcos," he said, eliciting another chuckle from his grandson.

"Yeah. I thought it would be a good place to meet. Get in a little history and sightseeing," David said while they moved farther into the lobby.

"Just like Cary Grant and Deborah Kerr," Randall Prouse said.

"What?"

"In *An Affair to Remember* Cary Grant was to meet Deborah in front of the Empire State Building. Glad our rendezvous turned out better."

"That a movie?"

"Yes, a real love tragedy," Randall Prouse said with a chuckle.

"What happened?"

"Deborah Kerr was hit by a car on the way to the rendezvous, crippled for life," David's grandfather said solemnly.

"Yeah, well, you be Deborah, okay?"

"One of your grandma's favorites, that movie, you know," Randy said, genuine sadness creeping into his tone.

David said nothing. They both felt the hurt of losing her too badly to go further.

"What's this all about, Grandpa?"

"Like I said. I—we—don't really know. But it involves events that happened those years ago, before you were born."

They stood with the others, watching the numbers light as the elevators ascended and descended.

"About that weird stuff going on in New Mexico and all that? Yeah, you and Grandma told us about all of that. Had something to do with UFOs, too."

"But not the extraterrestrial sort. These things, they are real. But they aren't tangible, except when they want to be material in appearance," Randall said, moving with David and the crowd toward the large elevator, which had just emptied of its passengers.

"Yeah, you said they were from the Benai Elohim—the fallen angel ranks," David said in a subdued tone, not wanting to attract the ears of those surrounding them.

"You remember that, huh?"

"Yes. You told us about it a lot, Gramps. Pretty spooky. I remember having Dad come in to look in my closet about five times after hearing about that," David said with a laugh. "Heck, I still have to look into the closets when I think about it."

His grandfather laughed. "Guess I did a pretty good job of storytelling, huh?"

"Yep."

"Well, it is all true; I assure. And, looks like it's happening again," Randy said while the elevator sped toward the Empire State Building's highest observation point.

"That's why I wanted you to get me to that advertising agency. The girl agreed to meet with me this afternoon about Morgan Lansing. They are best friends, according to what Lori and Mark—Morgan's mother and dad—told Christopher. Since I'm here, I need to find out what she might know about Morgan's…seemingly being missing."

They stepped out of the elevator and transferred to the next on their way to the top.

"But, it's only been a few days; you said Chris told you. Maybe she's just involved in some meetings and things that she can't break loose from," David said.

"But it's the other factors. Her brother, Clark, has been unable to be reached, too. The same time frame. Plus, both of those kids are in the Colorado Mountains, working, apparently, on things for the U.S. government that are secretive. At least their work involves things dealing with government projects. And, neither Clark nor Morgan knew—as of yesterday—that the other is in the same area working on those governmental matters, whatever they might be.

"We hope maybe this girl," he retrieved a piece of paper from his shirt pocket, then read the name he had penned, "Kristi Flannigan will be able to tell us something."

Washington, D.C.

The meeting in the bowels of the Pentagon had been both painful and angering, and George Jenkins simmered in silent rage while riding in the back of the black government sedan. He remembered Wayne Snidely's words, wishing he could cleave the head of the Department of Defense's smirky hatchet man like the mid-East terrorists were beheading all who opposed their version of religion.

"The apartment," Jenkins said, looking out the dark, tinted window to his left at the familiar monuments and buildings of D.C.

"Yes, sir," the driver said, switching lanes to begin the trip he had made many times for the covert operations chief.

"Pick me up at 1800 hours, Ted," Jenkins said, letting himself out of

the back of the car, slamming the door, and walking toward the building
without looking back.

Thoughts of the chiding, the "instructions," of the mental midget's
scathing words ate into the rawness that was already there from having
lost the opportunity to get the Saudi terrorist. He didn't know if the lecture had come from Rumsfeld or from whom. Had the little scab just
taken it upon himself to give the dressing down? The thought that such
a boil on the backside of Defense Department bureaucracy could have,
upon Snidely's own decision, called him from truly imperative matters
taking place in the mountain poured gastric juices directly upon his developing ulcer. He popped several antacids, chewing them while riding the
elevator to the eleventh floor.

At least he would have a few hours to catch up on some things. He
threw his suit coat across a chair and began looking through mail that had
accrued since he had been away from his D.C. home.

He felt the coolness of the slender fingers through the shirt. They
massaged the tenseness of the muscles from his neck to his shoulders. It
felt good, and he turned to look into April Warmath's eyes.

"You are so tense," she said, continuing the massage from his facing
position.

"Yeah. Quite tense," Jenkins said, closing his eyes and rolling his head
to help with the massage.

"Bad time at the Pentagon?"

"Hhmmm," he said, a combination of pleasure from the probing fingers and irritation at remembering the meeting with Snidely.

"What did they say?" the girl asked, changing the position of her
fingertips and beginning to massage his temples.

"It was only Snidely, the little puke. The Secretary was busy elsewhere, according to Snidely," he said, adding a swear word.

He noticed that April Warmath wore only a diaphanous negligee. She
pressed against him and kissed him, her fingertips continuing to knead
the back of his neck while her slender arms encircled him. She ran the
long fingers through his hair, her kiss becoming more insistent.

Jenkins started to remove his tie, unbuttoning the top button of his shirt. The phone's ringing broke the rising passion, and he moved to retrieve the receiver.

"Yes?" he said gruffly.

He listened to the colleague for several seconds, then said, "They will get him. Let them handle it. Do whatever they want to do."

When he hung the receiver on its cradle, he looked again into April Warmath's eyes. "Someone is doing reconnaissance from above the valley," he said.

Her eyes had turned from their normal color to solid black during the seconds he had been on the phone. His own eyes did likewise, and he smiled, continuing to unbutton his shirt.

Wilderness Su rrounding Crestone Needle, Colorado

He had seen unexplained, perhaps even unexplainable things. He trained the binoculars on the dark green against the vast field of white. It was just as if solid objects—flying disks—descended, then brightened to the point it hurt the eyes. And…they sat atop the forest, seeming to merge with the greenery, then vanished into the forests. All without disturbing the trees in any way.

Several of them had descended this way. None had left, but several had merged with the forest, and he saw no trace, even with the larger, more powerful telescope he used to check the mind-boggling scene.

Heavy thumping overhead aroused Nigel Saxton from his deep concentration on his spying activities. Snow cascaded in front of him from the ledge he had called home overnight and into this snowy Colorado afternoon.

They were onto him!

"He's in there," the voice crackled over the radio between the two small helicopters.

"It's not a cave. It's an overhang of some kind, looks like," the white-uniformed man said from the right seat of the copter one hundred feet

directly above the slope that descended sharply from the mountain
wall.

The bird's noise and wind-created turbulence caused a minor ava-
lanche to pour into the canyon below.

"We can't land. Too steep!"

"That's a roger," the voice of the pilot of the other helicopter crackled.

The pilot of the closely hovering chopper announced, "I'll move
around front. See what we can see."

Nigel heard the chopper's engine thumping louder while it rose
higher above the overhang. It began to move over the canyon that opened
into the valley beyond.

"Now I've had it," he said, grabbing the equipment around him and
scooting back on his elbows, pushing with the heels of his boots. Maybe
the deeper recess of the cave would swallow him in its shadows.

He saw, then, a distant light. A glowing, colorful sphere was seemingly suspended above the canyon. It moved to the edge of the recess,
then became a blinding light, and he crossed his forearm over his eyes to
lessen the pain of the brightness.

The chopper pilot swung the white copter to just above the overhang,
then moved out to above the deep ravine. He lowered the bird slowly,
until he hovered directly in front of the recess. He swung the aircraft's tail
to the right, so the man in the right seat could get a shot with the automatic weapon he readied, sighting it into the recess.

They saw nothing. An empty space.

"Ain't nothin' there," the man with the weapon said. "Thought they
said we would find him here…"

"That's what we were told," the pilot said, reaching to call the base.
"There's nothing here. It's just a ledge covering a cave-like space. Doesn't look
like anybody has even been in there lately," the pilot said into the helmet microphone, still searching the recess along with the gunner to his right.

"That's weird; they're never wrong," the voice on the other end of the
transmission said, as if to himself.

"Well, they are this time," the pilot affirmed.

"Sweep the area a few times; then come home," the voice at the choppers' home base said.

Manhattan, Late Afternoon

Two young women approached. One was a little taller with dark hair that was swirled into a bun and dressed in a well-tailored business jacket and skirt. The other was in a tangerine blouse covered by a stylish black leather jacket above dark gray slacks with barely perceptible vertical stripes. The girl with the auburn hair had to strain to keep up with her longer-legged companion.

"Miss Flannigan?" Randy looked at both of the girls, not knowing which was Kristi Flannigan.

"That would be me," she said with a big smile. "And this is Cassie Lincoln." She gestured toward the other girl.

"I'm Randall Prouse," the archaeologist said, "and this is my grandson, David."

"David Prouse," the younger Prouse said with a smile equal to Kristi's in its friendliness.

The four were soon sitting at a small café at street level just outside the skyscraper that was home to Guroix, Tuppler & Macy.

"Thanks for agreeing to meet with us," the elder Prouse said. "As I told you on the phone, it's about Morgan Lansing."

"We haven't heard from her," Cassie Lincoln spoke up, anxiety in her voice. "It's not like Morgan not to call Kristi," she said.

The men looked to Kristi.

"Cassie—she's been so sick, in the hospital, and so forth. We are Morgan's best friends. Cassie has some things to tell you, Dr. Prouse."

Randall looked at the girl in a surprised expression. He had said nothing to them about his degree…

"Morgan's mother, Lori, talked with me. Said you were a good friend. That's how I know. A doctorate in archaeology, I think she said?"

Randall smiled and nodded yes.

"Something strange is going on, Dr. Prouse," Kristi said. "Tell them, Cass."

They looked to the young woman sitting across the table from David, who saw in Cassie's expression a spark of animation he had seen in no other. He fought to listen to her words instead of staying lost in the visual pleasure presented by her loveliness.

"You will think I'm crazy, Dr. Prouse," she began, her voice animated with excitement to get the story told.

By the time she finished telling of her experience, from the night when she passed out to awakening in the rehab center, Randall Prouse's mind blazed with realization. This girl had had an experience like that of Morgan's grandmother. Laura Morgan had lost consciousness and remained comatose for weeks, then suddenly had emerged totally unaffected.

"But, that's not all," Cassie said, a degree of uncertainty in her voice while she glanced nervously at Kristi, who sat beside her, then across the table at David.

"Just tell us, Cass," David said, reaching to take her hands that fidgeted on the table's top.

"I'm seeing…things."

"What things?" David asked.

"Dark, cloud-like forms. Human-like monsters that are made of boiling, black smoke. And, they aren't dreams—at least, I don't think they're dreams," she said, looking into David Prouse's gaze for validation.

"Tell us," he said. "These forms—do they say anything?"

"They say, they, like, growl the words, 'The kingdom has come.' Not only that, I find written on my computer screen, in red letters, the same thing. Whether the screen is on or off, I can be working or not, and this message will appear in red letters—'The kingdom has come.'"

Randall's brow wrinkled in concentration. He leaned forward. "These…cloud-like beings. Do they ever take you places…in your mind, I mean?"

Cassie nodded her head yes but seemed reluctant to say more.

David, looking deeply into her eyes, said, "It's okay, Cassie. We've seen them too. That's what this is all about."

His grandfather wished, without saying so, that he could agree with David on his assurance that it was okay. One thing sure, he mused. Someone of higher authority had brought everybody involved together for some yet unknown reason…

Colorado Mountains

He had waited for two hours after the choppers left before leaving the protection of the ledge. Another couple of hours found him moving with great effort through the field of white.

Clouds, thick and gray, hurried the coming night-darkness along. He stumbled and fell in the deep snow. Having to high-step was wearing him out, and the backpack was becoming a burden he would soon have to shed, despite the fact he needed the things inside to survive.

Nigel Saxton looked at the compass on his right wrist. He was headed east—back toward the complex. Well before entering that forbidden zone, he should encounter the crags and cliffs, places where he could find shelter, places the snowfall couldn't cover with its life-sapping depth and coldness.

And, the snow came again in profusion, huge white flakes that made everything opaque in the growing darkness. The wind began to whip angrily, causing the mountains in the distance to look to be mere ghostly images that occasionally appeared as if apparitions, then to fade again to nothingness. He must find the rocky places, the craggy areas with their hiding places from those hunting him and from the potentially life-ending blizzard.

The Brit sensed it then, something even the frigid wind couldn't completely obliterate while it blew with raw, icy force against his face. The vile smell added to the stinging effects the cold gale inflicted upon his breathing with each burning intake by his nostrils. A foul scent—of something beyond death's sickly odor.

He had sensed the smell before, two summers earlier while climbing in the Swiss Alps. Or had it been the Himalayas? His convoluting brain, half-frozen and meandering between reality and delusion, fought to remember. The natives—must have been Sherpas—must have been the Himalayas—had fled. The smell...the same...The powerful little people running...Screaming in terror the word "Yeti!"...

Saxton stepped higher, trying to run in the thigh-deep accumulating snow field. The thing was tracking him. Getting closer. He tried to turn to look behind at his pursuer, but the attempt was painful. The big backpack caused him to lose his balance, and his back twisted painfully, his lower half remaining stuck in the position of moving forward.

He struggled to stand and finally managed to do so. The exertion of running through the snow, and the effort to right himself once fallen, exhausted his last burst of energy. Whatever wanted him could have him. Resistance was no longer within his power to offer.

He fell backward, his body engulfed by the snow pack. He looked upward into the darkness of the overcast. The smell was overpowering. The thing must be near; it would be upon him at any moment.

He thought it strange. Fear of the thing pursuing left him. He no longer felt the chill that had hurt to the bone, no longer felt the sting of the biting wind that relentlessly assaulted the flesh of his face. He was growing euphorically groggy. It would be wonderful, just to climb into the high-tech tent and sleep. He could sleep forever...

Nigel shook his head, blinking widely. He indeed WOULD sleep forever, he reminded himself. He would sleep for eternity if he didn't stay awake. His life would end, after thirty years, in these frozen regions. He would die an ocean and half a continent away from his England...

"What ya smell, feller?" Zeke smiled at the rottweiler, who stood sniffing at the cabin's only door. Jeddy barked in answer to the old man's question, standing stiffly with his nose pressed against the crack between the rough-hewn door of oak and its facing.

He growled a deep, throaty growl and whined his distress. The smell—he had inhaled the hateful scent before. It evoked primitive urges within the deepest reaches of his canine being. Did the odor mean the creature was there? Did its nearness mean, too, that his mistress needed him? Was she nearby, too?

"Okay, okay, feller. Everything is okay. Let's have a look at our visitor..."

When Zeke opened the door, the wind invaded with blowing snow, which gathered on Jeddy's thick, black fur. The dog peered into the whiteness that contrasted starkly against the heavy gray-black clouds. He bounded high through the snow, Zeke grinning, his eyes twinkling while he saw the canine's tail-docked rump lifting and falling with each leap.

"Good boy!" He shouted, urging the dog onward while Jeddy neared the fallen man.

Momentarily, Zeke stood behind the dog.

"It's okay, boy," he said. "I'll take it from here," the old man added, patting the rottweiler. Jeddy looked up at Zeke, then back at the other man, who lay unconscious, face up in the blizzard winds that increased with each passing second.

THIRTEEN

The New NORAD Inner-Mountain Complex

Takeoff had been delayed for eight hours because of snow over the Denver area. George Jenkins was in a seething rage by the time he walked into his office just over five hours after his government jet departed Andrews Air Force Base.

"Where's Kline?" His words were shouted at the squat, balding scientist who followed him into the office.

"He's preparing the subject for tomorrow morning's experiment," Clyde Bledsoe said. The PhD stood, fidgeting with a clipboard while his boss stood rummaging through the middle drawer of the desk.

"Where is the damned thing?"

Jenkins moved his hand angrily through the long drawer, his face reddened with blood pressure-raised frustration.

"Ah! Here it is."

He pulled from the drawer a slim remote device, pointed it toward the right of the desk, then pushed buttons that activated several monitors set within the wall.

"Do you need me?" the scientist asked. "I need to help with the Project Scotty subject studies, if I'm not needed here."

"Yeah. Go to the rest of the pointy-headed…"

Jenkins's castigating words were cut short when he saw on the largest of the screens a close-up of the young female being led to the stainless steel table. The woman assisting her, dressed in a white lab coat, steadied the girl while she moved up the two steps, then helped her lie down, face up, on the table.

"That the Lansing girl?" Jenkins asked.

"Yes. The brother—" the scientist looked at the clipboard "—Clark Lansing—is scheduled next."

"Why is she so calm? Surely she's not volunteering for this."

"She's had no sedation. I can't account for her state. They did something. Whatever it was, she's been cooperative."

He knew what they did. Had seen it before. They had done it to him many times. He knew they had done it to him, but he never remembered. It wasn't uncomfortable, just…nothing. Just a blackout of some duration. It had bothered him at first but no longer did. The…strange interlopers…would help him accomplish his goals. Would help his nation develop the RAPTURE through Project Scotty. Develop it to the point that armies could be produced that had no fear, that were dispensable, because they had no families, no loved ones, no consciences…

The girl and her brother were the only two who had the precise genetic makeup to complete the work successfully, according to…them…Morgan and Clark Lansing's grandfathers, then their parents…The genetic tampering, manipulating, and rearrangements had been done long ago. He didn't understand it all. Didn't care to understand it all. So long as one George Jenkins came out on the top of the heap…

The camera from above the table zoomed in to frame Morgan Lansing, now strapped to the table. Her eyes were closed beneath the surgical head covering while people in operating room garb worked over her body.

Jenkins watched with fascination while they prepared the girl. His thoughts ran in often-used neuron-to-neuron synapse routes throughout his brain. Routes that he had cerebrally retraced many times.

The two imperatives. His imperative and…theirs. This was the beginning of those two, distinct, all-important purposes of the project coming together. He wished at this moment—seeing the scientists pull back the cover to expose the girl's midsection—that he knew exactly what the imperative truly entailed…

New York City

Paul Guroix stood over the credenza back-bar looking out the window that gave him a vista of the streets far below. The city moved with sidewalk pedestrian life, the many vehicles bumper-to-bumper, crawling between traffic lights along Madison Avenue.

The intercom on his desk buzzed, and he turned to pick it up after rolling the desk chair to one side. He sat down as he answered.

"Yes?"

The advertising executive listened to his secretary, then said, "Okay, I'll be right out."

Randall and David Prouse stood when Guroix walked into the waiting area.

"Dr. Prouse?" he thrust his hand in Randall's direction, smiling, and glancing at the younger man.

"Yes. And, my grandson, David Prouse," Randy said, gesturing toward David, who took Guroix's hand.

They entered the executive's office after amenities were finished.

"You are worried about Miss Lansing, I'm told," Guroix said in a questioning tone.

"Yes. Her family hasn't heard from her in days. And neither have her closest friends here in New York, Kristi Flannigan and Cassie Lincoln," the archaeologist said, after being seated in the burgundy leather chair offered him in front of the executive's desk.

"Yes. Kristi and Cassie are both employees here, as you know," Guroix said, seating himself behind the desk.

"Morgan is one of our brightest. We placed her in a very important public relations position, with one of our top clients."

David looked at his father, indicating with his expression that he wanted to quiz Guroix.

"We were hoping, Mr. Guroix, that you could give us details about Morgan's interaction with the company to which you've assigned her," David said.

"I can tell you that she is in good, safe hands," Guroix said in a businesslike tone. "Transportec is a top 500 company, with billions in assets. The company has a number of contracts with the U.S. and other governments around the world. But, as far as specifics, I'm afraid I can't go much further. They deal in some highly classified technological matters—particularly for the U.S. Department of Defense."

Guroix took a sip from a cup of coffee on the right side of the desk. "Can I offer you some coffee?"

Both declined.

"These DOD projects, are they within the country?" David asked.

"Oh, yes. I can tell you that they are being carried out mainly in Colorado, around some new NORAD installations. That's all public information, of course. But, that's as far as I can go. For one thing, I don't know any more than that. I haven't got the clearance to know much more than that. But, of course, I couldn't say, if I did know."

"And Morgan—does she have the clearance?" Randy put in.

"Yes. I'm sure she had to pass background checks. She has to have at least a modicum of clearance to even enter those areas. Even though her area of work deals only with public relations in a campaign they are developing for public consumption, she, like everybody involved, must have governmental clearances."

There was a pause while David framed the next question in his mind.

"Have you heard from Morgan?"

"No. But, that doesn't concern me. I've assigned people to work with Transportec and other companies that do business with government agencies. Sometimes we don't hear from them for weeks at a time. So, I'm not the least concerned. It's nothing out of the ordinary," the executive said, taking another sip of the coffee.

"I hope you understand, Mr. Guroix, that it is highly unusual for Morgan to go more than a couple of days without calling her parents. They are extremely close. And, the girls—Kristi and Cassie—they tell me she would have contacted Kristi by now. Cassie, of course, was ill, so Morgan wouldn't have thought to call her on her cell," David said.

Guroix let his eyes wander his office, obviously in thought about David Prouse's words. He kneaded his chin and played with his silver-gray mustache with his right thumb and fingertips. "Only thing I can think, then, is that for some reason she is temporarily out of touch because of the concentrated nature of her work. I'm sure they will let her make the calls to family, and so forth, when whatever she is working on lightens a bit."

There was an uncomfortable silence, prompting Guroix to speak again. "Tell you what, I'll see what I can do to get in touch with the Transportec people. See if we can find the reason for her not calling," he said, reaching to the intercom and pushing a button.

"Sherri, make a note for me to call John Harris at Transportec."

He looked back to David and Randall Prouse.

"Give me a call later this afternoon, and I should have some answers. Is there anything else I can do?"

"As a matter of fact, there is, Mr. Guroix. Could you give Miss Flannigan and Miss Lincoln some time off to help us a bit, if your findings when you call the company are...less than satisfactory?"

David's words caused the advertising executive to study the question for a moment. He again reached for the intercom.

"Sherri, if Kristi Flannigan isn't working on something too vital, authorize her a week's leave, with pay."

Guroix looked at David, a tight smile on his lips. "Miss Lincoln is already on leave for a week or two, just to make sure she is fully recovered."

The thought struck both the elder and younger Prouse. It sounded like Guroix knew that his findings, upon talking with his contact at Transportec, would prove unsatisfactory.

Phoenix—1:22 a.m.

Christopher had been nauseous since dinner at six the previous evening. The tuna casserole felt as if it had come up again and now lodged at the top of his esophagus, the gastric acid burning bitterly at the base of his throat. He looked into the bathroom mirror, seeing the pallor on the seventy-four-year-old face. He swallowed the watery white-powder mixture he had prepared, hoping it would do the trick. It would be the last time he would eat tuna casserole, he promised himself, sticking out his tongue to check its condition. He didn't know why he always did that when feeling poorly. He guessed it was because that's the first thing the doctor always wanted to look at, during his seemingly endless trips to his physician lately.

It was no fun getting old. His Susie, he was thankful while gargling mouthwash to rid his mouth of the foul taste of the medicine, was as beautiful, as young as those years ago when they were dating. Well, maybe not quite as young in appearance but every bit as beautiful.

It was the prayer life, he decided in silence, pulling his lower eyelids down a bit to examine for the redness that seemed more pronounced than usual. Yes. It was his sweet Susie's prayer life and dependence on the Lord that kept her young and vital—while he himself continued on the down-ward spiral his failing flesh was taking him, toward antiquity...

"Oh, Lord," he began the prayer, without speaking it. "Please help me to pray as I should."

He thought then of something to add. "Please give us direction to know what these things are all about. How we can be of service. To know your holy will in these devilish matters...Please, dear God. In the name of your Son I pray..."

He flipped the light switch off and began walking down the long, darkened hallway. Randy Prouse's words replayed in his head while he en-tered the bedroom, sat on the bed, and swung his legs beneath the covers.

"The guy at Morgan's ad agency—Paul Guroix—said the people in Colorado couldn't divulge her whereabouts. It didn't seem to bother Guroix at all. Said it's not unusual," Randall had told him.

Christopher shut his eyes, but they popped open. He couldn't stop thinking about the conversation. His thoughts ran in quick bursts while he stared at the ceiling.

Randy had told him that Morgan's friends said she would never go more than a day without talking to her mother—they were adamant about that fact. No way would Morgan not keep Lori abreast of what was going on in her life for more than twenty-four hours. Lori had told Christopher the same thing during their phone conversation last night before bed.

Lori was insistent that she must find where her daughter—and her son, for that matter—were in Colorado. That the kids were there without each other's knowledge was just too coincidental. And, both Randy and Lori had driven home the facts: The events that happened those years ago with Lori and Mark. The experiments done to them in the underground labs at Taos. The visions, or dreams, or whatever they were that had haunted the whole family since that time. The invasion into their children's lives. The Bigfoot creatures that dominated their son's career pursuits. Clark's seeing his sister and some male figure in the lab in a dream or vision…the vision Clark had described not unlike the vision or dream Christopher, himself, had seen in the desert. The vision of both of Lori's and Mark's children, strapped to gurneys, head to head in a laboratory setting. The dark creatures that inhabited the dream-visions…that Morgan repeatedly saw in her dreams…Randall Prouse's encounter while flying from Phoenix to New York, like the things he himself had seen in 1967 while flying home across the Atlantic. Strange, otherworldly sights…

Christopher shut his eyes and massaged them gently with his fingers. "Oh, dear Lord, give us direction…"

Susie Banyon sat up partially to lean on one elbow toward her husband. "Chris?" she said just above a whisper. "Christopher?"

There was no response. She turned back to find her own sleep again, after leaning further forward to kiss his cheek.

Colorado—the Next Day

The helicopter swept the mountain range in a slow, low orbit. The TV camera, held by the uniformed man in the right seat, trained on the many dark creases in the mountain side that might serve the interloper as hiding places.

Satisfied that the intruder wasn't in the crevasses, the pilot tilted the chopper in a sharp, banking sweep to the right, hurrying to cover yet another of the search-grid coordinates plotted the night before.

George Jenkins looked through the camera's perspective while the copter moved swiftly toward its next area of search. He watched on the other screens on the wall across from his desk different helicopter camera views of other areas being searched.

The operative would be found. He had to be found, even if Jenkins had to call those of other-worldly intelligence to do the finding…

He held down a button on the strip of controls affixed to the top of his desk to his left.

"Have you tried the Xavier Gorge area, closer in to the complex?" His question screeched into the headphones of the pilot of the lead copter.

"No, sir. Haven't tried that yet. Over."

"Get somebody over that sector. It has some areas where he could hide," Jenkins commanded, ignoring protocol for back and forth with the pilots.

"Roger, sir. Will do," the pilot said, maintaining a professional flyer's tone, then proceeded to order two choppers in the direction of the main complex of Defense Department facilities.

Jenkins followed the flight of the birds on the screens monitoring the helicopters.

Nigel Saxon, at the same moment, heard the thumping sounds. The choppers were very close, and he scanned the sky in the direction from which the noise came.

Jeddy stood beside him, looking into the sky, trying to scent any odor that might tell his senses something about what was troubling the man.

"They can't miss the cabin," he said, ducking back inside Zeke's small dwelling. The old man sat by the fireplace in the rocking chair, apparently oblivious to the choppers that now swept above the cabin.

"I'm sorry, Zeke. Looks like they've found us. Don't want you involved in this. I'll break for it. Get them away from your place," the Brit said, looking at Zeke, then going to the lone window to try to see the birds.

"No, Son. You stay here. No harm will come to me, to any of us," the old man said, continuing to rock in the chair while chuckling, and snapping his fingers at the dog.

Nigel heard the thumping fade. He eased the door open, and again swept the sky through the binoculars for the helicopters.

"They seemed not to have seen us," Saxton said, with perplexity in his declaration.

The old man was too busy laughing while playfully wrestling with Jeddy to pay attention to the Brit's observation.

They kept their date to meet at noon. Cassie wasn't sure, but she thought she had detected some interest he had for her. She had asked Kristi.

"Are you kidding me? He couldn't take his eyes off you," her friend had said. "Why do you think he wants to see you again?" Kristi laughed, amused at Cassie's naiveté.

Well, she thought, she wasn't so confident while she hurried toward the Empire State Building's Fifth Avenue entrance.

David Prouse remembered his grandfather's words about the tragedy in the movie. What was it? *An Affair*? Or something like that—where the stars were to meet at the Empire State Building, but the girl was crippled for life in an accident on the way to meet the guy. Maybe he shouldn't have asked her to meet him in the lobby of the Empire State Building! But, it was the logical place. It was near his office and not too far from where she worked. But, she was not back to work yet, so the trip further downtown from her apartment building required a bit of effort.

Did he really see a spark of interest for him? She had agreed to meet him, so…

"Hi, David!"

He turned to face the broadly smiling young woman, who reached to grip his offered hand.

"Boy! Some traffic at this hour, huh?" she said, patting his arm.

A very warm greeting, he thought while putting his big hand over hers. Maybe he had been right about her liking him…a little, at least.

"Yeah. I'm glad to see you. I was beginning to worry. My granddad told me about this movie. The guy and girl were supposed to meet here, but the girl was crippled in an accident on the way over," he said.

"Oh. You mean *An Affair to Remember* with Cary Grant and Deborah Kerr!" she said brightly.

"Yeah. That's the very one. Couldn't remember the names of the movie or of the actors."

"Guess some guys don't remember very well about the romantic movies. And that's a really old one."

"Granddad remembered it. Of course, I'm sure it was because my grandmother told him it was her favorite."

Cassie looked upward at the handsome face, whose eyes sparked with obvious pleasure in seeing her.

"Well, here I am. Safe and sound!"

"Now, if we can just get through the sightseeing from the top without King Kong getting us, we can grab a bite to eat," he put in with a big smile, offering his arm, which she took while they walked to the escalator leading to the elevators.

Forty minutes later they sat separated by a small table inside Heartland Brewery, each's growing interest in the other closing the distance between them. David's thoughts turned to things that might help him better understand Cassie's relationship to Morgan Lansing.

"How long have you been friends with Kristi and with Morgan?"

"Since college. We were suite mates at UCLA."

"You and Kristi don't sound like Californians," he offered.

"Oh, no. Kristi and I are from New York. We're both from Long Island."

"UCLA is a long way from Long Island."

"Yep. About as far as you can get," she said, then sipped her Coke.

"Cassie...these dreams..." He hesitated, his attorney's mind trying to meld with his desire to win her affection. "Exactly what are the things that stand out in them? I'm trying to understand what's going on. Is this all related in some weird way?"

She looked upward in thought, still sipping from the straw. She put the glass in front of her and played with it by half-twirling it with her fingertips while in obvious thought about his question.

"I guess what stands out most, besides those dark creatures, is the laboratory setting," she began, pausing to reflect for several seconds. "It's the little sea horse–looking shapes in the glass containers that look like fish tanks. They are immersed in some kind of bubbling, greenish liquid.

Kind of the consistency of—you know that stuff that keeps your car engine from freezing? What do you call that?"

"Antifreeze?"

"Yeah," she said, her pretty face wrinkling with laughter at herself. "Yeah, antifreeze. That's it."

David studied her for a few seconds, then asked, "And these seahorses...these fish tanks, are those all you see in the dreams?"

"Oh, no! There are these, I guess they are globes or balls of glowing lights. They are always in the dreams. But, they aren't really dreams. They don't seem like dreams. It's like I'm really there, and when I awaken in bed, it is as if I am still there...in their presence. At least for a few seconds. I can still see them. They don't just suddenly pop from my mind like dreams. I can see them, these big globes of light floating around the bed. Then, they just..." She gesticulated with her hands. "Just fade to nothingness..."

David asked, "And, these seahorse-like things in the fluid, do they just fade from the picture?"

Cassie rolled her brown eyes up in concentration. "Oh, there are also these people. Dressed like doctors. You know, doctors ready for surgery, or something. They are bending over the glass tanks. They obscure my view. I can't see what they are doing."

She paused, trying harder to remember. She shook her head negatively. "That's all I remember. Then the lights are all around me, and I'm coming out of it."

Colorado—Near Midnight

They were coming. They would be here at any moment. George Jenkins paced his office carpet, glancing at the clock.

"Eleven fifty-eight," he said in a whisper, feeling the anxiety well within his stomach. He reached to his coat pocket to retrieve the Rolaids. He popped several in his mouth and crunched them, shut his eyes, turned his face toward the ceiling, and rotated his head to relieve tension in the thick neck muscles.

This was it. Something special. They summoned his thoughts to this early morning meeting for something different. Something that he instinctively knew was a leap beyond any dealings he had had with... them...before.

They seemed all-powerful, could do anything with impunity. Yet they could—or would—do nothing when he called them earlier that day to intervene in the capture or killing of the operative who hid in the snow and crags of...

The clock began chiming, and he stopped to glare at the instrument above the credenza against the wall. Midnight! They were never late. Never...

Before the clock's chime struck its twelfth tone, the room darkened to near black, and in the next instant, a single figure appeared out of the air, standing directly in front of Jenkins in the black suit and tie, like always.

The DOD covert operations chief felt his knees weaken. He caught himself and straightened, his emotions flush with fear and, at the same time, with exultant anticipation.

The human-like figure stood stiffly, its mouth a black line that expanded and contracted upon the pasty white face.

"Time has come, George Jenkins. Now we begin bringing the kingdom to this sphere."

"What kind of kingdom?" Jenkins's question was offered meekly.

"The subjects are prepared. Now is time to introduce the seed that will complete the process begun in the antediluvian age. It is the moment for you to come into the fullness of fruition of that which must be hereafter. It is time for you to understand these matters in their totality."

Jenkins tried to form another question—to ask what the things spoken about involved. He could but stand, unblinking, watching the black slash of a mouth writhe in expansion and contraction while his mind somehow absorbed thoughts from this—he knew within his deepest reaches—ancient intelligence beyond any that was human.

"Come," the pasty humanoid form said.

He felt himself shrouded in warm mist that obscured everything around him. Still, he could not speak. He could but be engulfed, and somehow invaded, by the caliginous mist from which he received dark knowledge—understandings from regions where light did not penetrate, where no flesh and blood being could long survive.

Then, just as quickly as it came, the boiling mist dissipated. He stood, he knew when he could again see his surroundings, in the silvered, gleaming oval room. The room where the experiments—the strange experiments had been taking place for, he somehow now understood, eons of time…

He knew exactly what was happening while he watched the tall male he now knew was a long-ago planted subject within the European Union clandestine cabal—within American private commercial enclaves. He watched Blake Robbins, his eyes black, glistening spheres within the handsome face, first sit, then lie beneath the white covers atop the surgical gurney. Next, the young woman, in a zombie-like state, moved, with the help of surgically-garbed people, to the table near the gurney upon which Robbins had just reclined. Morgan Lansing was strapped to the table while instruments were moved beside and above her body. The same procedures were performed surrounding Blake Robbins.

A faint smile crossed Jenkins's lips. He now had absolute knowledge, and it was indeed an inspired plan.

FOURTEEN

Zeke took the plate he had just filled with bacon and eggs from the big frying pan on top of the old wood stove and handed it to Nigel.

"How do you get the things to make breakfast like this?" The grateful Brit didn't waste time for an answer to the question. He dug into the food, glancing at the rottweiler, who had his muzzle into the deep bowl of dry dog food the old man had moments before poured.

Zeke treated the question as rhetorical, and said, instead of answering the question, "They'll be sendin' out folks to look for ya, young feller."

He peered out the window into the whiteness that surrounded his cabin. "But, y'all will be long gone 'fore they get a chance ta get at ya," he continued.

The old man walked to the fireplace and stoked the burning logs with a poker, causing sparks to shoot up the chimney.

"Got this place I wanna show ya. We'll start when ya've finished yer eats."

When Saxton had sipped from the coffee mug, he asked Zeke, "Have they…these government types…never bothered you out here? Seems you are right in the middle of some secret things they are doing."

"Nope. Ain't never been bothered by any of 'em. Never once."

"Hmph…" Nigel, with his mouth now full of food, grunted his incredulity. He spoke again when he had swallowed.

"What do you do out here, Zeke? I mean, especially in these mountain winters? Seems there's little to do—especially with having to go so far to…civilization."

Zeke was again at the fire, stoking it to life, so that it glowed red, then blazed brightly, the sparks again flying upward.

"Ain't so far as ya might think, young feller," he said. "I'm gonna show ya what I mean."

The old man snapped his fingers for Jeddy to come to him. The rottweiler happily complied, sitting at Zeke's knee while being stroked.

"Gonna miss ya, Peanut," he said in a quiet voice.

Near Phoenix, Arizona

Reds, browns, and many gradations of tans colored the mesas and buttes to the west. The sun was still high, but its quick traverse of the afternoon sky caused rapid changes in the crooks and crevices of the distant promontories lying across the horizon. The desert between Christopher Banyon's third story studio/study and the ridges beyond seemed but a short expanse.

He hadn't stopped scanning the sky above the ridges, looking for another glimpse of the things—the disks, or balls of lights, or whatever they were, that had beckoned him that day, had tugged him toward the cave that had become, somehow, the area of Qumran, near the Dead Sea.

He felt the bump against his leg, then bent to scratch Klaus behind an ear. "It's about time to take our walk, Christopher said, putting the volume he had been studying back in its place on one wall of shelves. He looked around the large study for the dog leash, seeing it on the floor near the massive ceiling-to-floor window that gave him the magnificent view of the vista he had grown to love.

He was a blessed man, he thought, bending to attach the leather strap to Klaus's collar. The Lord had indeed been good to him and to Susie. Had given them three children and seven grandchildren, with another on the way. He had provided for the family. Not many were so fortunate.

But, it was not fortune, or luck, he mentally pinched himself to remember. There is no such thing as coincidence in the Lord's vocabulary, he thought, remembering the well-worn apothegm.

His uncle had left several million dollars to his great aunt. She had turned it into millions more. He was the sole inheritor of the estate—the properties in Maine and the stock market investments that had burgeoned over the past several years.

"Unto those to whom much is given, much is required," he thought, paraphrasing the Bible's reminder to those who might think wealth gives them special privilege but no responsibility.

But, he didn't want to be like the philanthropists who threw their money down the rat holes of social do-goodism. His—blessings—must be put directly to God's work here on earth. The words of John F. Kennedy's 1960 inaugural address echoed through his mind's ear, "...here on earth, God's work must truly be our own..."

"Come on, Klaus. Let's get you to your favorite spots."

The dog happily led him from the study, then to the small elevator at the end of the long hallway.

"We need to start using the steps, boy," he told the canine, an admonition to himself, which he gave every time he stepped onto the elevator floor.

At 74 and getting older, he mused, it wasn't likely that using the steps more often was going to happen. Maybe it was time to downsize, to get a one-story home, like most of the other residents in this desert community. The kids and grandkids still loved coming and spending time with Susie and him, though, so downsizing wasn't a likelihood.

The Lord had indeed been good, he thought again while the elevator clunked against the floor and Klaus led him into the large foyer toward the double-doored entranceway.

Yes, he had decided. If they wanted to do it. It was all that had occupied Susie's mind lately. And, he worried, too, about the kids—Laura's grandchildren, Mark and Lori's children. Yes. He would offer to charter a plane to pick them up and fly to Colorado. He hoped they would accept. The Lord was prompting Susie and him to offer to do it. It was settled...

"Jenkins is in for a not so pleasant wake-up," Wayne Snidely said, snapping shut the attaché case and rolling the tumblers on the locks on either side of the handle.

Jeremy Lasceter watched the smirking administrative assistant to the deputy secretary of defense jump his suit coat onto his body, then straighten the tie at its knot after buttoning the coat's top button.

"You think they'll fire him?" the young man asked, following his boss into the hallway outside the basement office.

"Well, let me just say this, Jeremy, my boy, be ready to pack and move your things into covert operations. There's enough in here to hang him."

"You think the budget overruns are enough to do it?" Lasceter asked, holding the door at the end of the long, linoleum-covered hallway leading to the old building's elevators.

"Not the overruns. The hiding of funds in black projects that have nothing to do with the project he's heading," Snidely said, walking ahead of the taller man into the elevator doors that had just slid apart.

"I'm taking this directly to Rumsfeld. Not going to stop until I'm at the top, kiddo."

"How can you get to the secretary? I mean—not many even want to get to the secretary," Lasceter said, only half-joking.

"Got an appointment, my young friend. Rumsfeld wants to see me at 2:30," Snidely said smugly.

"How'd you manage that, boss?"

"Told his appointments secretary the black ops was about to cause DOD to experience a scandal that will rival Watergate. That got 'em moving, I'll tell you."

"And, you've really got that kind of information?"

"Sure do. Been gathering for more than six months, and this last thing—can't tell you about it—is the proverbial straw that…"

Snidely stopped mid-sentence when the elevator doors parted, and they faced several men wanting to enter the conveyance.

"You'll know about it soon enough, kiddo," Lasceter's boss said, hurrying ahead of the younger man while they moved toward the doors that led outside the building and to the awaiting car.

Jeremy Lasceter opened the door of the left rear, allowing his boss to seat himself before slamming the door. He hurried around the rear of the dark government sedan, then got in behind the wheel. Moments later, they started toward the Pentagon, Snidely smiling tightly with self-importance, pleased with his weeks of getting the goods on one George Jenkins. If he had it figured correctly, he, Wayne Snidely, would very soon be the new black ops chief.

Neither saw the darkly clad man with binoculars trained on the vehicle, standing in the huge window five stories above them while they drove out of the circular drive and merged with the heavy afternoon traffic.

Mark and Lori Lansing rode in the Tahoe from their cul-de-sac and entered the LA Freeway eighteen minutes later, merging with the vehicle congestion traveling toward LA International Airport. The smog hung heavier than usual, causing traffic in the distance to be swallowed by a coagulant haze.

"If Randy and Christopher want to meet us in Colorado, that will be great," Mark said, glancing into the rearview mirror at the line of traffic that disappeared in the maze behind. "Just can't wait on them. We've got to find out something."

Lori said nothing. She could think only of Morgan and Clark...Of why they had not called, had not answered their cell phones.

"We should be there by five, or so, Mountain Time."

"I just don't see how we can find out much," Lori said, tears in her voice as well as in her eyes.

"I'll raise enough stink. We will find out something," Mark said glancing at his wristwatch. "It's 11:19. Randy and Christopher couldn't do anything that we can't," Mark said. "They can join us whenever they can make it."

"But, don't you see, Mark? We're, somehow, tied together in all of this..."

Mark glanced at his wife and reached to put his right hand on her hand.

"And, I agree, babe. I just can't sit still any longer. I've got to get something going, in order to find out about those kids. If it weren't for all the weird happenings, there probably would be no need to worry. But, like you said, we're all tied together. Tied to what? We've got to find out."

"I know the Lord will take care of them," Lori said, straightening a bit.

"But, the Lord expects us…"

Mark's spoken thought was abbreviated by his cell phone's chime.

"Hello," Lori said, answering her husband's phone while she continued to blot at her eyes.

"Christopher!"

Christopher Banyon said, from the other end, "You guys want to go to Colorado?" His tone was bright, meant to lighten the gloom he knew must hang over the parents.

"As a matter of fact, Chris, we're about to do just that," Lori said.

"Oh?"

"We're headed for LAX right now, to fly to Denver. We were hoping you, Susie, and Randy would join us when you can."

Banyon said, with laughter in his voice, "Well, to paraphrase, your ticket, not to mention your money, is no good. I've chartered a plane for all of us. Randy got it for us in New York, and it's on the way. They'll pick you up at LAX in a few hours. Then you'll pick up Susie and me at Phoenix International, and we'll fly out together."

Jeremy Lasceter steered the dark gray Chevrolet onto the entrance ramp and into the flow of traffic on the interstate. Wayne Snidely thumbed through a number of the documents in the open attaché case sitting atop his lap. He grinned his pleasure with each page he turned. The evidence was simply overwhelming. Jenkins was diverting funds, using them to abuse prisoners from Guantanamo for experimentation. And, it was all in black-and-white on these pages and in the video his operative had snuck out of the complex. It was printed directly from computers manned by Snidely's own mole within the Colorado mountain complex. After saving DOD's—

Rumsfeld's—hide, he, Wayne Snidely, would be given the black ops position. No doubt about it. There were those in the Pentagon who had guaranteed that if he got the goods, they would deliver the position. This was a no-miss proposition.

Snidely's young driver glanced at his boss's face. He hadn't seen the usually somber or, at best, smirky Snidely look so gleeful.

"You will get a pay grade higher, Jeremy-boy. Maybe two pay grades…" Snidely's words brought a smile to the driver's face, his eyes meeting those of his boss in the mirror.

"Yep. We will soon be directing things from Colorado. You ever skied, Lasceter?"

"Oh, no, sir. I've never been around snow much, until I moved to Washington," Jeremy said, glancing first at the traffic ahead, then into the rearview mirror at Snidely.

"Neither have I. But, we can learn together, if there is time. There's so much I want to do with these projects, kiddo. But, we'll find time for some recreation."

"Yes, sir," the younger man said, knowing firsthand Snidely's preference for male companionship over female.

Jeremy forced the sedan to pick up speed, the traffic having thinned considerably along the usually congested interstate.

He noticed, then, a semi-tractor-trailer truck in the rearview mirror while it approached the tail of the government car. The truck would swing around them, Jeremy thought while keeping the speedometer on the permitted seventy mph.

Traffic ahead, he could see, was growing heavier, and he had to start braking or would soon be in a position that braking would have to become more dramatic in order to avoid rear-ending the cars ahead.

He slowed to sixty-five, then to sixty.

The huge tractor rig suddenly loomed larger and larger. The driver of the big rig would begin braking at any second—surely…

But the truck continued to get bigger in the mirror, getting dangerously close. The cars ahead demanded that Lasceter brake immediately. The guard rails on both sides of the beginnings of an overpass now hemmed in the car driven by Lasceter, as well as all in front of him, between heavy concrete and metal railings. There was no place to go to get away!

Jeremy's wide, terrified eyes saw only the massive windshield when the truck closed in on them at eighty miles per hour. No one was behind the wheel. The truck was driverless!

Less than an hour later, George Jenkins sat behind his huge desk, sipping black coffee an assistant had just poured for him. He watched the center monitor that was twice the size of the other monitors inset in his oak-paneled wall. His gray eyes squinted from between the nearly closed eyelids, the hot liquid painfully making its way to his ulcerated stomach.

"Our Washington, D.C. affiliate traffic helicopter caught the tragedy as it unfolded," the network reporter said from the monitor's speakers.

"The truck, as you can see, is a gasoline tanker that was fully loaded. For some reason, the driver couldn't brake as the other vehicles had, because of congestion ahead, come to a standstill."

Jenkins sipped again while he watched the gigantic tanker rig crash into the dark gray vehicle directly in front of it, then quickly become one with the first car contacted and a number of vehicles in front of the first car hit. The whole scene erupted into a tremendous fire ball, gasoline exploding and sending a wave of the burning liquid over the decimated vehicles and over the bridge onto the roads crossing beneath.

George Jenkins's lips raised at the corners only slightly while he sat with his feet crossed on one corner of the big desk. He lifted his cup in mock-toast to the late Wayne Snidely.

Xavier Pass—Same Hour

Nigel Saxton checked his backpack for the third time. You were taught to always check three times as part of MI7 training. To check less would be to be remissive. To check more would be compulsive—obsessive, a waste of time agents could, in most crisis situations, not afford.

The GPS device was critical. That must be kept in operational order at all cost. Even if Nigel Saxton met an untimely end, the satellite must be able to relay to those in London where it happened, where the body could be located.

"Ya 'bout ready, there, young feller?"

Zeke's words pulled Nigel's thoughts from the pack, which, after all, had been checked three times. The old man's question interrupted the Brit's urge to check for a fourth.

Jeddy stood by Zeke's right leg, looking up at the man while he questioned Saxton.

"Got everything ya need?"

"Think so. Except one." He pulled from the pack a camera. "Do you mind, Zeke? Can I get one of you and the big fellow?"

"Don't see why not," the old man said.

Zeke stood looking at the camera, his left hand on the dog, who looked up at Zeke, then at the camera. Saxton snapped the picture.

"Thanks. Something to remember you by, my friend," the Brit said. Saxton knelt, stored the camera, then rummaged through the backpack.

"Yes. All seems in order," he said, snapping a pocket on the back shut, then putting his arms through the straps before jumping the backpack high on his back.

"You say there is a short cut to the town?" The Brit inquired while buckling the clasp that secured the pack at mid-chest.

"Yep. That I do, sonny. There are places ain't nobody but ol' Zeke knows 'bout within that big rock."

"How much time can I save by cutting through?"

"Days, sonny. Ain't no way ya could get to that town by hikin' over that mountain pass. Not with the white stuff so deep."

"Well, let's get started, then," Nigel said, putting sunglasses on the bridge of his nose.

"What about the dog?" the Brit asked. "He won't fare so well in that snow, as deep as it is. Haven't got any high boots, have you, big guy?" Saxton said, rubbing Jed between the ears with the thick gloves.

"He needs ta find his friend," Zeke said. "Gotta let him go, bad as I hate ta. He'll be okay. Ain't but a short distance ta where I'll take ya. Ya will be on dry ground, then, and outta the wind."

The canine licked Zeke's hand when the old man rubbed the dog's chin.

"Shall we be off, then?" Saxon asked.

The snow was again falling, but the sunglasses were a good idea, Nigel thought. The brightness, despite the clouds and profusion of snow, hurt his eyes when he thought at first to remove the dark lenses. He noticed that the glare didn't seem to affect the old man. Neither did the cold, and wind, apparently. Zeke led the way through the deepening snow, cutting a trail for Jeddy to follow. He wore neither sunglasses nor a heavy coat. He was a very strange old man but a wonderful one, Nigel thought, walking the path that somehow seemed more heavily trodden than one cut only by one old man and a dog.

They approached a sheer cliff wall within ten minutes, an opening becoming visible as the snow shear thinned. It was a small opening but one that would easily accommodate a man and backpack, Saxton surmised.

"Here's a flashlight, young feller," Zeke said handing Nigel a long instrument. "This'll get ya through the mountain."

He knelt in front of Jeddy and hugged the dog, who returned the affection by licking the man's face. "Ya take care of this feller," Zeke said.

"I'll take good care of him, Zeke," Nigel said.

"Weren't talkin' 'bout ya takin' care of him," Zeke said, a twinkle in his eye while he stood. "Off with the both a ya, then," he said.

"Will you be okay?" Nigel grabbed Zeke by the shoulders and gave a brief hug.

"Don't worry 'bout me, Nigel. Just do what must be done."

When they had moved within the mountain opening, Nigel searched the tunnel with the flashlight beam. A sound of thumping just outside the cave entrance caused him to switch the light off and hurry to the opening.

Several white helicopters hovered high above. They would get the old man. The thoughts ran quickly through his mind. What could he do to save the old man? But, the copters moved on, and soon the thumping of the chopper engines faded to silence.

Nigel searched the snow field. The snow had stopped. Zeke was nowhere in sight. Neither was the pathway they had cut through the snow.

The undersecretary of defense spoke in a consoling tone; although, he knew the man on the other end of the secure transmission was most likely jubilant with the news. He didn't care. George Jenkins was a man who had the knowledge and the ability to get the job done. Those who mattered within DOD agreed. The loss of Wayne Snidely was a blessing, not a thing to be regretted. The undersecretary knew that Jenkins felt even more that way, knowing the frustration the black ops chief must have had to endure, with Snidely acting as the filter between Rumsfeld and every jot and tittle of the top secret matters involved in Project Scotty.

"George, I know this is a hard time for you, as for all of us. But, we are depending on you to now keep things on the positive track, even more than ever,"

"Yes, Mr. Secretary. We must move on through this tragedy," he said solemnly, barely able to contain his glee over Snidely's fiery end.

Jenkins listened to the undersecretary's words but kept watch on the monitors. He couldn't fully enjoy the moment, for the things transpiring at Xavier Pass.

"Yes, sir. Access directly to you and the Secretary will greatly expedite our efforts here at the project."

"And, the BORG imperative?" the voice from the Pentagon said. "Is that…moving along as well as Scotty?"

"There are a few snags with the biology, sir. But the technology, the RAPTURE, I'm assured, is right on schedule. BORG should be fully operational within the time frame we've discussed," Jenkins said, frowning at seeing the helicopters moving away from their prime area of search.

His mind returned to the BORG imperative. He was not nearly as confident as his words to the man closest to the Defense Secretary implied. Battlefield Operations Ready Giant, he forced himself to admit to himself, if not to the undersecretary, was not under control. The creatures could only be handled through the RAPTURE devices, and development of an army of BORGs would, it seemed from his present circumstance, take longer than had been discussed and promised.

With their phone conversation about his now having direct access to the Secretary of Defense through the undersecretary completed, the black ops chieftain returned his full attention to the troubling matter in the mountains.

April Warmath opened the door to the office. George Jenkins stood in the middle of the room, glaring at the monitors within the wall. He cursed, slamming his right fist into the palm of his left hand while the white helicopters scanned Xavier Pass, then broke off their surveillance of the high-mountain plain to move to other areas. Why did the day that was going so well have to be marred by the incompetents' inability to find the intruder? The eradication of his thorn in the flesh in D.C. and now the operative from—from where? From the EU? From Great Britain?—just disappearing. All of the satellite data said he was in the Xavier Plateau, the area of the mountain pass where they should easily be able to spot a man against the field of white. Especially with having been given coordinates and special infrared devices. Why had the beings who had given the coordinates not been able to lock on the intruder?

April Warmath said nothing but moved behind Jenkins to the desk, where she searched through a stack of papers.

"They won't find him now. If they haven't spotted him with all the help they've been given; they won't find him," Jenkins said with disgust. "He just seems to have disappeared."

"Maybe he's buried himself in snow, right there in plain sight," April said, glancing at her boss, then at the monitor screens.

"No! No…"

Jenkins scowled his disagreement while he walked to behind his desk. "The infrared detectors would detect body heat under the snow. Those things can find a rabbit in an underground nest beneath that snow field, no problem."

"Well, let me cheer you with a bit of good news. The first phase of the insemination seems to have gone quite well," April said, picking up the papers she had been searching for.

"They will be thrilled with that," Jenkins said with dismissive irritation in his tone while he continued to glare at the monitors, thinking of the failed attempts to catch the intruder.

"Still the self-absorbed creature," the voice growled from the girl's throat.

The words caused Jenkins to jerk with startled spasm. April Warmath's possessor manifested itself in the glare from the eyes, which now blazed with blackness from the eternal pit.

"You obsess over this human microbe. Our imperative seems not to matter, Jenkins," the entity inside April Warmath's body said.

George Jenkins stumbled backward slightly, the force of the sarcastic anger causing his knees to weaken.

"No…I…I just know he can cause us problems, can cause your imperatives great problems, that's all…"

"You don't successfully lie to the chief of liars, Jenkins," the voice growled. "You care about what we can do for you. And that will amount to nothing except major troubles for you if you cannot get your priorities straightened."

A chloros-colored mist grew darkly within Jenkins's office, engulfing him and April Warmath. The cloud boiled and became stifling. They did not possess him this time, he thought with trepidation rising while the sickly yellow-green coagulance seemed to lift both him and the girl, finally obscuring her form totally.

He moved through bone-chilling cold darkness, feeling as if he tumbled, the winds of the mist becoming a vortex-like movement that spun him, then seemed to settle his body on solid footing again.

He recognized it immediately. It was the place he had not been allowed to physically visit. At least not as he remembered. It glistened, like polished steel. It was huge, and oval, its top a hundred feet above him, curving seamlessly, forming ovaled walls of stainless steel-like …was it metal?

The surface felt like metal against the leather soles of his shoes. Stainless steel or something more…

The obscuring mist dissipated, and he stood beside April, whose eyes were wide and again human.

Neither said anything, their senses frozen by astonishment and fear. They were paralyzed by the rationale-confounding sights they witnessed.

The black, boiling creatures appeared and disappeared from the very air within the chamber. They seemed to pay Jenkins and the woman no attention while the pair gawked at the eerie movements and activities of the cloud forms, which seemed to manipulate the two human forms upon the surgical gurneys at the center of the massive chamber.

Why had they not possessed him? Why did they no longer possess April Warmath, who stood at his side, as amazed as himself at the mind-boggling sights before them?

The light in the chamber, to this point bright but with an amber tint, grew darker, as if turned down by a switch somewhere on the fantastic array of technological wonders he had never seen, not even at the heart of NORAD's computer control centers, which housed the most advanced technology on the planet.

But this chamber was on the planet, he reminded himself. Or was it on the planet? The invaders, they did their work—or were for the moment doing their work—in the valley. Somewhere, somehow, within the forest, where there was no room for such a disk. Yet it was among the forest, the valley. The thick, evergreen forest beyond Xavier Pass. Miles from his own office, from the complex, where their…experiments…so different from his own Project Scotty, would be taken to grow, to gestate, to incubate.

Why had they brought him here? Brought April Warmath here? They had given him view, through the monitors, of the things transpiring within this—what was it? This ship? This conveyance from other worlds?

"So many thoughts," the voice rang out from the darkened laboratory. Light exploded from a singularity in mid-air, and in a millisecond a human-like figure strode from the portal that seemed to rip the dark fabric of the room's ambience.

"You have many questions, George Jenkins."

The form was human, yet not, Jenkins immediately knew. The man-like face was possessed of beauty beyond any, and Jenkins knew, or feared that he knew, its owner.

"You will experience the true imperative of this creation, Jenkins," the cavernous voice of the ultra-human said, his golden eyes aglow, penetrating the man's soul. "We have completed one-half of the imperative. This woman at your side will provide the second half, making the whole. We will show you all that comprises the imperative, Jenkins. You will understand the crucial nature of the position you will shortly occupy within the puny human governments."

Jenkins found little pleasure in the creature's words, words that pierced far deeper than the mind's ear. They were words that infiltrated, that pervaded, and seemed to want to explode every cell of one's being.

He could sit still no longer. He walked to Susie, bent to kiss her cheek, then snapped his fingers at Klaus.

"Come here, boy!" His excited tone caused the Vizsla to hurry happily to his master's side.

"Can't you be still for just five minutes?" Susie remarked, watching her husband kneel to rough up the dog's fur, trying to provoke Klaus into snapping in play at him.

"Wish he would call," Christopher said, standing, placing his hands on his hips and stretching by leaning backward to relieve tension in his lower back.

"He said the delay shouldn't be too long," Susie said.

"Well, it's already been too long. They were supposed to take off by 4:30. It's almost six here…That would make it nearly eight o'clock there," he said, walking to the window to see the darkening evening sky above the distant plateaus and ridges of the Estrella range.

"You wouldn't want the pilots to do something dangerous, would you?"

"Makes no difference what I want. The JFK people have delayed all flights until the thunderstorms have passed. Randy says only a couple of flights have been allowed out. It's very unusual for that airport to shut down that long."

"Then it's Providence. Can't you see that?" His wife's matter-of-fact faith made Christopher smile—as it always did. He walked to her chair, extended his right hand to her, and when she took it, pulled her gently from the big recliner.

He embraced Susie, her face turned against his chest and shoulder while he wrapped his arms around her and held her tightly.

"You're right, sweetheart, of course. It is the Lord's decision, not ours."

"We should try to get a little sleep," she said. "Randy will call soon. We will need to be rested. It might be well into the morning before we can meet them at Phoenix International."

"He and I agreed that they should stop by to get us first, then fly to LAX to pick up Mark and Lori," he said. "That seems more efficient than our original flight plan, according to the pilot."

Ten minutes later, Christopher, followed by Klaus, walked through the French doors to his study. He scanned the shelves of his many books but decided to pick up from his desk the most important volume to his life.

It had been on his mind, probably since he first saw the figure that night in the torrential downpour near San Antonio—the dark, giant, man-like form that slogged toward the picture window of his home. The other manifestation, bright and sparking like lightning itself, had intercepted the beastly one. The resultant, electrifying light show had been blinding. Then, there had been nothing, just the horrendous rain, lit occasionally by brilliant flashes of lightning from the thunderstorm.

Then the dreams he had heard time after time from Mark, Lori, and their kids—

Morgan and Clark. The dark creatures, like the ones Mark said Clark was investigating. Bigfoot, Yeti, Sasquatch—many other names for the creature that seemed more myth than reality. Yet they were, somehow, linked to the dark, smoke-like masses, to the creatures of clouds that were from…where? From the fallen supernatural world? From the world described in Ephesians?

He thumbed through the old Bible which fell almost automatically open to the passage he was looking for. He read the words from the book of Ephesians, chapter 6, verse 12, in a whisper: "For we wrestle not against flesh and blood, but against principalities, against powers, against the rulers of the darkness of this world, against spiritual wickedness in high places."

He closed the Bible while he stood at the big window that gave view to the desert sunset. The thought troubled him. Why had Clark Lansing's quest to learn about the creatures led to the Colorado governmental complex? Why had Clark's sister's job led her there? The creature her mother reported Morgan seeing on the pathway. A Bigfoot type creature? The description certainly seemed that of a Bigfoot, or Yeti, or whatever they were called, depending on the part of the world where they were reported.

But, there were never any bones, hides, or evidence that such beasts lived upon the planet.

The thing had vanished, Morgan told her mother. What kind of creature—perhaps eight feet tall—simply disappears from sight? Was it something the government was keeping secret? Why could they want such a creature? How could they make it just vanish into thin air?

Perhaps they would find answers in Colorado—if they could ever leave New York, Phoenix, and LA.

His thoughts kept prompting him to think more deeply. The U.S. government, the eight-foot creatures that seemed to be at the same time of physical matter and ethereal. They could make deep, sixteen-inch footprints in snow, or in the earth, yet could vanish to nothing. Carcasses had never been found; yet, sightings of them had been reported, even by witnesses whose reports were trusted, thus had credence.

The government. What did governments do? They maintained treasury, monetary supply. Government gave governance to the people, maintained order in society, in culture. It provided for the common defense…

Defense…Yes. That was the small spark of troubling thought behind it all. These creatures—could they somehow be used in a military way, if, indeed, they did exist and the United States government…and no doubt other governments chose to develop…to somehow bring them into being?

All the other signals of the end were there: Israel was at the center of the end-of-days mix. Yes. Israel becoming the cup of trembling…the burdensome stone predicted by Zechariah the prophet. Israel, at the center of the war on terror, declared shortly after the 9-11 attacks in New York City and D.C.

He and Randall Prouse had discussed it many times. Were these UFOs Jesus's words beginning to come to pass? His prophecy that it will again be "As it was in the days of Noah…" at the time Christ comes again to earth?

In "Noah's Day," the Bible told that the Benai Elohim—the fallen angels—looked at flesh and blood women on earth and saw they were alluring. The minions of Satan—some of them—somehow, had sexual relations with the human women. From the unions were produced the Nephilim, the supernatural giants of the time. The beings from which, Randy believed, the legends of the Greek, Norse, and Roman gods were spawned. Hercules, Hera, Zeus, Thor, all the rest…

Could this be another visitation between Satan's minions and human beings? Could these unions, in some way, produce an army for the human governments of the world?

The thoughts came in rapid succession, culminating with his searching his memory for a specific prophecy of end-time things. He thought back through studies he had done, then combed several concordances he took from the shelves nestled against the four walls of the library.

When he was satisfied that he had found the book he was looking for, he quickly found the verses in the Old Testament book of Joel, chapter 2, and read in a whisper:

Blow ye the trumpet in Zion, and sound an alarm in my holy mountain: let all the inhabitants of the land tremble: for the day of the LORD cometh, for it is nigh at hand; A day of darkness and of gloominess, a day of clouds and of thick darkness, as the morning spread upon the mountains: a great people and a strong; there hath not been ever the like, neither shall be any more after it, even to the years of many generations. A fire devoureth before them; and behind them a flame burneth: the land is as the garden of Eden before them, and behind them a desolate wilderness; yea, and nothing shall escape them. The appearance of them is as the appearance of horses; and as horsemen, so shall they run. Like the noise of chariots on the tops of mountains shall they leap, like the noise of a flame of fire that devoureth the stubble, as a strong people set in battle array. Before their face the people shall be much pained: all faces shall gather blackness. They shall run like mighty men; they shall climb the wall like men of war; and they shall march every one on his ways, and they shall not break their ranks: Neither shall one thrust another; they shall walk every one in his path: and when they fall upon the sword, they shall not be wounded. They shall run to and fro in the city; they shall run upon the wall, they shall climb up upon the houses; they shall enter in at the windows like a thief.

Christopher slowly closed his Bible, his gaze trained into the now almost totally dark desert. This was a strange army the prophet Joel predicted for the last days. A very strange description of the troops, very strange, indeed…

"Randy is on the cell!"

Susie's words disrupted her husband's immersion in thought, and he turned to look at her.

"He says they've been cleared to leave JFK!"

FIFTEEN

Kristi Flannigan had never seen her city from just this angle, the lights of Manhattan sparkling like a diamond-encrusted piece of black velvet. The Criterion X climbed steeply over the Atlantic, turning at the same time back over the city, the pilot setting course for Phoenix International.

Jeb Strubble pushed the throttles forward with ease, the 2 Rolls-Royce AE 3007C turbo fan engines pushing the four passengers and two crewmen back into the rich leather seats of the customized bird. The pilot watched the many colorful screens, their displays blazing with information that automatically set the plane on its preprogrammed course of flight.

Strubble loved it, as did his copilot, Hamilton Lamb, who, himself, would be in the left front seat of just such a plane within three months when his training was completed. Both men had nothing more to do than sip coffee and keep watch; yet, they were far from bored. The aircraft was just too exciting in its every facet.

The Criterion's engines were huge. Appended on each side of the fuselage at the back of the plane, they seemed almost as big around as the fuselage itself. They were simply the newest and most powerful, period. The airplane had the highest thrust-to-weight ratio of any corporate jet and was almost in the same realm as some of the fighter jets of days not too long ago, jets that both men had flown—Strubble in the U.S. Air Force and Lamb in the Navy. Even though the engines were powerful, their strength of thrust yielded a remarkably low specific fuel consumption. The corporate manager's dream—high speed efficiency and performance far better than anything in its class ever designed.

It was the most aerodynamically advanced airplane available. Every contour had been precisely designed for luxurious, high-speed, high-altitude flight. You could only move up if you went to an F-22 Raptor, Strubble considered, sipping on the black liquid from the Styrofoam cup.

Randall Prouse forced his eyes from the glorious view of the city out the large porthole window. He had a lot of reading and writing to do in the hours it would take to fly to Phoenix International. He wished he had taken the brief course the flight attendant had offered while still on the tarmac at JFK, the course in which she instructed about the many advanced electronic accoutrements on board.

He sat in the roomy seat that reminded him of a full-size recliner covered in luxuriantly soft leather. He counted eight of them in the elegantly appointed fuselage, whose high ceiling allowed even his grandson to walk upright. Wonderful electronics were at his fingertips—a computer with a twelve-inch screen and wireless keyboard, telephone, Playstation portable gaming machine, all built right in either the arm rest or on the bulkhead.

The attendant had complained after he asked if he could just please have a legal pad that that request was what everyone always made, and she couldn't understand why passengers didn't want to avail themselves of the wonderful technologies. She was not much past her teenage years, and that was why she couldn't understand, Randy mused, nonetheless wishing he had learned how to use the system.

He glanced at Kristi Flannigan, who thumbed through a magazine, since the city and its magnificent view now receded into the distance behind. She sat in her own big recliner, seemingly lost in a story that had stopped her thumbing the pages.

"Glad you could come with us," Randy said from across the aisle.

"Thanks for inviting me. It's great getting off work for a while," she said with a forced smile.

Randy could tell something was bothering the girl, who looked at him but seemed reluctant to say anything.

"Something wrong?" he asked.

Kristi hesitated but spoke after several seconds. "Not…*wrong*…actually," she stammered. "It's just that I'm worried about Morgan. It's just not like her to completely cut herself off. She would have found some way to contact me, especially to contact her mom. Guess I'm wondering, too, what we can accomplish by going to Colorado. Oh, I'm glad you're going and that I can go—but, if it's a secret government thing, or something, how can we find her?"

"Good question. Can't say I have any answers for you. But, if we don't try, we for sure won't find out anything," he said.

The answer seemed to satisfy her, and the set of her pretty eyes framed within her expression of agreement said she was accepting of the rationale.

Four rows forward, just behind the cockpit, David Prouse put his right hand on top of Casandra Lincoln's left hand. "Morgan is lucky to have such friends as you and Kristi," he said.

"Yeah, I think we are the lucky ones. I feel that I'm the lucky one, at least. Morgan is special."

"You three roommates?"

"When I got sick, Morgan and I were apartment mates. Kristi lived with a couple of other girls. She eventually moved in with Morgie while I was…out of commission," she said with a subdued laugh. "We were roommates back at UCLA. Well, off campus, near UCLA."

"Morgan, was she…is she somebody who is adventurous? I mean, could she put herself in harm's way, just being caught up in the adventure?"

"Oh, no. Not Morgan. She is one of the most…aware…people you'll meet. And one of the most responsible. She would never allow herself—intentionally—to be cut off from her friends. And especially not from her mom and dad. That's what's got me so worried. This is so unlike her. I don't know her brother, Clark. But, she says he is even more thoughtful when it comes to staying in touch with their parents, and, especially, he keeps up with his little sister. That always irritates her, in a teasing sort of way. She really loves Clark."

"She have any guys she was particularly interested in?"

"Of course, we haven't talked in several years. But, she was very…

choosy…when it came to the guys. Her dad's and Clark's training, I think."

David was quiet for several seconds, then squeezed her hand slightly. "I'm sorry I ask so many questions, Cass…It's part of my training…and being just plain nosey, I guess. That's one reason lawyers are on the "least popular" lists, I think."

Casandra turned her hand palm up and grasped his fingers in a gentle touch. "I think you are the exception, then," she said, looking at the handsome profile while David glanced at her, then straight ahead.

"Glad you think so," he said.

Training had prepared him for many things, but this was not one of them.

Nigel Saxton moved into the increasingly cramped tunnel, Jeddy close on his heels.

Had the old man known what he was talking about? The tunnel was getting smaller, and he had to bend his head forward uncomfortably to keep moving along the narrowing corridor within the mountain.

Fortunately, the self-cranking light devised especially for him by MI7 was performing nicely. It more than adequately illuminated the areas ahead he needed to check out in order to make sure of safety for himself and the rottweiler.

"At least you don't have to walk doubled up, my friend," Nigel said, forcing his head even lower, causing his shoulders to ache.

And, the backpack was now impeding their progress, dragging at points along the tunnel's ceiling. He unclasped the device at his chest and slid the straps over his arms.

"Guess I'll have to carry this along," he said, holding the big pack by the straps and dragging it behind between him and Jeddy.

"See what you've got yourself into, boy?" He said to the dog, who didn't like the pack dragging in front of him.

"We should be through before long. Zeke said it was less than eight kilometers. Seems like a hundred, eh, chap?"

They had been moving for hours, sometimes the man having to squeeze through openings and force the backpack through openings that the dog could easily manage. They came to such a place, and Nigel went to his knees, placed the backpack in the hole, then forced it through the opening.

"I hope Zeke knew what he was talking about," Nigel said for the hundredth time since beginning the journey through the mountain.

He crawled through the opening on his hands and knees. This was the smallest of the tight places yet, but he managed it with only a back muscle cramp, caused by the awkward position he had to force his body into assuming.

Once through, he moved farther along so the dog could negotiate the passage. He shined the bigger light the old man had provided and was gratified at what it revealed: a huge cavern, one that went beyond the beam's powerful reach.

"This is more like it. Indeed! This is very good, boy," he said, patting Jeddy's head before slipping the backpack straps onto his arms, then jumping the pack onto his shoulders.

San Antonio, Texas—Same Hour

Laura Morgan laughed beneath her breath, despite the pain from the rheumatoid arthritis that wracked her joints. The cats always made the pain more tolerable when the bouts of the disease flared.

"Roy Luther," she said in a playful tone, which, in her mind, the cat took as a loving one. "Don't hurt Mrs. Hemingway," she said, watching the gray and white male cat playfully attack the female cat she had so named because of its six toes on each foot. Ernest Hemingway was reputed to have been quite fond of his six-toed felines, the line which, she knew through news accounts, still made their home in the Hemingway house in Key West.

They had promised to keep her up to the minute on their search for the kids. Still, it hurt—as much as the arthritis—that she couldn't join them. The pain was just too great. They would all be together as soon as they found Morgan and Clark; Lori had promised during the phone call two hours earlier.

Laura fumbled with the bottle's cap—one engineered especially for rheumatoid patients. She downed the dose of methotrexate and prednisone. She made a mental note that tomorrow she would take the folic acid dosage to deal with the drugs' side effects.

She looked at her hands as she always did. Maybe they would begin to show improvement, would become less gnarled and feminine again, not so ugly. But, as always, they were deformed, the knuckles and fingers twisted red with inflammation and swollen from the disease's years of working on them.

"Oh, Lord. I do trust you. I know you will take away pain and tears in Heaven. Please help me to get through this on my way back to you—the One who created me." Her prayer was given in her thoughts, not through spoken words, and was accompanied by thin streams of tears that trickled from the corners of her eyes.

She chastised herself for feeling sorry for herself. This pity party was NOT demonstrating faith in her Lord to see her through all of life's…unfairness.

"Forgive me, Lord," she whispered. She would buck up and do better.

"Roy Luther!" she shouted at the cat who had made Mrs. Hemingway scream with his roughhousing. Seeing that the female was okay, she returned to finishing the pills by swallowing them, washing them down with water.

When the cell phone rang, she moved as quickly as her painful hip, knee, and ankle joints would allow.

"Mom," Lori said from Los Angeles, "We've had a delay. The plane just left New York. It has to stop in Phoenix to pick up the Banyons; then they will get us."

"Still no word from the kids?" Laura asked, starting to sit in a chair but deciding that the effort of getting up later would be more than she cared to bear.

"No. We've talked to Mr. Guroix, again. He was unable to get any answers from Transportec or the Defense Department. He said the security is about as high as it comes. He was assured that Morgan and Clark are okay and that they're safe."

There was hesitation before Lori spoke again. "I don't buy it. I've been in these projects. I've never known—even back in those days at Taos—when a family member couldn't contact other family members outside the projects. That is, except in cases of lockdowns for a day or so."

"What does it mean, then, sweetheart? What do you think is happening?"

Laura's tone displayed her growing anxiety, and Lori—sorry she had added to it with her words, knowing her mother's medical condition—moved to assuage her angst.

"Mom, come to think of it, it's probably as simple as a temporary lockdown because part of the experiment has been misplaced. I remember once that a few slides of particularly virulent bacteria we were using went missing. They had all the doors locked for half a day. I couldn't have called you then if I had wanted. All scientists were kept sequestered until the bacteria were found. It's probably something like that."

Laura, like her daughter, wasn't buying it. It had been three days now. It was far more serious than some missing parts of experiments.

"If we don't get some answers," Lori said, hearing in the silence her mother's unresolved worry. "We'll go to the press, get them involved and anyone else who will listen."

They were finished in another two minutes, Lori promising to call Laura at every step of the search's progress.

A block away from Laura's home near Fort Sam Houston, the man took the device from his ear and checked to see that the digital recording was secure. He placed the device into an attaché case and drove the van into the black Texas night.

The black ops chief spoke with the operative from San Antonio, then switched phones when their conversation ended. He was very pleased. Things were going much smoother than with the search for the EU operative, whom no one could find. The thought of the spy wandering

around somewhat dampened Jenkins's mood, which had been on the
upswing with his people's most recent efforts at surveillance.

"You got a fix on that plane?" His tone harbored the irritation that
renewed thoughts of the spy in their midst had sparked.

Jenkins listened for a few seconds, then interrupted the man responsible for coordinating the mission of keeping track of the Criterion that
had left JFK within the hour.

"I don't want excuses, Brazil. I expect you to have a fix on that aircraft
every inch of every leg of that flight plan they filed. Do you understand?"

He raised his eyebrows and eyes toward the acoustical tiles of his office ceiling, hearing John Brazil at a central NORAD satellite tracking
chamber try to explain some technical details of the track they had on
the jet.

"Yes…yes. That's great, John. But, all I will look at in the final analy-
sis is the bottom line. Will you have that thing under proper coordinates
and so forth on its final leg to Denver International?"

He listened a few seconds longer, then said, "Good. Great. That's
what I wanted to hear. Our friends…are depending on it."

Satisfied all was in place for following the movements about which
his operatives had learned from the tappings and tapings, Jenkins hung
the phone on its cradle and moved to the lavatory doorway on the wall
opposite that of the walls inset with monitors. He would freshen his shave
for the meetings with the DOD people he would have to entertain in an
hour or so.

He didn't switch the light on, preferring to not have the light above
the huge mirror shine into his eyes. His head ached, and he looked in one
corner of the long countertop for the Advil tablets. He retrieved three of
the capsule-shaped medicant and started to put them in his mouth while
preparing the glass of water.

Remembering his order of procedure in taking the pills he swallowed more and more of now that pressures had increased, he placed the
three tablets on the countertop and reached into his pants' pocket. He
pulled out the Rolaids, broke three from the package, and chewed them.

The step was meant to buffer the burning effects medications caused otherwise.

He reached for the soap pump to the right of the cold faucet knob. He would wash his face, then shave with the electric razor.

It stopped him in mid-reach. A point of light that appeared in the center of the blackness that was the mirror. The light sparked like a match head flaring following a strike and seemed to burn a hole in the glass while growing—a large, incendiary hole in the blackness, becoming larger.

Jenkins could but watch, strangely calm while the light mesmerized his senses, then suddenly disappeared, the mirror again black—darker than before, the light having done its temporarily blinding work on his retinas.

Then a glowing—at first glance very dim—expanded within the mirror to become a scene before him. He watched while the gleaming metal object penetrated a girl's abdomen, just beneath the navel. The taut skin expanded to accommodate the probe, like a hot knife blade slicing through butter.

The probe invaded her body deeply and then slowly withdrew. When the probe had withdrawn fully, the skin closed to appear as if the penetration had never been accomplished. It didn't leave a mark on the body.

He knew. His thoughts were those of the ones doing the procedures he witnessed. The girl was April Warmath. The procreative receptacles, as the inner voice explained, were now entrapped within the instrument.

Other procedures—this time on the young man beside the girl—were performed, the cerebral voice informing that the life-introducing essence was being withdrawn from the male's body.

The mirror-scene next moved to a setting Jenkins couldn't make out. It was a scene that he instinctively knew was otherworldly, dimensional—not of earth. The man's life-essence—that of Clark Lansing—had been given, and the procreative receptacles—April Warmath's eggs—had received their life force. He knew, too, that the mixing of Luciferian immortality with human mortality had been accomplished.

The subjects had been prepared. The plan had taken root in the form of conception once accomplished long ago. He knew that he felt, in this moment of euphoria, the elation the minions had experienced in that antediluvian moment when ". . . the sons of God came in unto the daughters of men, and they bare children to them," and "the same became mighty men which were of old, men of renown."

The voice the same as that from times antediluvian and further in time past, much further, echoed within Jenkins's cranium. And he loved, savored every moment of the ancient knowledge.

How foolish he had been, considering his own selfish, pitiful imperative to be important. Producing an army and a means of teleporting it was nothing. This—this was staggering in its import. This was the thing for which he was born: to serve the master-creator of such a universe-changing paradigm!

He knew, too, (the voice implanted this knowledge in a way his synapses could never let him forget to dwell upon as most important to his mission) that the girl's—Morgan Lansing's—receptacles and Blake Robbins's life force essence would not do.

It was the man the Creator had produced out of the earth—out of the most basic of elements. The man came first, not the egg—the woman's procreative force. This is what the otherworldly beings had discovered, why they couldn't successfully introduce their own seed into the human women in that antediluvian time. The results had been giants—Nephilim. They were soulless and had supernatural powers, just like the great master-planner desired. But they didn't fit in, physically. They were twice the size—or more—of the humans of those pre-Flood days.

It was the human male who must first be prepared through careful genetics tampering. This had been done, early on. Both the man's paternal and maternal grandfathers had been tampered with, their genetics changed in some way only the master-planner could fathom.

The man-child's own father and mother had been prepared decades earlier, before they themselves were contaminated by the Son of God and his…salvation. There would be no salvation for these, not for the beings that would come from these life forms produced by Clark Lansing, April Warmath, and…them…

The scene within the mirror faded, and the mirror became again dark, void of all but the blackness of the lavatory. He flipped the switch, lighting the executive washroom. Jenkins looked into the mirror as his own senses, his own thoughts, were returned to him by the keepers of the secrets, secrets to which he was now privy.

Why was he so privileged to know their plans? What would be the danger involved in carrying such knowledge around with him? Was the exultation engendered by such privilege worth the dangers he faced if he failed to produce their desired goals? Goals of which he had been given only a slight glimpse, no doubt.

The words he had been given were biblical. He knew enough about Scripture to know that. They were prophetic as well. He knew that. He would look through the Bible for words he had been given when there was time.

For now, his job was formidable, and that was without even knowing fully what would be expected of him.

Jenkins looked in the mirror that now reflected his own grinning image. It was a smile of self-satisfaction. Whatever they required of him, he was the one person on the planet who could get it done.

Inside Ezekiel's Mountain, Colorado

He held his wrist in front of the flashlight's beam. The big-faced scuba watch read "8:35."

They had been a long time traversing the tunnels and caverns of Ezekiel's Mountain, as Nigel had mentally named it. How much farther? His hard, highly trained body had done well, he considered, but the backpack was wearing like a pack loaded with rocks now, and he longed to find the end of their trek.

The rottweiler lay down when they stopped, the man dropping the load for a few minutes of rest.

"You tired, too, boy?" Nigel reached to scratch the dog's face.

"So am I, my friend, so am I," he said, sitting upon a portion of the backpack and shining Zeke's long flashlight beam into the distance.

The cavern had narrowed and the ceiling had lowered since they had entered the huge chamber. But, the passage was still ten meters wide and probably five meters high Nigel surmised. It looked that way for as far as the beam would shine.

What were these nether regions? Who had walked the tunnels, which, Zeke had assured, ran the length of the mountain's interior? Perhaps Native Americans had scurried these channels that seemed a natural part of the rock structure—not carved by instruments of any sort. Besides, he cogitated, who—especially primitives with primitive tools—could bore such a hole? Such a task would be monumental, even with the most modern tunneling technologies available now.

He had watched the making of the "Chunnel," the passage beneath the English Channel bored from England and France. The fascinating documentary had showed the engineers' constant adjustments and maneuverings with the powerful, high-tech equipment to make sure the two holes met at just the right point. They had implemented special preparations in order to keep the channel waters from flooding once the connection was made.

At least there had been no water in the making of this tunnel. However it was made—by God? No, by nature. There was no water to complicate matters.

Jeddy stood and walked away in the direction they had been traveling. Saxton followed him with the beam. The dog broke into a trot, then a run, disappearing into the distance beyond the light's reach.

"Hey! Boy! Come back!"

Nigel stood, jumped the backpack onto his shoulders, and walked at a fast pace to follow the canine.

The beam soon shined on a solid wall of creviced rock, and he moved the light along the stony pathway covered with dry silt that had accumulated over the millennia. The dog's sprinting footsteps had disturbed the ancient soil, but the disturbance had lessened as the canine had obviously slowed his pace.

There it was, a hole to the right of the rock surface, just behind an outcropping boulder. An opening about three meters high and probably a meter and a half wide, the Brit figured, seeing that the dog's footprints led through the hole.

"Here, boy!" Nigel called, bending with the backpack to shine the beam around the area beyond the opening.

This was a diversion, not the path they should take. They needed to bear right, to continue through the big tunnel.

"Here! Come here, boy," he repeated several times, whistling and making smacking sounds with his mouth to entice the rottweiler out of the tiny passageway he thought the cavern to be.

Finally, with the dog unresponsive to his call, he shed the pack and slipped through the opening, taking only Zeke's flashlight.

The light met yet another dead end. Or, so it seemed at first. Further investigation showed that the canine had slipped through yet another opening, this one smaller than the previous. But still manageable.

Nigel passed through it with little more effort than he had to exert passing through the previous hole and was met by the crisp night air of Colorado.

"This is cool," he said with a broad grin. He scanned the darkness, searching for the dog.

Jeddy rounded a large rock face in the distance and loped to the man, who knelt and welcomed his friend's jubilant tongue kisses upon his face.

"Good chap! You got us out of there. A very bright customer, mate!" Saxton said, standing to again survey their surroundings.

The area seemed perfect for covert exit from the mountain. After he had retrieved the backpack, he and the dog could rest under the Colorado night sky, which sparkled crisply with brilliant stars. Even the temperature had changed. It was considerably warmer. They could bivouac without detection, surrounded by rocks on all sides.

The old man had been right so far. They had gotten through the mountain. Zeke had promised he would find a village not far when they had come from the tunnel.

But, they had taken a side tunnel thanks to the dog. Did the old hermit mean this opening or one that was at the end of the larger tunnel, had they taken it instead? The answer would have to wait until sunrise. For now, he would share with the rottweiler the food Zeke had provided them those hours ago.

The lights of Phoenix spread beneath them. Jeb Strubble was pleased when he checked the highly advanced console panel that housed the digital readouts that compared second-by-second increments of flight. The ETA result was about as good as they got. They arrived over Phoenix International at precisely 2058. The ETA was 2059.

"Darn near perfect," Strubble said to his copilot, who didn't understand, having his mind on instructions the bird was receiving from the Phoenix International air traffic controller.

"Sorry, Jeb, what did you say?"

Strubble shook his hand in a wave of never mind. "Not important," he said.

"We got assignment, Boss," Hamilton Lamb said, bringing the pilot's mind back to the task of preparing for landing the Criterion on the runway they had just been assigned.

Christopher Banyon paced slowly in front of the massive terminal building window. The newly constructed facility was the lounge for the many business travelers who preferred—and could afford—the convenience of private air travel in the array of business jets that routinely pulled to the concourses just outside the windows that circled the huge area's interior.

He stopped to stare into the distance at the transfixing strobes and other lights that illuminated the Phoenix night. The chartered jet would be landing at any second, and he wondered, with each set of landing lights that approached against the darkness, whether it was the one.

Susie joined him. "Their ETA was 8:59. It's now 9:11. Wonder if they're on time?"

Christopher's cell phone chimed, and he probed his shirt pocket for the instrument, finally able to pull it out with two fingers.

"Bet this is Randy, now," he said, flipping the phone open.

"Boy! You've got to get a load of this flying Rolls Royce you ordered up," Randall Prouse said in his usual boisterous greeting voice. His eighty-two years had scarcely dampened the archeologist's enthusiasm for life, Christopher thought.

"Pretty fancy, huh?"

"You bet! Don't know how to use all this impressive stuff in this baby. But, the kids have managed to use it all, I think," he said.

"Good flight?"

"Great. Excellent! Beats standing in those lines and getting poked and probed, I'll tell you for sure. This way of getting around is something I could become accustomed to!"

"Good, good," Christopher said, peering hard into the lights, trying to see if he could determine which was the aircraft conveying his friend toward the terminal.

When they had broken off the conversation, Christopher said softly to his wife, "We have about an hour and a half flight to LA, I think. Maybe you can catch a few Zs."

"I'm okay. I'm too excited about getting to ride in that swanky jet to sleep," Susie said, returning her husband's hug.

"Just pray that we aren't just wasting time and money," he said, more to himself than to Susie.

The Criterion's takeoff was smooth, the bird climbing at 250 knots past ten thousand feet, toward the temporarily assigned fifteen thousand. Jeb Strubble asked departure for a center frequency, changed over and filed an IFR round robin flight plan with them by touching a few buttons on the integrated flight management system. Just for fun, the pilot requested flight level five one zero, fifty-one thousand feet. He did so more to hear the awe in the responding controller's voice than to show off this fantastic plane's capability.

Strubble dialed in "510" on the altitude reminder read out and the airplane accelerated to 320 knots, 30 knots shy of the max operating speed of 350. At some thirty-one thousand pounds, well below the max takeoff weight of thirty-six thousand pounds, the plane shot up into the blackness.

The vertical velocity indication on Strubble's CRT pegged above thirty-five hundred feet per minute, and it took the Criterion less than twenty minutes to reach altitude. Leveling off at mach 0.92, the articulated throttles moved to set their own fuel flows, and again, all Strubble and Hamilton Lamb had to do was watch it happen.

David Prouse's wrist was beginning to hurt by the time the aircraft leveled off. Cassie's slim fingers gripped him so tightly that he wanted to remove them. That was the last thing he would do, however. Gripping his arm helped her cope with the anxiety of the tremendous thrust that had rocketed them after lifting off from Phoenix International.

He reached to put his big hand over her small hand.

"You're not scared, are you?" he teased.

"A little," she said, feeling calmed by his warm hand covering her hand. "I've never taken off like that before. That's quite a ride!"

"Yeah, I heard the pilot asking Chris if it was okay to stretch it out a bit on the takeoff. Guess he about maxed it out," David said with a chuckle.

"And you didn't warn me?" She playfully slapped his arm in a show of disapproval.

"I thought it was fun," he said, pulling her hand back to under his.

Cassie, sitting next to the aisle, craned to look at Kristi. Their eyes made contact, and she was glad to see that her friend's expression said that Kristi's stomach remained somewhere below, with her own. Kristi raised her eyelids to a wide-eyed expression of amazement.

Kristi had traveled extensively by air but had never felt an ascent like this one. She felt she was getting sick to her stomach. But, momentarily, after several seconds of level flight, the nausea settled, and all was well.

"Well," Christopher said to Susie, who had heard him give Jeb Strubble permission to "have a little fun" with the takeoff. "I wanted to get our money's worth."

She punched her husband's arm. "Maybe you won't think it's so much fun if some of us throw up all over the plane," she said, laughing at his little boyish amusement over the spectacular takeoff.

"We'll ask if they can make her do more when we depart LAX," he said.

Although George Jenkins detested, even was always anxious about, the times when the bigwigs from the Pentagon wanted to meet at the complex, his renewed confidence put his mind at ease. The confidence was born of his special friends giving him the otherworldly look into their imperative for history's future. What other human being knew such things? The thought was exhilarating while he quickly walked the hallway that led to the big conference room.

He wished for April Warmath. But, she was still with them. They didn't say why she couldn't be released back into his service. Just that there was follow-up that required her to stay with them for a while longer.

She always acted as a buffer between him and the bigwigs from D.C. The middle-aged, over-sexed men were easily put off the scent of blood because of one gaffe or another some of his staff might have committed. She could flirt and cajole like no other woman he had known, and it was an asset that he needed now while he approached the large oak door with the gleaming brass door handle plate.

Several men stood in the anteroom just inside the big door. They broke off conversation when they saw Jenkins enter. He smiled, offering his right hand in greeting. He knew them all, except one—a man younger than the others. "This is Ernst Kline," one of the DOD special ops directors said, guiding the younger man toward Jenkins.

"Pleased to meet you," Kline said in German accent. Probably Austrian, Jenkins thought, taking the man's hand.

"Glad you could come," the black operations director lied. He was never glad to have new people to deal with. They usually had turfs they wanted to protect—egos that needed scratching. Who was this one? And, what was his particular itch?

"Thank you," the German said, his facial expression remaining solemn.

"Ernst is here representing the European Union, George. They want a little better understanding of things involving Scotty and the BORG projects and so forth," Lester Graves, the DOD director who had introduced him, said. "The secretary, upon the president's suggestion, thought this would be the forum that could…provide enlightenment in the quickest, yet most thorough way possible."

"We will do our best," Jenkins said with a clenched teeth smile. "I've asked one of your own to help explain things," he added.

They sat in large, recliner-type chairs especially arranged to face the giant monitor screen inset within one wall of the enormous conference room. Jenkins sat in another of the chairs, one with a small console that he swung from the right arm of the chair, to in front of him, once he had settled into its seat.

He pushed a few buttons and manipulated some levers, and the screen lit up. The DOD officials watched it fill with different graphics and colors while Jenkins tested the various components for selecting what he wanted to emphasize during the presentation.

He could, with a movement of a lever, precisely project a thin, laser-like pointer that streamed in a line from the monitor screen's edges to direct attention to whatever he needed.

Jenkins pored over the several aspects of things he deemed would satisfy their inquiry.

"Project Scotty includes all things involving the Rapid Atomic Particle Transmolecular Unification Reassembly Energizer technology," he said, pointing to the term with a vivid red line that streamed from the screen's edge. We call it the RAPTURE. Seems there's a popular fiction series on that around right now…"

The men chuckled their agreement when Jenkins paused for effect.

"The project is named for the obvious—Mr. Scott and his much-beloved Transporter aboard the Starship Enterprise…"

Again, the black ops director paused for effect, and the DOD visitors obliged with laughter that expressed their amusement.

"We have made spectacular progress over the past few years, despite some serious problems. The physicists involved have—as you know—been able to break through some of the problems elucidated by the Heisenberg indeterminacy principle."

Jenkins looked at the faces, some which, he noticed, reacted as if they didn't have a clue.

"Briefly stated," he said, "the Heisenberg indeterminacy principle outlined the problems with time and space and the movement of matter at the molecular level. There are certain atomic rearrangements that are…were…required that were not possible…or so it was thought…in order to effect a translation. That is, the taking apart of an object's atomic structure here…"

He manipulated the controls and colorful graphics on the large screen displayed through realistic animation the disintegration and disappearance of a wine bottle, then its reconstitution and reappearance on the other side of the screen.

"Mr. Scott's Transporter," he said with satisfaction in his voice.

"Most specifically," Jenkins continued when the screen was electronically wiped clean, then the picture replaced with a visual of a man-like creature that reached from top to bottom of the monitor screen, "the RAPTURE has been applied to our creation and development of the BORG, the Battlefield Operation Ready Giant."

He again looked at the faces, and this time saw deep concentration etched in each. All eyes were upon the enormous man-beast shown on the screen, all ears attuned with rapt attention to his every word. This is the reason they had come to the complex. The military application. Always DOD wanted results to accomplish war-making ends.

"We have had immense success as of late with the teleportation of the BORG, the product of a special genetic manipulation of certain primates. Certain components from human Deoxyribose Nucleic Acid are also figured into the mix. The results: a being that can circumvent or bypass the Heisenberg indeterminacy principle. To a large extent, at least."

When Jenkins started to continue, Lester Graves interrupted. "These BORGs, they will be the troops of the future? Is that what we're talking about here?"

"Only for special operations. And, I don't see these operatives ever becoming much more than used in very special instances. Right now, their prime worth is that their genetic makeup makes them ideal for experimentation with RAPTURE."

"What kind of special operations?" another of the visiting DOD directors asked.

"Things like fighting in high altitude, in extremely unfriendly environments, where our troops would be ineffective," Jenkins answered.

"Like in the mountains of Afghanistan and Pakistan?" the same man asked.

"The war on terror will benefit greatly, once this army is fully battlefield operational," the black ops chief said with conviction in his voice.

"How long before these…creatures…are ready?"

"As complete biological beings, they are as ready as they will get," Jenkins answered. "But as programmed to do specific jobs in battlefield situations, we have a ways to go. This involves new methodologies, new instrumentalities we are working with to program these creatures' brains for the jobs that are expected of them.

"This much, the European Union has knowledge of," Ernst Kline said. "But, other things trouble us. We have not been given knowledge of this technology as it involves the—transport—of people. Why not?"

Jenkins was not taken off guard. He had been forewarned that the question would come.

He pushed a button on the console in front of him. "Send him in," he ordered.

A door swung open behind the group facing the screen, and a tall, youthful man walked in front of the big monitor screen. He faced the others, framed by the brightness of the electronic graphics that somewhat obscured his features.

"Good evening, gentlemen," he said. "I'm Blake Robbins of Transportec Industries. I'm here to, I hope, answer your questions."

SIXTEEN

It was love at first sight. He devoured its beauty through the big window that looked down on the concourse parking ramp. Mark's eyes sparkled only slightly less than did the Criterion X, which was pearlescent white, the same color of those new Cadillacs that sometimes roared along the California freeways, he considered. The bird was magnificent, indeed!

Jeb Strubble parked the Criterion, pulled back the throttles with a flick of his fingertips, and, after checking several instrument controls for proper shutdown, followed the copilot into the cabin, standing by the big door while his passengers disembarked.

"This is quite the airplane," Christopher Banyon said, talking to Strubble and Hamilton Lamb. "Loved the takeoff," he grinned, causing Susie, holding to his right arm, to push him in mock irritation.

"Hope we didn't scare you, ma'am," Strubble said. "We love to show off what the Criterion can do."

"Nothing frightens this woman," Christopher said, moving past the pilot to step down the few rungs and onto the tarmac.

"I was scared," Randall Prouse said. "Don't mind telling you. That was quite a kick!"

"Glad you enjoyed it," Lamb said, seeing the laughter in the archaeologist's eyes.

David Prouse stood at the bottom rung, extending his hand to help Cassie and Kristi onto the concrete. He and Cassie walked arm in arm toward the terminal's doors, out of which Mark Lansing was emerging.

Lori, who preceded her husband out of the doorway, embraced both girls, then Susie Banyon, talking in animated cheeriness with them while Mark and Christopher talked, Mark greeting Randall Prouse with a hand-shake and hug.

The former Delta pilot was anxious to examine the plane, so the three men continued in the conversation while approaching the craft.

A yellow fuel truck was refilling the main tanks while Jeb Strubble and Hamilton Lamb walked around the bird in a pre-flight check. Several maintenance personnel opened the big hatch just forward of the port engine. They stashed the Lansings' bags into the space that could hold more cargo than any comparable business jet.

Mark, watching with fascination, had studied this jet and knew that area could be used to transport the pets of those of privilege who would travel in style aboard the Criterion. The compartment was pressurized and heated, and there was easy access to it from the rear of the cabin, near the bathroom.

He remembered reading that the Criterion had temporary fuel tanks that would extend the aircraft's range to unimaginable numbers. The plane was already well known in magazines and on the news as something that could travel coast to coast above fifty thousand feet at mach 0.92—92 percent the speed of sound. That, he silently calculated, worked out to be about 350 knots indicated airspeed.

Those huge engines that looked to be—he thought—out of scale somehow were rated at sixty-seven hundred pounds of thrust each, more than adequate to lift the machine up at its max gross weight of thirty-six thousand pounds. It had been designed to hold nearly thirteen thousand pounds of fuel. The additional fuel add-on capability seemed to be a curious extra cost, but he figured that somebody wanted to provide the feature for those who might want to stay up a long time or go somewhere far, far away.

The three men met the pilot and copilot at the plane's rear, where Mark stood peering into the back of the left engine.

Mark saw the epaulets on the taller man's shoulder. It had three black stripes with a gold star at its center. This was, he knew, the pilot—probably the chief pilot of the charter service.

"Quite a bird," Mark said, moving away from the engine's exhaust opening. "How long you guys been flying this one?"

"It's my tenth flight. It's the newest and the best," Strubble said.

"Ham, here, he's new to the aircraft but will be assigned one in a few more flight hours."

Handshakes and shared information soon prompted the Criterion pilot to say, "Delta, huh? I flew for American but just couldn't resist this one."

"An offer you couldn't refuse, huh?" Mark said with a chuckle, running his gaze over the seventy-two-foot beauty, one of the most unusual aircraft he had seen.

Mark was, for the first time in days, thinking of things other than Clark and Morgan. This was pleasure, a brief respite from the troubled thoughts that had, for the moment, melted into total concentration on this jet.

He marveled over the unique engineering, like the attachment point of the wings. This cleared enough fuselage space to give the plane a full-length, stand up aisle that stretched twenty-four feet. This looked odd, at first. In fact, it reminded him of how weird the F-4C Phantom had looked to all of the pilots—including himself—as they caught their first glimpse of the warbird back in 1964. They soon learned that the Phantom might be ugly, but it grew on you the first time you shoved the throttles forward and got mashed into the seat.

Mark followed Strubble and Lamb while they walked around the plane, starting at the integrated stairs just aft of the cockpit area. The pilot showed Mark the access panel to the environmental control systems and, just aft of that, the larger door that covered the electronics bay. The two-foot-wide hatch was open for inspection and one of the ground crew had been loading the computer with new flight information and data bases.

"The new data base will make the nav systems completely independent of any input from the ground while in flight," Strubble said with pride. "The bird has dual Honeywell GPS and the newest Laseref V IRS," he added. "You can't get lost," the pilot said. "The GPS knows where you are at all times, and, if you're in doubt, the radar even has a ground-mapping mode."

Just like the F4, Mark thought. Now there was something that could get you into trouble, he grinned to himself, remembering how the F-4 pilots would sometimes engage in—extracurricular strafing activities. Had to be careful with such a tracking system…

"When's our takeoff?" Christopher asked, interrupting the pilot's impromptu lecture.

"Eleven-thirty, sir," Hamilton Lamb said after Strubble looked at him for the precise time that he himself didn't know.

"And, when is our ETA?" Christopher asked.

"Two forty-five, sir," Lamb said. "Remember, we lose that hour we gained."

"Oh, yeah. Back to Mountain Time," Christopher said absentmindedly while turning and walking back toward where his wife stood with the others.

"We'll leave at 11:30," he said to Susie. "That's about…" He checked his watch. ". . . eighteen minutes or so."

David Prouse and Cassie had walked a hundred feet to the east and stood watching the strobes and other lights that provided a spectacular light show against the black sky over Los Angeles International.

David reached his hand toward Cassie, who gladly took it. They began walking slowly back toward the others.

"You know, Cassie, you coming along makes my having to put off that work on all those cases okay."

She said nothing but glanced at him with a quick smile, then back to the tarmac in front of them.

"We're going to find Morgan and Clark. Then…I hope that won't…" He found himself uncharacteristically at a loss for words to express his thought. "I hope we can still see each other," he said.

He felt her small hand grip his hand tighter while they walked toward the Criterion.

"I want that, too," she said, her heart racing. David Prouse was a special guy, she thought, a warm feeling she had never felt before welling within her.

He felt the same, and they said nothing during the rest of their hand-in-hand walk to join the others.

Mark listened to the pilot proudly educate him on the superiority of this doubtless among the most advanced of all corporate jets. But while Strubble talked, his mind took over, his eyes devouring the bird's every nuance of sophistication as he ascended the stairway of not very many steps. Nothing like getting on an old 727 or 707. This plane was close to the ground for now but held great potential for going very high real soon.

It took just one breath to know that there had been a change for the better. No more exhaust fumes or airport noise, just that new-car leather smell that every man knows and loves. A quick glance to the right revealed a somewhat narrow, but tall aisle that was big enough for most anyone to walk down without stooping over.

There were eight passenger seats, in groups of four along the bulkhead, right and left, in the cabin. Each was elegantly covered in the finest leathers. They reminded him of eight full-sized Lazy Boy recliners. Strubble pointed out that each seat was, in fact, fully reclining and had integrated computers, entertainment consoles, and telephones. There was a bar and compact galley in the rear, and at the farthest point, the door was open to a large restroom with a vanity and mirrored closet door. Desks between each seating group were built in, but retractable. The creamy pearlescent white of the interior plastic surfaces were complemented with wood trim made from redwood burl.

This wasn't the kind of seating he was used to—traveling space available as a perk, being a retired Delta employee. He could get used to it; he thought to himself.

The view to the left was what Mark wanted to see more than anything else. He had heard this cockpit was also the newest and highest-tech available. His first impression was that most of the room had been given to the passengers. That was the right priority, he guessed, but the cockpit access and seating seemed pretty tight. It was beautiful, and that more than made up for the snugness.

The five, seven-inch-by-eight-inch colored screens glowed with electronically generated representations of familiar instruments. Two pairs of identical flight management systems appeared on the outermost screens, and the one in the middle was the new standard in EICAS display.

The engine indicating and crew alerting system showed the fan speeds in percent, engine temperatures, oil temps and pressures, digital fuel readouts and all of the other things a pilot needed to know to operate this aircraft safely.

At the bottom were a couple of what he and other pilots called "idiot lights," the ones you never want to see illuminated. Just below that, the duel Honeywell GPS pilot input and readout consoles had already been turned on and set up for the flight to Denver.

Radio frequency readouts and every other conceivable bit of information seemed to be presented digitally on other displays through out the cockpit area. No space wasn't covered by some sort of control, readout, switch, lever or handily placed coffee cup holder.

The throttles were correctly placed, and the reverse thrust levers were integrated in the same style that had been in every design since the first. Flaps on the right, speed brakes on the left, fire control panel just aft of that, and other miscellaneous controls filled out the center console.

The space immediately below the large windscreens was filled on both sides with what seemed like hundreds of circuit breakers. These were those pesky little safety devices, which "popped" at the slightest indication of an electrical anomaly or over voltage or over heating situation. Every system in the plane, from nose cone to APU exhaust, was protected by one of these simple, trusted, devices.

Mark thought how it was a universal trait among pilots to also use these circuit breakers as on/off switches sometimes. The easiest way to disable some kind of noisy warning horn or integrated pilot monitoring system was to use the breaker as a switch. Convenient, but not a good thing to do. Looking straight ahead, out the large windscreen, you couldn't see the nose of the airplane. You were really at the front end of this thing. Below the glass was a glare shield and underneath, the emergency lights. There weren't very many of them, less than a dozen, compared to the other aircraft he had flown where there had been lights enough to read by, if something went horribly wrong. Just below the warning lights was a row of tiny but familiar instruments. A standard attitude indicator, comfortably two-tone gray, like they had been for forty years or more and to the right, a single, twin-needled, radio magnetic direction indicator. There was even a compass!

He took heart that there was still something here with which he could identify.

Colorado—Twenty Minutes Past Midnight

The big screen, inset flush with the dark oak wall, filled with the image of the meeting of several hours before. The DOD black ops chief watched the replay from the plush recliner.

The tall young man stood before the D.C. group and Jenkins, answering questions. Jenkins fast-forwarded to the spot on the video recording he desired. The German representing the EU asked the question when Jenkins stopped the fast forward.

"It is our understanding that there is much more to these teleportation matters than we've been led to believe, Blake. You have been the go-between for the United States government and the European Union since the projects' beginning. What is the full story? Why haven't we been given the whole thing?"

Blake Robbins smiled, but the effort was strained.

"Need to know, Ernst. You know the priorities, the protocols. Those who are working on these things at the core level simply aren't prepared to say, with certainty, that all the things involved are...completed...in the sense that they feel comfortable releasing the facts. That will come—soon, I think."

The man could be a great presidential candidate, Jenkins smirked to himself, hearing Robbins's evasive answer. But, it was the next question and answer that the black ops chief was truly interested in.

"I wonder how the core folks would feel if I—if we—recommended the things you hold so close to the vest be either fully divulged or all funding for them be cut off? Answer me that," Lester Graves said in a hostile tone.

The room had been silent, Jenkins remembered while he watched the video replay. The silence had seemed much longer—the tension thicker—in real time when it was happening, he thought. His eyes narrowed in concentration, watching Blake Robbins's face take on a very different countenance than before that point.

His complexion became shadowy, eyes black—devoid of human warmth. His voice now seemed to undulate in his throat and to rumble from deep within the body, rather than spill easily from the voice box and tongue.

"Tell your people that if they cut off funding…" Jenkins heard the sinister chuckle within the words that preceded the warning he knew was coming. "…all reverse engineering knowledge will be instantly withdrawn. Every project will be instantaneously scrambled, garbled beyond recognition."

Jenkins watched Graves's face become ashen. He had inferred, and thus implied, the unmentionable—that those who held the knowledge of the ages could be manipulated, could be held up to extortion by the puny treasures of human government. The attempt to so threaten them amused Jenkins while he continued to view the replay of the previous evening's meeting.

"Oh, I didn't mean…"

"We all know exactly what you meant, Mr. Graves," the voice growled from Robbins's throat. "This is all the explanation you and your governments will have, for now."

George Jenkins had heard enough of the meeting, which had culminated with Lester Graves profusely apologizing to Blake Robbins, and to those Robbins represented.

The black ops director switched off the video and on another. He watched with transfixed interest the scientists while they worked within the laboratory to which the…objects. . . had been moved. From the huge, gleaming, oval chamber that was, he was almost certain, a conveyance from another world, the recorded video quick cut to a close up of the forms in the greenish yellow liquid. They had grown—grown tremendously.

These were the matters to which Lester Graves…Ernst Kline…were not privy. Matters that would one day be known not just by governments but rather by the world. These were man's future…

Jeb Strubble had a vector to Denver. He engaged the autopilot, after confirming that Denver International Airport was programmed into the computer, then set the air speed at mach 08.87. The Criterion was now at thirty-nine thousand feet, exactly meeting the preprogrammed cruising altitude. Well above all standard commercial travel.

In the Criterion's main cabin, Mark talked across Lori to Randall Prouse, who sat next to the porthole on the other side of Kristi Flannigan. He was pleased that the super-quiet engines and cutting-edge insulation technology made it easy to converse at a near normal level.

"What do you make of what happened on your trip to JFK? The things you saw? The words on the nonactivated monitor?"

Prouse let the questions roll around in his mind for a few seconds, before saying, "Don't know, specifically. But, I'm convinced it's all about spiritual warfare. "For we wrestle not against flesh and blood, but against principalities, against powers, against the rulers of the darkness of this world, against spiritual wickedness in high places—Ephesians 6:12.""

"What about the dark screen, the red sentence on a dead monitor?" Mark probed.

"Beware the sons of God, daughters of men," Randy said, as if simply cogitating upon the sentence. The archaeologist's facial expression made Mark know that Prouse still hadn't come to any conclusions in the matter.

"It has something to do with Lori and you, Mark, and with Morgan and Clark."

Both Mark and Randall Prouse looked to the seat just ahead of Lori's, surprised at Susie Banyon's interjection.

"Genesis 6. These things are back. Or, their hellish brethren are back—like the minions that tried to change human genetics in times before the Flood," Susie said.

"Yeah. I've thought about that, Susie. Somehow this is all tied together with what's going on in those mountains of Colorado," Randall said. "We seem to be right in the middle of an end-of-days war," he said.

"The kingdom come," Susie said. "That's what Christopher saw in his…vision. Could he have been told the satanic kingdom is coming to earth?"

"Well, it's not God's kingdom. That's for sure. That won't happen until Jesus comes to bring God's kingdom to this cesspool of a planet," Randall said.

"Kingdom come!"

Kristi Flannigan's words interrupted the archaeologist. All eyes turned to the girl, who sat forward, her eyes wide in epiphany.

"That's what was written on that old man's sign!" she said with excitement.

"What old man?" Mark asked.

"That old guy—an old man wearing a robe, tied at the waist with a rope or something. He looked like a cartoon of some old prophet you see sometimes. It was a big cardboard sign on a stick. What do you call it? It was like a placard or something. He was holding it. He jumped right in front of Morgan and me, actually, in front of Morgie. He said something, I can't remember what. He pointed at her, holding that sign. It said, 'The kingdom cometh.'"

Kristi's face brightened, her eyebrows rising again in the remembrance. "Oh, yes! He said, 'Daughter of man. Child of darkness.'"

"What happened then?" Lori asked.

"The old man—he just, acted like he was choking. Grabbed his throat, then fell to the sidewalk. Some people gathered around him. Morgie and I just went on to work."

"You see? It's all tied together somehow," Susie Banyon said from the seat in front of Lori. "And, we are all brought together for some reason by the Lord himself."

"And, it seems to have begun back there in 1947," Christopher said, almost to himself, his eyes gazing into his own thoughts.

Light burst in the cabin with vision-debilitating brilliance, whiting out everything. The light then dimmed, the things and people in the cabin again becoming clear in the passengers' recovering sight.

"What was that?!" came from each of them while they looked at each other, then to the night sky through which the Criterion roared.

Mark unclasped his seatbelt buckle and stood in the aisle, taking stock of each person. They blinked, trying to recover fully from the temporary blindness—but he satisfied himself that none suffered serious effects.

David Prouse, too, lurched from his seat, getting to the cockpit door a step ahead of Mark, who rapped on the leather-appointed door with his knuckles.

He knocked again, receiving no response. He tried to open the door, but it wouldn't budge. Locked from the inside, probably automatically. The door was a sealed hatch when closed—a "plug," he thought.

Something was wrong. All the copilot had to do was twist slightly to release the mechanism that would permit entrance. He had knocked several times, loudly enough that their wanting entrance could not be missed by the two men.

"Here, I'll open it," the flight attendant said, her eyes showing her anxiety while she slipped a key device into a slot.

The door opened easily. Mark, the girl, and David Prouse stood in open-mouthed astonishment. The cockpit seats were empty! Jeb Strubble and Hamilton Lamb were gone! Vanished!

"My Gosh!" the girl screamed, grabbing her mouth, tears streaming over her cheeks. "What's happened?!"

David wrapped his arms around her and tried to quiet her. He handed her to Cassie, who had moved to their side, seeing the girl's distress. She led her toward the rear of the cabin.

Mark searched the seats, even as he maneuvered his six-foot, two-inch frame toward the left seat.

The seat harness—the lap belt—both lap belts—were still fastened as if they had simply collapsed when the bodies they had been restraining had melted away...or whatever happened to them.

"What's going on?" Randall Prouse asked in controlled tone that was calm but anxious.

"Don't know, Grandpa," David answered, looking to the seats again.

"Lap belts still fastened," Mark said, hurriedly unfastening the belt of the left seat.

Christopher Banyon stood just outside the open door, trying to see over the others.

"They're gone, Chris. Just disappeared, looks like," Randy said.

"My good Lord," Christopher said, beginning a silent prayer for divine help.

He moved back to the women, wanting to assure them. But, what could he say? The pilots weren't there. The plane was thousands of feet in the air, moving at who knew how fast, and the plane was...pilotless...

"The pilot and copilot...they are...not there," he said to the women, whose gasps of fear he moved to address.

"Now, Mark is a pilot. He will get us down safely. He has a whole lifetime of flying experience," Christopher said, looking first into Susie's eyes, then into Lori's and into Kristi's, hoping he was using his best pastor's voice.

"The Lord is in control at all times. Let's remember that," he said, reaching to pat Kristi's shoulder lightly, not knowing the strength of her faith.

Mark maneuvered into the left seat, buckled the lap belt, and searched around for the headset. It was a Bose, the very best, and he could hear clearly, even before placing the ultralight earpieces over his ears, the voice of an air traffic controller somewhere calling to Jeb Strubble.

There was a microphone on the bulkhead among the circuit breaker panels. It was the same mike, only smaller, that had been installed in tens of thousands of airplanes. Mark hoped that the pilot's intercom was set up for transmit and receive. He pressed the talk button and responded to the center's call.

"This is Criterion X. We are still level at 240, but we do need a further descent. There's been some changes in personnel, and it will take a little time and distance to get situated." Mark explained his circumstances to the controller. The man acknowledged the pilot, and in a few seconds, gave him a discreet frequency to use for all of his further communication.

Mark looked around and found what appeared to be a radio control head on the center console. He dialed in the new frequency and was relieved to hear another man identify himself as a final controller for Denver International.

"Good morning, Criterion," the voice said. "This is DIA, and we will get you home this early morning. Please squawk one three four two and ident. I've got you on the scope, sir, and it looks like a couple of turns will get you right into a spot for landing."

Even though he had not been flying in this intense environment for years, Mark was reassured by the calmness of the controller's voice. The fact that he was not familiar with this complicated flying machine didn't matter. They would get down in one piece.

"We've got company," David Prouse said, standing in the doorway. "Both right and left," he said.

Mark glanced to his left, and then to the right. Sure enough, F-16s flanked the Criterion. He could easily make out the configuration of the aircraft by the glow of their position lights against the blackness. They had made no attempt to cut into the transmission. They were there for one reason. In case a terrorist aimed this plane in a direction other than the directions Denver International gave him. He knew the pilots were under orders—in these times—to shoot down anything that threatened to commit terror from the air.

No problem, he mused. *Ain't gonna give 'em reason to cut loose of that terrific ordnance,* he thought with an inward smile.

The controllers gave him a vector, which turned him somewhat, and said he could descend without restriction to seventy-five hundred feet. This would be, he calculated, about fifteen hundred feet above the ground—a good pattern altitude. The altimeter setting was 30.12, the winds light and variable. Temperature was reported as being thirty-two degrees, and the dew point was forty. One of those cold fronts from just beyond the Rockies was making its way down to spoil the relatively mild fall he knew Denver had been enjoying.

The controller mentioned that since the pattern had been established for landings to the west, he would vector the Criterion onto a fifteen-mile final approach to the newest runway at the airport.

The impromptu pilot reminded himself that complacency and ignorance were still trying to kill him and his assortment of passengers. Although he had flown a plane with this so-called glass cockpit before, this version was so far in advance of what he had known that it appeared almost totally foreign. Mark was glad that he could still see outside and orient himself to the airport from familiar points on the ground. He, while a Delta Airlines pilot, had logged many landings here. The experience was beginning to create a sweet mix of commercial airline pilot and jet jockey nostalgia. Flying the 737s around the mountains and valleys of Montana and Colorado in the summer would engender an intoxicating feeling. Certainly, low-level bombing missions back in Vietnam were equally tense.

Mark looked closer at the display on the small screen, and right there, in the center, was all of the information he needed to know. In fact, there wasn't anything for him to do except push a button, apparently, the one to the left of the letters "DIA" for Denver International Airport.

When Jeb Strubble had leveled the Criterion off at 240, he had not only selected a desired airspeed and altitude per the flight's clearance, he also had selected Denver International Airport in the FMC—the Flight Management Computer. The data was right there for Mark to select, as, he knew, the device followed the position of the aircraft and was always updating itself as to nearest suitable fields, distances to home base, fuel required, and dozens of other potentially needed bits of information regarding the flight.

Mark went silently over the knowledge born of decades of flight training and experience. It was crucial to remember…

When he pushed the button to the left of the screen's "DIA," the readout changed to one labeled "Approach Ref." This was the page Mark had hoped would appear at some point. Here was all of the information he needed to safely operate the aircraft within its airspeed limitations.

Mark had to fight the tendency to concentrate on the computer readouts and control mechanisms. He could not afford to neglect flying the plane. The first rule of any emergency management scenario is "Fly the plane!" he reminded himself. The second was harder: "Always be ready to land when you hit the ground!"

The gear and flap actuating switches were obvious, and now that he had the approach reference speeds he needed, he felt ready to continue.

It was getting darker because of the scarcity of lights now and more and more difficult to see back over his shoulder toward Denver. Mark was thankful that the screen right in front of him continued to display a familiar-looking attitude director, heading indicator, altitude and vertical velocity indicator, and (most importantly for the pilot) an airspeed indicator.

The Criterion was still whistling along over the high mountain terrain at 80 percent of the speed of sound.

He prayed that the F-16 pilots were aware of communications between ground control and him and would give him wide berth to do what must be done. Mark disconnected the autopilot and heard the snap of the switch, which engaged the system.

The airplane jerked a little. The jolt was actually comforting because it let him know that, in fact, the autopilot was off. He retarded both throttles back to idle and grabbed the speed brake control lever. It was just to the left of the throttles. When he moved it slowly up to put the brakes out, the airplane erratically yawed and rolled a little but settled into a steeper dive. This was just what was supposed to happen.

"Criterion X, I see that you have left flight level 240," the man on the other end of the transmission said. "Turn left now heading three five zero, this is a descent vector, and we will turn you back in for a down wind when you are lower."

"Have you been flying the Criterion very long, sir?" the controller asked.

"About forty minutes or so," Mark responded. He wasn't sure whether that was a funny thing to say or a serious response that came out sounding like a wisecrack.

Mark did explain that he had been flying since 1958 in one airplane or another and that he had been a Delta pilot for more than twenty years. They talked a little back and forth, since the Criterion had been given a discreet frequency and no one was listening. Radio procedures could be informal.

Mark's controller turned out to be the tower chief, who had been called in because of technical problems. He put Mark at ease somewhat by informal ice-breaking conversation. He was, he said, going to retire later that month, and he was glad to have something out of the ordinary to do to make his last month memorable. Mark was glad that the controller was going to be able to retire, but he didn't want the occasion to be too memorable.

Mark had been holding 350 in the descent and was shooting for 250 as the aircraft went through ten thousand feet. Two hundred fifty knots and passing through nine thousand feet. Denver said, "Criterion X, give me a turn left to zero eight zero, and if you can slow down to 210, I think I would appreciate it."

The speed brakes were still up, and the airplane slowed quickly, very quickly. He didn't want to stall out here, so he was glad to remember to put the brakes down. All of the vibration and shuddering that accompany a rapid descent smoothed out immediately. It got quiet, and the bird seemed to glide in a controllable descent, all the while in a thirty-degree bank to the new heading. As Mark left seventy-five hundred feet, the altitude reminder beeped, indicating that he was now within five hundred feet of his desired altitude.

His friend on the ground said, "Turn right heading one seven zero for a base leg that will give you a fifteen-mile final. When you roll out, the airport will be at your one o'clock, seventeen miles. Let me know if you see it."

Mark looked in the direction as instructed. He couldn't make the desired visual confirmation. A thick haze had developed and covered every landmark. This early morning, Mark knew that the proper frequencies had been selected in the FMS, but he hadn't a clue as to how to get the instrument to depict what he needed to get the craft on the ground.

Even though he knew he shouldn't be embarrassed, he was a little hesitant to tell the controller that not only could he still not see the airport, but he did see four other planes turning on a variety of headings, which were leading them to landings on the other runways. At this early hour, he had expected the prom to be sparsely attended. But, the dance—as the big jets' pilots called the hectic landings and takeoffs—was getting furious.

He began to put some flaps out as the Criterion slowed down; he finally selected fifteen degrees of flaps and settled in at 135 knots. Seven thousand feet above sea level. Current altimeter setting. Good.

Mark still could not see the airport, but he noticed two 757s—at least that was the type of planes according to the controller's information—had disappeared into the haze, about ten miles to his right.

"Turn right, now, heading 240. This will get you on a nice intercept for the localizer. Maintain seven thousand feet."

"Roger the turn, but I have to remind you that the ILS is inoperable!"

Actually, he was inoperable, Mark thought, but he didn't want to sound like a dummy or worse. The power setting was a little too high, because the Criterion's airspeed was going through two hundred, and the vibration of the air frame was getting very noticeable. He reduced thrust and got another deceleration going. *Look out for the airport!* he mentally jabbed himself. *Make sure in your mind not to land with the gear up.*

"You're crossing the center line," the controller announced. "Can you see the airport, sir?"

"Actually, no, I can't. Did I mention that the ILS wasn't working?"

"Yes, sir. I assumed you'd be using the inertial reference system and the GPS. Have you got those on board?"

"They are inoperative too"

"No problem, sir. Say, how old are you?"

What a strange thing to ask, Mark thought. *Here I am, screaming around the Colorado, mountain-filled countryside at 135 knots. There are at least a dozen airplanes within twenty miles of my present position, at who knows what altitudes or headings, and he wants to know how old I am!* The thoughts both irritated and amused him.

"I'll bet you're old enough to remember what we used to call a GCA," the controller radioed.

"Sure I do." A GCA, or ground-controlled approach, used to be the standard instrument landing scenario back in the '60s in the military. He hadn't flown one since he got out of the service in 1969. They never used them in the commercial airline driving business, so it wasn't something that was common anymore, except in the memories of old timers—like Mark Lansing. He had many of those memories. Landing on the wing of his flight commander in an F-102 in heavy fog. Bringing the F-4 Phantom into Ubon Thailand when those afternoon thunderstorms made a nice day into a grim time for flying. Good memories because he was still alive. Not so good if you don't listen and trust your controller.

"Let's finish this morning's flight with a show for the youngsters," the new friend on the ground said. "We've had this GCA system installed and operating here in the tower for years, and we use it for a backup. I can bring it up on my screen and get you down here just like I used to do as an airman first class at Itazuke Air Base on Kyushu, in the late '60s."

"Sounds good, considering the alternatives."

"Give me a right turn to two nine zero and maintain your seven thousand feet. You're about eight miles from glide slope intercept. You might want to begin slowing to approach speed."

Mark pulled back on the throttle slightly and selected twenty-five degrees of flaps. This combination of increased drag and lower thrust immediately acted in concert to give the plane a huge change in airspeed. He still had the altitude hold on. He jammed the throttles again and the powerplants responded with some good feeling thrust, and the airspeed settled in at 130.

A warning buzzer sounded and a woman's voice said, "Landing gear, landing gear, landing gear."

Ooops! He wasn't going to forget that, but it would have been forgotten without her computer voice to remind him. The computer wanted some gear down, and so did Mark Lansing.

He snapped the plastic wheel-looking knob mounted on a short lever to the down position. Three red lights came on followed quickly by three green lights, indicating that the gear was down and locked. The lady in the computer shut up.

"Turn back left now to two eight five. You are approaching the center line nicely, glide slope intercept in three miles," the controller said.

"Left to two eight two, and you're on the centerline. Glide slope in one mile. Call gear down."

"Roger, Criterion X, down and locked, three green."

"Approaching glide path, begin descent."

Mark pulled the throttles back to give himself about twenty-two hundred pounds of fuel flow and clicked the altitude hold off with his right thumb. The vertical velocity moved, indicating an initial descent.

"On glide path, on center line," the controller called out.

The air speed began to drop off a little, and the Criterion was descending at about nine hundred feet per minute. Too slow, too fast, he thought.

"Slightly below glide path, on centerline."

Mark nudged the throttles a bit. He had to stabilize and come back up on the glide path.

"Drifting slightly left, turn right now, heading two eight five. Below glide path."

He had learned to use the rudders to change the heading in these small increments. Usually the rudders are used only in dog fights, strafing, and taxiing in jet airplanes. He added a small increment of power.

"On center line. Coming up on the glide path. On glide path."

Mark reduced power one hundred pounds on each engine.

Let's see, now, he considered. *I'm in the clear up here in the early morning. I'm flying a plane that I have yet to log an hour's worth of time in, and I can't see the runway. The millions of dollars worth of avionics are one click away from taking control and making a safe landing unimpeded by the human touch. I don't know how to turn it on. Situation normal,* he thought.

"On center line and on glide path, one mile to touchdown. Winds are light and variable; you're cleared to land."

The power setting had been correct. Once trimmed up, one can adjust his vertical velocity with tiny changes of thrust. It works in an F4, a 737, and here, in the Criterion X. It might be something to teach everybody, he thought. Patience is a good thing to have, too. Don't chase any readout. If you're off course, correct but just a little. Wait. If you're low, add some power. Wait for the vertical velocity to change. See if it moves the way you want it to.

"On centerline, on glide path, approaching minimums, call the run-way."

Mark looked up from his circuit of instrument scanning. Nothing. A pretty orangish-gray in the lights, he thought. Smog.

"On center line, dropping slightly low on glide path, one hundred feet to minimums."

The airplane was smoothly cutting through the fog and smog. All parameters were nailed, just as if he had been doing this for years. It had been seven years, in fact, since he had moved the controls of an airplane, and then it had been a Cessna 172, on a sunny afternoon. Eighty dollars worth of fun. He knew there was an airport out here somewhere. They promised him when he and the controller started all of this.

"Holding slightly low and on center line. At minimums. Call the runway in sight or go around!"

Mark held his breath. He locked his grip on the controls. He waited. One hundred twenty knots, 550 feet per minute rate of descent. He waited. One click of nose up trim, tiny reduction of power, don't move anything!

The runway was, he remembered from reading in industry magazines that kept him up to date, 33 percent longer than the other runways at the DIA and approximately twice as long as runways at lower altitudes. He didn't know if it was the truth, or propaganda hype, but it was said that the sixteen thousand-foot long, two hundred-foot wide runway was so long that a jet parked at one end was not visible from the other end due to the curvature of the earth.

Now, the lights on either side narrowed in perspective in the black distance. The big landing light illuminated nicely. The huge strip still pretty clean, he considered, now able to see the broad expanse of concrete. There were no long streaks of rubber residue where hundreds if not thousands of airplanes had landed before him. That was because, he for some reason recalled from a distant conversation, it had been opened only a few months—maybe a year before. He was—he was certain—among the first ten thousand to land on this monster runway.

Christopher Banyon and the others watched the flashing red lights while the emergency vehicles roared to meet the plane at the end of the runway.

"Don't know why there's such a greeting," Lori said in a light tone. "The best pilot in the whole world was flying the airplane."

The passengers laughed at the proud wife's assessment and broke into applause.

"Absolutely none better," Randall Prouse agreed, reaching across the aisle to squeeze the left forearm of Mark Lansing's bride.

Mark taxied the Criterion off the runway and pointed it toward the terminal area. They wouldn't want him going further, he knew.

Now, what to say to them? How would he tell them he had to fly the airplane because the pilot and copilot had...disappeared?

Nigel Saxton couldn't sleep. His training had taught that one should be able to fall asleep under any circumstances, then awaken, fully alert, as if one had never fallen asleep.

Fine in theory, he thought. But, it didn't work as a matter of practicality. He was wide awake and had been for an hour. He had gotten some sleep, but now his core thoughts nudged him to move, well before the dawn began dissipating the darkness that surrounded the village of Alamosa.

The rottweiler was awake, too, lying near him, alert to the man's every movement.

"I think we better get a move on, boy," Saxton said, vigorously rubbing Jeddy's head and tugging on his ear. The dog shifted, then stood and stretched his muscular body.

"Let's have a look at what we have down there," Nigel said, taking the binoculars from the backpack and, after walking to the edge of the rocky area that had given them shelter from the frigid winds, trained the glasses on the sprawling village, whose lights were already ablaze with early morning activities.

"Alamoso," he said. "Just like Zeke promised."

The canine looked to the man, trying to get the human's meanings.

Did this mean that "Mommy" was there? Were they going to find his mistress?

"We had better move in that direction, mate. Before it becomes too light. We will get a room."

Jeddy whined, responding to Nigel's happy tone while Saxton patted him and playfully tugged at one of the dog's ears. "Shall we ask for two double beds?"

Mark thought it odd—as did Christopher Banyon and Randall Prouse— that they had not been questioned to any extent upon departing the Criterion. The lights of the Denver area whisked by while they rode toward downtown in the big van—first on Peña Boulevard, then I-70.

The man had flashed credentials and said he was with the Federal Bureau of Investigation, then "invited" them to accompany him and three other agents to FBI headquarters.

None of the men spoke to them during the thirty-five-minute trip into Denver, other than a forced smile of politeness and short answer when Lori asked the man who had flashed the credentials, "Are we being arrested?"

"Just want to ascertain facts, ma'am."

Lori and those old enough to remember looked at each other. Jack Webb—Joe Friday—*Dragnet* was the consensus of thought.

But it wasn't funny, Mark knew. The missing pilot and copilot was no joking matter.

Each had the same agonizing thought gripping their brains. What had happened? If they couldn't explain it to themselves, how could they make the authorities understand?

Mark's worries went deeper; although, his rationale went further, too. It was true that the Criterion began the flight from LAX with Jeb Strubble and Hamilton Lamb, and they weren't there when they landed at DIA. But, there was absolutely no way anyone was going to be able to open a cabin door at altitude, in a pressurized cabin. They would all likely be dead if that had happened.

On the other hand, what if they concluded that the passengers, somehow, for some fried reason, had thrown the men out before takeoff?

But, if that had happened, the pilot and copilot would have reported it—or their bodies would be found. The authorities couldn't produce bodies—not at LAX, at any rate...

His own father, Lori's dad—had vanished. That was the explanation. Part of the...things...that were ongoing...

"You folks just relax," the man with the credentials said, turning as far as he could to look at his passengers. "We just want to try to get to the bottom of all of this."

Momentarily, the van turned into an alley way and descended a long driveway, the driver stopping the vehicle in front of a huge, garage-type door. The door slid electronically upward, and the van moved into a vast underground parking area.

David pulled Cassie to his side by wrapping his arm around her shoulder. "This won't take long," he said, bending to joke, whispering in her ear. "I'm a lawyer, you know."

Jeddy walked ahead of the man, impatient to keep moving toward whatever destination the flashlight's powerful beam pointed. He occasionally stopped and glanced back at Nigel Saxton, having gone beyond a point he wanted to be separated from his human friend.

The slope was gradual leading from the rocky crags down the mountain's foothill toward Alamosa. At least Ezekiel had told him the town they saw after leaving the mountain would be Alamosa. The gradual slope, however, hid the rugged, boulder-strewn difficulty of negotiating the terrain.

Better than having to climb in the bone-chilling heights from which he had been forced by the "allies" of Great Britain and the EU.

It was the darkest time, the minutes while the sun's earliest rays were still sequestered behind the planet's curvature. The flashlight beam seemed to illuminate beyond any he had known. It was the combination of the powerful, many batteries of the long instrument and the deep blackness that surrounded him and the rottweiler.

Occasionally when he switched the light off to preserve batteries, the light-points of life in the village that was still far below were beckoning, welcoming jewels of beauty. They were stars shining up at him, instead of down from the black void of space.

It was impossible to estimate the distance to Alamosa. His thoughts were interrupted by the dog's whining bark—several yelps. Not barking of anger, or even excitement, but rather of important discovery the man must come see. The canine wanted him to see what he had found.

"What you got there, boy?"

Nigel aimed the light just off the course of travel they had chosen. The beam fell upon what looked to be a crumpled heap of cloth—a rolled-up ball of discarded something or the other.

"What do we have here?"

Saxton knelt beside the find, turning it and opening its folds with gloved fingers.

It was a sheep-lined jacket of some sort. He held it up and examined it. It was a fairly large jacket, a man's, one that had not been in these elements very long.

"Somebody out here without this is in trouble," he said, causing Jeddy to cock his head, then sniff the coat. The dog whined, then barked at the coat. His excitement grew while he half circled the coat, barking at it.

Could be the sheepskin—the fleece—the Brit thought, wondering what had sparked the dog's reaction.

"Have a good whiff," Nigel instructed Jeddy. "If this fellow is out here, we had better find him."

SEVENTEEN

The man was in a khaki shirt and cardigan. He still had that sleepy-eyed look. It was obvious that this man—most likely the top man, or near the top man in the Denver FBI hierarchy—had been called from his bed.

The agent sipped coffee from the Styrofoam cup one of the other agents had just handed him.

"Mr. Lansing," the youngish, middle-aged man said, seating himself across the small conference table from Mark. "They tell me that was a fine piece of flying you did, bringing that Criterion X to a safe landing. That's among the most sophisticated civilian jets in the world. And, you—" He picked up a manila file folder and thumbed through the pages it contained, after setting the coffee aside.

"You, I see here, haven't flown any jet aircraft since..." He put a finger down a page and stopped while he read the line. "Since 1998. Is that correct?"

"September, 1998, that's correct," Mark said, his irritation slowly burning in his fatigued senses.

"Now, come on, Mr. Lansing. You are telling us that there was a bright flash of some kind, and those two guys in charge of the flying—these fellows Strubble and..." he looked to the note appended to the file folder, "...Hamilton Lamb, they just vanished? Just weren't there when you and the others opened the cockpit door?"

"That's exactly what I'm telling you," Mark said.

"That's impossible! Surely you know that."

"Why would I say something so obviously...impossible? Don't you think I would try to come up with something more plausible, if I had done something like...murder those two guys, or whatever?"

"Oh, we have seen and heard some pretty wild stuff, Mr. Lansing. And some of those weird things have been to claim that people just… *poof!*…disappeared."

Mark said nothing but sat back in the chair, eyeing the FBI man.

"Problem is, in every case, they were proven to be lying. That's because people just vanishing, without the help of somebody, just cannot happen."

"Wish I could help, Agent Warford. But, all I know—that any of us knows—is that when we opened the cockpit door—which, incidentally, is a plug—those guys were gone. Their lap belts were still clasped as if they hadn't even released them."

"A 'plug door?'"

"A plug door is one that seals from the cabin while the crew is flying the plane, in case the cabin suddenly depressurizes."

"How did you get in?"

"The the flight attendant had the card key," Mark said. "And that's another thing. The girl wouldn't lie for us, would she?"

"I've seen people lie for perfect strangers for numbers of reasons, Mark. You'd be surprised."

"The cockpit was plugged, that is, it was pressurized fully, as the flight data recorders on that…sophisticated…bird will attest. If the seals had been compromised in the cockpit—or anywhere else in the plane—the sensors would have made that clear. The cabin would have to have been depressurized in order to open doors and throw bodies out. The recorders would have indicated that. You see the fallacy of thinking that we somehow threw those men out?"

Warford squinted in concentration, looking again into the file folder.

"Sir, Mr. Lansing's attorney wants to talk to you," another agent said, opening the door to the conference room where only Mark and the agent had been sitting.

"Send him in," the seated agent said.

David Prouse came in past the agent holding the door open.

"Sir, I need to know your plans, please," David said in a businesslike tone. "Will you hold Mr. Lansing and the rest of us? Or let us go on our way to attend to the business we have in the area? If you hold us, I will go to the federal office and secure a writ of habeas corpus."

John Warford didn't like bully tactics, to which he was so often subjected by lawyers—

a fraternity to which he himself belonged. But, he chose his battles carefully with them. He would fight this one obliquely.

"I'm not holding Mr. Lansing or any of you. We're just trying to determine the facts. When Homeland Security has checked out all of this, you may go about your business. But, we will need you to inform us of your movements around the area until these things are resolved."

A door behind Warford opened and a man standing in the opening said, "Agent Warford, it's a DC One."

"Excuse me, please," Warford said, rising from the chair and going into the room beyond the open door, which closed behind him.

David Prouse sat in the chair beside Mark.

"They can hold us for a number of hours—even days—under new Homeland Security laws. But that doesn't seem to be what they want...at this point, at least."

"What about habeas corpus?" Mark asked.

"That's suspended...or takes second priority in suspected aircraft-involved terrorism."

"Then, what do you think? Will we be allowed to go on our way?"

"Two missing pilots are unaccounted for. On the other hand, we don't present your typical terrorist profile. Obviously, he wants us close by..."

The door opened again and the agent hurried back to the table. His face appeared different, both Mark and David noticed. It was a gray, ashen look of a man in shock. Warford was quiet for a few seconds, looking at the men, then at the file he thumbed through, as if doing so without purpose.

"Here's what we have. Two pilots that have gone missing under absolutely inexplicable circumstances. This nation is under an elevated alert protocol—an aircraft is involved in this weird set of circumstances."

He again paused to look at the file before turning his eyes to look into those of David Prouse, then Mark Lansing.

"The others can go to…" he looked to the paper attached by a paper clip to the file folder, "…Alamosa. That's where it shows you plan to spend some time vacationing. Is that correct?"

Mark nodded yes.

"Mr. Lansing, Mr. Prouse. I have the legal right to keep all of you here for a considerable time, as you fully know, Mr. Prouse," the agent said, looking to David.

"Now, rather than have to do that, we need for you and Mrs. Lansing to stay with us for a time. Hopefully no more than twenty-four hours. We will then release you to join the rest of your party. We will provide hotel room, food, and so forth. We'll even helicopter you to Alamosa, if you wish—at our expense."

Both men studied the proposal, which wasn't really a proposal, David Prouse realized. Mark looked to David for answers.

"And, the alternative?" Prouse asked.

"Otherwise, we will have to insist that you all stay here—indefinitely—at your own expense."

Jeddy moved quickly through the sharp-edged rocks that filled the downward slope toward the lights that grew larger with each step taken by the dog and the man. The rottweiler had an obvious purpose, Nigel thought, seeing the black, tail-docked rump rise and fall, then turn from side to side, all the while sniffing the terrain.

"You got the scent, huh, chap?" the Brit asked in an excited tone that seemed to urge Jeddy forward.

Saxton held the fleece-lined coat while he followed the path broken by the canine, hearing the occasional whine. Any noise from the rottweiler was unusual, he knew now from experience, so it was wise to pay attention.

"That's a boy! Let's get the guy who owns this!"

The rottweiler neared scrub brush that thickened into a gnarled grove of trees. He stopped, the dark fur expanding into a bristling mass of black that covered the bulging muscles of the neck, chest, and shoulders.

Growling rumbled in short, furious bursts from deep within the canine's throat while he stood, his massive head bowed and dark eyes trained on the interior of the thicket.

The hair on the back of Nigel's neck seemed to stand on end, too. Chill bumps pimpled his back, neck, and arms. Something that posed a threat hid somewhere in the barely visible forest of brush and smallish trees.

Nigel knelt, pulling the infantry knife from a pocket of the backpack he had dropped. He reached beyond where the knife had been to bring out the .40 caliber semiautomatic pistol.

He gripped it on either side of the slide and pulled back; the action, upon releasing the grip with his left hand, chambered a thick round.

He pointed the pistol's muzzle skyward, his elbow cocked, ready to in an instant thrust the weapon's business end toward the menace the dog perceived.

He grabbed a small flashlight from the pack when he couldn't locate Zeke's flashlight quickly enough. He flicked the beam in the direction Jeddy pointed. The light exposed a large patch of reddish brown hair.

The fur moved, and when he ran the beam upward, to a height of, he estimated, eight feet or more, the creature screamed, its hideous, expansive face opening into a monstrous gaping hole. Fangs dripped with drool; its eyes glistened—seemed to spark—with hellish, blood redness!

"Back off!" Nigel shouted at Jeddy, never letting his own eyes move from the demonic face, whose mouth and dagger-like teeth gnashed at them.

Saxton leveled the pistol, cutting loose with a burst of five rounds into the center of its huge, heaving chest. There seemed no effect, so he poured three more rounds into the head.

The beast turned, screaming, then leaped into the forest, knocking saplings aside. Saxton followed, but it seemed to just not be there.

The Brit stood dumbfounded. The creature had to have weighed five hundred pounds. No, probably more. It had knocked trees down. But it just…vanished from the beam!

The stench was overpowering; he hadn't noticed that in the excitement. It smelled like nothing he had smelled…something beyond death's sickly odor…

"Mate...You okay?"

The dog was again friendly, no longer in the attack mode. Nigel rubbed Jeddy's head.

"Good boy. You are a brave soldier, my friend. You didn't have the weapon, I did. Of course, it didn't seem to do any good, as they say."

The beast...the animal, or whatever it was, he knew now existed. The Yeti—the Bigfoot. But, it had vanished!

He searched the direction the creature had gone, seeing the broken, bent evergreens. The thing seems to have disappeared at this point he thought, shining the light around the area where the trees were no longer skinned and torn apart.

Jeddy was whining again, and Nigel broke off his light search of the forest where the monster had just disappeared.

The rottweiler stood over something. He nuzzled the crumpled heap with his muzzle, his whining at a higher and higher pitch while the Brit approached.

"What you found?"

He again scanned the forest behind him before turning to look at the dog's find.

A body! It was a man, a man who groaned—he was alive!

"It's okay, friend. We are here. You are with friends..."

He gently turned the man's face toward the light.

"You are the American. The journalist!"

He had to urge the dog to move aside. Jeddy licked at the face, continuing the high pitched whine of concern.

"My friend, looks like you found your Bigfoot," the Brit said.

"The Lord will take care of them, Chris. This is all happening for a reason, for God's purpose," Susie Banyon said. "These things are not in our control, never have been."

Christopher sat on the edge of the hotel bed, his thoughts spilling verbally from his growing worry. "What have I gotten them into, Susie? Gotten us into?"

Susie came to her husband from hanging clothing on the bar of the closet. She bent to hug and kiss him on the right temple. "Don't you see, hon, this is all beyond us. When things are out of your control, it's time to just sit back and watch the Lord at work."

"Yeah. Well, I'm having trouble letting go. All I can think of is that it was my idea to charter that plane and come to Colorado."

"What about the…visions…the Lord has given you? That He's given both of us? And has given the others? The mark of God is so obviously on all of this, Chris. Don't you see that?"

He said nothing, rather sat staring out the big window into the Alamosa morning that looked as if it would grow into a bright day—at least physically. Christopher's own dark mood could use some of the sunshine that radiated from his sweet Susie…

A knock at the door disrupted his introspection.

"Just heard from Mark and Lori," Randall Prouse said, walking to the bed and slapping Christopher on the shoulder.

"Mark said someone from Homeland Security had gotten them released…"

Christopher's face brightened. "Terrific!" He stood and grabbed Prouse by his arm. "That's great…"

"Wait a second, though," Randall said, patting his friend's arm to quiet his exuberance.

"They've invited him and Lori to the government complex…"

"Who's invited them?" Christopher asked.

"Really not sure. Mark said he wasn't sure, either. But the offer was made in front of the FBI guy and the Homeland Security person, Mark said. Said this other guy came in from the Department of Defense—a special branch involved in projects for DOD in concert with civilian technological suppliers or something like that. We didn't have long to talk."

"So, Mark and Lori are going with this government person…where?" Susie asked, her concern beginning to rise.

"Don't know that either," Randall said. "Like I said, we just didn't have much time to talk. The decision had to be made right then. The guy with DOD, or the special projects, or whatever, said he would do what he could to locate Clark and Morgan if they were involved in the projects at the mountain complex."

"Well, yes. Their children…That's all it would take to get me to go with them, too," Christopher said, his eyes staring into his own thoughts while he spoke them.

Susie understood Mark's and Lori's thinking in accepting the invitation, too. But she was troubled. Things had developed just too conveniently. "Doesn't it seem odd that this guy from the Department of Defense, or whatever, just happened to be at FBI headquarters to make that offer?"

"I thought the same thing," Randall Prouse said. "It wouldn't be so odd if it weren't for this history of weird things, the visions, or whatever. There is definitely something strange going on."

David Prouse and Casandra Lincoln walked hand in hand in front of the quaint shops that were just opening for the morning's business. The Tyrolean motif of the shops presented the image they were intended to convey by the architects who conceived them. The white-washed lattice work shone brightly in the morning rays of sunlight that streamed from between the mountain spires and reflected off the wooden strips that crisscrossed the window panes and the building's façade.

"This is a long way from Manhattan," Cassie said. "I think I could make this my home permanently."

"Quite a difference," David agreed, bending slightly to examine a miniature Tyrolean village model displayed in the window.

"Maybe we can let you take your new home back to New York with you," he said, tugging her by the hand.

They walked through the Swiss chalet-type sculpted door of rough-hewn wood, causing a small bell to tinkle.

He walked, with Cassie still in tow, to the counter.

"Hi. Say, how much for that little village model over there in the window?"

His question caused the short woman, wearing the antiquated dress of the Alps, to move from behind the counter to the window display.

"This one?" The clerk bent to touch the model.

"The very one," David said.

The woman went again to behind the counter, checked price listings, and said, "Two hundred fifty dollars and forty-five cents."

"That's too much," Cassie said before she could catch herself.

"Yeah. That is a lot," David said. "Tell you what," he said, looking at the woman and squinting, as if he were squaring off for a bargaining session. "You knock off the forty-five cents, and we have a deal."

"That sounds like a deal to me," the clerk said, David Prouse having won her salesclerk's heart with his charm.

"What's your brand?" He took out his wallet and began thumbing through the many credit cards.

Ten minutes later they sat at a small outdoor area of a coffee shop.

"Thanks for the gift," Cassie said, seeing the handsome face through senses that had, she knew, already fallen under this wonderful guy's spell. Could this be the one? Could he?...

"Always wanted to have my own town," he said, sipping the mocha latte. "Maybe you could call it Prouseville..."

"Prouseville it is," she said, sipping from her cup of hot chocolate.

Silence sat between them for several seconds, their eyes meeting. Hers dropped to the chocolate, then shifted nervously away to the mountains.

"This is meant to be, you know, Cassie?"

She looked at him, a puzzled expression on her face—the most beautiful he had seen.

"God puts things...situations...people...together, you know?"

She didn't know how to respond. She believed in God. Didn't know him very well. But believed there was a God, a Heaven...

"He's brought us together. And, I owe him big time for that," David said, reaching across the small wrought iron table to take her hand.

"Do you think you could ever...Come to feel about me...the way I feel about you?"

"How—how do you feel about me?" She didn't know how else to answer.

"I love you, Cassie."

Nigel Saxton wondered why the rottweiler refused to move more than a couple of meters from the man's side. He had to stop and rest every fifty meters or so because the backpack was cumbersome while trying at the same time to support the man, who could limp beside him but couldn't speak.

They stopped at the point just where the concrete of Alamosa met the beginning of the mountains foothills. This was the time to do it.

He removed the backpack after helping the man lie on the snowy grass. The canine came and lay behind the man, sniffing his face and giving a lick and a high-pitched whimper.

The dog knew this fellow, the Brit assured himself, taking off his right glove and holding it in his teeth while he rummaged through a pocket of the pack.

"Ah. Got it!"

He brought out a small, leather-covered notebook.

"Yes!" He patted the man, who tried to lift his head but shut his eyes and drifted to semiconsciousness again.

"Your name is Clark, Clark Lansing," Saxton said, pleased with himself that he was always faithful to jot down the names of those he met, no matter the circumstances. This was Clark Lansing, the journalist he had met on the ride into this very town—the Bigfoot hunter. And, a successful one, at that.

His thoughts were becoming giddy, he recognized. They had to find rest and get Lansing some medical help. No telling how much damage that…whatever it was…had done to him…

When he had put on the backpack and convinced Clark to begin limping again toward the town, they moved through what appeared to be a small park with children's playground equipment that obviously would be unused for the foreseeable future because of the onset of the mountain winter.

He remembered something he had meant to do.

"Stand here, Clark," he said, letting go of his companion, then taking the backpack from his shoulders.

He took from the pack a long, thick cord.

"Come here, boy," he said, kneeling to meet the rottweiler, who at first pulled away from Nigel, seeing the cord.

"We've got to have you on leash, old chap," Saxton said in reassuring tone. He tied the cord around the dog's collar at the metal loops, then again jumped the backpack onto his shoulders.

"We don't want the constables putting you in doggie lockup," Nigel said, taking Clark's left arm and putting it around his own neck and shoulder above the backpack.

George Jenkins was up early and fuming. He strode in short, quick steps toward the main laboratory, a roll of papers in his right hand. He slapped the palm of his left with the papers. When he burst through the big double doors, several men and women in lab coats hurried to intercept him.

"Why didn't you wake me up?"

His words were not shouted; they were seethed between clenched teeth. But everyone in the immediate vicinity knew he was livid.

"Sir..." One of the men started to offer an explanation but was interrupted by the angry black ops chief.

"You have him on video, don't you? You were supposed to always keep the subjects on video."

"Yes, sir. We have the recordings."

"Let's see them," Jenkins said, walking faster toward the area in which all experiments were monitored.

The others struggled to keep up with their boss.

He exploded into the semidarkened room.

"Which monitor?"

"This one, sir," a woman said, pointing to the big monitor near one corner of the room.

"Run it."

One of the scientists sat at an inclined control board and manipulated the essential controls. The video began to roll.

Jenkins's eyes flashed with anger between slitted eyelids while he viewed what had happened in the previous early morning hours. He twisted the roll of papers with both hands, then, realizing they were important papers, released his grip and tried to undo the damage he had done.

"We can't figure what happened, sir," the woman said. "You see, here the subject sits—

more or less like he has been since the introduction of the sedatives. He seems barely able to function."

The screen suddenly grew bright, so much so that the whole recorded image was whited out, the image completely lost. The room darkened as quickly as it had burst with light, and the man who had been sitting was no longer there.

Jenkins's eyelids narrowed even more. He growled his angry displeasure.

"What happened? Was this the RAPTURE? Who did this?"

"No, sir. The RAPTURE had not been used in more than twenty-four hours. That is, previous to the subject's being gone from the holding room. We used it to send a BORG after him."

"He was not to be damaged, you fools! That thing will tear him apart…"

"Sir, we retrieved the BORG before he could harm the subject."

"Are you sure of that?"

"Yes, sir. The device within the subject's body shows his vital functions are good. He does remain in a sedated state. He didn't escape. He was somehow taken from the holding room."

They must have taken him for some reason. Removed him from the lab setting for their own purposes. Jenkins's thoughts caromed in his now fully awake brain.

"You have his location?"

"All we know is where the BORG was placed, then retrieved. The subject didn't yet have a GPS chip."

"Great! Just great!" Jenkins slammed a nearby wall with the heel of his fist, further crumpling the rolled-up papers. "Then he IS escaped!"

Alamosa—11:43 a.m.

"David is with Christopher and Susie and his dad. You want to go get a bite?"

Cassie stuck her head out of the hotel bathroom, looking in Kristi Flannigan's direction while brushing her auburn hair.

"Well, I guess I won't have my feelings hurt by taking second place," Kristi said, then looked back to the laptop screen at her e-mail.

"Well, you are the one who said you wanted to make sure David and I had time to be together. We offered to have you tag along," Cassie said, her use of the words "tag along" emphasized for the purpose of playfully irritating the girl who was, along with Morgan, her best friend.

"Yeah. I'll 'tag along' with you for a bite—since Mr. Wonderful is busy."

Cassie, still brushing her hair, walked to Kristi, who continued to scan the monitor.

"Seriously, Krissie…you are so sweet to give us space. But, you ARE welcome with us."

Kristi turned and laid her face against Cassie's arm. "No, you two need to get to know each other. I'm fine, really."

"What is David doing with the others?" Kristi asked, turning from the screen, then standing and stretching her long limbs and body.

"They're trying to contact Mark and Lori by their cell. They thought they would have heard from them by now. David's checking in Denver with the FBI people, I believe."

"What in the world is this all about, Cass? What are we into? Two guys just…disappear?"

Susie is convinced it's something to do with the end of days. I just don't understand it, the things she and the others are talking about…"

"Yeah. What does that mean, the 'end of days?'"

"Something to do with the Second Coming of Jesus or something."

Cassie returned to the bathroom, and Kristi looked to the mirror of the closet door. Her body was shapely enough, she thought. A little skinny, maybe. But, that was due to her height.

She moved closer to the mirror, looking at the pretty face that looked back at her. Only, she thought, it isn't so pretty. It's losing its tan, and she thought that a touch of blush was in order. She would take care of that when Cassie vacated the bathroom...Jesus. The Second Coming. What could that have to do with all of this? She would look into that, she assured herself, turning sideways to examine, then assess, her shape in her pants. "Not bad," she thought. "Right!" she said to herself, then. "Then why are you alone while your friends have the guys going after them?"

Fifteen minutes later, the girls walked a block from the hotel's entranceway. The shops were now in full swing in the downtown tourist area. They looked longingly at the many trinkets for sale, amazed that the prices were higher than such things would be in Manhattan.

Cassie bent to look at a painting that interested her. Kristi started to look more closely, at Cassie's insistence, but before doing so, she caught glimpse of something dark rounding a corner twenty feet away. It was a dog leading a man.

"Cass!" Kristi pulled at her friend's sleeve.

Cassie stood and looked in the direction Kristi was looking.

"That dog, did you see it?"

"No. Where was it?"

"Going around that corner," she said, pointing toward a building of brown stucco and trimmed in white wood.

"What about it?" Cassie asked but knowing by her friend's tone that Kristi had seen something amazing.

"That was a rottweiler. And, I swear, it looked just like Jeddy. It looked exactly like the Peanut!"

"Let's go!"

Cassie ran ahead of Kristi, who soon caught up.

"They were headed this way," Kristi said taking the lead, her longer legs, used to afternoon runs, striding smoothly.

Rounding the back corner of a large building they caught a glimpse of a man moving just out of sight into what looked to be an alley way.

"There he is!" Kristi pointed and broke into a full run, leaving Cassie behind.

She entered the long, narrow alley, seeing the man walking ahead, led by the dog.

"Hey! Sir! Wait, please!" she said breathlessly.

Nigel Saxton pulled on the new leash he had just purchased for the rottweiler. "Hold up, chap," he said, causing the dog to stop, then turn to see what the man wanted of him.

"Jeddy! Is that you, Jeddy?!"

Kristi's shouted words made the rottweiler come to attention. He lifted his ears in alertness, then leaped to action, moving with great strength toward the female, startling Saxton, who almost lost control of the powerful canine.

Cassie had caught up and knelt, as did Kristi.

Jeddy rushed to them, his huge black body shaking in the greeting wiggles of a puppy. He licked their faces, going from one girl to the other.

"Oh, Peanut!" both said in unison. "Is it really you, Peanut?!"

David Prouse snapped the cell phone shut. He turned to his grandfather, Susie, and Christopher Banyon.

"There's no breaking through this from this end," he said in a resigned tone. "Grandpa, you might have to call on a couple of your friends in D.C. to find out about what's happened to them."

"I was afraid that would be the case," Randall said. "They treat these secret operations—

these black ops things—as almost sacred."

Christopher Banyon looked to Randall, then at the younger Prouse. "There is nothing to be done—other than try to get someone with influence in Washington involved?"

"Oh, I have some ideas," David said. "These people don't like publicity. Newspeople aren't crazy about governmental secret projects, especially

not about those of military significance. And, they don't like this admin-
istration. We know that."

"Of course. Stir up some publicity!"

"Or, even better at this stage, Grandpa. Threaten to stir up some
stuff…"

The cell alerted David, and he flipped the phone open. He listened
for a second after the greeting, then said with excitement, "You've found
Clark? And Morgan's rottweiler?!"

The words instantly riveted the others' attention to David's face while
he continued to listen before speaking again.

"We'll meet you."

Less than fifteen minutes later, Kristi led them into a small individual
motel unit. She calmed the rottweiler, who stood and began to bristle
when the door opened.

"It's okay, Peanut. They're friends. It's okay…" Cassie's words seemed
to put the dog somewhat at ease, and the five people moved closer to the
bed.

"Clark," Christopher said, coming to the side of the bed and reaching
to touch Clark Lansing, who blinked, glanced toward him, then seemed
to lapse again into sleep.

"Nigel Saxton," the Brit said, offering his right hand to David, then
to Randall.

"I think he will be fine," Saxton said. "Circumstances prevent me
from getting him medical assistance at present."

"What happened to him?" Susie asked, feeling Clark's face with the
back of her right hand. "He doesn't seem to have fever."

"Actually, the dog and I ran into him quite by chance on the way
down from the mountain," Saxton said. "The big fellow there sniffed
him out—in a bit of wood, a small forest area just off our course. The dog
smelled him…smelled something…"

They all heard in the Brit's words a hint of mystery. Randall Prouse
spoke for the others. "There's more to it than you're telling, I think," he
said.

Saxton said nothing, but they could see the truth of Randall's supposition in the Brit's eyes. Nigel said after a few seconds of considering the elder Prouse's words, "Yes. Most definitely."

He paced, obviously looking for just the right words.

"Seems our friend—Clark—found what he was looking for," Saxton said, finally.

He fell silent again, and the others looked at him, making him uncomfortable, knowing they expected a fuller explanation.

"You know him. Perhaps you know about the nature of his work."

"He's a reporter, a journalist," Cassie said.

"Yes, but I mean, specifically, the type things he is investigating—at least that he told me he is investigating," Nigel said.

"He told his father and mother he was looking into these Bigfoot sightings. He's been doing this since around 2001 or so, I think," Christopher Banyon said. "He seems to have actually seen one...in Idaho or somewhere in the Northwest...in 2001, I think, on some remote road while going to talk about sightings of these creatures in that area with a farmer somewhere up there."

"Well, I can tell you he found one. I saw it on the way down early this morning. We both saw it, didn't we...Peanut?" Saxton talked while moving to the rottweiler and patting him. "The creature was grotesque. Like a giant Chewbacca, a Wookiee, that thing in *Star Wars*. Only it was uglier, and he wasn't friendly—was he, mate?" He again patted and stroked Jeddy's head.

The sitting rottweiler glanced up at the man and emitted a high-pitched expression of agreement.

"Come here, Jeddy," the softly spoken command came from the bed, and all eyes went to Clark Lansing, who tried to rise on his elbows while calling to the canine.

"Come here, Peanie," he said.

The dog went to him and stood with his front paws on the bed beside Clark, who, though weakened, threw an arm around the thick neck and hugged Jeddy.

"Where's Morgie?" Clark asked Jeddy the question but turned his eyes to Christopher and Susie, who had come to his side.

"Where's my sister?" he said to the humans in the room.

"We will find her soon, Clark. Just rest," Susie said.

The disk descended and dissipated when it entered the tops of the evergreen trees. It grew pale in contrast to its former luminescence, then disappeared.

He was at first observing from a position just above the strange scene. His perspective changed, and he was looking at the ivory-hued face of the girl—April Warmath's lovely face, her features changing while she smiled at him.

She sipped from a golden chalice and wiped her lips with a scarlet scarf. Still, from the corners of the full lips, trickles of crimson ran in thin streams.

She opened her mouth, and her teeth metamorphosed to those of animal-like configuration. Fangs projected in vampire fashion, her countenance changing into a ghoulish mask while she laughed a hideous, gaped-mouth cackle.

"You okay, chap?"

Nigel nudged Clark's shoulder, causing him to struggle to a sitting position on the bed.

"What's wrong?" Clark asked, straining to get his bearings, then looking at his roommate.

"You were moaning. Was that Yeti after you?" Saxton said in a light tone. "Thought you were going to do something drastic."

Clark sat on the edge of the bed, rubbing his neck and shoulders, feeling the bruises from his encounter on the mountain's foothills.

"It's the girl," Clark said. "She gave me something in that hot chocolate."

"That's what's causing the nightmares?" the Brit asked, putting a hand on Clark's shoulder. "You going to be okay?"

"Yes. I'm okay," Clark said, standing and walking into the bathroom to splash cool water on his face.

He looked into the mirror and mopped his face with a towel. He knew the truth, now. Remembered everything that happened in the snowmobile cab.

"You are a fool for trusting her," he said to himself. She almost succeeded in getting him killed by the thing he had stupidly trusted her to help him investigate. He would get to the bottom of the betrayal. His would be the last laugh.

W here are our son and daughter?"

Mark Lansing's question elicited no response from Niles Gregory, who had brought them from Denver to the complex by helicopter. Gregory pressed the necessary buttons after inserting the chip-implanted card in the slot. The actions caused the doors to slide apart, and the black ops agent stepped aside to allow Lori and Mark to precede him into the elevator.

"Are they in this place you are taking us?" Lori's words brought a slight frown of concentration to Gregory's face.

"All in good time, Mrs. Lansing. You will have your answers, I assure…"

The platform on which they stood bumped to a stop, and the doors slid open when Gregory again inserted the card in a slot to the right of the right door.

They negotiated several hallways, the ultramodern facility seeming to wind forever and split into multiple other hallways off the one they walked.

"Where are we going?" Mark asked, beginning to get perturbed with the DOD agent's refusal to be forthcoming with information.

"You will see, momentarily," the agent said, leading them onto a hallway to the right that then angled off the main corridor they had been walking.

"Just another few turns," he said in consoling tone. "And, here we are." Gregory stopped in front of a door, inserted a card, and the door opened when he twisted the levered handle.

They entered a short foyer that opened into a spacious suite. The area had three rooms, Lori counted, her eyes taking in everything almost at once. It was like the expensive hotel suite in which she had stayed when on a trip at the underground complex at Taos, the time when she had been a rookie molecular biologist.

"We hope you will be comfortable here," Niles Gregory said, tapping the palm of his left hand with the credit card-sized suite key he held between his right index finger and thumb.

"It's very nice. But, what about Morgan and Clark? What about our daughter and son, Mr. Gregory?" Lori, too, was growing impatient. Her concern for her children was growing by the second.

"Let me assure you, Mrs. Lansing, sir," the man said, looking at Lori, then at Mark. "Your son and daughter are just fine. You will see them very shortly. First, we have a few things we need to talk over with you. Important things involving service you might be able to provide for your country."

Alamosa—7:05 p.m., the Same Day

Randall Prouse paced, his frame still straight and large, Susie noticed. She remembered the times in Jerusalem all those years ago. This was a very brave man. A world traveler, an archaeologist, a man of God. She imagined that, like Moses, his strength remained even into his eighties.

"Got 'em!" Randall's excitement caused Christopher Banyon to stand from the hotel room chair.

"Mark! That you?"

"It's me, Randy," Mark said from the other end of the cell transmission.

"What's been wrong? Where have you been? Couldn't get you on the cell."

"They just returned it to us, Randy. Some sort of things they had to check out first."

"Yeah, well. Let's not discuss anything top secret, okay. Probably have some special stuff in it now."

They both laughed, but Mark knew Randy's words weren't altogether meant in jest.

"Have you found your daughter yet?"

"Supposed to let us see her and her brother tomorrow first thing, according to this Niles Gregory guy, the agent who brought us here."

Susie walked through the hotel door, after going into the hotel room several doors away to retrieve Clark Lansing.

"Clark!"

Mark's words of greetings after the archaeologist had handed Clark the cell phone made the younger man smile.

"It's me, Pop. How's Mom?"

There was silence on the line.

"Dad? You there?"

Mark cleared his throat of emotion, then replied, "Yes. Yes, Son. I'm…your mother and I…are fine."

Again silence while Mark assessed the fact his son was on the other end of the cell call. He wasn't in the complex after all.

"Clark? You okay? Why are you there? We thought…"

"I was in the mountain government complex, Dad. It's sort of a convoluted story. I'm here now, safe and sound. Have you talked to Sis?"

"No…no. Not yet," Clark's father said, still in a daze from hearing his son's voice. "They said we can see her in the morning…"

There was hesitation in the transmission for a few seconds.

"Mom wants to talk," Clark's father said.

"Clark? Are you okay, sweetie?" His mother's words were put with tears.

"Yeah, Mom. I'm fine. Just a little bruised."

"What happened?" Lori's question was issued with urgency.

"I…I remember going to a certain spot with a girl…her name is April Warmath. We were in a snowmobile of some sort. A really fancy one. We stopped overlooking a valley, a forest."

He paused to reflect on the memory.

"It's all surreal. Seems like something funny was going on in that area with all those trees. And seems like there was unusual activity above the trees—above the valley—in the sky."

"Like what?" Lori asked.

"I really don't remember, Mom. Next thing I knew I woke up in the snow, with Peanut licking my face. Then I kind of went in and out of consciousness. Nigel, this new friend, he and Jeddy brought me into Alamosa where the rest soon joined us."

"We'll find your sister. Don't you worry about that, Son. I'm furious about all of this cloak-and-dagger stuff. They nearly let my son die, and now I can't find my daughter. What on earth is this all about? Got any idea?"

Clark let the question move around in his thoughts.

"Has something to do with the things I've been tracking all this time, Mom. Nigel and Jeddy saw one. Nigel took a few potshots at it with his pistol. Said he hit it directly. It just screamed at him and leaped into the trees. Then…just vanished."

"Vanished?!"

"Yep. He says it just disappeared. They brought me into Alamosa where I finally came to early this morning."

There was silence for a moment on the cell transmission, then Lori spoke. "They told us there is something we will be asked to do for our country. I remember hearing that kind of garbage a long time ago. They are up to something, and it involves you and your sister. You stay put with Christopher and the rest, sweetheart. Your dad and I can handle it here."

"Yeah, right. Like I'm going to do that, knowing the things you and Dad have told me about what happened with those experiments. Knowing the nightmares Sis and I have had all these years."

Lori said nothing for several seconds, knowing their son shouldn't be expected to do nothing under the circumstances. The history was so fresh in everyone's memories.

"We're supposed to see Morgan tomorrow morning. They've returned the cell phone to us, for now, at least. We will check in every two hours at the very minimum, Clark. If you don't hear from us within that amount of time, you will know we need help."

"Yeah, well, sorry, Mom, but I don't promise to wait on you to call me before we do something."

—

Ten minutes later, Clark sat on the edge of the bed in his and Jeddy's room. He had, he considered, just sworn off ever letting himself get close to another female. But Morgan's apartment mate—without expressing the slightest interest in him—was breaking down his resolve, and he welcomed the dissolving of his self-imposed moratorium on women. He chastised himself with the thought that he was acting as fickle as a teenaged girl.

Kristi Flannigan instructed him in the use of her cell phone.

"Just consider it yours until you get another," she said while fingering a button on the instrument's key pad.

"Really loved that phone. Knew it as well as my laptop," Clark said, not looking at the girl's index finger manipulate the phone's numbers but rather at her pretty face. She glanced at him and saw his attention was on her, not on her instructions.

When he saw she was onto him, he looked back to the number pad. "So, you have to push this every time in order to hang up?

She smiled, her beauty cracked a bit by the laugh lines that crinkled her peach-perfect face. This was a girl who liked to laugh...

"Clark. You know better. I'm not talking to my granddad," she said through her amusement. "Now, pay attention..."

He folded the phone and laid it aside on the bed. "I am paying attention, Kristi. Boy, am I ever paying attention!"

She saw in his blue eyes a twinkle that told her he was indeed. The lips were solemn but gently so. She was a woman of self-confidence, she thought. A cosmopolitan female who didn't fall for the first look or come-on. But, this guy made her feel funny. Not like the wise-cracking guys of her office...of the city...

"What's your story?"

"Pardon?" she asked, her eyes reflecting her surprise.

"Anyone special in your life?"

"Oh! You mean a guy?" She wasn't used to blushing, but she felt her face redden with warmth. Clark Lansing was even more straightforward than some of the Manhattan men she knew.

"No, not really. Just friends..."

"Good, that's good," Clark said, the serious expression on his face melting to an extremely pleased smile, his heart pumping with a lighter beat.

Nigel Saxton folded and placed the few changes of underwear in the backpack, having just returned from a nearby Laundromat. He missed the rottweiler. He would have to perhaps get one when he returned to England. Still, it wouldn't be the same. The dog was quite special. Helped save his life. The dog and old Zeke, he thought, zipping the pack shut.

He had, safely within the backpack, the photos from the ground reconnaissance they sent him to gather. He was fortunate to escape with his skin, much less with these important proofs of the fact U.S. allies were being kept from the whole truth about the black ops projects.

He could never take these through the Homeland Security checkpoints—through customs. He would hand them off to the one who could get them to Great Britain...

His thoughts were disrupted by a knock on his motel cabin's door.

"A moment, please!" Nigel shouted toward the door, removing the recon package and looking around for a place to put it. If they were unwelcome visitors, they must not find these. He lifted the top mattress and shoved the thin package as far to the center of the box springs as he could manage.

He rummaged through the bag and brought out the semiautomatic and stuffed it between his belt and waistband under his shirt before pulling the peephole cover from the door's center and putting one eye against it.

It was the old fellow, the archaeologist, and the two other men. He unlocked the deadbolt lock and welcomed them inside.

"Welcome to my humble abode," Nigel said, shaking hands with each.

"Looks like you're packing," Randall Prouse said, seeing the backpack zipped and in order atop the bed.

"Yes, sir. I must be off, I'm afraid. Got a plane to catch tomorrow morning."

"Aren't you the slightest bit curious about all of this?"

David Prouse's question caused the Brit to straighten, then stretch his head and shoulders while he looked toward the ceiling in reflective thought.

"There are many things about this that fascinate me, I must say. But, I'm expected back in England by my…company," he said. "I really would prefer to sniff things out with you chaps. I feel a certain camaraderie. No disrespect meant, but I especially feel such with that dog…Jeddy… Peanut, if you wish."

"Wouldn't you like to see Peanut find his mistress?"

Christopher Banyon's question made Saxton smile. "He saved my life. Yes, I would very much like to help him find his mistress."

"Can you not put your trip off for a few days?" Randall asked, seeing in Saxton's demeanor that as unimportant as Christopher's rationale for the Brit helping should have been, it proved the correct tact to use.

"Nigel, you are the one who knows your way through the mountain. You've done it. We will never be able to get access to the NORAD complex by a frontal assault. But, going back the way you and Jeddy came—through the mountain tunnel—we can maybe, somehow, enter the complex the back way."

David's words caused the Brit to again look toward the ceiling in thought.

"Actually, I've not been to the complex. Just dropped by helicopter to within a few kilometers of the valley area."

The three men were glad to hear him thinking out loud on the matter. At least he was open to the idea. David moved to try to seal Saxton's agreement to lead them.

"Clark has been there. He and the girl moved from the back side of the complex to that same valley. He can, we hope, retrace his and her movement back to the complex."

"Do you think he's physically up to something like that? It's quite a long, arduous journey, you know. Although…" he paused for further consideration. "…the weather is warmer—much better now…"

—

The amenities were all there. The inner-mountain complex's accoutrement couldn't have been any more hospitable. The thoughts ran through Lori Lansing's mind while she and Mark rode the conveyor belt-like surface that whisked them along at a rate slightly faster than one could walk at a brisk pace.

"This escaway inclines almost imperceptibly; doesn't it?" The man who accompanied them interrupted her thoughts.

"How far to where we're going?" Mark asked with impatience.

"Another quarter kilometer," the man, dressed in a black jumpsuit, said.

True to the black ops man's word, the conveyance stopped at a point where the passengers could move from off the surface by holding to handrails that led down several steps.

The three walked down a twenty-foot-wide corridor, the agent then making an abrupt left onto a much narrower hallway.

"In here," he said, stepping aside and holding open one half of the big glass, steel-framed doors so Lori and Mark could pass through.

Control boards and monitors were arranged ubiquitously, yet were well ordered throughout the cavernous room. The area was dimly lit. Lori immediately recognized the room as an experimental station for a much more intricate and involved complex of such control rooms that must surely lie beyond. It wasn't unlike the Taos underground of those many decades earlier, she surmised. But, the gadgetry was much more advanced...exponentially so, she calculated, scanning the enormity of the room.

"This doesn't seem structured for anything to do with military application," Lori said, not looking at, but addressing their chaperone.

"Very perceptive, Dr. Lansing," the man said, leading them through the room toward its center.

The middle of the gigantic chamber was open floor, completely encircled by the many computer control boards. A carousel-like drop-ceiling housed monitors above them while they stood directly at the center of the room.

"Don't be alarmed. We will descend now. There will be only a slight bump," the man said, manipulating a remote device he held in his right hand.

The platform circle on which they stood lurched with a slight jerk, then began a slow descent, just as the agent had promised.

After a light bump at its stopping point below, the man stepped from the circle and said, "This way."

They negotiated several hallways and smaller control rooms, the black ops man stopping at another large door, inserting a card that caused the door to slide into the wall recess, allowing passage through the opening.

"Please be seated," he said, gesturing toward large, comfortable-appearing chairs that were two of several such chairs and sofa-type seating that graced the room's plush décor.

"I'll leave you for now," he said. "Someone will be with you in just a minute."

Mark stood while Lori sat in one of the chairs.

He looked at their surroundings while he spoke. "One thing for sure, this place should be bunker-buster-proof."

"Just wonder why it's not military in nature, Mark. The NORAD is supposed to be all defense," Lori said, sitting forward on the chair, fiddling with a small handbag she brought with her.

"Black ops—anything goes here, honey. We both know it's got to be weird; whatever it is. We've been there, done that," he said.

"They've got our daughter. That's all I know," she said. "Oh, Mark, is it the same thing all over again? They've got our girl…"

Mark put his arm around her and knelt on one knee beside her. He kissed her cheek and hugged her. "The Lord is going to protect us and Morgan, sweetheart…no matter what's going on here."

She said nothing while blowing her nose with a tissue taken from the bag. She spoke after she had gathered her emotions.

"But, she doesn't know the Lord, Mark. The demons…they…they can do what they want without that protection…"

"Listen, hon. We didn't have that protection when we went through all of that." He made Lori look into his eyes. "But, the Lord is full of grace and mercy, remember? Remember?" he repeated, forcing her to acknowledge his words.

Lori said nothing but nodded.

"He will show us what to do. We know Clark is safe. And so will our little girl be...soon..."

The wall in front of them slid apart, and Mark stood, as did Lori.

"Please come in," the pretty, young woman said with a smile. "My name is April Warmath, and I will take you to Mr. Jenkins, director of some of our projects."

Mental alarms went off upon hearing the name. This was the girl Clark had named as being with him when he blacked out. They glanced at each other but said nothing, following their escort while she made pleasant chitchat as they moved down more hallways and through other rooms.

"How's the weather on the surface? It's been a while since I've been able to get out," April said.

She wasn't lying, too much, Lori thought, noting her fair ivory skin. She looked like she hadn't seen sunlight for months. Except to take her son to the danger point...

"Okay," April said, before either of them could answer the question about the weather. She inserted a half-plastic, half-metal key card into a slot against a wall. "Let's see if it works this time. I've been having trouble with this card. Guess it's time for a new one."

It opened the sliding door, and they passed through into yet another of the highly advanced control rooms.

"Mr. Jenkins," she said, looking in the direction of a wall full of monitors, at the center of which sat a high-backed swivel chair. The chair turned to reveal George Jenkins, whose tight-lipped smile greeted them as he stood and offered his right hand to Mark, then to Lori.

"Mr. Lansing, Mrs. Lansing," he said, the grin showing teeth now. "May I call you Mark and Lori? My name is George Jenkins."

They said nothing, returning the greeting with solemn expressions. Their daughter had been hidden from them, and they were not happy.

Jenkins's countenance dissolved to a serious expression, recognizing they would not be influenced by his façade of conviviality.

"We've come to see our daughter, Mr. Jenkins," Mark said.

"Yes. May we please talk to her…now?" Lori's tone was businesslike, bordering on stern.

"All in good time. She is well. You will see. Nothing to be alarmed about…"

"Mr. Jenkins. We are her parents. You expect us to not be concerned when our daughter has been…hidden away from us?"

"We've not hidden her. She has been helping her country. . ."

"Yes, Mr. Jenkins. We once did that. And, we know that you know all about our past, the …missions…we were asked to accomplish for our country."

Lori's voice was, she feared, quivering. But it expressed her anger in a calm tone. "Now, what do you want of us…"

"Yes, Mr. Jenkins. Cut to the chase. We aren't stupid. We're familiar with the way you guys operate," Mark said. "We want our daughter. We know we aren't here by accident. The thing with the airplane, taking only us and not the others for interrogation and now bringing us here. As I said, we aren't stupid, Mr. Director. What is expected of us in order to get back our daughter?"

Jenkins said nothing for several seconds, walking from the chair and pacing with his head down in thought, his thumb and fingers kneading his lower lip and chin.

"That's good, Mark. That's good. You know that we wouldn't have asked you here unless it was most important. You are among a very few—outside of those with the proper clearances—to be allowed this far into the security circle of this operation," he said, the tight-lipped, pseudo-pleasantness returning when he looked into Mark's eyes, then into those of Lori. "We will just cut to the chase, to use the well-worn phrase."

He looked to April Warmath who walked back into the room when Jenkins pressed a button on a console.

"Miss Warmath, please prepare our…guests…for the lab visit," he said, then turned and walked through a split that developed in a wall to his right.

The rustic façade of the hotel two hundred feet ahead gave the appearance of a Swiss chalet while Clark walked with Kristi, holding Jeddy's leash in his right hand. He switched the leash's leather loop to his left hand and reached to take the girl's hand with his right.

"Do you mind?" he asked, looking at her.

Kristi glanced at him and squeezed his hand, then looked again at the rottweiler, who walked at a slower pace in front of them than he preferred. He stopped to sniff one area of turf that was clear, the snow having melted in the increasing warmth of the day.

"Are you really up to going with them?" Her question brought a moment's reflection about things as they were.

His mother and father were somewhere in the area that hid secrets some clandestine types would kill to protect. His sister hadn't been heard from, and they had made no apparent effort to contact her family. He didn't remember—exactly—what had happened to him after he drank the hot chocolate with April Warmath. But, Nigel had said that something— a Bigfoot?—nearly killed him. Then there were the sights he himself saw while in the complex: the top secret matters of the RAPTURE technologies. Those of covert operations intended him to be found dead on the mountain slope. He had almost complied with their wishes.

"I've got to. My sister is being held. Mom and Dad—I don't know their status. And, I want to know more about all these things, about why they left me out there to…die, maybe."

"Then I'm going, too," Kristi said, her tone firm, not open to argument.

"That's cool."

She stopped and looked at him, her eyes wide with amazed delight. "You mean that?!"

"Of course I do. You're in great shape—and I DO mean great shape.

And, I don't want to be without you." Clark let his last few words drift into soft affirmation that he really meant them.

They didn't speak for awhile, starting to walk again, slowly following Jeddy, each momentarily lost in the magic that had just happened between them.

Susie Banyon looked down from the third floor of the hotel, a smile crossing her face.

"What are you looking so pleased about?" her husband asked, walking to the window.

"Look at those kids. Isn't that a picture of young love?"

Christopher looked past her to see Clark and Kristi, hand in hand, sauntering behind the rottweiler toward the hotel.

"Well, we are still like that," Christopher said, taking Susie's hand and bending to kiss her cheek.

"I know. But, isn't that a picture?"

From a half-block away, and in another hotel room window, a big man held powerful binoculars to his eyes, watching Clark and Kristi walk away from him. He pulled the glasses from his face after a few more seconds of watching, then talked into a cell phone.

"It's him. No doubt about it. What you want us to do?" he said, putting the field glasses to his eyes again, watching the two and the dog walk from his sight and into the hotel.

Lori emerged from the decontamination chamber, walking in a quick stride to her impatient husband. He turned from looking through a wide, rectangular window into the laboratory they, apparently, he thought, were about to enter.

He felt relief, seeing Lori. She looked none the worse for wear. He knew she had been through the same procedure they had inflicted on him. If hers was any more stringent than that to which he had just been subjected, it didn't show on her.

"Well, here I am, babe. Sorry to subject you to your best girl with absolutely no makeup. But, what you see is what you get."

She stood in a gleaming white jumpsuit, her hair, still the color of sunlight, with only the slightest hint of gray, he thought, pulled back and banded.

"You are more beautiful, not less," Mark said, looking into the bright blue eyes her nearly six decades of life had not dimmed.

She joined him in peering into the lab chamber, seeing the many lab-coated scientists going about their business, surgical-type masks covering their noses and mouths.

"What kind of lab is it?"

"Something biological. There's no doubt in my mind," she said, seeing in the setup things that could be in place for only one ultimate purpose. "It's a gestation lab of some sort. At what level of life, I don't know. Maybe microbial, maybe higher forms; I won't know until I get a closer look."

"And, so you shall," a short, bald man approached them from the de-contamination chamber that they themselves had left not many minutes before.

"I am Hans Sheivold," the man in the lab coat said in an accent nei-ther Mark nor Lori could make out.

"You will please pardon my not shaking hands," he said. "That would defeat our purpose with the decontamination unit," he said, gesturing with an open-palmed wave toward the decontamination chamber.

"Of course," Lori said with a nod. She understood the protocols of trying to maintain as pristine a lab as possible—especially where attempts of such things as fertilization and gestation projects were concerned. Such had been the primary nature of the Taos complex and of a number of other lab situations in which she had been involved during the years following.

The special knowledge she held only heightened her anxiety. What were they doing to Morgan? What did all of this have to do with those events of 1967? What about those occurrences going even back further in time to Mark's father's disappearance from the Cessna and her own father's being forced into clandestine activities after he reported the disappearance? And, what did this have to do with her and Mark's own involvement with the otherworldly inhabiters of the bowels of the Taos facility?

Although she asked none of the questions aloud, the scientist knew she had them. "You will know what is necessary for you to know in a very short time, Dr. Lansing," Sheivold said. "Your procedural attire is right here, in these sealed lockers."

He walked to one wall and pressed a button, causing the wall to split apart and a row of stainless steel-looking lockers to emerge and protrude into the room.

"I'm sure things have not changed that much, Dr. Lansing. We still suit up two legs at a time." The scientist laughed heartily at his own attempt at the joke while opening the lockers with a flick of a button at the side of one of the locker's handles.

"Voila!" Sheivold exclaimed when the door whirred open. "And, yours reacts the same, Mr. Lansing," he said, urging Mark toward his locker with an open hand gesture.

The back wall of the walk-in lockers of chrome-like metal had armholes. Lori knew the routine. Mark watched.

"This is how it's done, Mark," Lori said. "I'll help you when I'm finished."

The scientist looked into the lab through the window and then at an electronic clipboard, manipulating the number pad between glances at the activity in the chamber beyond the glass.

Lori slowly thrust her arms deeply into the holes while standing upon the foot pads that constituted the centermost part of the locker's floor. White material appeared to surround, then wrap itself around Lori, who remained calm until the procedure was completed. She stepped backward from inside the locker and reached with her gauze-like gloves that surrounded her hands. She snapped a white plastic fastener at her right side, then at her left, and the white, germfree suit was complete in its fit to her body.

Less than ten minutes later, Mark and Lori walked through an elevator-like door that hissed and popped when it opened and closed, breaking, then reinflating its vacuum seal.

They both wore, like all others in the lab, white surgical masks. Lori knew the masks were much more than ordinary such contrivances. "These masks are the latest, Dr. Lansing—or do you prefer your degreed name of Morgan?"

"Lansing," Lori said, surprised that the man had delved to that extent into her background. She stepped ahead of Mark but behind the stocky Sheivold while he led them farther into the room. The others seemed oblivious to the three, going about their duties of monitoring various computer generated numbers.

Sheivold spoke as they moved deeper into the vast chamber. "The mask actually tracks down and destroys each and every bacterial microbe that we might be harboring, then it filters the air and returns the cleansed air to our respiratory systems. This level of purity has never been attained before; thus, the reason why we don't have to have the old head-and-body coverings— with self-contained life support mechanisms—that made us look like men on the moon, deep sea divers, or something."

The scientist slid the card-key into a slot when they reached an elevator. They descended for ten seconds and exited into a scantily lit area, which, when Mark's and Lori's eyes adjusted, appeared to be an unfinished cave-chamber, the walls looking to be of mountain stone.

Hans Sheivold walked to the rock-face wall fifteen feet from the elevator door. Mark and Lori stood amazed when the man stuck the card into a slot they hadn't seen in the surface, and the massive rock split. They followed him through the schism, the rift closing once they entered an area that presented an even more astonishing sight. They stood looking down a gun barrel-like tunnel, whose rounded surface had a continuous panel of lights at its topmost section. The amber-hued light appeared to be a laser stream that narrowed until it vanished in perspective.

"Dr. Lansing, Mr. Lansing," this is our transport to the truly wonderful marvels of the complex," Sheivold said, leading them up three steps onto the platform to a gleaming metallic vehicle with plush seats. The vehicle, sitting atop a monorail that ran the length of the tunnel as far as the eye could see, was encased by rounded, transparent, glass-like material that fit the tunnel's contour.

"Fasten your belts, please," the scientist said, doing so to his own seat harness where he sat. "It's about a twenty-minute ride."

NINETEEN

Jeddy strained on the leash while Clark fought to hold him back. The canine was in a hurry to get to the patch of vegetation just behind the hotel.

"Guess he's held it about as long as he can," Clark said, laughing, then breaking into a faster walk to let the dog get to where he wanted to go.

"Yeah. I've felt like that before," Kristi laughed, her long legs easily achieving the increased pace.

Jeddy marked first one tree trunk, then another, before settling into sniffing out the area and enjoying the grass, now dead due to the onset of winter.

The shadows of the late afternoon covered the wooded area. Above the tree line of mostly conifers, the high mountain spires glistened magnificently in the late afternoon sky. The deep blues and purples mingled with the whites, grays, and glinting reds and oranges while the sun rays swiftly passed the Rocky Mountain peaks.

Kristi took it all in. She had seen nothing like it in her twenty-six years, and she breathed in the Colorado essence, sensing it for all it was worth. She loved Manhattan and its mountainous skyscrapers, but she never wanted to leave this beautiful place, she considered, glancing over and slightly upward at Clark. She didn't want to ever leave his side, either, she thought while they followed Jeddy, who himself seemed to drink in as much of the ambience as was possible.

"I thought Cassie and David were going to join us," Clark said, giving the rottweiler his head while he poked his black and brown muzzle beneath an evergreen bush. The dog jerked his head out, shook it, and sneezed before moving farther along.

"Bless you!" Kristi said with a laugh.

"Yeah, Peanut. Gesundheit!" Clark said, trying to maintain a firm grip on the powerful dog, who pulled him forward with a jerk.

"Guess they won't be joining us," Kristi concluded. "Guess they prefer their own company to ours."

"Well, that's more than fine with me."

Clark stopped when the dog stopped and seemed content to remain sniffing one small patch of ground.

Clark took Kristi's hand and pulled her closer, then put his free arm around her. "You really are something else," he said, his eyes penetrating deeply into her returned gaze. "I would much rather be here, alone with Kristi Flannigan."

She wanted to respond, to shout how she felt the same. But for some reason she pulled back. She let her gaze drop from his and turned to kneel and snap her fingers toward Jeddy.

He responded, walking to her and accepting her hug, then sitting in front of her while she stroked his head and playfully pulled at his ears.

"Why are people afraid of rottweilers? He's the sweetest guy there is," she said, hugging Jeddy by putting her cheek against the side of his head and pulling him to her.

Clark reached down to take her slender fingers, then nudge her to stand by pulling gently on her hand.

"I'm a sweet guy, too, you know," he said, again looking into her blue-green eyes.

Their lips met in a soft kiss that made her throat tighten with the flush of emotional rush.

Randall Prouse followed Susie and Christopher Banyon into the room from the balcony. The temperature was dropping, the night invading Alamosa.

"Still haven't heard from them," the archaeologist said, seating himself in a chair near the bed closest to the French doors that opened onto the balcony.

"I have a bad feeling, Randy," Christopher said, sitting across from his friend and crossing one leg over his other knee. "This whole idea seems...to have been a wrong one on my part."

"That's nonsense," Susie said, reaching into the closet to retrieve a rose-red cardigan, then put it over her shoulders. "The Lord has led us every step of the way. We are here for His purposes."

"Well, there's such a thing as getting ahead of the Lord, sweetheart..."

"I agree with her, Chris. The things that happened on that plane— they're just incredible. How does one explain that to anybody?"

Randy's words bolstered Christopher's spirits, and he sat a little straighter while thinking aloud.

"Certainly couldn't be just coincidence that Mark was there to bring that jet safely down. Randy, what on earth happened to those two fellows?"

"Well, they weren't raptured. We are still here," Prouse said. "I would be worried if it were just you and me here, Chris. But, Susie's being here makes me know their...vanishing from the cockpit wasn't the Rapture. If anyone's going in that event, it will include our sweet Susie."

Susie smiled but changed the subject. "They want Mark and Lori for specific reasons. It has always been about the Lansings and the Morgans." She spoke as if more to remind herself than to include the men in her conversation. "And now it's Lori, Mark, and Morgan in that top secret mountain area. It's got to have everything to do with all of the beastly happenings of those years ago and the recent dreams, visions, or whatever they are. And, we are included, have been brought here as part of it."

She looked at Randall, then at her husband. "Whatever this is about, the Lord is about to bring it out in the open. Don't you sense that, Randy?"

"You know," the archaeologist said, "I've been giving it some thought."

Christopher smiled inwardly, knowing that his big friend had indeed given the matters much thought. Randall Prouse was never without opinion. That was one of his most charismatic qualities.

"And, I'm convinced that these things aren't altogether from the enemy. In other words, it's not so one-sided. You are right, Susie." Randall paced the length of the walkway from the room's front door to the French doors that opened to the balcony.

"These dark things—the dreams, visions, the kidnappings, or whatever of the Lansing children—these are frightening, extremely troubling. But, you, Chris, were shown, in specific terms, what was happening to them—or apparently so."

Prouse sat on the end of one of the beds. "Each and every one of us has had a purpose in coming this far, dating all the way back to Jerusalem, to Qumran. That supernatural...storm; I don't know how else to explain it. The storm—the clash between...were they angels? The battle you witnessed just outside the aircraft on our way back to the states. My own UFO experience flying from Denver to New York. All that has happened since you got the idea to get us all together in coming here. The disappearance of those guys from the cockpit, running into this Nigel Saxton guy with the dog that belongs to the Lansing girl...it's all positively exciting!"

Christopher couldn't help laughing. His friend—in his early eighties—was as exuberant as ever, as passionate as those days ago in Jerusalem when he hornswoggled the Islamic fanatics during the time of the Six Day War in 1967.

Prouse paid no attention to Christopher's chuckle; his epiphany was too overpowering to notice. "What I'm saying is that I agree with you, Susie. It's obvious that the Lord is bringing all of this to light at this late hour of human history. But, what excites me is that our God will meet force with force. In other words, he won't let the dark dominion influence matters involving mankind without meeting those devilish activities with equal supernatural force from his heavenly realm."

Knocking on the hotel room door interrupted the archaeologist's ponderings. Nigel Saxton moved from the hallway into the room upon Susie's invitation.

"I've decided to have another go at them," he said, looking first at Christopher, then at Randall. "Where are Clark, and the others?"

They had waited longer to leave the wooded area that covered a quarter mile behind the hotel, and they picked their way back by keeping their eyes on the lights of the distant windows and of the blue lights high atop the light poles bordering the streets of the town.

Clark and Kristi scarcely felt the cold that pervaded Alamosa. The emotions of their growing feelings for each other warmed them while Jeddy led them toward the lights that shone between the tree trunks ahead.

"Do you think we can find Morgan by doing it the way they are thinking?" Kristi's question was one that had been on his mind.

"We can't do it through the front door. I remember nothing much of what happened to me after drinking that hot chocolate overlooking that strange place, but I won't be so stupid again as to go in there thinking there's nothing to worry about. I'm not sure how we can find her, or find Mom and Dad, but I don't think we will find out what's going on by doing it in the open."

Jeddy stopped at the end of the leash, his fur starting to bristle, his throat emitting a deep growl that grew in resonance with each breath he took.

"What's wrong, Peanut?"

Clark's words had no effect on the rottweiler, whose muscles swelled with the intensity of his concentration while he glared into the trees and vegetation ahead.

"Jeddy? What's wrong, boy?"

Clark moved to the dog, kneeling beside him and fingering his collar.

"What are you doing?" Kristi's apprehension grew in the darkness that had grown more noticeable within the past minutes.

"I'm setting him free of the leash. There's something up ahead."

Clark released the clasp that attached the leash to the metal rings of the collar. When he did, the rottweiler exploded from in front of them. He moved into the darkness but not straight ahead, as Clark had expected.

"Where did he go?"

"Don't know," Clark said, trying the impossible—to locate the mostly black animal in the darkness that now engulfed them. He mentally kicked himself for not bringing a flashlight.

Crackling of the underbrush ahead brought his and Kristi's senses to full alert. Was it the dog? No. The rottweiler had bolted from their sight in a second—to their right, not toward the area ahead—the direction in which the dog first indicated something was wrong.

"Jeddy?!" Clark's call brought no response.

"What is it, Clark?"

He gathered Kristi to his side and held her close while still trying to catch a glimpse of the dog, of any movement in the scant light between the tree trunks.

There! A flicker in the lights of the town!

He didn't know why, and there was no time to analyze why. He forced himself and the girl to the partially snow-covered weeds and grass, hearing the air go out of Kristi when he landed on top of her.

Shots thundered, and he heard the rounds whizzing above them—heard the bullets crash into the trees behind them.

"Stay down, Kristi! For Goodness's sake, stay down!"

He heard feet shuffling toward them and heard the assassin pull back the slide of the pistol for another round of firing.

The woods just ahead erupted with snarling and vicious noises of attack. The man behind the weapon screamed while the rottweiler tore into his body. The panicked gunman popped off several rounds into the woods in reflexive action before the dog's powerful jaws closed on the side of his face, then his neck.

The man screamed in pain and terror, doing all he could to defend against the rottweiler's determination to kill him.

Clark, satisfied the man was no longer capable of using the gun, sprang from his protective covering over Kristi.

"Stay down!" he instructed, keeping a low profile while carefully approaching the scene of the fight. The struggle stopped just as he arrived on the site, the dog standing over the gunman's unconscious form. The rottweiler continued to growl between labored breaths while poised rigidly over the body.

"It's okay, Jeddy; it's okay, Peanut."

The dog let out a slight high-pitched response and relaxed when Clark tugged on the collar and pulled him away, then attached the leash.

"Good boy!" Clark hugged and roughed the dog's fur while trying to get a look at the man.

Clark's boot toe hit something hard, and he felt the object by running his sole over it. The pistol! He reached into the snow and retrieved the weapon.

Holding Jeddy close to the collar, he bent to examine the man, a large man with blood covering his neck and face. Unconscious, he was breathing in low, shallow bursts.

Clark pulled his glove from his hand and reached to the unbloodied side of the face, placing his fingertips just beneath the jaw. The carotid pumped slowly...very slowly.

"Let's go get Kristi," he said, turning to walk the twenty feet to where he had left her. She met them before they could get to the spot where they had crashed into the snow.

"What happened, Clark? Who...what was this about?"

Clark put his arm around her. "Are you okay, Kristi?"

The darkness burst with vision-debilitating light in a fraction of a second. Then the night again encapsulated them.

When their eyes adjusted, they walked to the place where the body lay. But, it was gone. The man who had been totally incapacitated was no longer there!

"Clark! You there, Clark?"

The voice of David Prouse.

"Yes, David, it's us!"

Moments later, David and Cassie hurried to where they stood.

"What happened?" David asked. "We heard shots."

"What was that light? Looked like an explosion, but we didn't hear one," Cassie put in.

Clark took the flashlight from David's hand. He directed the shaft of light across the area of the scuffle. The attacker was indeed gone. But, much of his blood remained.

Mark and Lori had been whisked from the monorail as soon as it came to a stop. They knew it, even before the actuality of the things involved set in. All concerns Christopher, Susie, and Randall had held—all worries they, themselves, had harbored—were true.

They had not been asked to do anything since arriving at this strange place but rather were put in quarters that were little more than a cell.

At least they were together, not kept in separate holding rooms—not yet, at least.

"There are things that must be prepared," Hans Sheivold had told them when they were put in the small room. "Please be patient with us."

It was the last contact with anyone. It had been more than two hours, and they sat in the sterile room, still in the white, gauze-like attire given them those two hours and many miles ago.

"Where do you think we are, Mark?" Lori's question was asked in a voice that betrayed the stress on her emotions, which she had begun to lose control of an hour earlier.

Her husband reached to put his hand on her cheek. "We have to find our girl, sweetheart. This was the only way we could do that. We are at the center of…whatever they're up to. It's not by accident that we're here. Don't you think the Lord who got us this far can see to it that we complete our mission? That we find and get our daughter out of this place?"

"Yes. You're right, of course," she said, her tone more confident. "I just want Morgan with us."

"I know. I know, Lori. She'll be with us soon."

Mark stood and walked to the place where the wall had slid apart. The crack that ran from the ceiling to floor was almost imperceptible. He had to feel the place where the door halves met with his fingertips.

Like all the other times he had examined the surface of the wall, he turned away in frustration and returned to the small sofa and sat down.

The room was painted in white. Its austere décor provided the bare essentials: a bed; two small, white, vinyl-covered sofas that faced each other; a white metal chest of drawers framed by polished steel; and a tiny bathroom with a commode, a shower in one of its corners, and a triangular sink in the other. Curtains from ceiling to floor, only slightly less white than the rest of the room, hung against one wall. When Lori had pulled them apart more than an hour before, she discovered another wall of white.

"Tell you one thing," Lori said with a wry inflection that helped break the sterility and monotony of their surroundings. "White will never be the same..."

She jumped with a start when the wall parted.

Two large men dressed in black uniforms walked through the opening.

"They are ready for you. Come with us," one of the men said in a firm voice that somehow, Mark thought, seemed void of humanity.

Mark took Lori's hand and followed the man who had spoken while the other uniformed man trailed behind them. The men wore dark, goggle-like eyewear so that their eyes were veiled. Mark noticed that there seemed to be no weapons. He started to ask their destination but decided he would likely receive no response from their robotic escorts.

They walked through several small hallways, then into a large corridor, at the end of which was a massive wall that automatically split apart while they approached. They stood, then, inside a gargantuan chamber that flashed and glinted with light of every imaginable color. The room was a gigantic half-oval, its walls and ceiling unbroken by corners, angles, or windows.

The chamber seemed to be of polished metal with shimmering that changed in hues from deep copper to silvered chrome from moment to moment.

Despite the lights and the colors, the very atmosphere of the room created a sense of shadows—a dark ambience that somehow defied physical logic, Lori thought.

There was scant human presence at first, but from the moment Mark and Lori entered with their escorts, the chamber began to fill with activity, lab-coated people going about whatever business was at hand. All seemed to have the darkly tinted, goggle-like eyewear.

They had been given no such eye coverings. Lori wondered what might cause the need for such covering. And why had she and Mark not been given the protection—if protection was needed?

"Dr. Lansing, Mr. Lansing…"

Hans Sheivold walked to them from somewhere among the now milling crowd of lab-coated people.

"Sorry for such a long wait. But, preparations must be precise for our procedures…"

"What procedures?" Lori's question was adamant.

"Remember, Dr. Lansing. You and Mr. Lansing were told that you would be asked to help your country. Your cooperation will be most appreciated and rewarded."

The scientist's reminder was issued with a grim expression. Many of the others had gathered in a circle around Mark and Lori.

Sheivold reached to his dark goggles and removed them. At the same time, those surrounding them removed theirs. The man's eyes—like the eyes of the others—were black, the eyes of something other than human.

TWENTY

Christopher Banyon signed the credit card purchase slip, replaced the card in his wallet, and walked with Randall Prouse from the store.

"That was quite a bill, Chris," Randall said.

"Yeah, well, it's the Lord's money. Just hope we're putting it to its best use."

"That's why you have it, my friend," Randall quipped. "He knows you are the only one among us who could handle the responsibility."

The buying was done, and they walked toward the hotel where the others were preparing for whatever lay ahead. The thought of what the young people might face troubled Christopher.

"I can give them the clothes and things. Only God can give them what's really needed," he said while they stepped off the curb to cross the street.

"Yeah, well, he did that last night in those woods, didn't he?" Prouse said.

"Yes, yes. Oh me of little faith," Banyon said with a chuckle.

"That Saxton guy—he's a strange one. You think he's just out here to practice for climbing the Alps or whatever he claims?"

"Why? Do you think otherwise?" Christopher asked while stepping upon the other curb and onto the sidewalk that led to the hotel.

"He's awfully old to be so young, if you know what I mean."

"No, Randy, I don't think I do."

"He's more than just some kid out to climb the mountain just because it's there. At least, that's my perception of the guy."

"You think he's got an ulterior motive for taking them into the mountain?"

"Don't know what it is, exactly, Chris. Just seems more...experienced...than some young man out to see how many peaks he can climb."

"All I know is that he—along with that dog—saved Clark's life. And, it was you and I who talked the boy into sticking around. He was ready to go back to jolly old England, remember?"

"Yeah. I know," Prouse said, letting the rest of his thought go unsaid but wishing he could find a way to learn more about one Nigel Saxton.

"It sure isn't very pretty," Cassie Lincoln said ten minutes later while she and Kristi tried on the red, lightweight goose-down and miracle-fiber ski suits.

"Mine isn't exactly something Tyra Banks or Heidi Klum would wear, either," Kristi offered.

"And, they expect us to wear these?"

Cassie held out another garment—an off-white pair of large stretch pant-like trousers—

while she asked the question.

Kristi said, "Nigel wants to be—what do you call it? Camouflaged—as much as possible. The off-white will do that in the snowy areas, once we get through the mountain, he said."

Both girls checked the rest of the things from the shopping trip paid for by Christopher Banyon.

"Are you scared, Krissie?"

Cassie posed the question while plopping on the bed and, resting on her elbows, held for examination another less than attractive piece of apparel at her fingertips.

"Yes. I'm scared, Cass," Kristi said, turning sideways to look in the long mirror inside the closet wall.

"Krissie...What do you think...about the religious stuff? You know, the prayer that Mrs. Banyon...Susie...prayed for our safety?"

"What do you mean? She just thought it was the thing to do, I guess."

"Do you think there's anything to that stuff—you know, Christianity? Jesus and all of that?"

"Well, I've been a Catholic since I was born. They christened me when I was a baby. Yes. I suppose I believe in that sort of thing," Kristi said, moving to her bed to pick out another of the pieces of apparel she had purchased earlier that morning.

"David really does believe."

"What do you mean, 'really believes?'"

"He says Jesus is the only way to salvation—you know, to God and Heaven."

Kristi said nothing but rather stood before the mirror after trying on the hooded waistcoat.

"He says that…the Lord will protect us. "

"Yeah, but I'm hoping that the guys will do their parts in that," Kristi said, frowning—

unhappy with the reflection she saw in the mirror.

Randall Prouse was in a stew about things. He looked out the French doors of Christopher and Susie's room, past the balcony to the forested area in the distance.

Christopher talked with the three younger men.

"Are you sure you want to take those girls? Just seems like a thing best not to do."

"They insist, Chris. They're healthy—and in shape. We will take care of them," Clark Lansing said. "Morgan will want her friends with her."

Christopher said nothing but harbored trepidation about their chances for success in finding the Lansings and then getting out of the mountainous areas—areas Nigel Saxton had painted as rugged in some places.

"Well, I'm irritated, don't mind telling you," Prouse said, turning from gazing at the wooded region that led to the foot of the mountain.

"You want those girls to go with you. Yet you don't want me along."

"You know why, Grandpa," David Prouse said, shaking his head and grinning.

"Yeah. Too old…" Prouse stated his self-assessment with disgust.

"We're getting just a little beyond the years for such adventures," Christopher mused. He patted the archaeologist's shoulder.

"Well, I don't feel too old," Randall said but was resigned to the fact he wasn't welcome on the trip.

"Those girls will give a good account of themselves," Susie said. "Remember, Randy, I used to go with you guys."

"Yeah. And we were glad you were there, right, Chris?" Prouse said with a chuckle.

"When will you leave?" Christopher asked Nigel Saxton.

"Just before dark will be best, I think," the Brit said. "That should put us at the other end of the tunnel sometime around daybreak. Still give us a few hours of sleep."

The NORAD Complex—7:10 the Same Evening

"Lloyd Craxford is dead," April Warmath said upon entering George Jenkins's office. "He lived less than five minutes when they picked him up on the T-pad, the teleportation pad. But, it put him back together nicely. The dog did quite a number on him, though. They aren't sure yet whether it was the dog attack or the RAPTURE that was what caused death."

"Just as well," the black ops chief grumbled. "He failed miserably. I would have probably killed him myself."

Jenkins watched the monitors against the big wall to the left of the desk. The screens displayed the cavernous, half-oval room. Two monitors specifically homed in on the two "guests" who had been brought there for purposes of "assisting their country." Jenkins let the calming thought of Mark and Lori Lansing's fate run through his mind. Their son had gotten away. They and their daughter wouldn't get away—not until they were finished with them.

"What about the boy, the Lansing guy?" Jenkins asked, then sipped from a spoonful of soup from the bowl that sat on the pull-out tray just above the desk's top left drawer.

"He wasn't hit by any of Craxford's fire," she said, walking behind the desk. She stood beside the chair and massaged Jenkins's back and shoulders while he continued to watch the monitors.

"I told you that you should have let them take care of him. He knows a lot about things here. If the memories all come back, he can be a problem."

Jenkins slammed the spoon into the half-full bowl, swearing and standing after rolling back in the swivel chair.

"We've got his sister, his parents. He's not going to go to his reporter friends. Not as long as we have them."

Jenkins walked within several feet of the monitor that showed a close-up of Lori Lansing. She lay face up, her eyes closed, with a surgical mask and headdress that allowed only her eyes and parts of her cheeks to show.

"Collection of the woman's material should complete the gathering necessary to assure the child's DNA regime has what is required. What then?"

"They haven't made me privy to the next step in the process," Jenkins said, sipping from a cup April had handed him several seconds earlier.

"They just tell me it will be unlike any human who's ever walked planet Earth."

Mark sat with his wrists and ankles shackled. He had been in this position somewhere within the complex of corridors since Lori had been taken from him. He had struggled and was injected with an infuser gun of some sort. It had immobilized him but allowed his thoughts to remain cogent.

His questions to his guards the few times they had come into the small room had been ignored. Where was Lori? Where was his daughter? When would he see them?

The men, all in black uniforms—jumpsuits with strange insignias at the left shoulder—acted as if they hadn't heard his words. They wore the dark goggles, and he was just as glad. The memory of the eyes—the soulless, nonhuman eyes, black and glistening—haunted him. These were the monsters that had his wife, his daughter.

He had prayed as hard as he had ever prayed. His faith, he thought, was strong. But, it was wavering, and he had to do something to free himself, to get Lori and Morgan and—with the help of God—get out of this devilish place that was devoid of all that was human.

The wall that was the door slid apart and three men entered. Two of the men were his keepers. The third man, wearing a dark red jumpsuit, was taller. Mark was almost comforted by the fact the third one didn't wear the ominous goggles and that the eyes looked human.

"Mr. Lansing," the man in red said, smiling. "Sorry for the restraints. We simply can't have disruption within the facility. The work here is critical. We hope you will understand once you are informed."

The man gestured to the guards to remove the shackles.

"Your wife and daughter are unharmed, I assure."

"If everything is just fine, why wasn't I allowed to go with Lori? Why haven't we been allowed to see our daughter?"

The man held his hands up for calm while the guards lifted Mark by his biceps to his feet. "All will be explained, Mr. Lansing, I promise. You and your family are part of things that will mean a bright future for your fellow countrymen, for all of mankind."

His questions would be fruitless, Mark determined. He would play along—await his opportunity.

"Ours is a glorious mission, Mr. Lansing," the man said while walking from the room, then down the long corridor with Mark by his side. The two guards shadowed them just behind.

The language of fanaticism, Mark thought, listening to the young man. *Language of the brainwashed…*

George Jenkins had said little while they traveled at a rapid clip along the monorail. April Warmath thought it best to leave the black ops chief to the thought she knew was on his mind.

They couldn't blame him for the failure of the operative who missed offing Lansing. Besides, they needed him—George Jenkins—to complete the things they were set on accomplishing. They could find no one else as dedicated as himself to seeing that mission through to its completion.

The light of the tunnel ceiling seemed to stream into the top of the conveyance from its origination point far ahead while the glass-surrounded tram sped toward the valley. He was anxious to see the progress of the imperatives that those who had given the scientists the anomalous knowledge intended to accomplish in the lab, the laboratory that was not man-made and that had fabulous advancements beyond man's capability. Beyond man's comprehension, for that matter. He had never even been to the facility, had never even been allowed access.

But, he—George Jenkins—knew, at least much more than any other human, about the imperatives. The infants within the fluid were growing at phenomenal rates. The last of the genetic factors was about to be introduced into the subjects of the imperatives. Excitement raged within the DOD covert operations chief. His position—in practice—was at a height never before achieved by a mere mortal. He was far beyond being head of a top secret American Defense mission or even a joint Amero-EU Defense mission. George Jenkins was the key to their plans for mankind's future. He was indispensable because of the time factor. They wanted no delays in bringing the subjects of their plans to full growth in preparation to fulfill their destinies. These plans went exponentially past Project Scotty, past the BORG matters, and even beyond the RAPTURE technology.

"Something's ahead, George," April Warmath said, grabbing Jenkins's right arm. "We're going to hit it!"

The tramcar suddenly lost power and decelerated rapidly. The vehicle glided to a groaning halt within twenty seconds. They came to a stop just in front of three tall, thin human-like forms that seemed to hover just above the polished steel monorail.

All looked identical—the triune representatives of those who held his future and who held in their power all of humankind's destiny.

The middle figure emerged, seeming to float in front of the broad windshield. The thin line of a mouth upon the colorless face didn't move.

But Jenkins heard the thoughts while he stared at the large black eyes that looked as if they consisted of viscous, partly congealed liquid.

"George Jenkins. Your failure to eliminate the younger Lansing male has created complications."

A chill ran through the black ops chief while the girl clung painfully to his arm, her fingers digging into his flesh through the lab attire. He started to speak, but the pasty humanoid's thoughts preempted him.

"The one called Clark Lansing even now moves where they cannot be intercepted. They will cause problems if not destroyed."

"But, they should present no problem to you, with your powers and…"

Again his words were interrupted by the white-haired figure's thoughts. "For now, the ones of Abaddon are neutralized, George Jenkins. Forces of antiquity oppose Abaddon's imperatives. The Lansing group must be dealt with by your human efforts. You created the disruption. You will deal with the matter."

"Yes. Of course," Jenkins stammered. "But, how? Where are they—this Lansing group?"

"If that were within our knowledge, we would not need pathetic human assistance."

The form moved to stand again between the other two figures.

They said as one, their warning echoing within his thoughts while their images and words faded, "Do not fail, George Jenkins. Do not fail."

"Seems to me we might have come halfway," Nigel Saxton said, shining the long flashlight—one of several he had purchased with Christopher Banyon's money. The lights weren't as strong as Zeke's had been. But, he thought, he hadn't been able to open that strange flashlight. It had no place to put batteries—at least none that he could locate. So he couldn't take a chance on using it on the return trip.

The five moved along the tunnel, all squeezing with relative ease through the smallest of the passages that they occasionally encountered.

They had reached the point, Saxton recognized, that would require them to remove their backpacks, push the packs through the openings, then slither through the increasingly smaller openings in order to move further through the mountain.

The Brit wished the women hadn't come. His training and experience with MI7 had taught him one thing: Western man would protect women in a crisis. If crisis came, it might be difficult enough to simply protect one's self. Still, somehow, it seemed okay. The girls didn't seem out of place. There had been no complaints. Both seemed in good condition for the trek.

But, now they faced the first test. Not for the girls but rather for one particular member of the team.

"David, my friend," the Brit said, stopping in front of the smallest of the tunnel passageways to that point. "This is going to be a bit tricky."

The several flashlight beams focused on the hole through which they now must slither. All eyes studied the opening.

"Don't think I can make it," David Prouse said, seeing the hole in the base of the stone face that confronted them.

"Ah, yes. You will make it, my friend," Nigel said. "Anyone have some grease?" The joke brought muffled snickers that didn't change the looks of concern.

"I will go through first. Then the ladies. Then you, David. Clark, might need you behind to push."

Saxton pushed all of the packs through the opening. He then struggled through himself, having to put his arms straight out in front on the cave floor of packed earth. When he had cleared the hole, he moved the backpacks several meters along the tunnel.

Kristi Flannigan moved through the hole easily, her slim, athletic body scarcely touching the sides. Cassie Lincoln next snaked her way through, pulled gently by the Brit.

"Ah! Now for the engineering feat," Saxton said, going to his pack and removing a sharp spade, which he unfolded so that its short handle gave him the leverage needed to do the required work.

He dug into the cave floor, hoping the dirt was fairly thick. It was, and soon he had hollowed out a trench of eight inches or more from his side of the hole through its middle.

He handed the spade through to David Prouse. "Your turn, chap," he said. Within two minutes, the trench extended well into Clark and David's side of the tunnel.

David tried to move through flat on his belly, but his shoulders wouldn't fit, even when making them as slim as possible by holding his hands together, his arms as far outstretched as he could manage.

"Turn on your side. You should have room," Clark said from behind.

When Prouse tried the maneuver, it worked, and Saxton, with the help of Clark pushing and Cassie tugging, succeeded in moving the 235-pound attorney through the opening.

"We should be clear from here," Saxton said when they had again strapped on their backpacks.

"Where's Jeddy?"

Kristi's question caused all eyes to begin to search the cavern ahead, with their flashlight beams following the dog's paw prints into the distance.

"He's our scout," Nigel said. "He will be back. Another four and a half hours, I think, should do it," the Brit said, leading the group in the direction of the rottweiler's trail.

Christopher Banyon turned over first on his right side, then onto his left. He awoke from his restless sleep and felt for his wife to his left. Not finding her there, he sat up in the bed and turned on the lamp of the nightstand.

He swung his legs over the side of the mattress, his feet onto the carpet of the hotel room.

He looked around the room, then flipped the light on in the open-doored bathroom. He walked to the balcony and looked through the glass panels of the French doors. Susie sat in a double chair-swing, her feet curled beneath her, wrapped in a blanket. She was asleep. He opened the door and went to her, then touched her on the shoulder.

Susie awoke and tried to get her bearings. She smiled sleepily when she realized her husband was standing over her.

"It's freezing out here, sweetheart. What are you doing out here?" Christopher helped her to her feet and held the blanket to her body while he led her back into the room.

"I was praying…about the kids," she said, her thoughts still filled with drowsiness. She sat on the bed, shaking from the chill that saturated her body.

"Did you have to do it out there?" he asked, sitting beside her, then wrapping another cover, taken from the top of the closet, around her and trying to warm her with his own body heat.

"I wanted to pray out loud. You need your sleep, and I didn't want to wake you. "

"Well, you will get to talk to the Lord face-to-face if you're not careful, babe. And, your dying of pneumonia would sure keep me from getting sleep."

Susie said nothing but cuddled closer to her husband.

"Those young people are in good hands; I'm confident," he said. "Don't you have faith?"

"David is the only one among them who knows Christ," she said. "But, I know the Lord has this for them to do."

Christopher lay back on two pillows he first fluffed, then he pulled his wife to himself. She rested her head on his chest, still wrapped tightly in the blanket.

"I dreamed that something dark was following them, Chris," she said. "It was like one of those creatures they talked about; you know, the creatures Clark has been researching."

"Bigfoot?"

"Yes. That's it. I dreamed the thing finally found them…in that mountain, the tunnel, or whatever the place. It attacked them…"

"It's just the stories you've heard from Lori and Laura about Morgan and the thing that apparently stood on the path when the dog intervened and about the story Nigel Saxton told about what happened coming down the mountain."

"Maybe so. Maybe that's all there is to it. But, those...monsters...are real. Look what happened to Clark. They're in danger, Chris. We need to keep them in prayer."

The rottweiler lifted his head in the sphinx position beside Nigel Saxton. His forehead wrinkled and his ears came to attention while he stared into the darkness ahead.

The group lay sleeping in the hour just before dawn would break outside the tunnel. Saxton had figured out loud before they settled down to get much needed rest that—based upon the time traveled—they were less than a mile and a half to the hole in the cliff face he and the dog had entered before their previous trip toward Alamosa.

Jeddy's guttural growl awoke the Brit, who put a hand on the dog. The rottweiler stood, his fur, Saxton could feel, was bristled. The canine sensed something ahead. Nigel fidgeted with the snap on his backpack and withdrew the semiautomatic. He pulled back the slide with thumb and fingers, chambering a .40 caliber round.

He pulled one of the long flashlights from another part of the pack, knelt, and quietly stood to follow the dog toward the direction he led.

"What's wrong, Nigel?" Cassie, who was unable to sleep, whispered, startling the Brit.

"Don't know. The dog senses something up ahead."

Jeddy had disappeared from view, but when Saxton and the girl rounded a corner in the tunnel, they saw the rottweiler in attack mode, his body swelling by the second, his powerful muscles tense, spring-loaded for dealing with whatever threatened.

Nigel swung the flashlight beam around the sides of the cave, but neither he nor Cassie spotted the object of the dog's fury.

Then a form appeared, as if out of nothingness. It was a creature that stood almost the height of the high cave ceiling. The thing screamed, its mouth gaping to display canine teeth of several inches; its hideous, blood red mouth dripping drool; and its ruby-colored eyes gleaming in the flashlight's beam.

"Jeddy! No, Jeddy!" The Brit shouted to the dog, who stood his ground, snarling at the hairy, man-like form that hunched a bit, crouched slightly, then reached toward the dog and the humans, its huge arms and hands presenting a deadly challenge.

Saxton raised the pistol and sighted the almost-human head. He squeezed off three rounds, but the bullets seemed to pass through the creature's skull without contacting solid bone and tissue.

"Go back, Cassie!" Saxton poised for another series of shots while shouting the instruction to the girl.

Cassie turned to do as told but came face-to-face with another creature like the one Saxton faced. She shrieked, causing the Brit to glance behind him.

Jeddy launched his 115 pounds from his position between Saxton and the monstrous beast, past Cassie. The only thing she could see was the outline of the gigantic creature that blocked her way, its eyes catching the occasional reflection of the flashlight's ray bouncing off the cave walls.

Saxton fired several rounds into the beast that confronted him, to no effect. It leaped forward, and in an instant, grabbed the Brit, lifting him from his feet and crushing his arms with leathery hands five times the size of human hands.

The other creature started to move toward Cassie. The rottweiler feigned a leaping attack toward its midsection but quickly moved to the right, then locked his crushing jaws on the beast's leg. It screamed and hit at the dog.

The blow was glancing but still enough to knock Jeddy against the cave wall, stunning him. He recovered almost instantly and again locked his jaws on the back of the giant's left leg.

David and Kristi, led by Clark, scrambled toward the melee, navigating in the light of the flashlight's beam as Saxton used the instrument to flail against the creature's head. The beast nearest them, with the rottweiler hanging onto its leg, turned to face them.

David Prouse focused on the monster in the flashlight's rays. Its fangs gnashed while it let out an unearthly scream of fury. Then it half-turned, reaching a gigantic arm toward Cassie. David rushed forward in a crouch and slammed into the enraged creature. But his 235 pounds did nothing to move the giant, who grabbed him and held him level with its mouth, bringing him in range to rip him with the dagger-like canines.

Clark had forgotten about the flashlight he had grabbed from Saxton's pack when rushing to the noise in the darkness. He would use it as a weapon. He flipped it on, and the brilliant shaft of light shot to the monster who was about to end the life of David Prouse.

David dropped to the cave floor. The beast had...had vanished!

Clark's surprise wore off instantly, and he rushed past Cassie, who went to David. Kristi joined her in helping him to his feet.

The creature choked Saxton, whose face was reddened, the veins on his forehead standing out against the flesh while he continued to flail at the beast's head with the flashlight.

When Clark's light beam hit the beast and the man in their death struggle, Nigel Saxton, like David Prouse moments before, dropped to the floor of the cave.

Then the beast was gone! There was not a trace...

Mark Lansing called upon his Vietnam-era training to maintain his sanity. The torture wasn't physical, like some of his fellow pilots experienced in those days at the Hanoi Hilton, as the North Vietnamese chief torture facility was nicknamed. But, not knowing the status of Lori…of Morgan, was torture of the worst psychological sort.

The young, tall man in the red uniform had promised he would see his wife and daughter. But, the promise remained unfulfilled while he lay atop a hard bed, his head propped on a pillow covered in material he had never seen or felt. They had instructed him to get some sleep and said he would be reunited with his wife and daughter the next morning.

The wall parted, and he recognized the face he saw in the opening.

"Mr. Lansing…Mark," George Jenkins said. "Hope you haven't been too uncomfortable."

"Where's my wife and daughter?"

The question caused Jenkin's pleasant façade to melt to one of seriousness.

"That's why I'm here, to see that you are taken to them. But, first, we need to chat a bit, if you don't mind."

Mark sat on the edge of the bed while the black ops chief pulled a hard, plastic chair closer.

"Your nation is in crisis, Mark," Jenkins said, his facial expression becoming reflective while he looked to somewhere other than in Mark's eyes.

"You have served your country in a heroic way. During the time of Vietnam, the Six Day War. Those were times of crisis."

The DOD black ops chief stood and walked to behind the chair, gripping its back with both hands.

"But this nation faces one infinitely more complex today, Mark. You and your family are among the very few who can help with this war on terror that we face—that all of the civilized world faces, really."

Mark listened without expression but wanted to shout questions at the man whom he saw as an enemy, not as a friend. What about Clark? His daughter? His wife? Was this how citizens who are valued by their country are treated? What about all of the strange, demonic occurrences of those years ago, which now raised their hideous heads into his family's life? Sequestered, not allowed their freedom?

But he held his peace. There would be time to get answers. For now, he would go along quietly.

"I know that strange things have gone on in the past, and the events happening as of late are perplexing, Mark. But, they are not without reason, not without purpose."

Jenkins paced behind the chair while he talked.

"To get right to the point, it is all about developing technologies to deal with America's...and the world's, for that matter...crises brought on by the terrorism that threatens to overwhelm us all."

He sat down again in the chair and leaned back, seeming to gather his thoughts before continuing. "This war declared by President Bush is unlike any other in the history of mankind. Wars have traditionally had specific battlefields, battlefronts, specific beginnings and endings. Vietnam—with the Vietcong and their terrorist-like attacks—was a transition to the type we face now. Many times the lines were blurred in that one. But, it still had aspects whereby there were ways to project strategies for conventional forces to win against the enemy and so forth. This one—the war on terrorism—has no such aspects. There are no definable scenarios for conventional ways to end it—or even to fight it. And, it's worldwide. So, we must find ways to fight it that defies conventions."

Mark said nothing, looking into Jenkins's eyes while the black ops chief continued.

"It is true that we've had to stretch the boundaries of conduct and ethics in some cases in order to find solutions to this new kind of war.

But, with civilization itself in the balance, if there were ever a case of the ends justifying the means, this is it."

Mark interrupted but in a tone that was low key. "And, that's why my wife and daughter are kept from me? Why my son was used, then discarded, or whatever?"

The white wall behind Jenkins split apart. Mark watched the young woman walk to whisper in Jenkins's ear. She turned, then, and exited the room.

George Jenkins stood and said, "I'm sorry, Mark. We will continue this later. I've some urgent matters to attend to."

Two minutes later the black ops chief, followed by April Warmath, were met by Blake Robbins at the center of the enormous, half-oval room. The three stood looking out the bubble of glass-like material from a point high above the chamber's floor. The platform, encased in the crystal clear material, gave view of the activity below.

"What's this about their son? You found him but lost him?" Jenkins said to Robbins, who didn't turn toward Jenkins but rather continued to watch the bustle of lab-coated scientists going about the business of the chamber Jenkins was visiting for the first time.

"The coordinates on Saxton were correct. The satellites put the BORGs within the mountain passage. Everything went according to planning, until the BORGs were dispatched."

"Dispatched?!" Jenkins said with incredulity.

"They weren't recalled. Something ejected them from the inner mountain."

"What about the BORGs? Were they...damaged?"

"We don't know where they are or what happened to them."

Jenkins spit swear words, then said, "Incompetent fools! Are you all so inept?!"

Robbins turned from watching the goings-on below. He wore the tinted goggles, which he removed.

Jenkins's face became ashen, seeing Robbins's eyes were those of indwelling, black, ominous orbs that could plumb the depths of the soul when looking into human eyes.

"You have been made the overseer of security, George," the entity within Blake Robbins growled. "Your underlings have simply followed your leadership. Perhaps it is time for us to assess the effectiveness of that leadership."

Jenkins let his eyes meander from the abyss that was the young man's glistening eyes to April Warmath. He desperately felt the need for support. He found only two despicably black pools where the pretty green eyes had been moments before.

"Perhaps it is you, George, who is the incompetent fool." The words came from April's lovely, red lips, but the voice emanated from another place and time.

"We are instructed to bring forth Mark Lansing. It is time to put aside unproductive human diplomacy. It is time to explain what is intended and to show the Lansing sire the undesirability of the alternative."

Jenkins started to speak. His mouth, which had begun to form a word, transitioned into the hint of a smile. The DOD covert operations chief's eyes grew large and black while his soul gave up its humanity to possession.

First rays of sunlight glinted off the snowfield while Nigel Saxton surveyed Xavier Pass with the powerful binoculars. He handed the instrument to David Prouse, who scanned the area then gave the glasses to Clark Lansing.

"We came from that area," the Brit said, pointing toward a region that turned gray against the gargantuan mountain in the distance. "We were somewhere near the foothills of that peak," he said, taking the binoculars handed back to him by Clark and trying to focus on the place where he and the rottweiler had spent time in the old man's cabin.

"It isn't that far," he said. "But, it's so small, it would be impossible to make it out from here. Maybe if we had a telescope."

Kristi took the binoculars. "Well, there's nothing out there that's moving. Not that I can see," she said, handing the glasses to Cassie, who moved the instrument from right to left while Saxton talked.

"Somebody knew where we were. That means they still know where we are, my friends. Those animals, or whatever they are, were sent to intercept us. The thing that had me by the collar intended the same thing for me that the one who attacked you, Clark, had in mind for you."

"How can something just vanish like that?" David asked.

"That's been my experience—talking to people since I started looking into these sightings. No one can find a trace of anything. How is it that something that size gives everybody the slip? That's what happened to me in Idaho in 2001. That thing was in the headlights. It turned back to the woods and was just...poof! Gone."

"Are we going to try to find that old guy?" Cassie asked, handing the binoculars back to the Brit.

"Yeah. Guess we had better," he said. "He seemed to bring Jed and me a spot of good luck."

The snow field had melted considerably in the warmer weather and sunlight since the time Saxton and Jeddy had left it, traveling the tunnel toward Alamosa. Still, a path had to be broken through the foot-and-a-half deep snow, and Nigel—followed by the rottweiler, the girls, then Clark and David—led the way toward the spot where he thought Zeke's cabin was nestled near the mountain's foothills.

More than forty minutes later, the others stopped when the Brit put his right hand up after stopping to assess their location.

"This is the spot," he said, standing on the carpet of snow. "It has to be the spot. Those two distinctive trees sat directly behind the old man's cabin," Saxton said, looking perplexed while at the center of the area where he was certain he and Jeddy had stayed with Zeke.

All sense of time eluded him. How long had it been? Hours, for sure. His beard had grown to the prickly point.

Mark paced the room where Jenkins left him—how many hours ago? He had finally slept—from sheer time elapse, he considered. But, it had been rest well needed. Now he had a fresher mind since waking up after bouts of fitful sleep that had preceded the deeper, longer sleep.

The big wall roared apart, causing him to spin in surprise toward the black-uniformed men.

"Let's go," one of them said solemnly from behind the dark goggles.

He started to question them, to ask where they were taking him and why. But he decided against it, not wanting further delay in learning about whatever was going on. He would at least be out of the cage that masqueraded as a sterile hotel room. Maybe, just maybe, they would take him to Lori...To Morgan.

He walked between his escorts, observing the strange, undulating movements of the corridor surfaces. The atmosphere about them seemed to breathe with indefinable influence that made the air that surrounded him pulsate with pressure. Mark thought how the sensation was not un-like cockpit pressurization in the F-4 Phantom fighters he flew in Vietnam and the Middle East. But, then, the pressurization, once done, was fin-ished for the duration of the mission. This was constant pressurization, then release. Though it was not an unpleasant sensation.

The very air seemed to consist of colors when the oval-shaped gleam-ing metal wall split apart, and he walked between his escorts into the gigantic chamber. Hues of every description filled his eyes, the odors of the chamber, like the pressurization sensations, not altogether unpleasant. The psychedelic ambience tended to mesmerize one's thoughts, he con-cluded while the three of them walked past the lab-coated people, who sometimes turned to glance at him through the black, slitted glass behind which their eyes hid.

His escorts nudged him onto a round cylinder that stuck four inches high from the stainless steel-like floor. The cylinder began moving up-ward and soon came to a stop when the round platform surface was flush with the room floor. Mark scanned the area, seeing it was surrounded by a clear bubble that allowed 360-degree viewing of the chamber.

"Greetings, Mark Lansing," George Jenkins said, approaching him from a nearby console of control devices. But, the voice was not of the black ops director. It was strange, like an echo in an empty fifty-gallon drum.

"At last we can achieve good things for America, for the world," the entity inside Jenkins said in a strangeness of tone that implied its delight.

"Where are my wife and daughter?"

"You will soon see them. They are unharmed. And, whether they stay unharmed is...well...up to you, really."

"What do you want me to do?" Mark's rage was growing. He forced himself to remember the rules of capture. Remain calm. Only calm brings rationality. One accomplishes nothing by rage or panic.

"You will be inculcated shortly. You will then understand...the imperatives of our projects..."

Randall Prouse's cell rang. He looked at the caller identification display. "I think it's Nigel Saxton," he said, not able to remember the strange number Saxton had given him to expect if the Brit could get through to him. They had discussed that almost certainly an ordinary cell phone would be of little service. But, Nigel had a special phone that employed geosynchronous satellite technologies.

Christopher Banyon moved closer to Prouse while the archaeologist talked.

"Randall Prouse," he said, his eyes brightening and looking toward Christopher when he heard the voice on the other end.

"You're through the mountain. That's great! Run into any problems?" Prouse listened for a second, a frown taking the place of his earlier expression of optimism.

He listened for a minute to the Brit explain about things that had happened.

"Yes, I understand, Nigel," Randall said, finally. "Yes. We will be ready for your call."

He folded the cell phone and looked at Christopher, then Susie Banyon.

"A couple of those Yeti things intercepted them. But, then they just... vanished."

"My Lord, you were given a dream-vision," Christopher said. He looked at Susie and took her hand. "We are being shown that something is going on, something to do with the struggle against spiritual wickedness in high places…"

"Saxton says he has specific instructions for us, should he call and need us to help them. He will call if he wants us to implement them."

"What kind of plans?" Susie asked.

"Something to do with help that's available to him in the area if it's needed," Randall said.

"They are going to need it! Those…creatures…sent to destroy them. They are definitely going to need help," Christopher put in, a worried, puzzled expression on his face.

"Yeah, well, this guy, Nigel, isn't just a youngster out to climb mountains. It's just like I said, Chris. He's out here for other reasons. I'm betting it has something to do with all this government business, all these strange things going on. He's probably an operative of some sort."

"But, for who?" Christopher asked.

"Probably an ally. Maybe the UK, maybe the EU. Fact is, he probably indeed can call upon help to extract himself from…whatever situation he might find himself facing. But, I don't know how that would translate into removing four other nontrained types out of harm's way."

"The beasts didn't get them. They vanished. There's a much greater force at work here than those trying to stop those kids," Susie said.

Nigel Saxton's worries were growing by the minute. Why did he go against everything he had been taught—against everything he knew was the correct course of action? Four untrained people, totally unprepared for the dangers they might face, two of them women. Quite fit women, perhaps, but not with the kind of strength that would be needed to climb some of the rugged rocks of this man-killing terrain.

Everything was fine so long as they could move as they did now, along the relatively flat, smooth plain of Xavier pass. But, not in the cliffs and crags where they must find refuge if needed.

The weather was another matter. It could turn at any moment. It could go from the forty-five degrees and sunny to ten below zero and/or blizzard conditions.

The thing was done. They were his responsibility.

But a much greater worry filled his thoughts while he led the other four and the rottweiler toward the valley, if not all the way to the valley of the strange goings-on, at least to where they could give Clark Lansing—the Brit hoped—a reference point so he could by backtracking find the back side of the secret mountain complex.

The greater worry involved the weird things. The disappearing—what were they? Yeti? Bigfoot? Ezekiel, the old man who seemed, sometimes, as elusive as the hairy, four-meter tall creatures?

The cabin had been there on that very spot. The log home had been a welcome refuge after Zeke had saved his and the dog's lives. Had the enemy taken the old man? Destroyed, then erased the log home from the snow field of Xavier Pass? It didn't appear that that had happened. It looked as if the log building had never been there. But, Zeke had been real. Saxton considered that he had the old man's strange flashlight to prove it. Ezekiel did exist...

The big monitor screens were like none he had seen. They appeared to be holographic—three-dimensional in their presentation of the scientists while they engaged in the business of this mind-boggling laboratory.

Mark looked at one screen, then the other. Nausea rose from the pit of his stomach.

"I see you recognize the subjects of all the activity," Blake Robbins said, looking at the screens, then back at Mark.

"You see? They are being well cared for," Robbins said when Mark made no response.

"It is time that you are made aware of the importance of these procedures and know why we brought you and your family to this laboratory," Robbins said in a voice much older than it should be, coming from a man in his early- to mid-thirties.

Mark didn't hear him, his concentration on his wife's face while she lay face-up on the gurney they had just rolled into the area beneath the bright operating room lights. Then, his daughter, like her mother, was rolled into place, the blue-garbed men and women—all wearing the dark goggles—working over Lori and Morgan.

"You once interrupted our activities to improve upon humankind when you were Captain Lansing. You destroyed our pursuit helicopters that day in the Gulf. Remember?"

Mark glanced at the tall Robbins, who looked downward at him while he asked the question.

"Yeah. I remember," Mark said. "They were trying to blow the cabin cruiser to pieces."

"Yes, well, there must be no more such interferences with our desire to help mankind achieve its ultimate destiny."

"And, exactly what is that?" Mark asked with anger rising in his voice.

"Why, to improve mankind's genetics, of course. To eliminate disease, death, poverty...all that plagues your kind."

"What about you? Are you not our kind?"

"So to speak—when combined with the friends of earth."

"Friends of earth? From other planets, you mean?"

"From other...places, let's just say," Blake Robbins said. "Other times, other places..."

"Look, I know who you are, what you are," Mark said, starting to stand. The big guards behind him forced him to sit again.

"Oh?" the voice within Robbins's throat said. "And who—what—are we?"

"You've been here before doing these same things. You've been here all along."

"And, what else do you know, Mark Lansing?" the question was an echoing snicker.

"That the word of God talks about you in Genesis 6 and in Ephesians 6:12. That Jesus said it will again become like it was in those antediluvian days. That violence will fill the whole earth, that you will again try to change the genetic makeup of human beings."

The invader within Robbins cackled; then he removed his goggles, unveiling hideous black eyes that glared at Clark as if peering from the abyss.

"This is why you need our kids and my wife?"

"And, you...especially you, Mark Lansing," the thing growled.

When Mark didn't reply, the entity said, "The male contribution is needed to complete the project...our imperatives for bringing in the kingdom."

"What kingdom?"

"Well, certainly not the kingdom you and all the Jesus sycophants think is coming!"

"There's only one other possibility," Mark said. "And, it won't work. It didn't work before the Flood of Noah's day. It won't work now."

The indwelling voice grumbled its displeasure with the insolent human. "It will. And it is you that will make it work."

"How so?"

"The man was instrumental in the downfall of your kind. Adam was in disobedience—not deceived and deluded like the woman. It is the man who must provide the...to put it simply...the DNA for mixing with the Benai Elohim seed."

Mark's senses grew dark as his emotions of rage, combined with the enormity of what was happening to his family, hit him with full impact.

"Why my wife and daughter, then? If they can't help you in your..."

The entity's voice interrupted Mark. "They have both been programmed from long ago. Don't you know that? The woman called Lori has been programmed since her time in the labs of Taos. You and she were simultaneously programmed, given certain supernatural predispositions to provide genetic material necessary to bringing forth a special hybrid."

Mark again tried to leap from the chair but was forced to sit.

"Your offspring have been the beneficiaries of earlier rearrangements with you and your woman's cellular structures."

"What are you going to do with us?"

"The girl, your daughter, provided a young, viable ovum for use in receiving the seed of the coming kingdom," the hollow, echoing voice said.

"Your wife provided part of the DNA and other factors to introduce into the now-growing new earth dwellers. You will provide the final DNA that will complete the process begun before you and the woman were husband and wife. Before you became the follower of the abominable one."

Mark looked to the monitor screens—one containing the close-up of his unconscious wife, the other of Morgan. He looked to Blake Robbins, whose eyes were glistening pools of black.

"You will cooperate if you wish your wife and daughter to be set free," Blake Robbins's possessor said.

The early evening sky above the westernmost edge of Xavier Pass began to darken. The outcroppings of the cliffs that turned into the mountain a half-mile distant provided a good place to camp.

The temperature hovered at forty degrees, Saxton noticed after letting the thermometer hang from its chain from a point sticking out from one of the boulders. The sky was clear. No snow.

Cassie and Kristi sat near the small fire the Brit had made from twigs. They petted Jeddy, who lay between them on his stomach, enjoying the scratching.

"You think he misses Morgan?" Kristi asked.

"Of course he does," Cassie said, giving the dog's huge head a hug. "Poor baby," she said, receiving a lick on her face for her affection.

David Prouse handed Cassie a tin cup of coffee Saxton had just finished brewing. "Lucky doggie," he said, himself rubbing between the rottweiler's ears. "Some guys get all the attention," he said, sitting beside Cassie.

"Well, some guys deserve it," Cassie retorted, then sipped from the cup.

"Here you go," Clark said to Kristi while handing her the tin cup with coffee and powdered cream.

Nigel joined them, with the rottweiler between them.

"So, what's our plan, Nigel?" David asked.

"Haven't got a specific plan. We'll just play it by ear, as they say."

David looked at Saxton over the cup while he sipped. He had to frame the question in a way the Brit would—perhaps—respond truthfully. If David's suspicions were correct—as he and his grandfather had discussed—there were more reasons for the man's proficiency in this wild, mountainous country than simply that he was a climber in training. Finally, the lawyer in him surfaced to break the ice.

"Nigel. Grandpa and I were talking, and we both agreed. You carry yourself much too well to be just some practicing mountain climber."

David's bluntness surprised even himself. But it came from his legal training, he thought, watching the Brit's expression as he absorbed the question.

"Guess you wondered why I would come back here when I didn't have to do so, right?"

"Something like that. Yes," Prouse said.

Nigel's slight smile, then more serious demeanor made David believe he would get the manufactured version of the Nigel Saxton story—not the true one.

"You and your grandfather have good instincts," the Brit said. "Actually, I'm an operative for a—shall I say—a group that is friendly to governments of the West, including the American government."

All eyes widened and ears came to attention. Nigel's tone was matter of fact, not stiff or contrived.

"I was sent to learn about whatever it is that is going on out here in these mountains." He looked at Clark.

"Sorry, chap, about that tiny bit of fiction I gave you on that ride into Alamosa. At that time I didn't know you and didn't know what I faced."

He drank down the black coffee, put the cup aside, and sat on his backpack, his forearms and hands dangling from where his elbows propped upon his raised knees.

"Still wouldn't be telling you except that I'm going to need your help. And, you are going to need mine. We must trust each other because we all know it's something beyond the normal we must conquer."

"You have a number?" Kristi Flannigan asked. "You know...007 or something?"

"Something like that. But my activities haven't been in such exotic places as James Bond traveled, I'm afraid. They've been more like sheer agony, like in these mountains when it's freezing, and there's a blizzard blowing."

"Why were you sent?" Cassie asked.

"They...that is, the group I represent, have been concerned for some time about the intelligence that has been kept from them regarding the unidentified disks that have been moving in and out of these places—and about the fact that certain technologies, believed to have come from reverse engineering since Roswell, are not being shared with America's allies."

"What are you supposed to do?" David asked.

"Get photographic evidence. I'm hoping I can accomplish with the help of Clark what I couldn't do before: get into that area I saw the disk fly into and then (as it seemed) melt into the forest on that valley floor. I am hoping that you, Clark," he said, looking at him, "might remember something that could get me into the complex down in that valley, whatever it is."

Clark thought for a few seconds. "But, I don't really remember anything much after drinking that hot chocolate, except for some strange lights in the sky just above the wooded area."

"Maybe revisiting will jog the old memory, eh, mate?" Saxton slapped Clark playfully on the leg. "And we can backtrack to the area where you took that snowmobile ride—find the back side of the inner-mountain complex they guard so closely."

Then, all ears heard a thumping in the distance. A helicopter!

TWENTY-TWO

Nigel dove to the campfire and began shoveling snow onto the flames. David joined him.

"We've got to move from here. *Now!*" Nigel's shouted words set in motion a quick gathering of backpacks. With the flames doused, Nigel bolted from the campsite, followed by the others, who jogged to keep up with the Brit.

"Jeddy!"

He felt the rottweiler brush past him, headed in the same direction as he himself was leading the others. He didn't want the dog to provide a target for the helicopter's search lights. Jeddy's big, dark body would be easily spotted on the white field below. The dog must be reined in; he had to risk it.

Nigel flipped on the flashlight he had instinctively grabbed from his pack. Its bright beam struck the big dog's rump in the distance. Jeddy was moving into a dark area beyond the outcropping boulders. He didn't see a better spot to hide from the oncoming aircraft, so he followed the canine into the place that turned out, they quickly learned, to be a cave barely big enough to accommodate the six of them.

Once everyone was inside, Nigel removed the semiautomatic and held it toward the cave entrance. Clark pulled a pistol from his own pack.

"Didn't know you brought one," the Brit said.

"It's the one the guy tried to kill us with in the woods. The clip has a few rounds," Clark said.

Jeddy began to growl, expelling his anxiety-anger in short bursts that grew louder with each growl while he stood at the cave entrance looking past the numerous boulders into the vast plain of snow beyond.

"Easy, boy," Saxton said, easing beside the dog and kneeling as he tried to see into the dark distance.

The roaring of the helicopters grew louder. They were now within a hundred meters outside the outcroppings of stone. Powerful lights shone from the choppers' bottoms. There were two, and they hovered fifty meters apart, the Brit surmised. Big helicopters made for cargo, he figured.

"They must have troops," Nigel said over his shoulder to the others.

Clark stood at the opening, looking with Nigel and Jeddy into the brightness that illuminated the snow-covered ground directly beneath the choppers. Several large, dark objects dropped the ten feet or so into the snow. Then three more objects dropped from the other copter.

"Guess we've had it now," Clark said.

The rottweiler stiffened, his muscles bulging while his growling intensified.

"Looks like six of them," Saxton said. "That what you counted?"

"Yeah," Clark said but not really knowing, having not counted.

Nigel pulled the pistol's slide back and released it, chambering a .40 round. Clark did the same on his semiautomatic. He had only four rounds, plus one in the chamber. A gunfight wouldn't last long, he thought.

The choppers' engines revved to full power, and they lifted out of view. The area was totally dark now, and the group in the cave dared not shine their flashlights toward the advancing party of however many…

Within about sixty seconds, Nigel estimated, sounds of shuffling disrupted the silence. Even the dog had remained quiet, but now began snarling when he heard the noises, which the human ears soon heard above Jeddy's low growling. Whoever it was approaching had a fix on the cave and seemed to be moving in for the kill.

"Let's give them all we have," Nigel said to Clark, who trained the pistol at arms length into the opening.

The predators hadn't used light of any sort, yet. Nigel considered whether they had night vision equipment. Probably, he thought.

Jeddy burst from the opening at the moment movement sounded not fifteen meters from the cave entrance. Clark and the Brit heard the rottweiler growling. He had taken a position between the advancing force and the cave.

Growling screams of another sort broke in the distance. Both Nigel and Clark had heard the sounds before; it was the creatures!

"Let's do what we can," the Brit said. "Let's not turn on the lights until we are near them.

Both men briefly thought how the pistol fire would most likely be without effect. These creatures had been hit point-blank but had reacted as if the rounds had not touched them. Still, they had to do something...

Nigel broke to the left just outside the cave; Clark went to the right.

The beasts—some hunched for attack, others standing and screaming, hideous mouths gaping and closing in rage—were upon them.

Jeddy half-circled in front of the six creatures, one scrambling almost on all fours to get at the dog.

Clark switched on his multi-batteried flashlight, and the horror of the creatures made him and those watching from the cave collectively expel horrified gasps. David made the women get behind him. His would be the final line of defense, but to what purpose? The huge giants would tear any human being apart in one easy rip. And, there were six of them!

Nigel fired rounds into the creatures nearest him. Clark took aim more carefully. His 9 mm spoke less loudly. The result was the same as Saxton's efforts. No effect!

The monstrosities now had nothing to stop them. Jeddy had to retreat a meter at a time. He was no match for one, much less all of them, but his instinct was to divert, not to attack while he leaped forward several feet, then retreated, grabbing the attention of the beast nearest to the cave's mouth.

Saxton reached for the flashlight attached to his belt. It was the old man's flashlight. The batteries must be down by now. But he flipped the switch and a burst of light shot from its thick lens. The creature closest to Jeddy turned into unalloyed whiteness, then was no more.

Vanished! The realization suddenly hit the Brit. The light Zeke had given him—something was going on with that flashlight!

He directed the beam to each of the creatures, which erupted into light that made all in the cave have to shield their eyes. The monsters popped into nothingness as the light directly hit each one.

"Lord be praised," was all David, standing wide-eyed in front of the girls could think to say. "Thank you Lord!"

"The choppers are still out there," Nigel said, "searching the area for traces of the vanished beasts."

"What happened?" Clark asked.

"Same as in the mountain," the Brit said. The light from this flashlight hit them, and they vanished. What on God's good earth do we have here?" the Brit wondered out loud, looking at Zeke's flashlight.

He saw the cave at the top of the steep embankment, and he tried to make sense of his circumstance. A gem-like cylinder set against a dark, ominous sky, sparkled just above the ridge that was the roof of the cave. Light seemed to shoot in flashes of lightning from beneath the hovering gem and evidently penetrated the roof, slicing into the cave itself, because light could be seen within what had been darkness. Light shot from the cave and streamed outward. It was a lighthouse, not a cave, he considered.

He stood now not on a hard, sand-packed surface but upon a pebbled surface. A dazzling shaft of light was streaming from somewhere; he couldn't tell. The beam lit the area, and he looked around, as in a slow-motion daze. The Dome of the Rock? The Al-Aqsa Mosque? What was he doing on Moriah?

A monumental storm rolled and tumbled above him, its darkness descending and obscuring his view. These were the clouds of the sort he had seen roll across the plains of northwest Texas and Oklahoma; they were the kind that produced twisters. Twisters in Jerusalem? This was a nightmare, and he must pull away from it, must just blink and open his eyes and be at home in bed.

No, it wasn't a dream; it was something more. A vision of some sort?

The clouds began to scroll apart, and the sunlight poured through, a big column of light centering somewhere ahead on Moriah's top. He walked forward. The clouds continued to boil, but permitted the light's wide shaft to illuminate the flat surface where it struck.

The light grew dimmer—or the shaft more translucent—and he saw within the light the figures of two human forms. They were small forms at first. Infants, then toddlers, but figures that began to grow and soon stood beyond human height.

He stared, squinting to see. The forms were of young men. They stood tall and proud and had looks that exuded their arrogance in ways he just knew were the manifestation of something unspeakably wicked, something unholy.

The young men surveyed their surroundings. He saw it then, the hands of the beings. Blood was dripping from their hands, their finger-tips.

Christopher awoke, sitting up in bed, startling Susie, who reached to steady him.

"What's wrong, Chris?" she asked, seeing his forehead soaked with droplets of sweat. She hurried from the bed to the bathroom, returning in a few seconds with a towel. She mopped his face.

"What's the matter?" she asked again, seeing his eyes wide in a look of fright.

"Oh, a dream, I guess," he said, his expression relaxing to one of relief that he was in the hotel bed with his wife in front of him.

"Susie, it was so real. I think it was another vision or something."

He eased back onto the pillow. Susie climbed into bed beside him.

"These two young men, I guess they were on top of the Temple Mount. There was a storm and its aftermath seemed to have planted them there on top of the Mount's surface. A big shaft of light came from be-tween the storm clouds and just…stood the young men…"

He stopped to remember. No. They weren't at first men at all.

"These…young men. They were babies when I first saw them…like… floating or something just above the surface. Then, they were small children. Toddlers at first, then a bit older. Then, soon, they stood as full adults."

When he seemed to lose his train of thought in an amazed after-thought, Susie asked, "What did they do, Chris?"

"I...I don't know. I didn't see either of them...do...anything."

He sat up again, then turned to look into his wife's eyes. "But, there was blood—a horrendous amount of blood that dripped down their arms, from their fingers, Susie...What does it mean? What, in the name of all that is holy does it mean?"

"Okay," Nigel Saxton said, smiling to himself about his sleepy headed companions. "We must make haste. We have kilometers to go before sunrise, mates."

After a cacophony of groans and grunting objections, Clark Lansing joined the Brit and the rottweiler in nudging the other three awake.

"What about the flashlight that old guy gave you, Nigel? Do you really believe that had something to do with what happened when those things came after us?"

Saxton knelt to button up the big backpack.

"All I can say is that we've had a number of strange experiences I can't explain. The light was always integral to each of those experiences. I will keep it at my side at all times."

Clark packed his own bag while looking up at the Brit from one knee. "That is weird—the old man—there being no sign of that log house. You sure we were at the right spot?"

"Without a doubt," Saxton said, standing with the pack, then jumping it onto his back and clipping the straps together at the chest.

"It would be nice if we could find where he's moved, if it's nearby. I would like to have some of that breakfast you said he fed you and Jeddy," David Prouse said.

"Plenty of power bars," Saxton said with a grim smile. "Want one?"

The Brit offered it, and David took it. Nigel tore open one of the candy bar-sized packages and took a bite.

"Much better for you than all of those eggs and bacon, you know?"

"Yeah, well. I'm not complaining," David said, strapping his pack on his own large frame.

"What's the plan?" Cassie Lincoln stood beside David, holding onto his left arm while bending a knee to slip a boot onto her foot with the other hand.

"I want to get a look at the place where Clark last remembers overlooking that valley. Perhaps we can get some sort of a fix on what lies below from that vantage. Also, see if he might remember how to backtrack over the course he and that woman took in the snow vehicle."

Clark, helping Kristi lace her boots, said, "It's quite a way from that point overlooking the valley back to the backside of the complex."

"Are you sure you remember?" Kristi asked in a mischievous tone. "Seems to me you were paying quite a lot of attention to the chick. Maybe it wasn't as far as you thought."

"Or it was farther," Cassie chimed in. "Having such a good time, you might have lost track of the miles traveled."

"Sick'em, Jeddy!" Clark said, causing the rottweiler to come to him and playfully slap at his mistress's brother.

Kristi hugged the canine from her sitting position while Clark finished lacing and tying her boots.

"That a boy, Peanut. You know who to attack," she said, giggling while the rottweiler tried to return the affection by licking at her face.

They left within minutes, each wondering what this day, with its almost totally dark beginning, might bring.

Muted light that changed in hues of amber and red created a sense of helplessness within Mark's anxiety-accelerated brain. A feeling of something beyond his control, beyond the control of any human being.

Blake Robbins manipulated switches on a slightly inclined monitor board while sitting half-turned toward Mark.

"This is our problem," Robbins said, looking at the screens beyond the huge viewing glass that separated himself and Mark Lansing from the live video of Lori and Morgan Lansing.

"Your daughter was thought to have the—to simplify—genetic programming for creating a profile essential to produce the...hybrid of the highest order."

Mark, confined in a large chair by wide bands of metal that held his wrists to the chair arms, his ankles to the chair's supports, could do nothing while Robbins punched a series of buttons. The action lit a third large screen.

"You see here the product of our efforts that have been a project in development for…for many years."

The manipulation of yet another control caused the screen to project two tiny children, naked infants that looked to be no more than two or three months old. They were boys, their eyes bright, light blue but almost colorless, their hair nearly white.

"They are in a—for lack of better description—fluid that is the product of decades of intricate biological and chemical blending by engineering technologies that are—well, are beyond this world. These are geometrically progressing in growth—growing at a phenomenal rate."

Robbins looked to the captive's face. Although his rage was at the ignition point, Mark continued to remember his training for missions over North Vietnam. *Try to never let them see anger or fear…*

"These…males…are products of procedures only this laboratory is capable of implementing. To say it most succinctly, these boys are creatures superior in every way to any human being that has lived upon planet Earth."

Robbins, wearing the dark goggles adorned by all within the cavernous lab-chamber, turned again from looking at the beautiful infants on the screen to see his captive's expression.

"They were not…born. They were created from biological materials taken from—to put it bluntly—your daughter. And from yours truly."

Mark felt the gush of anger fill his carotid arteries, flooding his brain with blast furnace-level rage. His and Lori's little girl used in the vileness that could only be perpetrated by Luciferian minds.

"Now, I said there is a problem. But, you, Mark Lansing, are the one person on this vast planet that can supply what is needed to bring these children to the level of the ultimately evolved human."

Robbins removed the dark goggles. The eyes shimmered, hellishly black, the lids wide and nonblinking. With the goggles off, the voice within the throat changed into a guttural, echoing growl. Blake Robbins's facial features contorted into a grotesque mask of shadowy flesh that looked to be more animal than human.

"You, Mark Lansing, must agree to donate material that is a mixture of flesh and of spirit." The thing Robbins had become stood from the console chair and walked as it talked. "We long ago prepared your cellular composition for a moment such as this. The laboratory of Taos and before. The visitations. You and the woman you call Lori…prepared from the foundation. Before the offspring, which you and she so dutifully provided."

The contorted face that was once Blake Robbins changed while he talked, sometimes into the handsome face that belonged to the human, then to the creature indwelling the human flesh.

Mark sat, his mind reaching a peak of understanding. He and Lori, Christopher and Susie, Randall Prouse, Lori's mother, Laura…all had discussed this to one degree or another. The spirit-invasion of Ephesians 6:12, of Genesis 6, of Christ's prophecies in Luke 17:26-29—Jesus's words: "As it was in the days of Noah, so shall it be…" But now it was reality. The challenge of the ages stood in front of him, was displayed on the monitor screens before him while he sat, unable to break the bands.

Even if he could, what could he do? *Hold steady…wait…bide your time.* The thoughts came in rapid succession and somehow calmed him.

"The preparation began long before with your father, Clark Lansing, and with the woman's father, James Morgan, when they were children. Preparation that now will produce a new paradigm."

The entity inhabiting Mark's human captor emitted a soft snicker of pleasure at the revelation.

"We had to get you to the…laboratory, you see. We…arranged…to have the pilots taken away, knowing that you, being a well-proven flyboy, would bring the craft to a safe landing. We simply had our…people… meet you and convince you, and the wife, of course—cause you and the others to think we were concerned about homeland security and that that was our reason for detaining you. We needed you both to join us in our venture into siring ultimate man."

Mark watched the screen rather than the monstrosity Blake Robbins had become. His wife, his daughter appeared to sleep peacefully. The two beautiful babies that were hypnotic to look upon were floating in a fluid of nondescript color, their crystal-blue eyes staring at him through the glass-looking enclosure that held them. Were these his and Lori's grand-children? No! They were creations of an unspeakable progenitor...

"You and your wife have the vital nutrients within the cerebral cortex of your brains, which we will extract. It is the point where physical and spiritual elements, where body and soul, come into confluence."

Mark spoke for the first time since being bound in the chair. "Why do you need our daughter? Let her go."

The hideous face twisted in a grin of amused contempt.

"Why, to assure your complete cooperation, of course," the one in-dwelling Blake Robbins said with a seething chuckle.

"You should be very proud, Mark Lansing. You, your wife, your daughter, and your son have been given the privilege of contributing to the gods again coming to earth," the voice growled. "The quantum leap in the evolutionary process has been long anticipated."

"You know and I know that evolution is a lie," Mark said, trying to remain calm with his tone.

"Oh? That's not what the vast majority of your kind believes," the voice hissed.

"These...children...will have answers for the quantum leap...the taking away."

"What answers? What taking away?" Mark found seeking more about what the monstrous being spoke impossible to resist.

"Answers about the prince long ago predicted to come to this earthly realm. About the kingdom that has now come to this planet. About re-moving trash from this planet."

"There are facts you just must accept, Nigel," Randall Prouse said, holding the cell phone to his right ear and glancing at Christopher, then Susie Banyon.

"You have to admit that these encounters aren't exactly part of our physical existence. Yet, there they are, right in your face."

Prouse listened for several seconds to the Brit's words, then said, "The actions of that UFO, flying disk, or whatever you said you saw out in that valley—that doesn't happen within the physical realm. You said it just melted right into the trees. Became translucent, then just vanished, leaving only the forest sticking up out of the valley floor. That's not exactly something involving the physical sciences, my friend."

Randall listened, his eyes looking at, but not seeing, the carpet of the hotel room floor. His eyes then went to the Banyons before rolling toward the ceiling.

"Yeah, I do think the flashlight thing is something along the same order—beyond natural, physical science. Let me talk to David, please."

The archaeologist looked at Susie, then at Christopher.

"Nigel will never understand what I'm trying to say. Do you think Clark would understand?"

"Clark doesn't know the Lord," Susie said, resignation in her tone.

"He has the open mind of a journalist, one that isn't stilted toward totally liberal agendas. He will listen," Christopher said.

"David. Are you okay?" Randall asked when his grandson was on the Brit's satellite phone.

"Yes, Grandpa. We're only a few miles from where Nigel and Clark say we will find the ridge that overlooks the valley. Nigel is quite experienced at doing the geographical coordinate stuff."

"That flashlight. Is it true? Do you think it had something to do with fending off those Bigfoot-type creatures?"

"Gramps, not only did it fend them off; they vanished right in front of us every time the beam touched one of them."

"The others will never understand, David. These are very strange days. Prophetic days, I'm convinced. The Lord will not let the devil...these Benai Elohim use supernatural force against mortals without providing humans the ability to oppose them. He will meet force with force in the supernatural realm in these closing days. I'm convinced of it. Things that have happened to all of us over the past decades, especially in the last weeks, prove it."

"Yeah. You're right, Nigel and Clark think there's something pretty weird about the flashlight. But, I don't think they will see the spirituality in the battle."

"You must try to convince them, Son. That old man, have you come in contact with him?"

"No, sir. His cabin wasn't there. Nigel was amazed. Said we stood on the very spot. Yet there was only snow, same thickness as the rest of the snowy ground. Didn't look like anything was ever there."

"Whatever you do, David, keep that instrument closely guarded. It will be your ticket through all of this. I'm convinced of it."

"Sure, Gramps. They know it has...special properties. There's no doubt about that. But, I think they attribute that to being a government experimental device of some sort. Despite the fact some old hermit gave it to Nigel."

"I'm convinced otherwise. You take care, Son. We will be together soon," Randall said.

"Okay. Nigel wants to talk."

Momentarily, the Brit was on the cell.

"Dr. Prouse, we are approaching our target area. I will have to cut the transmissions for some time, I'm afraid. My...people...are tracking me by satellite, of course. The technology is of the most advanced sort. They are standing by to move in upon my signal."

"What about Christopher and me? You had mentioned our accompanying your...people...to the area beyond Xavier Pass when you deem it necessary."

"I'm not certain at this point, sir. With due respect...your age would be quite a factor out here if—God forbid—anything should happen, and the means of bringing us home should be mechanically disabled."

Hans Sheivold accompanied Mark and the two black-uniformed men who escorted the captive.

"A successful experiment today could mean a tremendous future for your nation, Mr. Lansing. You shall see."

The four men rode a small elevator to several floors below the laboratory's level, Mark guessed. The conveyance was unlike anything he had seen. Everything in this strange place was unlike anything he had seen.

Most everything—the walls, the floor of the elevator (if indeed it was an elevator), the fantastic array of equipment that seemed everywhere one looked—was of transparent, amber-colored material. One could look into the sparking, flashing, rotating, and revolving inner-workings of the machinery. All of the things he saw seemed to combine not in a mechanical way but rather in an organic way, somehow. It seemed to actually pulse with life, rather than grind, bump, and whir with mechanical inner-activity.

"The procedure, for lack of a better term to explain to you, will be painless, Mr. Lansing, as it was for your wife," the scientist said in German-accented English.

"What about my wife and daughter?" Mark asked.

"You will be reunited with them upon completion of the procedure."

A hatch in the gleaming chrome wall split when they approached, and they whisked the prisoner into a small corridor, then the guards held him one by each arm while the scientist stood in front of one wall and spoke.

"Sevius Klorum Ceptir."

The wall rose from the floor, providing entrance into a perfectly round room. The enclosure was dark, except for a chain of various-colored lights running the 360 degrees of the walls. The light blinked in precise order, giving the gestalt sensation of movement while Mark watched them light and go out in rapid sequence.

"And now, Mr. Lansing, if you will be seated, we can begin," Sheivold said while the men forced him into a metallic chair that shimmered by the reflected points of light in the darkened chamber.

Cassie limped behind the group, and only Jeddy noticed, accompanying her while she fell further behind.

David turned to look back when he heard the dog whine and let out a yelp.

David hurried back to the girl.

"Hey! You guys! Need some help here."

The others trudged the several meters back to where Cassie now sat upon her backpack as it nestled in the foot-deep snow.

"A problem?" Nigel Saxton asked.

"A problem," Cassie affirmed, looking up at the Brit, then the others, pain etched in her pretty face.

"Got a blister on my right big toe," she said, unlacing her right boot.

"We've got about another kilometer and a half, as I figure," the Brit said. "Think you might make it?"

"I...I don't know, Nigel. It really hurts," she said, pulling the cotton sock and then the heavy sweat sock from her foot.

Everyone looked at the oozing red spot between her big toe and the next toe.

"That's nasty," Kristi Flannigan said. "You poor little thing." She knelt to hold the toes apart and examine the wound more carefully. "It's a blister, all right," she said. "It's huge...the worst blister I've ever seen. How have you been able to walk at all? You got anything for this in that miracle bag of yours, Nigel?"

"Only that magic flashlight," he said with a laugh. "Guess a bandage won't do, eh?"

"I'll carry her. It's only a mile or so," David Prouse said. "If you can help with the extra backpack, Clark."

"That will be a lot of weight for you, David," Clark said.

"Watch it, Mister," Cassie said, looking sternly at Clark.

"Well, not all that much weight," he corrected himself, to the laughter of the others.

It was unthinkable. The intruders could not still be free to move around without being tracked. The technologies available to his own forces were impossible to penetrate without detection. Yet his underlings continued to report the British operative and now a bunch of…amateurs…had evaded his super-sophisticated security. Not just the technologies of human science but the dimensionals' technologies as well. He would not be held totally responsible. They had equal culpability.

The black ops chief heard in his memory the voices—the combined, cavernous voices—while he, dressed in a white, military jumpsuit, walked in quick strides, his face reddened in angry frustration.

"For now, the ones of Abaddon are neutralized, George Jenkins. Forces of antiquity oppose Abaddon's imperatives. The Lansing group must be dealt with by your human efforts. You created the disruption. You will deal with the matter."

He had questioned them. Why did they not just work in their paranormal way? Why did they not just "know" where the enemies were?

"If that was within our knowledge, we would not need pathetic human assistance," the combined voice had imparted to his mind in warning. Their chilling message had not left him.

Their response, in triplicate echo had been, as one, "Do not fail, George Jenkins. Do not fail."

His all-consuming drive now hurried him toward a personal frontline attack. He would lead the charge to find them, to see with his own eyes that they were stopped.

Five people, including two women and a dog. What chance did they have? Still, the others had not been able to find them or to eliminate them.

Why were the others—the Dimensional entities—so concerned with these five? The concern that the group could somehow affect the imperatives was ludicrous. But, the warning thundered in his head, and he knew the humanoid masters always, without exception, meant what they, collectively, said.

"Do not fail…"

Jenkins spoke into the device while he walked toward the mostly white helicopter. "Rendezvous with me over the coordinates you've been given," he said, snapping the device shut, then stepping onto the rungs leading to the chopper's cockpit.

The late afternoon sky made the snowfield an ever-darkening plain before them.

"Maybe you should leave us here, Nigel," David said. "She just can't go on with the foot. We can't keep up. I'm ashamed to say it, but I'm just not in shape for piggybacking, even her 115 pounds."

David Prouse let Cassie slide down his back, and Clark moved to put David's backpack in the snow, providing the fatigued Prouse a seat to rest.

"We can't leave you here, David. Neither of you would be able to find your way out. And, I don't know when I might be in contact with my people to have them pick you up."

All among the party studied the situation. David finally spoke up.

"Okay, I've been thinking about it. Might as well try it."

"Try what?" Cassie asked, sitting on her own backpack beside David.

"What Kristi and Nigel were talking about earlier, about the old man's flashlight."

"What about it?" Kristi asked.

"Its magic properties…as Nigel put it," David said. "Give me the light, Nigel."

"The flashlight? For what purpose?" the Brit asked but dropped his backpack and rummaged through the carrier. He handed David the instrument after several seconds of searching.

"Take off the boot, Cass," David said.

"Try to convince them," David thought, remembering his grandfather's words about witnessing to the power of God in dealing with his creation. Perhaps this was the time…the opportunity.

Cassie dutifully removed the boot, with David's help, then peeled off her socks. Kristi examined the ugly red broken blister between Cassie's big toe and the long toe next to it.

"Boy! That sure looks painful," she said, holding the toes apart.

"What's with the flashlight, Dave?" Clark asked, agreeing silently that the blister was terrible.

"Don't know. Just testing Grandpa's theory." He held the flashlight lens near the toes. The beam's brilliance made all, for the moment, lose sight of the foot. Kristi was the first to see the toes after the light's initial burst had allowed her eyes to adjust.

"Look at that!" Her declaration of amazement made the others check the toes closely.

A chill ran up and down David's spine. His grandfather had been right!

Four prongs extending from a transparent tube clamped against Mark's head at the forehead, the left temple, the back of the head, and the right temple. There was no pain, and, he noted, he was fully conscious.

Hans Sheivold looked at him through the blackened lenses of the goggles. "The material is not physical that we extract," the scientist said. "Rather, we are gathering electrical impulses, if you will. Data of a sort."

Mark felt a slight stimulus that made his face skin crawl with points of stinging. Then he experienced two more such feelings of shock.

"The…data…programmed into your cerebral cortex—that part that is the confluence point of mind and soul—will transfer to the children.

This is the remainder of what is needed to complete their...ascension to the apex of mankind's capability."

Mark heard the scientist's words, but he forced his thoughts toward Heaven, toward God. "Please dear God. Let your will be done. Stop this abomination."

"Your son contributed seed—before he...left us. Your daughter provided the egg for the one who is to be subservient to the other child," Sheivold said, continuing to monitor the screens before him, then the face of the subject attached to the procedure's gadgetry.

"Your wife contributed cortex data as well as chromosomal addition to the girl's chromosomes."

"Please, dear Lord," Mark continued to pray in silence. "Stop this blasphemous act."

April Warmath entered the small chamber and stood beside Sheivold. She wore the dark-lensed goggles.

"This, Mark, is the...if we are to keep this in human terms...mother of your grandchild...the grandchild destined to unprecedented greatness."

Mark's concentration on prayer broken, he looked to the girl's pretty face. But, he knew the eyes that lurked behind the black lenses were not so lovely—they were hellish.

"Her ovum and your son's genetic materials, combined with our miraculous process—thanks to the many years of dealing with our friends from other times and places—are the unifying keys to the conception. So, we have the highest man and the next highest. These will work in concert to engineer a utopian earth. Your grandchildren, Mark Lansing. You must be very proud!"

Susie walked just outside, behind the hotel, her hands thrust deeply into the pockets of the down-stuffed coat. The temperature had dropped below freezing, but she didn't notice. She prayed while she paced. She didn't hear her husband's call from the balcony while he leaned on the railing on the heels of his hands.

"Susie! You need to come in!"

"Dear Lord, protect those young people," she said, the harsh, stiff wind and the fur-lined parka pulled over her head preventing Christopher's words from reaching her ears.

"Whatever we can do to help them, please, dear Lord, give us the strength...the means to bring them back to safety. I pray you will provide the way."

Christopher was getting frustrated over his ignored call to her. He fetched his own hooded parka from the closet, then returned to the balcony. His eyes widened at what he saw, and he screamed. "No! Leave her alone!"

She was struggling with two large figures who forced her into the back of a dark SUV, one of the men getting in after her. The other hurried around to the driver's side. The man looked up at Christopher, then got in the vehicle, which screeched away into the quickening nightfall.

"I'm terribly sorry, Mr. Banyon," the man with a slight French accent was saying to Christopher nine minutes later when Randall Prouse hurried into the hotel lobby. "We are doing all that is possible to find the SUV, according to your description, sir."

The man, a constable, who before retirement worked in law enforcement for a Swiss ski resort city, looked at the archaeologist. Randall put his arm around his distraught friend.

"This is most unusual," said the constable. "We have never had such a thing happen, sir. And, I pledge we will locate your wife."

Christopher, his eyes filled with concern, looked upward at the archaeologist.

"Randy, they've got Susie. Why? What do they want with her?"

"It's okay, Chris. We'll find her. They are just trying to frighten us. We'll get her back real soon. You'll see."

They had ratcheted up the intrigue yet another notch, Randall Prouse thought, not nearly as certain Susie could be retrieved as his words of assurance implied.

—

George Jenkins turned up the volume of the satellite phone to hear above the whining thumps of the helicopter engines. He spoke after several seconds of listening to one of his lieutenants on the other end.

"Take her to the valley tram. Get her to the remote lab as soon as possible. And, Philbee, there is no margin for error in these things. Got that?"

He snapped the phone off and stowed it in a compartment.

The woman was leverage against the others—her husband and the archaeologist—doing something to interfere. Their activities were impossible to control when they were helped by the enemy. The power they wielded was equal to his own, and he needed the leverage.

He had her now. But until the snatching of the woman at the hotel, they had been thwarted from abduction of the three enemies. The prayers had made it impossible. But, what did it mean? They were finally able to grab her. He didn't have time to analyze...

There was the business of the others, the younger ones to deal with, Jenkins thought, looking at the red and amber lights of the large scope to the left of his left knee. He turned to the pilot in the seat on the other side of the scope. "What are they telling you?" Jenkins shouted to be heard above the noisy engine sounds, frowning in concentration at the Terrain Recon-scope.

"They've got them framed within a half-kilometer of the overlook, sir," the pilot reported.

"Good. Good..." the black ops chief said but in a volume too low for the pilot to hear.

The early evening had been clear. But, now dark, heavy clouds smothered the last light of the day. Jeddy broke the trail several meters in front of Nigel Saxton, who held the beam of Zeke's flashlight in the direction his compass told him the cusp of the overlook laid.

He thought about the instrument's brilliant light. It had not dimmed

since the first moment he turned it on those days ago when the old hermit
gave it to him. Yet, he could find no place for batteries.

If MI7 had something like the amazing instrument, he had never
seen it. And, he would have been among the first in the field to be issued
such a light.

Did it actually have the paranormal properties which the others—not
he and Clark Lansing—attributed to it? Did the vanishing of the hideous
creatures really happen because of the light? Was the girl's toe really healed
before their eyes? Or had the supposed miracles been the figment of the
imaginations of those who were desperate for help from any quarter, even
from the supernatural?

White puffs of breath expelled into the light provided by Zeke's flashlight beam. The temperature had dropped considerably, the Brit thought,
thinking on whether it would be good to look for shelter until close to
next daybreak.

No. All seemed relatively fresh, and all were young. Most of all, they
were all determined to find the girl and her parents. Best to press forward
to the overlook and see what developed.

The big helicopters rendezvoused to the west of the valley floor from
which they had lifted. The infrared scope in Jenkins's bird pulsed brightly,
giving view of the terrain below. Lights would not be needed while the
three choppers made their way toward the last given coordinates of the
five interlopers.

"Tell your men to stop them when they are spotted. I don't want a one
of them to survive!" Jenkins shouted to be heard. "They must not survive!"

The three craft cut through the blackness, their position lights turned
off. The advanced instruments available to the fliers made each other visible, allowing sufficient distance between each to be maintained while
they roared toward their human and canine targets.

"Don't worry, sir," the pilot in Jenkins's helicopter shouted above the
scream of the chopper engines. "Once we lock on the laser sights, the 30
millimeters will chew 'em up!"

—

Jeddy stopped a few meters ahead, and Saxton put his hand up to forewarn the others following to pull up.

"Looks like Jeddy has found the ridge overlooking that valley," the Brit said, walking cautiously beside the rottweiler, who looked up at him while Nigel shined the flashlight beam along the ridge.

David walked beside Saxton. "What do you think, Nigel? Looks like we can't go much farther than this."

"Looks like." The Brit continued to shine Zeke's light along the ridge, trying to see beyond the overhang. The light pierced the darkness of the drop-off but gave no illumination of any ground of substance. The drop-off was at least five hundred feet, Saxton figured silently. The cliffs had looked to be relatively uniform in distance to the valley floor when he had overlooked the area from his mountainside hideaway several days before. What to do now?

"Well, the action is, apparently, according to what you say, down there in that valley area, right? We've got to find a way down," David said. "The Lord brought us this far. He will show the way."

Saxton grinned, then said with a slight laugh in his voice, "Yes, well, chap. This is the time for…the Lord…to do his thing, because yours truly is at a loss as to how to attack this cliff with the ladies in tow."

Clark stepped forward and looked into the imposing ravine. He agreed; their objective lay below. There would be no need for the back-tracking of the snowmobile route after all.

The dog heard them first and growled a whine of warning.

"What's wrong, boy?" Nigel knelt and put an arm upon Jeddy's back.

They heard it, then: the whine of numerous helicopters.

Nigel switched off the flashlight.

"Even with the light off, they will have no problem finding us with the instruments—the night vision technology," the Brit said to David.

The others gathered around Saxton, who surveyed the night in the direction from which the thumping came. He knew they didn't have a chance on this open ground. The attackers' terrain-scanning night vision scopes would easily find them. Even if they were in a hiding place, the infrared would locate them, expose them to the gunships' withering fire, should the aggressors decide to use the weapons at their disposal.

He said nothing to the others. To tell them they were about to die—should that be the case—would be cruel. Better to just let it happen. The pilot in the lead helicopter spoke loudly into the helmet microphone. "You locked on?"

The other chopper pilots answered, "That's a roger."

"Get me in a position I can watch this, Captain," George Jenkins said in a pleased snarl. "Let the gunners have the fun. I want to watch."

The pilot ordered the others in to do the devastating job while he veered, lifted over the other two choppers, and followed them to their target at a higher attitude.

Nigel Saxton shouted to the others, "Down! Get down—flat on the snow!"

Clark held Jeddy while he awaited the inevitable stream of deadly fire from their attackers.

David reached to the nonactivated flashlight Saxton held in his right hand.

"Dear Lord, use this weapon…sir, in the name of Jesus!"

He pushed the button at its center, and the beam flashed through the night, just as the lead copters came within visual range. The searchlights came on at the helicopters' bottom portions just as the beam from the flashlight made contact with the pilots' eyes.

Both pilots screamed simultaneously, their eyes receiving the excruciating, fiery impact of the light.

The five in the snow saw the results at the same instant Jenkins saw the explosion and night-rending fireball. The two birds had collided, and then tumbled to the valley floor two hundred meters from the ridge. A chill of fear hit him with the realization, the thought dousing his zeal for the havoc he had planned to inflict upon the intruders. He was dealing with forces he could not control.

George Jenkins, his eyes wide with fear, screamed, "Let's get out of here! Quick!"

TWENTY-FOUR

Jeddy barked from somewhere to Saxton's right, causing the Brit to point the beam of Zeke's flashlight in the rottweiler's direction. He saw the dog's rear disappear over the ridge; the thought that the dog was lost momentarily paralyzed him. Had his friend gone over the edge to his death?

"Jeddy!" He called to the dog, whose head popped up above the edge of the precipice.

Saxton, followed by the others, hurried to where Jeddy now stood, looking back toward the place he had been moments before.

"The light illuminated the area, and they all moved closer for a look.

"It's a pathway!" Kristi's excited announcement drew all in for a close examination.

"Sure is," Clark said, his arm around Kristi and peering over the edge of the cliff to see the narrow path.

"Looks like it's been well used," Cassie said from beside David.

"Yeah," Prouse said, leaning over to assess the path once use for human traffic. "Probably Indians—pardon me—Native Americans used it for getting down to the valley."

"Good boy, Peanut!" Kristi dropped to her knees and embraced the rottweiler, who licked her face before she could pull away. "You found our path for us!"

Jeddy didn't understand the reason for the praise heaped upon him while they all congratulated and hugged him. He accepted it happily but really wanted to get back on the six-foot-wide road of stone that spiraled in serpentine fashion all the way to the valley floor.

——

Hans Sheivold had not returned to the room where Mark lay strapped to the gurney. It had been at least two hours since they removed him from the area that appeared to be an operating room.

The scientist and his colleagues had looked frustrated, even angered while they stared at their monitors and their data upon strange-looking screens inset within their control panels. They had adjusted and read-justed the pronged device Mark wore at four points upon his head while they labored to extract the things Sheivold told him they must have to complete the work on the two strange children floating in the viscous liquid. The white-haired little boys now looking to be two years old were, Sheivold had said, his and Lori's grandchildren. But who, what, were the others that contributed to the mixture that produced the little boys who were—according to the scientist—not born but rather created from genetic materials? Cloned? No. Processes far more advanced...more sinister...

Lori and Morgan. Where were they? He struggled in vain to free himself from the metallic bands that secured him to the gurney.

His wife and daughter. He had to get them. Get them out of this hellish place. He prayed for the—how many times had it been? "Please, Lord, help me to get them away from this place..."

"I'm sorry," Mr. Lansing, the man said, coming to Mark and looking down at him. "There are problems. But, not to worry. You will yet be able to contribute to our budding Nephilim crop..."

Blake Robbins, still wearing the dark goggles, looked to again be human rather than the monster he metamorphosed into when he had removed the goggles earlier. However, the topic of which he spoke was anything but human, Mark knew from his study, his conversations with his wife, her mother, and with Christopher, Susie, and Randy Prouse. The Nephilim were, many believed, the offspring of that antediluvian visitation during the time before the worldwide Flood of Noah's day.

Robbins used the very word, "Nephilim," without hesitation. He knew that Mark understood the term...

"These will soon grow to bring the kingdom of enlightenment—of light itself—to produce a new world paradigm," Robbins said, moving about the small room checking various computer screens while he talked.

"One will serve the other, will prepare the way. Much like the Baptist paved the way for the one called Jesus."

Mark's senses dimmed with the shock of the realization of what the monster within Blake Robbins was telling him. The story of Revelation 13!

"Nigel! What's going on out there?"

Randall Prouse had awaited the phone call through the night. The Brit's accented words were like a dose of caffeine injected directly into his octogenarian veins.

"We have reached the valley floor, Dr. Prouse. Sorry to be tardy with the call. We've had a bit of adventure, I'm afraid."

The British, Randy thought with a fleeting grin. Always unflappable—always the understated.

"What happened, Nigel?" he asked, impatient to know their circumstance.

"Helicopters attacked early this morning. We were sitting ducks, as they say. But, this instrument, this flashlight given to me by the old hermit, apparently has properties beyond the explainable."

"What properties? What happened?"

"It has—I can't think of an appropriate way to say it—saved us on several occasions. First during our encounters with the hairy Yeti-type creatures. Then, Cassie's toe: a blister that had crippled her was healed when the light fell upon the wound. And, then, a few hours ago, we were attacked by the choppers. David grabbed the light from me just as the machines were about to fire on us. He shone the beam at the copters, and the things, they just crashed into each other and exploded."

"Praise God!" Prouse said, rolling his eyes toward the hotel room ceiling.

"What's that?" Saxton asked, unable to hear the archaeologist's expression of thanks to the Almighty.

"Nothing, Nigel. What happened then?"

"Jed…the dog…found a pathway just over the lip of the cliff. It winds to the valley floor, which is where we are presently."

"What's your plan?"

"Well, it's just turned daylight. We've tried to get an hour or two of rest. We will begin to look toward that strange forested area where I watched those disks vanish into the trees."

"They've taken Susie, Christopher Banyon's wife," Prouse said after digesting the Brit's words.

"Say again," Nigel said. "Taken Susie Banyon?"

"Yes. They abducted her from the back of the hotel. Threw her in a vehicle and left. Chris and I are certain they will take her to wherever they are holding Mark, Lori, and Morgan Lansing."

Prouse heard Saxton explaining to the others the fact that Susie Banyon had been kidnapped.

"Grandpa. What do you think? What does it mean? What can we do?"

His grandson's voice gave Randall a shot of much-needed adrenalin, and his voice brightened. "David! Yes. They've taken Susie. Chris and I are convinced it's for leverage in this whole thing. For some reason, and in some way, there's a stalemate between the supernatural forces that oppose each other."

The archaeologist paused, considering his own words that sounded to him unbelievable, yet at the same time the truth.

"Seems the natural world—using a human hostage—is now the method they are resorting to in order to stop our interference into their interdimensional influence upon the things Jesus foretold in Luke 17. That the entities would return and it would again be like the days before the Flood."

They both let their thoughts run through their brains before David Prouse spoke. "Then we will find her, too, Gramps. The Lord has brought us this far. You just wouldn't believe how he has brought us this far…"

"Yes, Nigel told me about the things accomplished by that flashlight," Randy interrupted.

"Yes. And, he will accomplish the rest, as he wills."

Randall Prouse smiled. His son and daughter-in-law had done well with the young man.

The black ops chief had not gone to sleep. He paced the hallway, whose walls were curved to become ceiling and then the wall on the other side of the corridor. The rounded walls were of shiny, metal-like material, giving the long passageway the appearance of a chrome-encased tunnel.

"Is the Banyon woman here? Do you have her secured?" He asked the questions in an angry tone while he walked to and fro in the hallway.

April Warmath stood, watching him pace.

"Excellent. We will be there in a minute," Jenkins said, snapping the communicator shut while striding down the corridor, followed by the woman.

Susie stood by Lori Lansing, putting her small hand on Lori's face. She then walked to Morgan and laid the back of her hand against the young woman's cheek.

She turned to the black-uniformed guards, who stood on either side of the open split in the wall.

"What have you done to them? What's wrong with them?" Her questions were put in a tone of controlled anger. The guards said nothing but stood stiffly, watching her movements.

Susie turned back to the women, standing between Lori and Morgan, who lay side by side on separate gurneys several feet apart.

She placed her hands on each of her friends while she prayed with her head bowed. "Dear Heavenly Father, please bring Lori and Morgan to full consciousness and health. Protect us…"

"Your…heavenly father…has no influence here, my dear," George Jenkins said, coming through the split in the wall, with April Warmath trailing him.

His interruption caused Susie to turn, a startled expression on her face.

"Your God has no business here. This is a place for the government of the United States to conduct its business. And you and those others are interfering," the DOD black ops chief said, standing at the foot of the gurneys in the space between the comatose women.

Susie said nothing for a moment, her words then coming in a measured, calculated tone.

"We both know that it isn't the American government that sits at the head of your enterprise. We've encountered you before or someone just like you. A Mr. Robert Cooper. His spiritually dark board of directors, not his human government, dealt him a fate that was not something to envy. Sir, I don't know your name, but I plead with you. Let us go. Accept Christ for salvation before it's too late."

"Shut up!" April Warmath screamed at Susie, lacing her invective with profanity. "Do you know who you are speaking to, you human trash?"

Jenkins put his hand up for calm. "Now, Miss Warmath. We are in the land of the free and the home of the brave. Mrs. Banyon has a right to speak."

He forced a smile. "We will have to see whose…fate…will be the less…desirable."

"Your lord has already been defeated. My Lord has prevailed. There's still time for you." Susie looked at April Warmath. "And for you, young lady. Accept Christ before time runs out for you both."

Jeddy looked toward the patch of green far in the distance, his ears erecting with his wrinkled forehead. He whimpered once, causing Clark to look in the direction his sister's rottweiler was looking.

"What you see, Peanut?" The dog broke his concentration on his point of interest and gave Clark a lick on his face.

"Thanks. Nothing like a bath to get the day started off right," he said, roughing the dog's fur with quick fingertip movements.

"Kristi came and knelt on Jeddy's other side and put her arm around him. " Good morning, hero," she said in her sweetest voice.

"Thanks," Clark said, grinning at the girl, who now had his full attention.

"Yeah. Right," Kristi said in feigned disgust. "You can't hold a candle to Peanut." The dog tried to lap her face with his huge tongue but missed because she was too quick to pull back.

"The others ready yet?" Clark asked, standing, stretching, and looking toward the forest again.

"Think so. Except for the princess. She's still primping, I think."

"Well, David thinks it's well worth it," Clark said.

"They are cute together, aren't they?" Kristi said with deep affection in her tone.

"Yeah. That's David. Cute," he said with a chuckle.

"Oh, you know what I mean," she said, standing and coming to him. She put her arm around him while they looked into the distance, laying her cheek against his arm.

"I think that we're cute, don't you?" Kristi said, turning her eyes up to his, which were still affixed on the area of green far distant.

"Well, you are. That's for sure."

He held her tightly and turned to face her. He pulled her to him as he bent to let his lips brush hers. They kissed more deeply, then, a lingering kiss that ended with each gazing lovingly at each other.

"Looks like we're ready to move out," Nigel called from a short distance.

They moved several minutes later toward the outcroppings of stone that had doubtless fallen over the previous centuries and decades. The gray skies looked threatening for snowfall while they walked along the lower perimeter of the cliff's face, then toward the wreckage of the helicopters.

"You think it's wise to go this direction, Nigel?" David Prouse put the question while walking beside Cassie, just behind Clark and Kristi.

"You're probably right. Just wanted a quick look. I figure if they haven't come searching yet, they aren't likely to do so. This wreckage doesn't seem to be their priority."

"No, but we do seem to be their priority," Cassie said.

"Still, let's have a pass by, if you don't mind," the Brit said while they approached the black hulks of the helicopters that still smoldered from the crash of the early morning just hours before.

"Well, I don't care to lose the small amount of breakfast I've had, if you don't mind," Kristi said, choosing to look away from the carnage when they neared the fire-blackened skeletal frames of twisted metal.

The wreckages smelled mostly of burning petroleum. But, the stench of burned flesh occasionally assaulted the nostrils of the passersby.

"Looks like somebody's head is still in that helmet," Clark said, his reporter's curiosity piqued. He stepped away from Kristi to have a closer look and snapped several photographs with the digital camera he had asked Kristi to remove from his backpack.

"David, one of you bring the flashlight," Clark instructed. "There's something here I want to get a closer look at…"

Clark took the light handed to him by David and aimed its light into the darker recesses of the twisted chopper wreckage.

"Guess I didn't see anything," he said, handing the light back to David, then snapping more pictures.

He checked the camera's screen to see what he had.

"What's this?"

He looked at several of the other digital photos, seeing the same thing from different angles. Clark scanned the area of the wreckage with a quick glance, then looked again at the digital shots. For some reason, his eye hadn't picked up on the small opening in the ground, just at the edge of the mass of burned machinery and corpses.

"What?" Nigel came to look at Clark's discovery, as did the others.

"Behind the wreckage. Look," Clark said, pointing on the camera's viewing screen to the clearest snapshot of the disturbance in the rocky ground.

"It's a hole of some sort," Cassie said.

She walked around the edge of the blackened earth to where the spot should be.

"Yes. There's a hole back here," she half-shouted to the others, who were already nearing the site.

When Cassie took a step nearer the deficit in the earth, the ground gave way, and she started to slowly sink toward its depths.

David grabbed her arm in time and drew her out of the still-developing hole.

"Indeed, we have a hole," Nigel said, moving close to the edge. Feeling the ground begin to give way, he backed away.

"What have we here?" the Brit asked, shining Ezekiel's flashlight into the still-collapsing void.

The beam illuminated something that glinted, surrounding a blackened spot at its center.

Saxton couldn't make out how far the drop to the object might be, so he continued to examine the hole carefully, staying on ground he felt was solid.

"That looks like something man-made. Think it's man-made?" David Prouse asked, peering into the hole while standing a couple of feet from the Brit.

"Looks like. But, no way to tell other than by going in," Saxton said. He dropped his backpack, unsnapped a flap of the carrier, and pulled from the pocket a nylon rope. He began tying the rope around his waist.

"David, you and Clark will have to lower me slowly into the hole. It's the only way we can find out what it's about."

Within seconds, the Brit dangled into the hole while the men held the rope taut from well beyond the hole's edge. The earth continued to collapse, falling in around Nigel, whose feet finally touched the shiny thing that he now knew had been struck by a large piece of the helicopter wreckage that morning.

David and Mark could hear the Brit yelling, but his voice was muffled. They couldn't move close enough to hear because of fear of the ground collapsing around the cavity.

"Let's get him out of there," Clark said.

Within thirty seconds they dragged Saxton from the divot. When he was on firm ground, he got to his feet and began brushing the dirt from his clothing.

"It's some sort of huge pipe or something," he said. "Part of the copters landed directly on top of the underground pipe or whatever it is."

"What do you think it is?" Kristi asked. "Is it an oil line or something?"

"No, no. Much, much larger than that," Nigel said. "It's like some sort of underground tunnel that's man-made. I really couldn't see much beyond the wreckage that lay below. But from what I could see, it looks very much like some sort of monorail or something like that."

Susie Banyon walked back and forth in the small room. Lori and Morgan Lansing lay comatose, unmoving. Their unchanged conditions failed to dampen her faith.

"Dear Lord, you are our only hope in all of this. It is all in your hands. All I can do is to wait upon you, my Father. Your will be done."

She had learned long ago that when she could do no more, it was time to stop fretting—to turn it over to the one who could be depended upon to get things done. She sat in the lone chair in the semidarkened room, seeing her friends, unmoving, atop the gurneys. She let her mind run through what she knew about their circumstance.

She had been brought to the facility—kidnapped from the hotel parking lot—in order to...to what? To serve as leverage in getting their way with carrying out their demonic experiments? No. They had the subjects of their projects. To keep her husband and Randy from interfering? No. What could two aging men do? To keep the youngsters from proceeding toward this place of hell-spawned activities? No. They would not be stopped because the evil ones held one Susie Banyon captive. They wanted only to free Morgan...and, now, Morgan's mother and dad. Those were the hostages the young ones wanted to rescue.

What, then? Why take her hostage?

The epiphany struck. It wasn't that the evil ones had decided to take her captive. It was that the Lord had chosen to put in their thoughts to take her captive. Yes. That was it.

An enemy on the inside—*a la* Troy and the Trojan horse. But, why her? She was no Trojan horse full of powerful soldiers. Susie Banyon could do nothing beyond scold them and shake a finger at them.

"I can do all things through Christ, who strengthens me."

The passage of Scripture Ephesians 6:12-17 burst into her thoughts. The memorized verses from Paul's letter to the Ephesian Christians then played in thunderous decibel through her mind:

For we wrestle not against flesh and blood, but against principalities, against powers, against the rulers of the darkness of this world, against spiritual wickedness in high places. Wherefore take unto you the whole armour of God, that ye may be able to withstand in the evil day, and having done all, to stand. Stand therefore, having your loins girt about with truth, and having on the breastplate of righteousness; And your feet shod with the preparation of the gospel of peace; Above all, taking the shield of faith, wherewith ye shall be able to quench all the fiery darts of the wicked. And take the helmet of salvation, and the sword of the Spirit, which is the word of God: Praying always with all prayer and supplication in the Spirit, and watching thereunto with all perseverance and supplication…

They moved with haste through the tram tunnel. The monorail ran as far as they could see in the distance, down the center of the tunnel at eye-level with David Prouse, the tallest of the five.

Jeddy had been the most difficult to get through the hole and onto the walkway alongside the stainless steel monorail platform. He had not been lowered into the hole without protest, but he happily moved well ahead of the group now, stopping to sniff and sneeze at several points while he proceeded.

"This comes from the top secret complex, you think?" Kristi Flannigan asked while walking beside Clark, holding to his right forearm.

"Has to be," he said, liking very much Kristi's touch.

"Won't they be coming to repair that hole in the tunnel?" Cassie questioned.

"Yes. I suppose they will," Nigel replied while in the lead position.

"Might've chosen poorly in following the tunnel," he said further, thinking out loud after answering the girl's question.

"This is the way we are supposed to go. No doubt of that," David put in.

"Oh? Got a message from above, have you?" The Brit's question wasn't caustic but rather was optimistically curious in tone.

"I believe that if we were meant to continue above, going toward those trees, this all would have never happened. The helicopters crashing, breaking through into the tunnel..."

Cassie interrupted David. "You got to admit, Nigel," she said, defensive of David. "We've seen too much...weird...stuff happening to just write off what he's saying."

"Yes, suppose so," Saxton said, seeing the rottweiler move from side to side in the space between the monorail and the tunnel wall. The dog sniffed the concrete and earth while moving between points of interest.

"What you found there, chap?"

The human party members stopped to watch the canine sniff. Jeddy whimpered, digging at an area just beneath the platform that carried the monorail.

"Whatcha have there, Peanut?" Kristi asked, kneeling to look beneath the rail housing.

"Cassie! She pulled out a burgundy piece of cloth, stood, and smoothed the cloth. It was a watch cap. On its front was an insignia that featured a picture of a rottweiler.

"It's Morgan's toboggan hat!"

The dog moved about Kristi while she held the watch cap at arm's length. He rose to put his front paws on her shoulders.

"Here, Peanie," Kristi said. "You know who this belongs to, don't you?"

The dog sniffed the stretchy head covering made of wool. He barked and grew agitated.

"It's hers!"

Cassie Lincoln took the watch cap and examined it, all the while the dog trying to sniff it.

Cassie knelt beside the rottweiler, letting him have his fill of smelling his mistress's scent.

"See, David was right," she said, looking up at Nigel Saxton, then at David. "We have chosen the right way."

She noticed Clark, who stood looking at the watch cap. She offered it to him. He held it to his face, looking past his sister's hat into the tunnel's distance.

"Where are they?!" George Jenkins's words exploded into the communicator, the veins in his neck standing out with blood pressure driven anger.

He cursed violently, spasmodically twisting his body one way, then the other while he paced the periphery of the vast chamber.

"You've lost them?! Well, find them! Do you hear me? Find them, and destroy them!"

He walked from the big room, followed by April Warmath, his face a furious mask of crimson. He stormed through the wall's opening when it split apart with a vacuum hiss.

He punched buttons on the control board, then spoke into a microphone that suspended from a thin tube into the wall of instruments.

"Yes, sir?"

The voice emanated from the mountain complex black ops command center miles in the distance.

"What's the message?" Jenkins growled into the mike.

"Sir, there's been a breach in the tram tunnel. Looks like the helicopters that went down broke through the surface. We are monitoring movement. Looks like our intruders are moving toward the laboratory."

Jenkins grimaced a grin of satisfaction.

"Good. That's excellent!" He turned to the girl.

"Got 'em!" he said, his eyes ablaze with his pending victory over forces he previously thought unbeatable.

TWENTY-FIVE

B lake Robbins seemed to be in a state of agitation. Mark watched him from his semi-reclining position on the gurney within the small laboratory chamber.

Robbins glared at the readings on several small monitor screens. He snatched the goggles from his eyes and flung them aside. A growl came from his throat when he turned to face Mark.

The entity within the man gurgled with hatred, causing the human flesh to contort while yellowish, foamy drool dripped from the side of the mouth. The eyes were black, the man fully possessed, indwelt.

"Our instruments will yet find the material we seek in order to complete the Nephals, Mark Lansing. Do not think you shall escape your…grandfatherly duties," the entity in Blake Robbins seethed, a sinister giggle issuing forth with its words.

The thing Robbins had become came to Mark and stood glaring into the human's eyes. Mark knew that he was looking into times and places far distant. The orbs' black evil drew the human senses toward their depths—seemed to have a gravity of their own.

The monstrous countenance grew more grotesque while its rage increased.

"The…holy one…cannot protect you here, puny human." The mouth opened wider than any human mouth could open. The blood red orifice dripped with coagulant saliva while it laughed near his face. The purulent stench assaulted, singed his nostrils, causing nausea to rise within Mark's stomach.

"We will get what we need. And, when we are finished with you, it will be my very great pleasure to send you to your…holy one, " the beast's cavernous laugh echoed in volume that made Mark feel as if his eardrums would burst.

"Your…grandkids…await their grandpa's assistance, Mark Lansing. Shall we try again?"

The room grew darker, as if the very air about them was the gathering evil that Susie knew saturated this strange place, this otherworldly place.

She stood between her friends, barely able to see their faces when she looked first to Morgan, then to Lori. She held a hand on each, her prayer starting to well within her quickening spirit.

"Dear heavenly Father," she began. "Bring us safely out of this place—as you did when you delivered your chosen from the Philistines, from the Egyptian Pharaoh. Part this demonic sea for your children as in the days of antiquity…"

She hesitated when she felt Lori's left arm move.

Jeddy picked up the pace, his nose sniffing the air, his brow wrinkling when he seemed to catch an occasional scent of something that drove him onward.

"Let's see where Peanut takes us. I think he somehow can follow Morgan's scent," Clark said, now taking the lead, trotting to keep up with the canine.

Within five minutes, the dog swerved to the side of the tunnel and stood staring at the wall. He held the position until his human companions arrived. He looked nervously up at Clark and whimpered, letting out, then, a short bark of certainty. His mistress had gone, somehow, through this wall.

"Now what?" Nigel asked. "The wall is solid. Is the chap telling us your sister went through this wall?"

"Seems like," Clark said, running his hands over the smooth, metallic surface to look for a seam. He found none.

"Time for the flashlight?" the Brit asked in an almost comical tone.

"You're learning," David answered.

"Shine it on the wall," Clark said.

Saxton did so, the light beam seeming more radiant than ever when it struck and illuminated the metallic wall.

A split developed and the wall divided, sliding to left and right. Jeddy galloped into the breech, followed by his human companions. He slowed to a walk, leading the way down the only corridor, which appeared to branch right and left at its end in the distance. The broad walkway was lit by ceiling panels much like those that illuminated the tram tunnel.

"I don't like this," Nigel said, pulling back and releasing the slide on the semiautomatic pistol, the action chambering a round. He held the weapon at attention in his right hand. "There should be warning signals going off. Something to indicate unauthorized access."

"It's the cloaking," David said.

"Cloaking? What cloaking?" Nigel asked with incredulity in his question.

"The cloaking we've been given. Don't you sense that?"

"No, David. Can't say that I do," Saxton said, watching the rottweiler approach the corridor's end, the pistol cocked and ready for any surprise that might await them. The one confidence he had was that the dog would alert them to that surprise, if it was in the offing.

Lori Lansing seemed to be coming to for the first time since they had locked Susie in the room with her comatose friends. At least she moved her arm, and Susie saw some fluttering of Lori's eyelids, even though the room grew increasingly dark. She looked to Morgan's face. Still no sign of awakening there.

"Father, you loosed Peter, then Paul, and the others. You are the same yesterday, today, and forever. Please do it again if it is in your will. Unleash your mighty power; release your children…"

The arm moved again, causing the gurney to move. No! The gurney was trembling. It was the gurney that moved Lori's arm!

George Jenkins felt the trembling just as he turned to April Warmath to instruct her.

"Get them to intercept the intruders in corridor six…"

Both the black ops chieftain and the girl felt the shaking, their faces flush with uncertainty of its cause. The trembling grew stronger and a hard shock sent both against the control board.

Finally able to regain his balance, Jenkins pushed a button on the board. "What's going on?!"

There was no answer.

The intruders felt the shock at the same time, each trying to regain equilibrium.

"Earthquake!" Nigel Saxton said. "Everybody okay?"

The lights dimmed, flickered, then came to full illumination.

"We have to hurry," Clark said, following Jeddy, who had never stopped moving in the direction his instinct pointed him.

The entity within Blake Robbins's body screeched a howl of displeasure. The shaking increased, and the eyes grew larger, its mouth gnashing with profanities that growled from within the human.

"The Holy One! He interferes again!" the echoing voice within shrieked, cursing the name of God and all that was of God.

Mark reeled side to side as the tremor turned to hard shocks. The shaking caused the bands around his wrists and ankles to twist painfully at his skin. In the next instant, the bands popped and fell from the inclined table, freeing him.

The inhabiter of Robbins's flesh was turned, looking downward to the small monitors—the experiments that must not be compromised.

Mark launched from the board, the strength of his youth returning to his body. He raised his hands clasped together in a tight, single fist; lifted his arms high above his head; and came down full force on the back of Robbins's neck at the top of the spine.

The body collapsed, the entity within screaming in fury while Mark lunged through the split in the wall that developed during the quaking.

The room had grown completely dark. Susie continued to pray, her grip on the gurneys to her right and left keeping her from falling in the violent shaking, the shaking that suddenly stopped.

The room burst with light so bright that she couldn't see its source. Then it dimmed, becoming separate orbs of effulgence. Spheres of light hovered over the bodies of Lori and Morgan.

Susie backed away from the gurneys, her gaze transfixed on the fantastic display of light.

The orbs hovered and pulsed with life beyond the earthly. Thousands of lights of colors she had not seen in her lifetime streamed into the bodies of her friends. The spheres—when their work was done—merged to become a singularity, grew bright beyond comprehension, and dissipated to nothingness.

Lori and Morgan sat on the edges of the gurneys curiously examining their own bodies, looked at each other, then at the broadly smiling Susie Banyon.

"The subject has escaped!" the beast within Blake Robbins's body screamed into the intercom, causing the black ops chief to manipulate the controls on the board before him.

"The BORGs! Intercept the subject!"

Mark hurried through hallway after hallway, searching for openings in the walls. Any of the strange sliding-door breaches in the walls would do.

"Please, dear Lord," he prayed silently while hurrying through the corridors. "Let me find them…"

Another earth shock jolted Mark, sending him careening off the wall to his left. When his shoulder contacted the barrier, the wall split.

"Thanks, Lord," he said, picking himself up from the new corridor's floor after stumbling through the opening. "But, is there a more subtle way to direct me to them?"

The grin at his own little joke melted instantaneously when his eyes met with a nightmarish form that appeared as if out of the air. It had haunted his dreams for as long as he could remember. But it wasn't a monster of boiling cloud-like matter. It was a beast of immense size, covered in hair, and having fangs at least three inches long.

The creature stood to the corridor ceiling, its reddish, glistening eyes seeming to project the flames of the lake of fire. Its mouth opened, the jagged teeth chomping with jowls that could detach a man's arm with a single bite.

Mark backed slowly away, turning abruptly when he heard a noise behind him. Another creature blocked his path!

Both beasts crouched for attack. They would tear him apart in seconds.

Mark caught a glimpse of movement to his right—a movement he had no time to analyze. He leaped sideways toward the movement and through the wall's opening. Yet another door opened!

He glanced back while he ran down the new corridor, seeing the giant's massive forearm protruding through the split. Soon they would be through the breach. He had to find his wife and daughter and get them out of this maze of horrors.

"Jeddy went this way," Clark said, seeing the rottweiler's hindquarters disappear through an opening. They followed, stopping to look into the strange area into which the dog had passed.

The area was labyrinthine, the darkened, cavernous chamber alive with constantly changing lights of many ominous hues.

"Weird," Kristi said, peering into the room that looked to be as large as a domed sports stadium.

"Let's go," Nigel said. "We've got no choice."

Clark was already through the opening and moving behind Jeddy. He saw them, then. Hundreds of them! His nightmares come to life.

The broiling, sparking figures were everywhere in the chamber, moving in and out of the walls, the gleaming floor. They were the nightmare beasts of a thousand dreams he and his sister had endured...

He stood among them, as did the others, who had caught up with him and the dog. The five people and the rottweiler drew no notice...

"What is it, Clark?" Kristi asked, gripping his arm and holding him close.

"Can't you see them?" Clark asked, his eyes wide while watching the creatures milling about the vast chamber.

"There's no one there, chap," the Brit said.

"Yes there is," David Prouse said, looking about the massive room but seeing nothing. "They are here, all right. But, Clark is the only one who can see them."

"Let's just find Morgie and her mom and dad and get the heck out of here," Cassie said, holding on to David.

Jeddy started to move again, his nose sniffing the air. Clark followed him, warily eyeing the creatures that seemed oblivious to them. The others crowded close behind, letting the dog have his head in the matter of tracking the one he loved most.

Susie examined Lori and Morgan for any injuries. Satisfied there were none, she asked, "Do you remember what happened to you?"

"Where are we, Susie?" Lori asked, still woozy.

"What's going on, Mrs. Banyon?" Morgan echoed, her mind again fully conscious.

Morgan clung to her mother, looking at her, and brushing her hair from her cheek.

"Mom, what's going on?"

"I don't know, sweetheart. I remember being injected with something—and waking up."

"It's part of all that we went through long ago, Lori, remember?" Susie said, seeing in Lori's eyes the beginning of return to awareness.

Morgan said, "I remember being on a sleigh ride with...with this guy. Then, I saw some weird lights, like disks that were full of light—like UFOs or something."

"Yes. We were coming to get you and your brother," said Susie.

"Is Clark with you?" asked Lori.

"My brother? What is he doing here?" Morgan asked.

"Long story, sweetheart," Susie said. "You'll get your explanations. Right now, we've got to get out of this place—as the song goes..."

The five followed the dog to the center of the huge room, to a large, rounded walled area of polished metal. The massive cylindrical enclosure went almost to the domed ceiling.

Jeddy stood in front of the wall, pawing violently at its base. He growled and whined between moments of putting his nose to the bottom of the wall, then scratching at the floor.

Clark looked around them, seeing the beastly black, cloud-like creatures emerging and disappearing from and into the domed chamber. None of the entities indicated they noticed the five, all of whom, except for him, failed to see the creatures. Even the dog was oblivious to them.

"Okay. It's worked so far," Nigel Saxton said, activating Zeke's flashlight. The wall split upon the beam's illumination.

When inside, the air about their heads swam with strange vibrations that reached near painful levels. They pressed forward to an inner-chamber with a wall that looked to be constructed of the same type of metal.

Jeddy now was in a full state of agitation, slamming his paws against the wall and biting at the floor at its base.

Saxton directed the light at the barrier. The wall glided apart in a silent, sliding action. The rottweiler leaped through the opening.

"Peanut!"

Morgan's greeting had scarcely left her mouth when her friend was upon her, knocking her backward with his paws upon her shoulders, his huge tongue lashing at her face in uncontrolled excitement.

Kristi and Cassie's greetings were only slightly less enthusiastic, followed by a long embrace by brother, sister, and mother.

The room began to shake, nearly knocking them off their feet.

"We must be on our way," the Brit said, trying to nudge the group toward the opening by gently pushing them in that direction.

"Where's Mark?!" Lori's shouted above the rumbling sounds of the quake.

"This seems to be the center of their little universe," Nigel said, letting his eyes peruse the area. "You and your husband are central to their purposes. He must be in this general vicinity."

"You ladies stay put, if you don't mind," the Brit said. "One of you gents want to come with me to look for him?"

"I'm going," Clark said. "David, take care of them."

"No! I'm going, too," Kristi argued.

"No, Kristi. Stay with us," Morgan said, wrapping her arms around her friend. "Clark will be okay. He has to find Dad."

Jeddy looked to his mistress, uncertain of his priority.

"Go with Clark, Peanut. Go. Find Dad," she said.

"Come, Jed," Saxton said, his eyes meeting those of Morgan.

"We'll find your father," the Brit said, turning then to hurry out of the chamber behind Clark and the rottweiler.

The humanoid masters called to him in the constantly changing in colors, multihued semidarkness.

George Jenkins jerked around to see the trio—the thin male forms with white hair and pasty skin who spoke as one through the center entity.

"You are failing, George Jenkins. You were forewarned of consequences of failure." The words were issued in a cacophonous hiss from the slit that was the being's mouth.

"I—I am getting things under control…"

"You are failing," the figure said in echoing but calm resonance. "Only the physical can deal with the circumstance, Jenkins. We are helpless. The Elohim forces prevent our intervention. However, there is no such prohibition in our dealing with you."

"We have Lansing isolated in a peripheral corridor. It's just a matter of time."

The room convulsed with an earth shock that caused both Jenkins and April Warmath to grab for the control board behind them.

"As you see, Jenkins, time is fleeting. The earth-moment is now. Release the BORGs. The hybrids, although of interdimensional gentinasis, are permitted interaction within your world."

The black ops chief let the beings' words sink in. He didn't understand the terminology, but he agreed that the strategy was his only hope. It came down to a matter of brute physical force.

The room shook again, causing the human occupants to jostle against each other and the control board. When the quaking stopped, the triumvirate of entities had vanished.

Jenkins reached for the buttons on the board when he recovered. He shouted into the tube-like microphone suspended from high on the wall of monitors. "Release the BORGs! I want them in every corridor in sector Charlie! They are to destroy Lansing and the others!"

The earth convulsions grew more violent. David and the women clung to the gurneys or to each other with each subsequent shock.

"Do you think we should get out?" Kristi asked, looking to David Prouse.

"No!" Morgan said, then governing with a milder tone than her one-word answer that had burst with adamancy. "No, Kristi. Not until they find Dad. If we go from here, they wouldn't know where to find us."

"What about those who know we're here?" Cassie asked. "They will surely come to…deal with us."

"They didn't know we were here while we walked through the middle of them," David said. "We are under some sort of cloaking—just like I said…"

"What about them, though?" Kristi asked, gesturing toward the women. "They could see Mrs. Banyon, Mrs. Lansing, and Morgan."

"You're right, Kristi," he said.

"Lori, Morgan, get on the gurneys," Susie Banyon said. "They don't know anything has changed—except that there's been a whole lot of shaking going on…"

"Yes. And, you can stand between the gurneys like you said you were before the spheres, or whatever they were, brought them out of their sleep," David said, moving to help Lori and her daughter climb upon the tables.

Susie covered Lori with the covering as before while Kristi and Cassie smoothed the cloth over Morgan so that it covered their friend from foot to neck.

"All I have left in this," David said, holding the .9 mm pistol toward the ceiling—up for them to see, "...is three shots. But, at least it's something."

Saxton knew that they could move pretty much with impunity, so long as the rottweiler showed no signs that he sensed unwanted company within the hallways ahead. The Brit couldn't figure how the dog seemed to know exactly where he was headed. Jeddy had not been given Mark Lansing's scent—just one more strange instance in a series of inexplicable occurrences, he thought, walking several meters behind the dog, the pistol at the ready.

The flashlight! He grasped for the flashlight. Yes, it was there, attached to his belt. He felt a rush of relief. Zeke's strange gift—did it really have special...properties? The thought gnawed at him while he and Clark moved from one hall to another. So far, all was clear. Should he have left the instrument with David? To protect the women?

"Jed smells something, Nigel!" Clark Lansing's warning caused both men to stop, then move to near the corridor wall. They watched the dog stiffen, muscles swelling, fur bristling.

Something lay ahead, and the rottweiler poised to attack. Then, just as Nigel and Clark expected confrontation with whatever monsters awaited, Jeddy relaxed and bounded ahead. He moved in a friendly body language, and his human companions looked at each other while the dog disappeared around the corner of an intersecting hallway.

They proceeded cautiously, their backs to the wall. Seconds later, Jeddy jumped at a man in white attire while both the man and the dog rounded the corner.

"Dad!" Clark's shout of greeting brought him and his father together in an embrace that only a father and son, long separated, could manage. It was a moment of reunion each savored beyond what any words could express.

—

Blake Robbins walked through the split in the wall, followed by April Warmath and three black-uniformed men. David, Cassie, and Kristi jerked to attention at the sudden appearance in the opening. Susie turned from her position between her friends lying on the gurneys.

"You were wise not to run when the quake opened the door, Mrs. Banyon," Robbins said from behind dark goggles with a satisfied smile. "We couldn't have guaranteed your safety within the complex."

David and the girls stood away from the scene, astonished at the newest arrivals' apparent inability to see them.

"Why don't you just release us? What threat are three women to you and…" Susie gesticulated with a sweep of her hand, "…all of this?"

"You will be…released," Robbins said in a way that harbored sinister meaning. "But, we have things yet to accomplish with our friends, the Lansings."

"What things?" Susie asked, stalling—but for what purpose, she couldn't figure. *Just stall* was her only thought in asking the questions.

"We owe you no explanations, madam, but I'm feeling particularly generous. Miss Warmath, will you please open the Nephal IC?"

"Nephal IC?" Susie asked, watching Robbins's companion pull from her jumpsuit pocket a small instrument, which she pointed toward one wall that began sliding slowly apart.

"Incubation Chamber, Mrs. Banyon. The Nephals—well, let us introduce you."

The chamber's interior was of a dark, sanguine hue. At its center sat a large container that appeared to be a perfect sphere of clear glass.

Susie saw them, then, and they grew in size within the thick, clear fluid that surrounded them when they floated to the glass-like barrier. Two small children—perhaps two, maybe three years old. Their crystal blue eyes were wide, and they stared at her. The eyes telepathically called to her…to her maternity, to her humanity, to her spirit…

"These Nephals are the focus of our mission. Our imperatives for this entire project."

The children were beautiful, transfixing. David, Cassie, and Kristi—

like Susie—watched the irresistible-to-gaze-upon little boys while the children stared back in wide-eyed innocence. Their perfect, round cheeks exuded life and health beneath stunningly white shocks of hair. Their chubby, naked bodies: perfection—as if a master had painted them as cherubs in some ancient portrait of heavenly portent.

"These…children…are Nephals. They are offspring of the combination of, shall we say, this human realm and a realm of another sort," Blake Robbins said. "Mythmakers would say they are the children of the gods. And they are, of course, partly human, as they spring from the biological contributions of human women. Actually, one of these Nephals is from a combination of the Lansing offspring—the male, Clark Lansing. The other is from the girl, Morgan Lansing. From their genetic materials, at least. Those of…the realm of another sort I referred to—how can I simplify?—merged, for lack of a more descriptive term, to create the right combination of…god…and human.

"Why?" Susie asked. "To produce a new kind of man? Like Hitler and the Aryan myth debacle?"

Robbins hissed a disgruntled sigh of exasperation. "Of course you cannot comprehend," he said, becoming more pedantic in tone. "These are the first. They—one of them—is the prince who will rule the kingdom that has now come to this planet of human ineptitude and error. The other Nephal child will point to the first, to convince the world of who he is. The others who will be Nephals—many others—will serve as armies that can move about by new technologies. Teleportation, I think your entertainment geniuses call it. The Transporter of *Star Trek* fame?"

Robbins became less effusive with his words, turning almost introspective while he spoke. "The creatures that are the product of those other realms combined with certain animal life forms—the Bigfoot, Yeti, Sasquatch—whatever you have called them, can be moved about—appear and disappear through the technologies. But human flesh had to be…adjusted. That is, the combination of those of the other realm and human genetics have produced—or will eventually produce—a hybrid that can be taken apart and reunified at the molecular—the atomic levels. Like Scotty did each time he beamed somebody up…"

Robbins pulled the goggles from his nose, the chuckle coming from his now metamorphosing mouth transitioning into a growl.

The others gasped at the transformation. Although they knew the beastly creature couldn't detect their presence, they instinctively backed away from the monstrous being.

The possessor of the man was startled when Lori and Morgan shrieked. Both women pushed the others aside, their eyes affixed upon the little boys, whose bodies looked larger than life in the clear, viscous liquid in which they floated—magnified by the convex sphere in which they were encased.

Susie held Lori while Kristi and Cassie held Morgan, keeping them from rushing closer to the scene before them. The room shook violently, causing them to scramble to restore secure footing.

"Lori! Morgan!"

Mark's shout caused his wife and daughter to pull from the grips of their friends and hurry to him. Both were sobbing uncontrollably while they clung to him.

"Oh, Mark! They are our grandchildren!"

Lori's words caused the being within Robbins to cackle with guttural laughter. April Warmath, still wearing the goggles, glared at the scene of the three in each others' arms.

"How very sweet," she said in a tone that dripped with sarcasm.

Another shock, more severe than the previous, jostled all within the small enclosure.

"Let's get out of here," David Prouse said, grabbing Cassie's arm.

When Mark and the women turned to exit through the split in the wall, the big men in black uniforms stood between them and the opening.

They raised weapons toward Mark but lurched forward, their mouths twisted in death throes when several .40 rounds from Nigel Saxton's pistol tore into their backs.

The monster within Robbins shrieked blasphemous curses, Robbins's body lunging for Mark and the women. David Prouse rammed the indwelt body, knocking it to the floor with a tackling technique once learned at the University of Texas and addling his victim with the impact.

April Warmath pulled the black-lensed goggles from her face, her countenance changing into a grotesque mask of hatred.

The entity inhabiting her caused the body to grab Susie by the throat from behind. Kristi Flannigan, with the help of Cassie, pulled the arm from Susie and held onto the possessed woman, who screamed, unable to determine why she couldn't get free to attack.

Clark burst through the breech in the wall, diving toward the woman who had brought him to the complex in a drugged state.

"Grab those wires!" he shouted, hanging on to the spasming woman's body.

David grabbed several thin wires, causing sparks to flash when he ripped them from beneath the control console. He tied April Warmath's arms and feet with the wires while the others made their exits.

All but one. Susie looked through the split in the wall toward the sphere, the white-haired children staring at Lori Lansing, who stood looking into the little boys' wide, crystal blue eyes above the perfect little mouths that seemed to be trying to say something to her.

She sobbed, tears streaming down her cheeks while Susie, then joined by Mark, led her out of the chamber that began again to quake in violence greater than before.

The black ops chief braced against the wall with the palm of his left hand while punching the communications controls on the board. He shouted to be heard above the roaring caused by the violent shaking.

"The BORGs! Are they released?! Are they released?!"

Response was muffled and broken in delivery. He heard the man's voice from somewhere within the laboratory reply, "Yes, sir…they…"

Jenkins swore at the board's speakers, then calmed. "I want those people found, Clemmens. Got that?!"

There was no further response.

Jenkins slammed his fist against the wall and exited the room, again having to catch himself by grabbing the door facing when the floor convulsed.

———

Lori wiped the tears from her eyes, forcing her thoughts from the babies—
her grandchildren—left in the lab from which they hurried. She lifted
her head, making herself remember that her God was in control at all
times—in all things.

She held to Mark while the two of them walked in near-trotting fashion behind Nigel Saxton and Clark. They traveled just ahead of Susie and
Morgan, who were followed by the other girls and David Prouse.

Jeddy moved ahead of the group, apparently unfazed by the quaking.
The corridor floor and walls now rolled and shook while the group moved
to find an exit from the strange laboratory. The lights along the hallway's
ceiling flickered and went out.

Nigel handed Clark a flashlight, one of several attached to his belt.
The group slowed only for a moment, then followed the rottweiler, who
had stopped to look back, then hurried forward when the flashlight lit
the pathway.

"How do we know the way out? Cassie wondered aloud from behind
Morgan.

"Jeddy. He knows the way, believe me. Looking for a place to relieve
himself is all-important," Morgan said, her words breaking the tension of
the moment.

They moved through a number of hallways before Nigel and Clark
saw the dog standing just ahead. The rottweiler bristled, growling, poised
for attack.

They heard other guttural noises, then a loud shriek. Clark and the
Brit had heard it before, as had Morgan.

"The Yeti!" Nigel's announcement froze each in place.

The flashlight beam framed two of the gigantic creatures just ahead,
the monstrous beings standing almost to the ceiling.

"Jeddy! No!" The rottweiler ignored the men's command. The canine
crouched, his muscles swelling in preparation for launching against the
foul beasts just ahead.

David, Kristi, and Cassie whirled to look behind them when they
heard grunting, shuffling noises.

Cassie shrieked, as did Kristi when the flashlight David pointed into the darkness of the hallway revealed one of the hairy giants. Ruby-colored eyes flashed their hatred for the humans while the light caused the orbs to glow from the hideous, leathery face that looked demonically human.

Each of the nine instinctively moved closer to each other. The two creatures ahead began to shuffle forward, scowling through their gnashing, foaming mouths while they watched the rottweiler. The beast prepared for attack from the hallway in the opposite corridor's direction.

Nigel struggled to get the flashlight from the belt. It wouldn't come loose. Morgan saw the Brit's problem and unleashed the snag.

"Thanks," he said in the fleeting, circumstance-pressurized moment, their eyes meeting, each understanding the nuance of humor in Nigel's understated word of gratitude.

Nigel switched Ezekiel's flashlight to the on position. The beam struck the wall to the group's right. The barrier split.

"Guess that's where we should go," the Brit shouted, choosing the opening rather than to battle the beasts that threatened.

An ear-shattering shriek followed by a yelp of pain caused the other flashlights in the group to focus into the hall from the opening.

Jeddy lay in a stretched position, his dark body twitching in convulsions just in front of the opening.

"Take the light!" Nigel shouted, handing Zeke's light to Clark.

The Brit dove through the opening and moved to the unconscious dog. Nigel grunted in pain when a huge hand grasped his shoulder just above his right bicep. The beast's nails pierced the man's shirt, the pressure exerted by the powerful grip nearly pulling the shoulder out of its socket.

Clark put the beam directly on the creature that held Nigel a meter off the corridor's walking surface. The Brit crashed to the floor when the beast that had him in its grip shrieked and exploded into a million points of sun-like brilliance.

Nigel, although in agony, gathered the rottweiler and dragged him, with the help of David and Mark, into the room.

One of the two beasts reached a massive, hair-covered arm through the split just as the wall started to come together.

Clark put the beam on the arm, and it, like the creature before, exploded in light and was gone.

Jenkins's frantic eyes met those of the black-uniformed guards near the tunnel tram car. He had failed. He knew that the masters knew that he had failed to stop the intruders from coming into their laboratory. He had failed to stop the mere mortals from interfering with the imperatives they wanted to accomplish. The Nephals...

Jenkins said nothing to the guards before leaping aboard the tram. He inserted a metal card into a slot on the control panels in front of him. The action caused the vehicle to begin moving forward on the high monorail that disappeared in the distance, toward the inner-mountain complex.

Morgan cried, her tears falling on Jeddy, who breathed in short bursts of air. His eyes were open, the pupils at full dilation.

Lori and Mark hovered over her and the dog, her father reaching to examine the canine, checking for bleeding.

"He doesn't seem to be bleeding, does he, Dad?" Clark said, standing over his family.

"Don't think so," Mark said, his thoughts on his daughter, who sobbed over her canine son.

The room shook hard, causing all to grasp for something to brace themselves. The tremor continued.

Nigel, still in pain from the encounter with the creature, had to pick himself up from the room's floor, and then moved beside Mark.

"Okay," the Brit said, looking at Morgan, who turned from looking at Jeddy to letting her tear-filled gaze meet Saxton's eyes.

"Let's give Zeke's flashlight one more test," he said.

The girl cocked her head, not comprehending his words.

While the Brit turned on Ezekiel's flashlight, the others gathered. Kristi knelt just behind Morgan and her mother. She put her hands on them.

Saxton put the powerful beam on the rottweiler's head, then ran the light along the dog's muscular body.

Jeddy lurched, instantly trying to regain his feet, which he found difficult with the humans all gathered around and the floor around them trembling.

"Astonishing!" the Brit said, looking hard at the instrument. "Absolutely amazing…"

The room, illuminated only by a few small colored lights on yet another of the control boards throughout the laboratory setting, began a violent quaking unlike any of the previous. The very space about them grew white with light that obliterated all ability to see anyone or anything surrounding them. A loud, hissing noise sounded continuously while the air about them seemed to be sucked in vacuuming action from around their heads.

The hissing sound grew louder, the sucking of the air more powerful. Then it turned to droning, the light dissipating and becoming a lifting, whitish-yellow sphere of huge dimension.

The light, getting brighter above them, grew smaller while they all, sitting or reclining, looked into what was the ceiling, watching the light rise. The sphere lifted…elevating into and beyond the ceiling…into the air.

It wasn't the ceiling of the room! The light moved upward, ever upward. It pulsed and turned, the noise of its hum lessening in volume… getting ever more faint in the sky.

The sphere grew bright as earth's sun. It shrank in the next instant into a distinctive saucer shape, then streaked upward and out of sight.

Each of them examined the surroundings. They sat or lay on the vegetation of the forest floor. The room they had been in, the gigantic oval laboratory…it disintegrated around them while melting upward through the trees that now surrounded them, leaving them to try to make sense of what had happened.

The chrome-like monorail ahead hurried toward Jenkins while he sat in the tram car that sped toward the inner-mountain complex. The many angst-ridden thoughts sped even faster through his mind.

The project, the most vital of the imperatives, was thwarted. It wasn't his fault. He didn't do it. He had done all they asked of him. The failure to deal with the disruption was the fault of their realm—not his.

But, they had forewarned him. They would abide no failure. The fault—from their perspective—was his. He had failed them.

Sweat dripped from his pallid face, even though the tunnel had lost its heat. He didn't feel the cold that had manifested itself through his own white puffs of exhalation within the past seconds while he rode the rail toward his destiny—whatever that would be.

TWENTY-SIX

There they are!"

Randall Prouse shouted to be heard above the chopper's powerful engines.

Nigel Saxton's satellite phone call had procured for them a large helicopter, his government's MI7 chief convincing an American Army general to send the bird. The chip within Saxton gave the pilot the location, the GPS soon bringing Christopher Banyon, Randall Prouse, and three of the Army's crew over the valley beyond Xavier Pass.

"Looks like they're glad to see us," Prouse said, looking down at the waving group through the huge window.

"Thank God," Christopher put in, searching the group for his wife, seeing Susie standing, smiling up at him.

"What did I miss?"

David's grandfather sat beside him while the bird whisked them over the pass toward its landing pad miles away.

"Quite an experience," David said, shaking his head while holding Cassie Lincoln's left hand.

"Yeah, well, you'll have to fill me in on the good stuff," Randy said, grumpiness in his tone.

Mark held Lori close in the seats across from the archaeologist. She shivered with the emotion she had tried to overcome the past hours while awaiting the helicopter.

"It's okay, sweetheart," her husband said, hugging her tightly to himself. "God will help us with this."

Morgan sat beside Kristi who knew the same thing that so affected her mother, affected Morgan, even if to a lesser degree. Clark reached across Kristi to squeeze his sister's hand and wrist.

"You okay, Sis?" he asked, seeing the sadness on the pretty face, even though the tears had run dry.

She glanced at him and shook her head without saying anything.

Jeddy sat by his mistress's feet, leaning his big body into her while she scratched the top of his head.

Nigel Saxton sat beside Morgan, talking into the satellite communicator that had brought them rescue.

"Yes, sir. I'll be on the plane to London at first light," he said. "Shouldn't say more for now. Unbelievable, I assure..."

He listened while a superior spoke from London headquarters before speaking again.

"Yes, sir. It involves some of the things we thought—but not precisely as we had envisioned," Saxton said, signed off, and put the phone in his pocket.

He turned to Morgan. "Feeling better?" he asked.

"Thank you for what you did for Peanut," she said, ignoring his question while glancing down at the rottweiler, who sat straighter in order to receive his mistress's full attention.

"Least I could do for him. He got me through all of this..."

"That flashlight. Do you really think it has some...special capabilities?" Morgan asked. "Kristi and Cassie say you've done some amazing things with it."

"I must say, I have no explanation for it," the Brit said, reaching to his belt for the instrument. But it wasn't there on its hook. He looked around; it was nowhere in sight.

He unbuckled his lap belt, then half-stood, turned, and searched the area.

"It's gone! It's vanished," he said, continuing the search.

Somehow he knew, then. They all knew. They stopped searching, and he sat, reclasping the seatbelt.

"Served its purpose, I suppose," Nigel said, a sigh of disappointment in his voice.

"Some old man gave it to you, Cassie told me," Morgan said.

"Yes. An old prospector out near Xavier Pass. Jeddy found me half-alive and brought the old gent to me."

Nigel's eyes lit up with remembrance. He reached into his backpack beneath the seat.

"Yes. I have a photo of old Zeke…Ezekiel was his name. Let's see what I have." He manipulated the digital camera until he came to the shot he wanted to bring up. "Yes. Here he is with Jeddy."

He held the camera so Morgan could see the photograph. Her complexion paled to white, her expression one of being dumbfounded.

"Kristi," she said almost in a whisper, not taking her eyes from the photograph of the old man and the rottweiler.

Kristi Flannigan leaned to see the picture. "My Gosh! It's him! It's the old guy…the old prophet with the placard!" Kristi said.

Jerusalem—December 26, 2004

Randall Prouse walked with David and his new bride near the rubble being loaded at the base of Mount Moriah. Large dump trucks moved in one after another while machinery dug and scooped the ancient earth.

"That's where I was allowed to dig in the 1970s," the archaeologist said, pointing to a specific area still untouched by the machinery.

Cassie grasped her husband's grandfather's left arm, laying her face against his shoulder and hugging him.

"Thanks, Grandpa, for bringing me along," she said.

"Well, you are David's wife. Of course I would bring you along," Randall said, returning her affection with a quick kiss on the top of her head.

"That's not what I mean," she said, looking up, admiring the old man who again studied the despised digging going on at the bottom of the Temple Mount.

"I mean, thanks for introducing me to the Savior. Thanks for taking time to tell me about the Lord, then teaching me so much."

David walked to them from an observation point nearer the excavation.

"This looks to me as if it could cause the whole end of the mount to collapse, Grandpa," David said, turning then to again look at the digging.

"Well, if it happens and the Mosque crumbles, we know who will get the blame," Randall said. "I kind of believe that's what some of the Islamic fanatics want, as a matter of fact. Collapse the Dome of the Rock and blame the Jews."

"There they come," Cassie said, pointing to the group of seven people walking toward them.

Kristi Flannigan turned loose of Clark Lansing's hand, then jogged behind Morgan who hurried to Cassie's side, leaving the others trailing them.

"Did you know some of these places—especially in the old city—are built upon thirty layers?" Kristi asked with little girl-like excitement, letting her eyes fleetingly meet those of Randall, David, and Cassie.

Morgan grabbed her friend's arm and shook her playfully. "Do you know who you're telling that to, girlie?"

"Oh, yeah. Sorry, Dr. Prouse," she said, giggling.

It was a terrific trip. What had happened in the mountains of Colorado a few months before, though strong in the memory, served only as a reason to make the trip a reunion of sorts. Christmas time, basking in the ambience of the ancient place where Christ walked, taught, and gave his life for the sins of mankind on the cross at Golgotha—at Calvary—overshadowed those remembrances of the horrific goings-on in the valley beyond Xavier Pass. The youngsters obviously loved the experience, and Randall Prouse was pleased, watching them enjoy themselves.

"Looks like your idea for the trip is a hit," the archaeologist said to Christopher Banyon when the others stood beside him.

"Susie's idea," he corrected. "And, it was a wonderful idea," Susie's husband added, hugging her and planting a kiss on her cheek.

"Randy, I just can't help thinking there's a reason...a special reason for our all coming together again...especially since we've been brought here to Jerusalem."

Susie's words, if coming from another, would, Randall thought, mean nothing more than an expression of emotional high of the moment. Susie Banyon was...different...not one whose thoughts should be summarily dismissed.

"Oh? What do you think is up?" Prouse asked.

"It's probably just nothing," she said, her eyes taking on an uncharacteristic, faraway look while she gazed in the direction of the younger people, who, with Mark and Lori, moved nearer the excavation taking place.

"She thinks it has something to do with the babies in that...laboratory, Randy. All that has happened is so much stranger than any of the visions or dreams, or whatever, that any of us have experienced."

Christopher's explanation brought further thoughts to Susie's mind.

"There was something about the little boys, Randy. I can't describe it. They drew you to themselves. It was the eyes, I think. The most beautiful, big, blue eyes…Yet almost crystal clear—with a hint of blue…"

The archaeologist began walking slowly, as did Christopher and his wife, toward the bus stop where a group was gathering. The others stopped gawking at the excavation work and hurried in their direction.

"They called them Nephals?" Randall asked.

"Yes. They called the little boys the first of the Nephals," Susie confirmed.

Twenty-five minutes later, they all readied to step from the bus. Morgan's face brightened, her smile pleasing her father. He got out of her way, so she could be the first onto the expansive sidewalk that fronted their hotel.

She jogged toward the man and the dog he held by a leash.

"How did he do?"

"Only ate three pedestrians," Jeddy's handler said. "Spit one out. Must've tasted bad."

"Nigel! How can you say that about our Peanut?" Morgan knelt, hugging the canine's thick neck and received his wet, tongue-administered affection in return.

"You can't talk about your future son like that," she said, standing and embracing the Brit, their lips coming together for a brief moment.

"No public displays of affection!" Clark shouted from the hotel door, then disappeared through the entrance with Kristi in tow.

Christopher dropped onto the end of one of the beds in their room a few minutes later. His wife answered a knock at the door.

"You mind if I come in for a second?" Randall Prouse asked, walking in before getting an answer. He found the TV remote, pushed the *on* button, then channeled until he found the news program he wanted.

"You have to see this. There's been a tremendous tsunami—in the Indian Ocean, I think. A real killer," Prouse said.

They watched for ten minutes while the fast-breaking story unfolded.

"They're saying this one could be a 9.0 or better. Might kill a hundred thousand—maybe more."

"Lord, protect the people," Susie said in a whisper.

"I've been thinking," Randy said, "about those children you say were floating in that globe-like tank." He stood and paced while he talked. "Lucifer wants a people who are totally devoted to him. He would thus want to create—or counterfeit a creation of—human beings that are totally devoted to him."

Susie and Christopher followed him with their eyes while he paced and talked. "These…boys…are the first of their kind, I think you said you were told."

"Yes. The demon—and I know it was a demon in that man's body—said these two children will bring in a new paradigm for earth. They are the first. One will lead the way, the other will point all others to the first," Susie said.

"Mark said they told him the same thing. Thinks it has to do with Revelation 13," Randall said. "The Antichrist and false prophet—the two beasts. Is it possible? Have our friends, Mark and Lori—their son and daughter—been used for…trying to fulfill this end-time prophecy?"

"The son of perdition, lost from the beginning," Christopher said.

"What?" Prouse asked.

"Jesus says in John 17:12: 'While I was with them in the world, I kept them in thy name: those that thou gavest me I have kept, and none of them is lost, but the son of perdition; that the scripture might be fulfilled.'"

"Lost, without salvageable souls. No chance for redemption—like the fallen angels. The beast and the false prophet are the first to be cast into the lake of fire. They don't seem to stand before the great white throne judgment for the lost."

Christopher, squinting in concentration at the TV screen, interrupted Randall Prouse, holding his hand up for quiet. He reached for the remote and turned up the volume.

The narrator gave the news story while the video played on the screen. "...man said he was commissioned by Allah to carry out the decapitations because his victims were part of a vision he received on top of Mount Moriah at midnight on January 1, 2000, the turn of the millennium."

The video showed the Arab, his dark eyes flashing defiantly, mouthing words in Arabic while the Jerusalem police forced him into a van. He spit at the cameraman, and one of the officers pushed his burnoosed head down to avoid it contacting the top of the van's opening.

"The alleged killer has been reported to be preaching that in his vision, while standing guard when the millennium and the century rolled over, he saw two babies at the center of the Temple Mount. The children grew into manhood while a violent storm raged over Moriah. He reportedly believes it was his mission from Allah to rid the world of the prophesied Antichrist and his religious consort, whom he believed these men to be. One the false prophet and the other the predicted end-time, Hitler-like dictator of Revelation 13. The man's name is believed to be Yusfi Shabatt."